River Deep Mountain High

River Deep Mountain High

Gareth Calway

Published by bluechrome publishing 2008
2 4 6 8 10 9 7 5 3 1
Copyright © Gareth Calway 2008

First published in Great Britain in 2008 by
bluechrome publishing
PO Box 109,
Portishead, Bristol. BS20 7ZJ
www.bluechrome.co.uk
A CIP catalogue record for this book is available from the
British Library.

ISBN 978-1-906061-22-7

"It is impossible to live in the present.
At least, not in Wales."
RS Thomas

'How little that to which alone we give
The name of education hath to do
With real feeling and just sense.'
Wordsworth, *The Prelude*

The boy I was at fifteen
Came to me in the night and said
You have betrayed me…

Book One

Friday 1 March 200-

Chapter One

Old Taff

Every day when I wake up,
I thank the Lord I'm Welsh

1

Nel mezzo del cammin di nostra vita. Acting Headteacher Dafydd Thomas, drilled into wakefulness by an alarm he mistook for the school bell, found himself face to face with a sex doll. The archness of her expression was heightened by a sledgehammer application of green eyeshadow. Two coats of scarlet lipstick accentuated her fixed "O" of pleasure. She was dressed in the gymslip of "Mountain High" - The Llewellyn The Last Mountain High School, Trollbridge – at which Dafydd attempted to lead Humanities and a school-sized microcosm of the Welsh nation. Tied to her thigh was a gift label:

To Dai. Happy Birthday. From The Boys.

Dafydd screwed up his eyes on his colossal Black Knight Special Export hangover and tried to remember how Inflatable Morfydd, the Trollbridge Club Mascot –for it was she – had found her way onto his bed. She was normally reserved for stag nights. Dafydd frowned, his left temple throbbing.... His blind date, a 'lufly lady' like the one in his Open University study text *Sir Gawain and the Green Knight,* had leaned over 'sauerly and sadly'. And then there'd been a Male Voice Chorus of HAPPY BIRTHDAY FAT

BASTARD. And then eight tankards of Black Knight had crashed onto a table to join the romantic bottle of wine. And then presumably the lady had vanished. Dafydd did not share the modernist indifference to plot. *What had happened next?* He hadn't told The Boys about today's interview and inspection had he?

Piecing together the brilliant visionary fragments of The Night Before, a shameful scene clicked into his head. He hurled back his duvet, sending Morfydd bounce-bouncing off the bed onto the layers of dirty laundry that made up his bedroom carpet, her mouth maintaining a fixed "O" of protest. He glared down at his gonads. Nationalist green! The Boys had painted them! He scrambled out towards the bathroom to scrape away this unwanted show of emulsion and glimpsed his backside in the mirror. Even in his panic and dismay, he couldn't help admiring the splendour of the red Welsh dragon daubed there, its mouth arranged with perfect symmetry to coincide with his anus.

"Oh," he said.

"O," agreed Morfydd.

Four brim-full Tizer bottles stood immediately outside his bedroom door. Dafydd knocked three of them over in the act of trying to avoid the fourth. He righted each of them in a panic, soaking himself and the floor in the process. A note like the ones you left for the milkman protruded from the remaining bottle. *Quick. Joyce is comming pleese hide these botles of piss for me, Ta, Brig.* Brig - Brigadier "Bullshitter" Davies - had obviously had company again last night. Brig had equally obviously – despite several conversations about it – still not adapted his nocturnal urination rituals to the requirements of shared accommodation or post-neanderthal hygiene. Dafydd wondered whether it was simply the excess of alcohol in Brig's bloodstream that had prevented him making the short journey along the landing to the toilet four nights running or whether it was the need to work the petrified piston and ballcock by hand in the national absence of plumbers. Either way, it was crouching naked, holding an overflowing bottle of piss and woaded like one of Boudicca's finest that Dafydd now made the acquaintance of the lady in question.

"Morning my lovely," said the lady. "Happy birthday. I like the suit."

"Uh… Good morning. You must be Joyce."

She giggled. "Need the bathroom?"

"Uh - yes."

"All yours."

Dafydd tried to conceal his belittled manhood behind two bottles of Brig's fermented urine and hoped the incident would not reach the ears of any of his pupils, not to mention their fathers and mothers. He hoped in particular that Joyce did not actually turn out to *be* the mother − or perhaps that would be the grandmother - of any of his pupils. He didn't think so but at his age you never knew. Ever since that Parents' Evening he came face to face with a woman he'd last seen straddling him on a teenage-babysitting sofa, he had become conscious of the inescapability of the past. Or what if Joyce turned out to be a reporter on the local newspaper? LOCAL PISS HEAD FLASHES WOMAN?

Dafydd told himself to calm down. No reporter − let's face it, no-one with enough brain even to read and write - would waste time on Brig. Dafydd was letting his aching hungover imagination run away with him. Besides, he found enough compromising bits and pieces of Joyce on the bathroom floor for an out of court settlement even if she did threaten some kind of exposure. He looked at his reflection in the full-length mirror. "Ah well," he quipped − not to his imaginary friend exactly but certainly to an imaginary someone with his own sense of humour, "I may be 45 but I've still got my tits!" He laughed. Then spent five useless minutes compiling a list in his head of the three most useless things in the world.

1. A kick for touch that gains less than ten metres.

2. The Newport County offside trap.

3. The male tit.

He turned on the hot tap full pelt and sighed.

Half an hour later, chastened but squeaky clean, Dafydd reclined in a lukewarm bath laced with patriotic paint scabs, balanced his Open University copy of Dante's *Inferno* on the side of the bath to avoid getting its sacred pages wet, and completed a mental self-review. He was 45 today, maybe 5 years into the second half of his life, exactly 20 years off his pension. He was like the Afon Marw river, locked into what was once called a Youthful Valley - and now, in a more prosaic age, a "V shaped valley" – locked, nonetheless, into a narrow slide down coal-seamed pennant grit, rock-breakingly furious, fatal in the rainy season (September –August), and, for all the foaming fury, never getting anywhere. He was also already two decades past the male life expectancy in Merthyr in the 1820s and with about half as much to show. He was already ten years past the point where the 35 year old Dante Alighieri had been when he was "midway this way of life we're bound upon." In other words, well and truly stuck up "a dark wood/ Where the right road was wholly lost and gone." Again. It was time he grew up, got into a proper relationship with a woman, got *on*.

He sat up suddenly knocking Dante's *Inferno* into the bath with him. This was swiftly followed by the radio, Brig's green plastic battleship and a bottle of Blonde Hair Losing Radiance Shampoo that must be Joyce's since neither he nor the Bobby-Charlton-overcombed-with-emotion Brig had any use for it. Dafydd cleared the bath with some difficulty and then sorted through several bottles of Specialist Conditioner and/or Henna Enhancers before finding two bottles of shampoo that an ordinary man might use. He sighed twice. Both were empty.

He shut his eyes and wondered. He had been born here in Monmouthshire - around the time when it was still officially England - and grown up in the Sixties to a junior school soundtrack of folksy elegy and the cadences of "We Plough The Fields And Scatter" – the very movement of a line like "soft, refreshing rain" echoing everyday valley speech. "The Lonely Ash Grove" haunted his infant memories. His mother used to sing it to him in her wistful Monmouthshire-Welsh voice burdened with seven centuries of national sadness. He had grown up in a hair-rich age. The Beatle fringe, the Maharishi centre parting, the Kevin Keegan perm. He had once had so much eternally springing hair that he could wantonly scalp it with a punk rock razor, bleach it, throw glowing curly handfuls of it to the violent winds of change and still come back

14

for more a few months later. Now each hair was preserved with care, nurtured, trained for the marathon his sprinting youth had turned into. Such was life.

He wondered. He wondered if instead of returning "home" he should have stayed over the border in England, where his first two promotions had taken him, pursuing his career in a country where you could at least live in the present, albeit a present which seemed bent on becoming an increasingly diminished photocopy of America. That railway journey up the enormous Severn estuary and towards the heart of Lloegr had filled his mind with silver waters and the potential of wide liberating spaces. He remembered being unable to look back at the Severn Bridge, spanning the Severn's fearsome channel of whirpools and bores. Not just because it had become to him the tragic gravestone of the dead 1960s, the relic of a motorway age's suspension of disbelief, the fossil of a white-hot technological revolution gone cold - but because he'd been in the toilet at the time. The nation-piercing Severn Bridge! Like that sword bridge made of a single blade of steel that the all-conquering hero Sir Lancelot crossed into the romance land of Gorre in humiliating quest of some *princess* who insisted he 'throw' a tournament as a coward, just so she could ignore him.

Maybe Gorre was Wales? He sat up, accidentally rucking the soap. But wasn't Gorre a land that natives could freely enter and freely leave? And strangers could only enter? *Everyone* had to pay a bridge toll to get into Wales now –you could get out for nothing. And if he was a native of Gorre how come he felt so trapped here? Unless- At this point, the faulty tap ejaculated a small but highly effective measure of scalding water onto his foot. He sent half a bathful of water onto the floor. (If the Wenglish phrase for "Eureka, I've discovered the displacement of water, albeit several millennia later than is strictly useful" begins with an F-, he shouted it now.)

An interval of unchanneled consciousness followed. Then Dafydd coaxed his foot under the melting glacier issuing from the cold tap and resumed his meditations. True to the modern spirit of choice, the Severn estuary now offered two bridges to pay through the nose at - the dated, 1960s modern industrial miracle, and the 1990s post-modern, post-industrial sci fi fantasy. He wondered if the fact that he himself had spectacularly stalled his Lada at the *older* Severn Bridge toll booth on his 'triumphant' return to Wales to take up his third promotion, ready like Sir Lancelot to save her but causing an hour-long pile up behind as the emergency services rescued *him* - was a sign that his career had taken a fatal wrong turn.

He wondered if he should have continued to teach geography and history, a growth industry now in Heritage Wales, instead of being interviewed today for the post of Headteacher at a school whose Great Hall was still dominated by a portrait of Welsh Llewellyn (The Last), conquered by the Norman Edward (The First) over 700 years before. He wondered what little bastard in 9N had written "Mr Thomas the only gay in the village" on the back desk of his teaching room as a result of the latest episode of "Little Britain". He wondered why kids who did this invariably observed the proprieties of the 'Mr'. It was like the quaint "Piss off, sir" mixing insult with anachronistic deference, which had precipitated his first permanent exclusion in the final week of the previous term. He wondered why *Thomas takes it up the arse* had appeared widely in graffiti only since his promotion to Acting Head. He wondered why the Rygbi Clwb Sign with its picture of a New Zealand Lamb dressed in Wellington boots and panties as presented by the touring All Blacks in the Nineties was still considered funny enough to be given pride of place in the Clwb hall, rather than hidden in shame in some museum. Perhaps it was one introspective, rugby-playing, sheep-rearing backwater bleating to another? He wondered how many other candidates for executive teaching posts in Wales required a genital scrub in preparation. He wondered how mankind had come up with the space rocket but had still not managed to combine "safety" with "razor". He wondered whether to skip today's Full Welsh breakfast – meaning a Full English Breakfast of egg, bacon, sausages, baked beans, mushrooms, toast, fried bread, hash brown with mashed potato and onion - and go straight to the chaser (a pint glass of aspro.) And he wondered how he was going to stop three cuts from blooding his off-white collar whenever they reactivated their crimson flow at moments of crisis through the morning.

He got up to pee and managed to knock the limescale remover off the cistern and onto his penis. He wanted to sleep again, return to his dream of defeating Norman Welch for the Headship. Instead he had ten minutes to drive his 1978 Lada from "Seaview Farm", the ironically named viewless gaff he shared with Brig in Bridge St, past the ghost collieries and all the other cholesterol of Trollbridge's post-manufacturing heart, up the twenty minute road-rage to Work....

2

"...The quote *unrelenting pressure* promised by this Government is actually driving good teachers out of the very schools they're needed in. And every year, they move the goalposts – *again* - and apply the 'unrelenting pressure' in a completely different way-"

Today cut out briefly under the latest sequence of new road bridges and tunnels that was gradually replacing the former Trollbridge-Penmarw railway network. Dafydd fiddled with a knob, swerved violently, swore. He was still swearing sixty seconds later when the signal crept back...

"...In common with a third of teachers, I have buckled under this pressure and after 24 years as a Head, I've had to leave the job I used to love, working with our country's young people. How, pray, is this improving education? -"

"Thank you. And to respond, we welcome Schools Minister, George Smith. Mr Smith, what do you say to Mr Jones' points? What, for example, is your answer to his allegation that far from improving schools, you have actually made them *worse* by driving away, debilitating or destroying the majority of good conscientious teachers while having no affect whatsoever on the tiny minority of weak and workshy, who are expert at avoiding accountability and don't care anyway?"

A sound like a record on the wrong speed – say a 45 rpm vinyl single played at 16 rpm on a 1950s record player (for those who can remember such things) – or, perhaps, a mogadon-doped but still terrified walrus yelping in a slow-motion nightmare - began, then immediately stopped. This was followed by a silence and then an odd creaking sound. Then what appeared to be a Cyberman's voice answered, "$%*()££$%&*()£$%^&*()£$%&*()£$% "£$%^&*()_"£$%^&*()££$%*()££$%   &*()£$%^&*()$%^&* ()_£$%^&()!"£$%^&*()_!"£$%£$%^&*()"£$%^&*()!"£$%^*()!" £$%^&*("£$%^&*(!"£$%^&*(!"£$%^&*"£$%^&*"£$% ^£$%^ &*"£$%^&*"£$%&*!"£$%^&*"£$%^&*()"£$%^&*(@   @@~ ~::>?{}:>}{}>>{{::><}}@?@~??@~??@}@}}:@?:"£$%^&*() _{>{{>>{{>{>>{>"£$%^&*()"

Thank you, Minister. Mr Jones? Is that a fair response? There was a pause. "Mr Jones? Ah we seem to have lost Mr Jones. Mr Smith, perhaps you could tell us a bit more about the next initiative? I understand the Government is launching a programme of Education Concentration Camps during the school holidays to help Drive Up Standards? Perhaps I should describe some of the publicity material you have brought in for our listeners. I'm looking at a poster advertising The Caerwent Festival of Unrelenting Pressure. It shows a hot air balloon in a summer sky. Sailing past it is a large pig with a target on its backside. And I understand every child from the age of one month upwards is going to get a free place on these courses. Mr Smith?"

"%^&&*()_!"£$%^&*()"*"£$%^&*"£$%^ -"

Today cut out again at this point. Dafydd wasn't sure if this was a result of "technical problems at the BBC", his own vandalised car aerial or the reconfigured contours of the valley roadscape in this, the oldest part of Trollbridge, but, abandoning his attempt to live in the present, he re-tuned to Radio Ychafi. He all but lost the will to drive as he heard Harvey Nickers, a cabaret karaoke singer from the Rhondda, singing

Tell me the way to Aberyswyth
To the gwrl I 'ad my fwrst kiss with...

Then there was a sequence of 'amusing' adverts in a transatlantic whine for local hardware stores and 'quality' fast food outlets: *Dai The U Bend Trading For Those Really BIG Jobs: Get Your Traditional Welsh Cooking At Always Say Dai, In Continental Surroundings.* Incontinent surroundings that meant, if last night's geriatric clientele was anything to go by, muttered Dafydd. Given the choice of Welsh or, say, Italian cuisine how many are going to plump for the former? Dafydd glanced out of his car window at the bloated, duvet-clad forms moving along the narrow early Nineteenth century streets of Old Trollbridge Town Centre and found the answer to his apparently rhetorical question was about nineteen out of twenty. A *Big Issue* Seller provided the only touch of economic vigour and modernity in the street. Still, now that Dai The Big Issue had moved his witty one man pavement show up from Oldport maybe Trollbridge was moving out of the 1820s at last? Maybe other *Big Issue* sellers and similarly cool pavement lifestylists would follow. Maybe there was hope for the future?

The Voice of Llansoroti New Town then announced the time, 8.28. Dafydd was late. (Or perhaps, given that Radio Ychafi, The Voice of Llansoroti New Town, was broadcast from Pontymarw, that was 828 *AD*, in which case he was early). Apparently The Heavy Metal Morning Show was coming up after the alleged News, with former 70s guitar hero 'Toucan' Jones: "If he remembers to come in". He was last reported lost up a disused railway siding near the Blackwood ex-Miners' Institute unable to remember details. Or broad outlines. There was then an advert for The Crem Club – he assumed this was a club attached to some Muriel Spark Academy for Young Ladies but learned to his amazement that there was in fact an Aberacheron Crem*atorium* Club and that it organised events for the 'living'. But then the Voice introduced some "classic Pink Floyd" and Dafydd's heart leapt. He turned it up.

Kicking around on a piece of ground in your home town
Waiting for someone or something to show you the way.
Dafydd sang along lustily.
Tired of lying in the sunshine staying home to watch the rain.

You are young and life is long and there is time to kill today
And then one day you find ten years have got behind you
No-one told you when to run, you missed the starting gun....
The guitar soared. He drove faster. Someone beeped him for swaying between lanes and he gave them a Pantysycham salute. Both fingers. He rode three banks of red lights on the resultant adrenalin. That's probably the Inspector, he thought to himself. (And, of course, it was.)

3

Inspector Carmichael Hunt of County Hall – or at least on secondment to County Hall from "a department of the Home Office" (code name, Education) - was listening to the *Peer Gynt Suite* on Classic FM. His enormous hearse-black SAAB kept pedantically to every speed limit, and every crossed t and dotted i of the Highway Code – including, in the middle of Trollbridge, the one about running a cat down if it got in your path. At the same time, it caused fatal accidents to all who came near it. His rear windscreen carried a sticker urging its readers to VOTE CONLAB: VOTE FOR EDUCATION, an oxymoronic but masterly deployment of the acronym in the interests of his 'Consultation Laboratory's' political balance. (The kind of balance perfected by someone who has an equally large pillaging of lead, taken from the school roof, in each hand). The spacious interior of his car had been adapted to accommodate a man less than four feet six in height, just as the Inspectorial vocation to which he had been called had been adapted to his waspish tiny-mindedness. The great Victorian Isambard Kingdom Brunel had defied physical shortness by wearing a funnel hat and putting the enormous dreams of genius into acts of faith like the Great Western Railway. Carmichael Hunt (true to the crisp vowels of his Sale upbringing) preferred cutting the enemy down to his own size. Behind his tinted driver's goggles, his insect head daydreamed now of the future he planned for the troubled school he had been sent out to inspect. With himself in charge, of course, and with his scalp just visible above the school lectern. He rehearsed his introductory assembly aloud in his waspish whine for the final time...

"Good Morning. My name is Carmichael Nebuchadnezzar Brunel Hunt. NB for short. I am your new Head. I have been appointed here in the light of this school's less than satisfactory showing in the recent Inspection. Less than satis-factory. For "less than satisfactory" read an appalling catalogue of sloppiness and inefficiency that adds up to a national scandal! I did not come into the education business for redundant notions like thought and feeling. You are all here to work and to work hard. One leak of bad publicity – the first suggestion of any backsliding – and you will find yourself in my office explaining why I should continue to underwrite your presence in my firm. That's right, *my* office. Yours is now over there, the one with TO LET on the outside. That's right, the toilet." He crushed the big accelarator under his tiny foot. "Education is about results. My predecessor may have claimed that he too was interested in results but the Inspection has shown otherwise. I am here to balance the books and get our results above the multinational average. Let me make that clearer. Viciously competitive examination grades from all pupils! I am the new vanguard of education. Where there has been discussion, let there be strength. Where the school mission statement has piled up words, delete 'spiritual growth.' We will begin by cutting this assembly short. From now on lessons will begin at 0.600 hours." A second cat – this time a black one - cannoned off his bumper. "Move aside Mr Pussyfoot! This school is at a crossroads. It needs a man of destiny, a leader of narrowed vision, a tyranus rex who will trample the past underfoot. I am that man. Expect multiple briefings, proliferating mini-enterprise, bi-weekly mini-tests, minuscule inspections of all minutiae. These little feet refuse to be tethered on the mountain of circumstance by an accident of size. Let those who would pass me over on account of my height, beware. I've risen to Inspector leaving many a superior humbled in my wake. And now I want to do something *really* small." NB turned up "Morning Mood" to ear-stinging volume.

So you run and you run to catch up with the sun but it's sinking
And racing around to come up behind you again.
The sun is the same in a relative way but you're older
Shorter of breath and one day closer to DEATH....

Dafydd braked abruptly as he hit the 20 mile limit. "And that Favourite Record Choice was for Master Dafydd Thomas of Trollbridge, the Acting Headmaster of The Llewellyn The Last Mountain High School up there in the backwoods of Lloegrbach," drawled the announcer, his accent wandering somewhere between East Cardiff and Southern California. Dafydd veered between lanes again, hearing his name and the proud maternal version of himself exposed to the world. "Happy 45th birthday. You're doing a great job, whatever the figures say. Love Mam."

He shut his eyes on a thread of pain, opening them an instant later on a bumper racing towards his bonnet. He braked. Last night's post-meal Asian takeaway skidded around his stomach, somewhere between South Wales and South Korea, but also stopped just in time. He groaned, wrenched on the handbrake, and waited behind the hearse-black SAAB in the queue...

Somewhere below him a mountain stream followed its own sweet will. He was stuck on the bridge as usual. Not even the wooded hillsides, with their first green shoots blazing on the grey light, could soothe his split-site headache for the journey. The view from Pontesgairmoelfronwennyddbedwelltycwminiscoygarnaruwa unddumynyddmordor - "the bridge of nine magnificently high, wild-oats-and-barley-hued, October-stern, May-queenly, December-deadly mountains" (for short) - had always been blocked by a hoarding, a high-rise block, a dead bus-depot and a redundant cinema. And today there were at least two of each. It made clear road signs for the perpetually expanding road system crucial, especially as they were all now in two languages. (Dafydd had once spent the first two hours of his holiday in Swansea traffic jams looking for what he assumed was the charming Welsh fishing village of Abertawe). However, thanks to the council:

1. If you followed the signs to Ugh/Brynbugaoffifyoumenglish you never got there.

2. If you followed the signs to Lloegrbach you came out in Garnlloegr.

3. All non-local traffic for Trollbridge/Pont-y-trol was directed to a county town twenty miles away.

4. If you followed the signs to Garnlloegr you came out in Lloegrbach – provided you knew the short cut, and didn't mind going through Ychafi.

Dafydd accordingly left the queue at the Garnlloegr turn off and, following the Afonmyynyddmordor river upstream, willed his Lada up the dispiriting mountain road. After ten minutes of clutch abuse, the gallant Lada appeared out of a cloud of fumes and Dafydd had arrived.

The Llewellyn The Last Mountain High School, Trollbridge (now officially Pont-y-trol again), was actually in Lloegrbach - in the 5 hour shadow of the Marw Mountain. It sat, as Dafydd did now, under its giant stone statue of the Prince, at the valley head in Garnlloegr, brooding over the old Lloegrbach steelworks (in Trollbridge) three hundred feet under the Marw. Dafydd turned off the engine, but waited for a Tina Turner classic to finish before switching off the radio. He unfastened his seat belt, his belly groaning as he did so. He swung open the heavy Lada door, careful not to hit the beautiful new white mercedes a sixth former had swung carelessly in next to it. The sixth former –Darren Watkins-Jones - sprang out of his seat and darted on nimble trainers towards the building. It wasn't fair. Watkins-Jones, for all his two names, carried infinitely less baggage than Dafydd – not just several accumulated stone of anxiety eating but also 99% less work in his so-called schoolbag and a couple of decades less history. Imagine the brain space Watkins-Jones had free of all those useless bushels, furlongs, chains, yards, feet, inches, sines, cosines, tangents, co-tangents, shillings, pence, halfpence, ounces, pounds, tons, hundredweights, stones, led zeppelins and iron maidens. Imagine a mind free of all that dad rock. Imagine Ike and Tina's "River Deep, Mountain High" for the first turbulent time without all the silt – the market measures, the reaction, the back story, the break-up, the re-release, the traditions, the personalities, the Radio 2 features, the scandals, the CD box set, the 'history' – which its glorious groove had progressively churned up, petrifying that ground-breaking original current. Imagine Watkins-Jones's half a dozen drum and bass CDs instead of Dafydd's two ton ex-Beatles retrospective alone, its own drum and bass remnant (Ringo and Paul) doing nothing to stop the dead and gone anthology growing every year. All Things Mustn't Pass. Paul isn't Dead. Meanwhile, Watkins-Jones was twenty yards nearer the Key Skills Lecture block in the peep of an electronic locking system before Dafydd had even got his key to the passenger door.

5

Briefing was, as usual, anything but. The first five minutes were consumed by "Uncle" Joe Benson's stream of consciousness ramblings through the assorted pastoral conditions of half of his Year 7 "nephews and nieces". A Caring Frown counterpointed his Smiley Face T shirt. "TLC please for Kerry Jones who is feeling very low after her mid term holiday. She's behind with her work, has very low self-esteem and feels she has no friends so can't face coming in at the moment."

"Never stops me," quipped Michael Umbrage.

Dafydd bit back a grin. Michael Umbrage was an old-fashioned Head of Maths with the look of an ageing but still useful heavyweight boxer. Like most of the population, he still called Year 7, year 1; Year 8, Year 2 etc. He usually described himself as being in the guards van of education, mainly because it put him at the opposite end of the train from "Uncle" Joe's 'vanguard'. He also referred to TLC – Tender Loving Care – as TCP –Touchy Cuddly Pandering. Unfortunately his remark about being behind with work, low self-esteem and a lack of friends not stopping him attending school didn't stop Sensitive "Uncle" Joe either. There was an inexhaustible supply of juicy social problems out there for Joe to get his teeth into and he wasn't going to be distracted by anybody's paid job as a subject teacher. He wasn't even distracted when young Mr Grimsby's elusive mobile – with its specially programmed puerile voice tone "ANSWER THE PHONE YA BASTARD, ANSWER THE PHONE YA BASTARD, ANSWER THE PHONE YA BASTARD, ANSWER THE PHONE YA BASTARD" – went off, over and over again, though of course everyone else was.

After six other Year Heads' laments and exhortations – the news of "Bomber" Harris's permanent exclusion from Year 9 raising a rare staff cheer on behalf of the classes he'd terrorised for two years - it was Dafydd's turn. He coughed. A Headteacher's cough. Uncle Joe came out of his reverie. Mike Crowsoft, Head of Staff Surveillance, stopped playing with his laptop, a nervous habit made almost hysterical by the announcement of strangers in the school. Even Mr Grimsby gave Dafydd his attention.

"As you all know, Mr Carmichael Hall of County Hunt…" (histrionic staff laughter) "sorry, Mr Carmichael *Hunt* of County Hall… is observing us in action this week. In the absence of the Headmistress, it falls to me to show Mr *Hunt* - and his sniffy team of young dogs - around. Since I do not know which route they will be following, I am relying on you, my foxy staff, to give the best possible impression of Mountain High at all times throughout the day. The tabloid press will no doubt have informed you that our erstwhile Headmistress was appointed here thirty years ago under a certain subterfuge. County Hall has chosen to regard the achievements and developments of Miss Francis over those thirty years with scepticism, given the recent discovery that none of the letters after her name bore any relation to real examinations. County Hall was also less than impressed by my predecessor's final act, which was to invite police sniffer dogs into school to check Year 10 bags. Though suggested as a nothing-to-hide tactic by well-meaning Governors, this has given us some unfortunate headlines in the *Trollbridge Morning News*. DOPE HEAD MAKES A HASH OF IT seems to be a particular favourite among the children. Not to mention some of the worst puns on the word 'dog' in the *Lloegrbach Herald* since last year's Miss Ychafi Beauty Contest. But then, who wants to waste time looking at themselves in the dirty daily mirror of the tabloids?

"Everybody," said Norman Welch.

If grins could kill, thought Dafydd, feeling his face crack into one. "Thanks for your assistance as ever, Norman. Mr Hunt may well decide at the end of this week that the school needs taking into County hands. He may well decide that insufficient attention has been given to the excellent education strategies, which have for some time been chuntering out of Westminster. He may decide, as a man on secondment from "a department of the Home Office" in London, that a degree of Government control, or even a complete take-over, is needed: a measure which is unlikely to improve our staff: pupil ratio. I trust I make myself clear.

"So. Three -" he was handed a memo – "Four - priority announcements." He paused as the bell for registration sounded, deciding to omit his homily about punctuality and glaring at "Uncle" Joe's Buddha-like serenity. "First, the fact that London has chosen to thrust Mr Hunt into the midst of our school Eisteddfod celebrations is, I am sure, an oversight and there should be no retaliation on behalf of The Free Wales Army. Second, there will be a Noise Exclusion Zone around my office all week. There will be signs up to remind pupils and those who do not wish to spend the rest of their lives with Mr Trolley copying out the Books of Deuteronomy, Leviticus and Numbers would do well to observe them. Third, there will be an immediate issue of the latest education strategies on laminated display cards. Pupils should post these in each teaching room and remove any out-dated education strategy placards forthwith." The bell for assembly sounded. "Fourth, Mr Trolley, I notice the Gallows from the school museum remains in place up on the school stage. Could it please be removed, as previously requested? I'm not sure the parents understand it. And we wouldn't want the Inspector thinking it's a pupil intimidation device would be?"

"It *is* a pupil intimidation device!"

"Very droll, Mr Trolley. But please remove it before Morning Assembly."

Trolley scowled. "And what about that wretched vaulting horse?" Mr Trolley had no intention of removing the gallows, which was a school tradition that had stood there since 1510, but still bitterly resented the vaulting horse Dafydd had added to – partly - obscure it.

"That stays where it is, please." Another bell rang. " Right, I suggest a more than usually speedy registration and then getting them into assembly five minutes ago. Joe, if I might have a very quick word about time limits…"

"Just one from me, Headmaster," simpered Miss Handle. "There's a Get Well card on the board there now for Tim - Mr Jenkins - who as you might know is off school suffering from a 'stress-related illness'." Mr Jenkins was in fact 'off school' with a complete mental breakdown brought on by dealing with Darren 'The Blade' Kelly and 'Bomber' Harris last period three times a week two years running – as timetabled by Miss Handle. He had been 'off school' for two terms, the time it took for a card to appear and to be mentioned during the TLC For Pupils Festival that was Morning Briefing. The 'stress-related illness' was the teaching career he was 'off school' from and which he had in common with everyone present. "The card is still there waiting to be signed," said Miss Handle. "If you've got a minute, please try to sign it." The stampede past Miss Handle to the door for the next routine drowned out the rest of her speech.

6

Bob The Caretaker, Coriander Cinnamon-Roberts, 11A, and Giles Nobob, Head of Music, ("The Three Bobs") were leading the school through the final strains of "Hen wlad fy nhadau" for the second time as Dafydd swept to the rostrum in his Acting Headmaster's gown, every inch an Aching Head. The gallows was still there, of course - though the vaulting horse was gone. Not for the first time, Dafydd wished it could be lifted forty feet into the roof-space of the Great Hall and dropped directly onto Trolley's ash-grave deputy head.

He regarded the school with withering hostility. His gown was borrowed from the drama department; his hostility was real. "Excuse me. I don't understand why you are talking. Not a good idea. I have a mess-" The bell for first lesson sounded. There was laughter. He roared it into silence and continued roaring at the silence for another five minutes. Apart from the vacuum cleaner that began its morbid drone about half way through, courtesy of a maintenance worker whose countenance would make a daschund look cheerful, it was an effective performance and the pupils were suitably subdued by it. Eventually Dafydd reached his messages. "I have a message from Mr Trolley who has the unfortunate need to remind you about the correct use of planners. This is a point I am sure Mr Trolley will take up with you in a moment. These planners cost the school a great deal of money and are designed to give you a sense of pride and orderliness in your work. They are not to be used as a sketchbook where you try out graffiti, personal ads, explorations of sexual crudity, cartoons of members of staff or all four at once. However, I have an even more important announcement than Mr Trolley's." (Mr Trolley sneered at this slur on his magnitude). "A County Inspector is joining us this week and will be casting a sharp eye over how we do things. I am sure that you will all rise to the occasion." Dafydd watched Rhys Williams make what he guessed was a penis joke behind his hands to his neighbour and glared. "And anyone who does not rise to the occasion will have every opportunity to explain to me, in my office, why he or she has not done so. I trust I make myself abundantly clear. In a moment, I will be asking the Sixth Form to dismiss, setting a standard of quiet efficiency for the rest, which was less than evident in the way you all came in. The rest of you will not dismiss. You will listen very carefully to what Mr Trolley and then Miss Handle have to say and then wait in absolute silence until your Year Head releases you. Now, Sixth Form- "

Year Heads dived into action on all sides. Tommy Jones was taken into custody along with the usual suspects. Dafydd stood watching the disintegration of Morning Assembly into the constituent parts that were always poignantly less than the whole. He felt himself go under for the fourth time.

But he showed nothing of this. His expression was as still and fathomless as the Afon Marw River below the cliffs of Craig Ddu, as settled into stasis as the overlapping sedimentary and metamorphic bedrock, their deep-seated struggles long past. Not that he was seeing anything any more. He was standing in assembly himself thirty years before, being reprimanded like Tommy Jones. And not for the first time either....

He was developing into rather a deep boy, torturously good at arts and humanities; torturously "lacking clarity" in science and maths – he always wanted to know *why* the square on the hypotenuse equalled the sum of the squares on the other two sides, *why* we should "let x be 3" - rather than 999 for instance - why Log Cotan sounded so much friendlier than Log Sin – and not so much what the rules that governed the use of Log Cotan were (he could do that) but what the hell it was. And of course he was torturously *bad* at technical drawing, the only subject (apart from metalwork) that his dad valued or understood. Naturally he was top of the class at metalwork *theory* but had recently cost the school over £300 trying to follow Mr Hacker's opaque instructions on how to differentiate the gear lever from the on/off lever (which, helpfully, were in reverse positions on his lathe only). Metalwork practical, which his steelworker dad said was "worth all the cowin' theory in the world" was beyond him. His dad was, in fact, furiously proud of his son's more academic leanings. But having had to pretend all his own life that the practical side of things was his own forte, he couldn't let anyone, not even himself, suspect this. Meanwhile, Dafydd lagged behind the lags in the simple chat-up line and disco "smooch". He was too wet, too uncertain, and too much of a dreamer to "make real progress" or even "achieve his potential" - what Mr Trolley the Deputy Head of Pastoral annually labelled his "very limited potential" in the school report. The boys were frustrated by his pretensions ("pass it, mun") and the girls frowned at his crypto-Leonard Cohen attempts to 'know' them in the Biblical sense. But it didn't matter because just in front of him sat M…

"or Mr Thomas!"

Dafydd came back to the present: his surname in Pastoral Deputy Head Victor Trolley's voice sneering across the hall.

"It's *frighteningly* simple! I repeat, report to Miss Powell or Miss World respectively – for History this afternoon – with the exception of Butcher, Davies, Morgan, Powell, Preece, Probert, Prosser, Tinker, Taylor, Wanker, Watkins, Williams and Young (who should see me) – *all* those pupils who usually have Mr Welch or Mr Thomas, and are not normally withdrawn by Mr Watkins or *Mrs* Thomas (or today *Miss* Thomas) unless they have already been told otherwise by Mrs Parry-Price. There is no *possible* room for confusion. Anyone who decides to use this minor alteration in the drill as an excuse to create a carnival for Carmichael Hunt's benefit will spend the rest of his school career in Deputy Headmaster's detention.

Mandy Hancock, Jodie Hill and Michaela Mallett exploded out of their front row places into giggles. Chloe had passed them a rude note, to which Christa, Nikita and Stacey objected in fierce female whispers that as usual, like the girls' giggles, and all the other myriad evidence of a feminine presence in school, did not register in Trolley's hearing aid. (Nor did Pansy Handle's sweet microphone-amplified whisper with which she attempted to close the assembly).

"That's all," snarled Trolley. *"Dismiss."*

Pansy regarded the assembly with cow eyes. "Now how many of you ever walk into a field on a daffodil-yellow March morning like this and just...*listen?*"

The stampede in all directions to the doors for the next routine drowned out the rest of her speech.

7

Seated in reception next to a skinhead parent and a girl who looked too young to be out on her own (but who in fact was also a parent), Luke Seer of the *Trollbridge Morning News* watched, fascinated, as Pansy was taken offstage in tears by her partner, Madge Watkins. The journalist's mobile phone rang. He stood up to answer it.

"Luke, it's Brian Jennings. The editors are just about to start our 9 o' clock conference. Carol wants to know whether you can get that Piss Head story for the education pages or whether it's even strong enough for the Splash?"

Luke imagined the scene back at Morning News House, home of the *Trollbridge Morning News*, the *Cwmcysgodionmarw Argus* (for whom he wrote theatre reviews under the byline Blind Pew), the gossiping *Mouth of Monmouthshire* and a long list of 'sibling' and/or 'rival' publications all desperately trying to stem the ebb tide of print journalism. Frowning over the neglected coffee pot along the conference room table at his team of editors, Brian would look exactly like an Assistant News Editor should look...

8

Brian Jennings was fifty five, skinny, suited and wide-tied without looking any less savage, had a thick head of grizzled black hair, dark eyes magnified behind thick square lenses, a handlebar moustache and the general air of a dinosaur who was nevertheless nowhere near as dated as he looked. He knew his way around a computer keyboard just as he once knew his way around a typewriter and he knew a good story – and a no story - when he smelt one. He lived in the real world and he wanted his journalists to write about it, the way it really was. "I don't have a degree in journalism but I know about media law," he would tell his interviewees (who usually did have a degree in journalism and didn't know media law). He also knew his rights as a journalist, knew public ad-

31

ministration - knew a select committee paper from a private member's bill – knew what was libel and what wasn't. Local councillors and bigwigs who tried to wave words like 'confidential' and 'not in the public interest' at him usually didn't get very far. He had a (large and hooked) nose for the right line and a (bucket) ear for the right - sharp – phrase. And his shorthand was in excellent working order.

"I'm not so sure," said Luke Seer at the school lobby end of the mobile line. "I'm beginning to feel for the bloke to be honest. I've just seen his assembly and he seems to be trying his best for the old place. He's got an Inspection on, he's being interviewed for the Headship today and we've already crucified the school over the drugs check, which was well meaning, if stupid, and was his nutty predecessor's idea after all. Also, I'm not sure we can trust Joyce's version of events. I mean, would you sleep with Brig 'Bullshitter' Davies just to get a private view of a local Headteacher's home life? We could try to get to the story *behind* the news here."

"Hmm. Well, keep on eye on things. If it's a no-no, Shirley's got a story about Ychafi High where parents are being taught how to forge more convincing illness notes for truants. Then there's always the woodwork teacher at Millstone Colliery School – what are they called nowadays? – who's got his pupils producing bird boxes for Barret Houses. He's got a lucrative national contract for the school and massive approval from the Environment lobby – but there's still the small issue of whether kids doing GCSEs ought to be working 8 hours a day on a business contract. Not to mention the two hundred people at Lloegrbach Timberworks who have been made redundant as a result and lost their pension on a technicality. Maybe we'll go with that."

Luke didn't want to lose his Splash if he could avoid it. "What about a bit of a success story here if this bloke does bring it off though? Local boyo made good gets the job, saves the school? That sort of thing."

"And gets the girl as well, I suppose? Give me a break, Luke. This is the *Trollbridge Morning News*, not Grimm's fairy tales. I don't want *writers*, I want campaigners like Joyce. Never mind the chamber music. Give me the piss hitting the pan." Brian paused. "Still, I like the idea of him turning his past around. Stay with it and see where it goes if the Piss Head thing doesn't - and let me know what you've got in time for the midday conference - "...

9

"Can I help you?" Dafydd was frowning at Luke.

Luke closed the call. "Hi. Yes. I'm Luke Seer, *Trollbridge Morning News*. I wondered if you could spare us five minutes about the Inspection?"

"Actually, no. We have an Inspection on. "

"I know." He held out a photo. "And before you tell us about it, do you want to give your side of this flasher holding a tizer bottle of piss story?"

But Dafydd had already gone.

10

Dafydd confronted Assistant Headmaster Norman Welch in his office. He had so far avoided arranging for Norman's name plaque (NORMAN WELCH - DIRECTOR OF DELEGATION) to be placed above his own on the office door, and Norman was "far too busy" to arrange it himself, but it aggravated an already strained relationship. The air prickled between them. It was the Four Minute Panic between Morning Assembly and Period One and between them they had seven people to see and a dozen tasks to do. Norman's single task was his Five Term Plan for improving the English Department's 'attack' on the Statistically Wayward Attainment Tests (SWATS) – a nationally 'audited' exam yielding no Exam Board qualification for the children it tormented, nor a marking standard that anyone could take seriously, and therefore a priority in all British schools. Norman's single task was printed out elegantly in three colours on a spreadsheet clipped to a clipboard. Dafydd's (eleven) tasks weren't.

"No mention of the new-era SWATS in your 'morale-boosting' assembly, I notice, Dafydd. Tut tut tut. I've just been talking to Norman Clark, Carmichael Hunt's Literacy Tsar. We can't be seen to be welching on our public duties in the presence of a Government Inspectorate, old boy!"

"Welshing is *exactly* what we should be doing with that load of toss."

Norman flinched as some Welsh English hit him in the eye.

"And while we're on the subject of appropriate behaviour," Dafydd's voice rose a few more notes, "that's my bloody chair."

" Temper, temper, Dafydd. You really must try to rise above these irrational flights of - "

"Now listen, boyo."

"Please don't call me *boy*o. I can't speak for present company of course but I left my boyhood behind a long time ago." He rose gracefully and affected to dust off his blazer. " I know you live in Bridge St. with your bevy of bohemians and boors, but surely even that lot start to grow up as they reach their forties?"

Dafydd was about to tell Welch to fuck off back to his pretentious new prefabs in Llansoroti New Town with all the other plastic carvery-scoffing Chelsea tractor snobs from Upper Llamydia before he got his big fat fascist gob smacked in - but decided not to prove the big fat fascist's gob's point. He drew in a deep breath instead and asked, with what was for him a near-saintly patience, "And what experience of civilised social life are you judging that on exactly? The Llamidia Neighbourhood Watch? That's about the only community responsibility you mutual back-scratchers seem to acknowledge. You certainly don't work for a living. "

"At least we don't all clench our fists and start cursing like Mr Stampabout when faced with a little pressure."

Dafydd watched his challenger launch into a corridor crammed with about two hundred too many pupils and just about managed not to slam the door after him. He made a conscious effort to unclench his fist – it stayed clenched until the third attempt – and then sat down heavily in his chair. Then he remembered he was covering a class first period and shot out of his office and along the corridor abusing whole lines of refugees for being late to their lessons, all the time making himself later for his. He was spliffingly beamed at by the least bad of the three 'Samarituns' and comprehensively snubbed by the Head of Inclusion. Finally, he entered his teaching room only to find it empty, ransacked his self-made slag heap of papers, books and urgent notices in frantic search of a cover timetable and realised he wasn't supposed to be here until period two. He sat down, perspiring savagely. He undid his shirt and was blowing cool air through the impressive curls of his bared chest when Ms Morgan burst in.

"Oh! I'm sorry. I thought this room was empty." Although she'd hardly spoken an informal word to Dafydd in the ten years they'd taught together, she touched her hair as she spoke. "The room timetable says it's free."

"It is – except for me. Trying to get a Development Plan done."

"Sorry. Have I disturbed you? Why don't you do it in your office?"

"Because I share 'my' office with Norman bloody Welch."

"Oh. Only I've got Carmichael Hunt coming in next and I've got a chair missing. Can I – possibly - borrow one of yours?"

"NAW! I've got thirty three in my next class as it is."

"Thirty three! That's three over the limit, Dafydd. Quite apart from the fact that the room only holds thirty children, you're breaking Union guidelines on workload. As Union rep, I have to ask why you've- "

"Allowed it to happen? I've got three kids extra and nowhere else to teach them. And there aren't enough chairs! What else can I do?"

"Don't get defeatist."

"Why not?"

"Because - I know it doesn't fit in with Employer targets for killing us all off before we get to our pensions but I still remember something called Job Satisfaction, even if you don't. As we spend most of our lives at work, it would be nice if we could have a bit of breathing space to do it in while we're here. Look, can we discuss this later?" She tried not to flinch. "Maybe when I bring back the chair?"

"Nothing personal Megan but the last time someone said that I had three kids standing at the back all through the lesson."

"But I mean what I say. You know that."

Dafydd made a panicky calculation. "OK." Hardly able to believe her luck – Dafydd never surrendered a chair to anybody – Ms Morgan grabbed it quickly and scuttled out. He shouted at the slammed door. "But I want it back!"

Ms Morgan reached the safety of the lobby and cannoned into Tommy Jones. Tommy carried his teenage world-weariness with a certain grandeur, and wore his acne tragically, like a leper without a messiah. A certain light of mischief in his eyes always made Megan want to laugh. "Is Old Taff in there, Miss?"

"Mr Thomas to you." Old Taff to me, she thought. "Yes. Why aren't you in a lesson?"

"Didn't he see you take the chair?!"

Ms Morgan was racing towards Main School. "Yes! Get to your lesson!"

"I've got to see him, Miss."

"Oh. Well, good luck!"

With a heavy heart, Tommy knocked at the door.

Knock knock knocking on heaven's door. Dafydd looked up from his Nineteenth Nervous Development Plan, the agitation reflected in his face clearing again to the anthracite calm of the Afon Marw on a December morning about thirty years ago. He was standing outside that door himself, flares flapping on the iron wind, knocking on the door like Tommy Jones....

11

The other two 'mobile' classrooms were full of sheep. There was a rusting coal trolley in the Technology-block hedge. The Rugby field had a horse and a hillock of unmelted snow on it. The Edwardian factory of Main school – with MINING AND TECHNICAL INSTITUTE 1868 still carved in stone over its main entrance - was stranded half way up the sky, yet still overlooked by worlds-end moors on three sides. An ancient time-worn limestone carving of the word BOYS stood over one entrance, a much brighter and more recent GIRLS over the other. New 'mobiles' were scattered at the building's feet. A blizzard full of sleet and the tang of coaldust and ironrust blew into his eyes making them water. The water froze. He would have cried only boys didn't and, in this case, at those temperatures, couldn't. He worked his way into the vandalised entrance lobby, appalled at the crumbling plasterboard punch holes, and heard voices on the wind. "Blackberry Way" by The Move was playing on a radio somewhere. He hesitated, entered, croaked: "Is this 2L please?"

"Shit, I thought you was Troll for a minute. What's in the suitcase?" A big kid in daps and denim jacket, muscular chest puffing out the red dragon pocket badge, emerged from behind a desk and lumbered over. A dogend was cradled in one paw and a handbook of open-crotch women in the other. The room temperature was, if possible, lower than outside.

The room's only other occupant joined them — a girl in the correct pinafore dress but with the dreamily-shortest hemline he had seen in his life. She held a transistor radio up to her ear, held it at arm's length, shook it and returned it to her ear. "Are you new?" she asked. He looked away and nodded. Ramo tugged the guts from his dogend and spluttered. "Course he's new. He's wearing a cap."

"That's not one of ours. Our boys' caps are red and green like the blazer, with a maroon badge. Not that anyone seems to wear them anymore. " She was new to the school and her attitude to the uniform had the zeal of the recent convert. "Then there's the maroon, black and green tie and charcoal trousers. *His* cap is brown and bright orange to go with the brown blazer, white shirt and grey trousers. And he's got a tie that looks like a turd with orange peel in it."

Ramo shrugged then helped himself to the cap. "How does it look?"

"Good - on you."

"Maybe I'll keep it."

"Please -. I've never seen a school like this before," said the newcomer. "All these demountables."

"Demountables!?"

"He probably means the mobile classrooms," said the girl.

"And I've never been at a school with girls before. There's about twenty girls outside. 2L isn't a girls' class is it?"

"Yeah," wheezed Ramo.

"No," smiled the girl. "Don't worry. All the boys are watching the fight."

He dropped his briefcase, "What fight?"

"The fight to see who's the second hardest kid in the second year."

"Who's the first?"

Ramo grinned. "Got any fags?" He yanked open the newcomer's briefcase and flung its contents across the floor.

"I've given up."

Ramo lifted him up by the throat.

"I'm starting again at Break."

"Fair enough."

"The Pastoral Deputy showed me around. He was smoking a woodbine!"

"That's funny," mused Ramo.

The newcomer looked at him relieved.

"'e usually smokes Capstan Full Strength when 'e shows new kids round."

"What? Jeez, I've never seen a school like this. All these towers and high windows where they keep the light out of kids' reach, and all these corridors and godforsaken demountables with their guts hanging out. And the toilets. They're thirty years old and they smell like an open sewer. And they freeze your arse off."

"They're a *hundred* and thirty years old, they *are* a open sewer and believe me you don't want to smell them when the thaw sets in."

"And that weirdo with the Woodbine. I thought he was having a heart attack but then I realised that was just his expression. By the way, what's all that growth on his eyelids and nostrils?"

"That's his face."

"And what language was he speaking? Was he trying out Welsh on me or something?"

"Do they speak Welsh where you come from?" asked the girl.

"No, but at least when they spoke English you could understand them."

"That's Troll's *Talk*. He always does that with new kids and their parents. Don't worry about him. He's senile. They'll be pensioning him off soon."

"I certainly hope so. Why does everything look so *hard* here? The mine, the moors, that metalwork block. It's more like a factory than a school. And your school shop...."

"What about it?"

"I can't believe it."

"What?"

"I said, 'I can't believe it.'"

"I know what you said. I meant what do you mean?"

"It sells fags!"

"Course it does. In singles, pairs, fives and tens. What d'you think we do with our dinner money? No-one in their right mind is going to spend it on the shit they serve up in the canteen."

The canteen was required by law to provide nutrition to the pupils. It did so by providing punishment veg heaped beside meat that tasted like the pigswill it would become, followed by suet puddings and sweet pink custard. Though Dafydd would subsequently find it inedible, because his mum found time to cook, it was still a square meal and thus better than what some kids got at home. Ramo looked at him more kindly. "You'd better get your stuff picked up before the others come in and trample all over it. I don't know what kind of school you're used to but you can't afford to leave anything lying around with these bastards. "

The girl squatted beside him and helped him repack his brief-case. "These are smart books. What was your last school like then?"

"A Grammar school."

"This be a Grammar school an all," grunted Ramo.

"A bilateral School," corrected the girl zealously. "It's a Grammar Tech."

"Aye, we'm that an all."

"So there you are. Nothing to worry about."

"Yeah but my Grammar school was built in 1284. It was tradi-tional."

"What does that mean?"

"Some of the original masters were still there."

"Really? Were they strict?"

"Well, you had to wear your cap at Break and go round the quad anticlockwise or you got 1,000 lines. The sixth formers had special black uniforms with Sauspanfach School badges and gave out detentions for everything – we called them The SS. I thought the Head Prefect was Hitler until I met Mr Questingbeast. Apart from that- "

"Mr *Questingbeast?*"

"The Head of Divinity. He said as I was permanently late for his lessons, he would arrange for me to be permanently late for my bus home. And now I'll always be late because I'm four terms be-hind everybody else!"

"Don't worry. I came here late too. From the rough school on the valley estate. And look at me!"

Ramo nearly choked. "We do, Megan, we do."

Taff paled. "The *rough* school? You think this one isn't rough!"

" Aye, compared to 'The Slagheap' it isn't."

"Millstone Colliery Secondary Modern," Megan corrected Ramo primly. "It wasn't that rough. *I* was a Modern Girl. So was Trish."

"Trish was a Modern Girl. *You* were the School Slag," an-nounced Ramo.

Megan smiled at Dafydd again. "Don't listen to 'im. I'm just friendly."

"But I've already ruined everything. That Year Head asked me if I was in the top set at my last school and I said 'Yeah'."

Young Megan and Ramo looked at each other. "So?"

"So my old man nearly killed me when we got outside. He says I should say 'Yes' to a teacher and not 'Yeah'."

"Ramo!" yelled a voice.

"Yeah!" answered Ramo.

"Troll," hissed Megan, waving at the cigarette smoke.

Troll strode in smoking a Capstan Full Strength. "What are you doing in here at break? Why aren't you outside watching the fight?"

"I'm in detention sir."

"Oh yeah? With 'oom?"

"You sir."

"Megan, you're not in detention. Get outside." Mr Trolley noticed Dafydd. " And you boy, cowering there like a mouse, WHERE'S YOUR UNIFORM?"

"This is my uniform Sir. You asked me before. My new one hasn't arrived yet."

"Oh. You're new are you?"

"Yes. Yeah."

"No one tells me anything. What's your name?"

"You asked me before, Sir."

"Really. And what did you say it was?"

"Dafydd Thomas."

"Taff", said Ramo.

"You again! The new boy from the Taff valley is it?"

"No."

"Has anyone shown you the ropes?"

"Sir?"

Megan intervened. "You showed him before, Sir."

"I mean, has a *pupil?*

"No sir."

"Ramo."

"I'm in detention."

"Megan."

"Yeah?"

"*Yes,* what?"

"Yes, I'll show him the ropes."

"'Yes, I'll show him the ropes' *what* ?"

"Oh! Yeah, I'll show him the ropes Sir."

"That's better. Ramo, come with me." Ramo did so, not that bothered.

Young Dafydd reached up to his neck, "What ropes?"

12

Dafydd's loosened his tie absently. The thunderous knocking returned. He roared, "What are you trying to do, break the f- (he repressed the expletive) door? COME IN!"

Tommy Jones pushed the handle but it wouldn't budge. He gave it a shove and the damp wood ripped along the hinges and crashed onto the floor inside. He gaped at Dafydd. "I wasn't even there!"

"Jones! You're a waste of space."

"Yessir!"

Dafydd started laughing. Hearing his own voice echoing Mr Trolley's description of himself at Tommy's age, "Old Taff" (as the kids called Dafydd) sat down and unclenched his fist. "All right Tommy, you needn't run away. As my predecessor once pointed out to me, all flesh fails, all things must pass, all pleasures wane. The only thing that lasts forever is a temporary classroom. Maybe they'll finally get me a new door now."

"Yessir! Sorry I'm late Sir." He went through his repertoire. " I was looking for my bag. Talking to Mr Welch. My form tutor kept me in. I had to go to the office... "

"You *have* been busy. Well?"

"You wanted to see me, Sir."

"Did I?"

"Yes. Mr Trolley said you wanted to see me after assembly. Is it about the homework, Sir?

"No. It can't be."

"Are you sure?"

"Of course I'm sure! I didn't set any. I haven't set any for weeks."

Tommy was shocked. "Why not?"

"Too busy with the Inspection."

"Oh." The boy took a deep breath. "I'm sorry, Sir."

"Sorry? What for?"

"For whatever it was Sir. I won't do it again."

"Well as I have no idea of what you're talking about, we'll leave it until Mr Trolley fills in the requisite paperwork."

"Sir?"

"Or we can cut out the middle man and you can just tell me yourself what you were doing wrong."

"You're not supposed to do it like that, Sir."

"Perhaps not but as I'm a grown up and the Acting Head-teacher, I can do it any way I like."

Tommy was a bit put out. "But what about my incident slip, Sir?"

"One more added to your substantial collection is hardly going to make a difference."

Tommy sighed. "I was 'insolent', Sir. When Mr Trolley told me to exit immediately in a straight silent line out of the door, I told him to disappear slowly in any kind of line he fancied up his own arse."

Old Taff shouted with laughter, then pretended it was a coughing fit. "Not the brightest of ripostes, Tommy."

"He gets on my nerves, Sir."

Another coughing fit. "What lesson have you got now?"

"RE, Sir. But I've been excommunicated so I have to work on my own in the library in those lessons instead."

"You've been what?"

"Excommunicated, Sir."

Old Taff chuckled. "I think that's one of Mr Riley's little jokes, Tommy. He just means you're excluded from his lessons. Is he still teaching that the essential core of all religions is the same?"

"Yes, Sir."

"That we are all one, like three in one oil?"

"That we are all two, like three in *two* oil."

"Ah he means 'one'. Mr Riley's heart and soul are in the right place but he's never been terribly numerate. Is he still refusing to teach the new RE syllabus?"

"Yes, Sir. He calls it sociology in sandals. He says that if God had meant us to study the letter of all the different religions rather than to sincerely practice the spirit of two of them then we'd all have been born in Esperanto."

"Have you any idea what he's talking about?"

"No Sir. And what is three in one oil, Sir?"

"Nothing: an old-fashioned allusion to God having something to do with *industry*, which is something that we used to have round here. They probably don't make Three In One any more... Have you any work to get on with in the Learning Matrix System?"

"Where, Sir?"

"The Library."

"No sir. I normally go for a walk, Sir."

Dafydd leaned forward and extracted a packet of Capstan Full Strength from Tommy's red dragon pocket, noting the SMOKING CAN KILL YOUR BABY in scary black capitals. "With these?"

Damn. "Yes, Sir."

Dafydd turned them over idly and read: SMOKING CAN STOP YOU GETTING PREGNANT. "I hope you and your girlfriend are not relying on these for contraception, Tommy."

"Chance would be a fine thing, Sir."

"Like that, is it? Well, virginity is quite normal at your age, whatever your peers might suggest. And, um, unlike property you can only lose it once. Right. See my desk?"

"Not really, Sir. It's hidden under a pile of books."

"Exactly. Now a County Inspector's due here in twenty minutes. I want that desk so tidy I can see my lesson plans on it. Understand?"

"Yessir!"

"Right, get to work."

Tommy duly obliged. Dafydd moved back, dislodging another stream of books and papers, and watched him for a moment, relieved to find that, unlike the usual detention fodder, Tommy *wasn't* making everything even messier and less coherent than before. Then he moved to a pupil's desk and spread out his papers. "You know, I asked Myfanwy Madoc to clear that lot up at the end of yesterday's lesson and she said she'd rather eat her own face? Unbelievable. "

"I don't blame her, Sir. Your desk is like a pigsty."

"Pigsties are actually clean and ordered, Tommy, provided the pigs are left to their own devices. Almost everything in that bonfire of vanities you're clearing up has been dumped there by bureaucrats. It is a filing system/waste-bin in which everything they throw at me is always either to hand or pending the built-in obsolescence they deal in. My own needs are rather simple and related to real children. Plus I do have rather a lot of real things to do, Acting Headteacher and Real Head of Humanities. Not to mention Head of Drama."

"Head of Drama?"

"What did you mention Head of Drama for! I've got enough to do as it is. Besides," he sounded bewildered and hurt, "even if the desk is like a slag heap, Myfanwy's *always* tidied it before."

"She's been getting a bit of stick for it, Sir. From the class."

"Really, why?"

"They say she's got a crush on you, Sir."

Dafydd laughed. "A crush! Myfanwy! But she's just a little girl. She's…"

"Fifteen, Sir."

"Fifteen! God, when did that happen?"

"You must have noticed. The hair, the make-up- "

"Exactly! Girls here aren't allowed to wear make-up. I'm just re-emphasising that very fact in the Development Plan."

"And now I'm getting stick as well for defending her. Really bad stick because they all think I'm out of her league, which is true enough. Not that I mind. If she'd just give me one full-on smile, I'd die happy."

"For goodness' sake, Tommy, this is a school, not a harem. We don't want you dying, or happy for that matter: remember you can't multi-task like that. Girls always do well in the end, no matter how many times the Gentlemen of QCA House mangle the courses to make them boy-friendly. Because – and no educationalist can fix this – girls actually *work*. Boys like you must start focusing on courses instead of on girls and other distractions. That's something else I've re-emphasised in the Development Plan. I gave Myfanwy a rocket about the make-up yesterday."

"Yes Sir. She was really miffed."

"Miffed? Why?"

"Because whenever Ms Morgan used to go on at her about tidying your own desk, Myfanwy defended you. And then you have a go at her."

"But I never asked her to defend me to M- "

"And because she knows you were just having a go at her because she'd refused to tidy your desk."

"Look, Tommy, if she is going to spend school time making something look nice, it would be a lot more educationally useful if it was my desk rather than her face, ok? And I don't mean to be ungrateful but girls are a lot better at tidying desks than boys. They enjoy it see. Homing instinct."

"That's sexist, Sir."

"Aye, it probably is. Most things are nowadays. It also happens to be true. Just as it's true that teenage girls are much safer drivers and women make better astronauts." He held up a glossy pamphlet. "It's all here. Read the statistics. Or even more convincing, try to read *any* boys' handwriting between Years 8-11. Strewth! I don't know where I am with it all anymore. All I know is there was a time when you could come back after Break and there your desk would be. Everything in apple pie order. Every book, folder, paperclip and piece of chalk arranged. With love. It made you feel at home. A joy to sit behind."

Tommy extracted a whiteboard marker from a fungus experiment that had once been a cup of coffee and put it in its correct place.

"Now it's just battle lines everywhere. And if that wasn't enough, every time I look round some poisonous dwarf from the Government wants to inspect me." Dafydd repressed the desire to look round now. "It's a mess. I'm so far behind, I don't know where to begin."

"Does that mean we won't have a lesson, Sir?"

"No, no, it's lessons as normal I'm afraid. Or better than normal I should say. Keep the Inspectors happy. Do you like my lessons?"

Tommy shrugged.

"I expect they'll make me change them. Again. Do you know, since the Great Kenneth Baker Prep School Curriculum Swindle of 1988, I've had to change my lessons more often than I change my underpants? It's one great stampeding white elephant after another. I don't even know what teaching is anymore they've moved the goalposts so often. Or is that targets now? Moving targets?"

Tommy didn't know.

"It's so hard to remember when everything comes at you in bullet points instead of sentences. And in metaphors violent enough to satisfy the First World War Generals who play the education games you and I have to live and work in. Did you realise that you're a hittable target these days, son? No? And the daft thing is everyone's so traumatized – and they change it all again so quickly - no-one even knows if anything's changed for the better. Or if they haven't just changed it all back to what it was in the first place! Believe it or not, Tommy, I came into teaching to change the world but I spend most of my time just changing the names of the subjects. And coping with the fact that all of them now seem to measured by League Tables and performance graphs, which used to just happen in PE. In fact what with all these 'team' meetings, summer camps, 'focus strategies', 'training regimes', 'fast tracking' exercises, bite-size assessment objectives, 'going that extra half mile' conferences and education booklets with cover gloss thicker than the actual contents, why don't we just turn the whole timetable over to Sport and have done with it? You have to be a PE teacher just to understand what's going on!" Dafydd paused, wondered if he'd gone too far in front of a pupil. "Apart from that, nothing's changed as far as I can see. No kid likes school or wants to go there at the time and then really appreciates it a few years later; girls keep coming top in school and everyone's worried sick about it; and ten years on, the boys – or some of them - are still running the world. Or the valley anyway. And," Dafydd became more vocational, thinking of the overflowing tap in his bathroom at Seaview Farm, "everyone's trained and retrained to the teeth until they're retired, but you still can't get a plumber for love nor money."

"I want to be a plumber, Sir. It's why I want to leave."

Dafydd watched as Tommy straightened out the last few items –including the Capstan Full Strength - on the now pristine desk. "And the kids of course. They're still the same. Thank God. The desk is great, Tommy. Thanks.

"Can I have my ciggies back?"

"No."

"Where's your bin?"

"I haven't bin anywhere!"

"Very good, Sir, but we haven't time for jokes. There's an Inspection on." Tommy held up a giant bin bag of rubbish, most of it from a previous term, a previous set of priorities, all now redundant or past help.

Dafydd pointed to the corner where a frightened little bin waited like a shy bride on her wedding night. As Tommy dealt with the rubbish, Dafydd sighed and asked, "What happened to that little girl in Year 7 – Myfanwy I mean – the one with the shining face and big smile who used to be so eager to help?"

"Why don't you ask her?"

"Thank you, Tommy. I might just do that."

The bell went for period 2.

"We've both got you now anyway." Tommy took his seat.

"Geography cover! Tommy, with an Inspector coming in! I had a foolproof lesson plan here. What have you done with it?" Dafydd started scrabbling for his lesson plan, papers flying. Tommy closed his eyes as he saw all his good work coming undone. "It must still be in my office. You'll have to go – no, you wouldn't know where to start looking." Deep patches of perspiration began to spread from Dafydd's armpits and prick out across the front of his shirt. A shaving cut burst into life over his collar. His lip split and bled continuously, so that, checking the damage in his cupboard mirror he seemed to be wearing scarlet lipstick on one side of his mouth. This meant – with his now cropped-and-greying hair – one side of him looked disconcertingly like his mother. Dafydd was beginning to find it difficult to remember his own name. "Don't let any one in until I get back!" he said, licking blood and applying tissues to his mouth. "And if they do get in, tell them to wait quietly."

Norman Welch looked in on his way to his orderly Key Skills seminar with the Sixth Form. "Everything all right, old boy? You know what they say: genius is one per cent inspiration, ninety-nine percent perspiration. Or, judging by your shirt, a full hundred in your case. Go on – hit me. What does a kid in this school get who does that? Three weeks off isn't it? Go on."

Dafydd's fist clenched. "And the teacher who does it to a cheeky kid gets the sack. But it still might be worth it in your case," snapped Dafydd, walking through the sneer which confronted him. He left the room in a blizzard of papers.

Tommy sighed.

13

Ms Morgan entered the staffroom and lit a cigarette. "Thank God for free periods."

"You mean thank the devil," laughed Angharad. "Satan has some mischief yet for idle hands to do."

"That's just what Troll thinks. The days of frees are numbered anyway."

Angharad looked worried – but then she always did – "Why, what's happening now?"

"Norman Clark, one of the inspectors, says you've got too many."

"What?" Angharad got up from her mountain of marking and scrabbled on perilous high heels to check the cover board.

"I was teasing you, Angharad. For God's sake relax."

Angharad returned to the table. "I can't, not with Satan here."

Megan peered at her through the eddies of smoke. "How was the Inspection? Did he ask to see your gerunds?"

"Why would he ask to see my- Oh, you're joking again" she smiled in relief. "I don't know how you can stay so laid back about it all."

Megan shook her cigarettes in answer. "Want one?"

"No, and you should put yours out too."

"Worried about my health, babe?"

"No, mine. There's a law against passive smoking you know."

Megan breathed out a lazy lungful of blue heaven. "Don't do it then."

"Megan, I'm serious. You'll smoke yourself to death." Angharad got up and checked the cover board again.

"Better than worrying myself to death. Will you sit down and do some marking. You are not on cover"

"Sometimes they make last minute changes. I get worried."

Now that *is* bad for your health. Have a ciggy and relax. Tell me about the Inspection."

"It was fine. I decided to teach the whole lesson in Welsh so he didn't have a clue what was going on. I greeted him with *Iechyd da, Saesneg*. And when he asked me about SWATS, I said *Fe fydd y prawf nesa yn wahanol.*"

"Which means?"

"The children are doing another test."

"What did he do?"

He said "*Merci beaucoup mes enfants* and left."

"Why?"

"The lesson was torturously difficult for the pupils, a living hell for the teacher and completely pointless for both. Maybe he thought it was French."

"Hmm. What's Welsh for a complete waste of time? Like a snowball in hell sort of thing."

"Nogobaith. Why?"

Megan wrote it down.

And 'modern art'?"

"Gweli traceyemincrap. *Why?*"

"And Renaissance Man?"

" Dyn port-talbot. What on earth are you going to be teaching? "

"Dunno. But with any luck he'll think it's Welsh and leave me alone. Sure you won't have a ciggy?"

Angharad shook her head tottered over to the cover board again. Megan whisked through another three exercise books with calm efficiency. Angharad came back and stared in utter misery at her pile. As often when the two women were together they shouted their interchanges in an accusative sing-song about three times as loud as was strictly necessary. It was something to do with confidence, a mutual affirmation against each other and the world. "How many do you smoke a day?"

Megan kept marking. " One or two. All right, twenty if I go out. All right, fifty if I go out to The Emperor's Clothes for the latest nouvelle cuisine and non-entertainment like last night. Cigarettes aren't my problem"

"What is?"

"Are. Men."

Angharad breathed in sharply and checked the cover board again.

"Last year you were chain smoking because you thought you had cancer. These days you've got ants in your pants because you think *I* might. Sit down. You've got a pile of books to get through. Make the most of the time."

Angharad sat down and sucked at her pen. "Who do you think will the get the Headship?"

Megan sighed. "Old Taff won't."

"Dafydd? Why not?"

"Because he's local, he's Welsh and he's an Old Boyo of the school."

"They sound like reasons why he should get it."

"Maybe out in the Wild Welsh West where you come from."

"I'll have you know Pantyfforch is in the Wild Welsh North!"

"North then. But in these relatively civilised parts, having an inferiority complex the size of the Bristol Channel carried round on your shoulder like a chip to be proud of is a distinct disadvantage where running a school is concerned."

"Really? I hadn't noticed."

"Really. Connie had at least proved herself in other schools."

"Meaning she had managed to dupe other schools as completely as she duped us?"

"If you like. But can you really imagine our esteemed present Acting Head running the school on a permanent basis?"

"At least he says good morning to you."

"Not to me he doesn't."

Angharad sighed. "What about Welch?"

"He's from Llamidia, the old bit of Llansoroti New Town. It's the 'real' Llansoroti tourists want to visit, complete with Llansoroti Socks, Cwmcysgodionmarw Tea-towels, Pantyponce Pinnies, Aberlyn Sweaters, real plastic cows in real plastic fields and a plastic middle-class living in giant versions of the Newtown doll's houses the rest of Llansoroti lives in."

"What does Trolley think of him?"

"He thinks he's hilarious. It's the only time I've ever seen Trolley smile in amusement. He keeps a list on his office wall headed, *Norman Welch's Silly Ideas*. The last one was giving out yellow cards for misbehaviour and a red card once four yellow cards had been awarded, resulting in a hell for leather competition by most of the upper school boys to see who could get the first red card, and then who could get the first 10 red cards and so on all the way up to 100. Jon Henderson was on 99 and about to press the school fire alarm one last time when the system was abandoned, causing him all the grief of a cricketer cheated of a certain century by a spoilsport captain. Added to which, Welch has no understanding of Rugby nor of its importance, he can't sing a good coalfield tenor and he doesn't vote Labour for the right reasons. He has completely the wrong background."

"And even Trolley doesn't like him. So?"

"So he'll probably get the job."

Angharad picked up Megan's cigarettes and fiddled with them. "Better than Troll getting it I suppose."

"Troll won't forgive Taff getting the *Acting* Headship over him let alone either of these 'youngsters' getting the real one. The only person who thinks Troll wasn't too old for the job when the devil was a boy let alone now is Troll himself. So 'better than Troll' is hardly a recommendation. Now may I please try to get this marking done before the bell?"

Angharad marked one book, thought about checking the cover board one more time, then looked up at her friend, "When are the interviews?"

Megan swore softly and gave up. "Today. That's what this morning's assembly and the zone of silence were all about. It's the official reason why Goliath is here."

"Goliath?"

"The surreally diminuitive Carmichael Hunt."

Angharad laughed, then looked even more worried, "What's the unofficial reason?"

"You know. Information gathering."

Angharad looked relieved.

"Information gathering as the first stage of taking us over! As from tomorrow and tomorrow and tomorrow. She lit another cigarette and inhaled deeply. "Angharad, even anxiety junkies like you sometimes have some real things to worry about."

"I'm worried about the headship now as well. I'm surprised you weren't put forward for the job."

"I'm not. I'm just an old girl of the school."

"I didn't know you came here!"

"Well – I did. Then I got as far away as possible. Driftwood Comprehensive, Norfolk, and Dis Community College, also Norfolk. Streatham Boys' Secondary Modern in London, the only female on the staff. And a great time was had by all. And then I came back. Sucked into the vacuum of the Eastern Valley."

"Why?"

Megan looked at her.

14

The Green Mountain, Spring 1972. Radio One was still playing "My Sweet Lord" by George Harrison. Young Megan was singing along, "I really wanna know you, really wanna go with you" (which she used to think meant 'go out with you'). She remembered singing it patta-cake with Trish outside of Biology, turning petticoat-revealing handstands and other minxy lapses against the school dress code with all the boys watching. She felt Ramo's hand brush her leg as he leaned over to turn it down.

"So what do you think of the car then?"

"It's great."

"You really think so? It's just the old man's banger. He's been more generous since the strike."

Megan said nothing.

"What's the matter?" said Ramo at last.

"Nothing." She looked out of the window and took in a view of the Western Mountain and the pricking lights of the valley below. She was tired of it. The banks of the streams plunging riverwards across the igneous pavement tops of Craig Ddu were a sickly after-the-goldrush orange, ghost-buildings and broken up winding gear beginning to sink into the dusk; a wilderness of ferns interspersed with slag; a disused railroad; a dead sheep rotting acridly on the wind, and bones everywhere. The stump walls and wind-bitten lintel of a solid but roofless old limestone farm, so old it may have pre-dated the industrial revolution and been ruined by it, were still just visible among the dead bracken and leaves of a century of autumns. Trees fell away below and mounted above, the lines of evergreens nearest the lane and the old railway conveying an atmosphere of resentment and hostility. Two former brick works spewed their memory of industry and energy, one of the many bi-products of a thriving coalfield and ironstone valley, pouring it imperceptibly away into this tributary of the Afon Marw year by year, a treacherous slide of decay down the steep valley sides. Slag heaps and waste tips had begun to take root and bear gorse, whimberry and heather, and next to the one remaining pit-head there was an old miners' cooler. A big rusty sign still proclaimed DA GER: DO N T SWIM – but it had seen its last unauthorised swimming boys in the miners' water a couple of years before. It had not seen *miners* bathing for even longer. Shale and iron caught the last daylight. The whole place seemed to be rusting.

A ghostly but sheepish figure in a white sweater emerged into view out of the gloom, jumping from one bit of abandoned rolling stock to another, chattering to itself among the pit waste. "Mmmmmehhhh! Mmmmmehhhh!" Megan at first thought it *was* a sheep and, when it stopped, a boulder, still as the dead centuries. A boulder brought to life by a trick of the dusk or maybe some older scarier earth-magic.

But no, it was just a boy wandering his lonely cloud of longing, making silly noises, looking for some coalfield princess.

Megan was alarmed. "Ramo, Someone's coming."

Ramo peered. "It's just a kid."

"It's Taff!"

"That ponce! He's probably come to play with his toy aeroplane. Come on, let's go somewhere else."

"I think he's seen us." She called, "Taff!"

"What are you calling him for?"

"Why not?"

Ramo reached into the back seat and lobbed a missile at the intruder. The intruder watched them, petrified into a boulder again.

"He's not coming anyway."

"He'd better not." Ramo clenched his fists. "Come on, I'll show you how fast this thing can go round the hairpins. We'll look at the lights and 'ave a laugh in town. I'll show you how the seats fold back. I'll- ."

She sighed. "We never talk about anything, Ramo. Let's sit here and talk for a bit."

Ramo's brain ticked over...The Headmaster telling Troll earlier that day that coal miner's sons never made anything of their educational opportunities... Troll agreeing...Ramo overhearing, taking them at their word...Dusk and silence...

An owl hooted in the gloom. Somewhere far off in the valley below a teenage car beeped and another replied. Some iron railings several miles away, painted by Ramo's grandfather, slowly dried in the damp air.

"Come on then. Let's go." He let in the handbrake.

Megan caught his hand away from the controls and held it against her, glancing once more in Taff's direction. "No," she breathed, "let's stay here."

15

"Megan?"

Megan Morgan had been staring intently at Angharad without seeing her. She realised and grinned. Angharad grinned back cheerfully and then froze. Megan guessed that Troll had entered the staffroom, sniffing for sedition. Permanent Pastoral Deputy Victor Trolley – universally known as 'Troll', or in his five and a quarter foot presence by the ironic code "The Man Mountain" - had that effect on staff and students alike. Megan felt as cold in his presence now as she had as a hot-thighed rebel of fourteen, and at 45 she naturally resented it. She wasn't that naughty schoolgirl anymore but Permanent Pastoral Deputy Victor Trolley, like the Marw Mountain, never budged on any issue – hadn't got where he was today by changing his opinion. He had core beliefs and a heart of pennant grit and a career that seemed to last forever. He had opposed Megan's appointment at the school on the same petrifying principle he had opposed Dafydd's. He would oppose Dafydd's *promotion* even more. He was the dead weight of the status quo, the solidified might of the past. He was *Wales*.

He was on a well-worn path, the stone-floored warpath he trod every morning from his Orifice to the Cover Board. He was haranguing a girl waiting outside the staffroom door.

"…And, seventhly, why are you in the Administration Corridor at all?"

"D-don't know, Sir."

Two friends – and a kid who happened to be passing and spotted a chance to stay out of her lesson - stood with her. Trolley's voice was a sustained snort, sneering dalek-like down its nose at the human world. "Name and form!"

"A-Athene Jones, Sir. 8 TH"

"Why aren't you in lessons?"

"She can't breathe, Sir."

"Don't interrupt." Mr Trolley persisted, "Why aren't you in lessons?"

"Sir, I've been trying to - "

"Don't interrupt. Why aren't you in lessons?!"

"C-can't breathe, Sir. I was sent to reception by Mr Welch but they said I had to get a note from a member of staff. I've got an exeat."

"Oh, you've got an exeat have you? In that case, I apologise." His sneer intensified. "Jones! Look at me when I apologise!"

"Sir!" choked the panicky voice. She pointed wildly.

"What?" And *don't,* " – he pointed a finger at her face–" *point!*"

"Ch –choking!"

He consulted the Staff Room Duty Board. "Who's on First Aid Duty?" he rapped.

"Sir, Sir!!" choked the child.

"Don't interrupt!" he ordered her. His increasingly high pitched sneer addressed the staffroom in general, "I said, "Who's on First Aid Duty?"

"Sirrr!!! " The child began to go red.

Unable to bear it any longer, Megan ran to the door and brought the wheezing child in.

Angharad rubbed the girl's back, "What is it, Athene? Do you suffer from asthma or anything?"

The girl, who seemed about to expire at any moment, swayed away from them.

Megan took her firmly by the shoulders. "Have you swallowed something?"

Mr Trolley was still scanning the Information Boards, his expression that of a man attempting unsuccessfully to pass flint.

Athene's friend Kazara-Jade was on the edge of tears. She looked at Megan. "She... swallowed my chewing gum."

"Athene Jones, 8TH. Nothing here about asthma or anything else," snapped Trolley as if that ended the matter.

Megan clapped the child sharply on the back and the gum shot out from her throat and – with wonderful accidental aim – into Trolley's pigeonhole. Megan breathed a sigh of relief. So did Athene. Megan hadn't been entirely sure this was the right thing to do but as the alternative seemed to be asphyxiation by procedure, she acted from instinct. The pupil began to calm down, then to cry. "Than- thanks, Miss."

"Perhaps you'll think twice about eating gum in lessons, Athene, eh? Especially PE lessons. Come on. " Megan gave her a hug.

"This is precisely why we have chewing gum all over the playground," interrupted Mr Trolley in a glow of triumph, his entire world-view vindicated. He steered Athene firmly back out of the staffroom towards her anxious pale-faced friends. "You are the most obnoxious set of litter louts it's ever been my misfortune to address. A self-respecting rabbit would be ashamed. Yes, Jones, a rabbit eats its own excrement. But you wouldn't think of clearing up the detritus of wrappings and fag ends you excrete everywhere in sight even if you were rabbits. If you're not very careful, you're going to see another side of me."

"'But - this is that side!" said Athene.

Megan – sending the girl back to her lesson with a note – agreed, and she'd known Trolley a lot longer. "From the rising of the sun to the going down of the same," – the very definition of permanence Trolley had snorted in a hate-filled voice through every School Morning Prayers the youthful Megan could remember – summed it up very well.

Mr Trolley's progress through the staff-room continued as if nothing had happened. Several of the old School Internal Communications System Crap Attractors winced as he passed them, instinctively trying to conceal their openings. In the long quiet nights between school days, they shared horror stories of Troll ramming their defencelessness with his documentation. The new (larger and smoother, plastic coated) Crap Attractors, recently built alongside, weren't so sure whether they believed these stories or, frankly, whether they would even mind if they were true: it might be rather thrilling to have one's hole stuffed so purposefully. They even debated among themselves why the old wooden Crap Attractors avoided the name Trolley used for them. Dafydd's Crap Attractor bravely asserted that "We must never be pigeon-holed in that way," though she had of course suffered more than most - even the new ones conceded that.

"Miss Morgan, you haven't filled in the correct documentation for your recent theatre trip!" Trolley held out a five-page form. "You'll have to do it all again. And don't," his mouth smirked like something wedged between a rock and a hard place, "deface the appendix this time."

Megan had once in sheer frustration inserted "grumbling" before the word "appendix" and filled in some of the more ludicrous boxes with references to anal retentiveness and having *piles* of work to do without having to fill in this toilet roll of a form, which was all very childish but then Trolley treated her like a child. All her life in this school, on both sides of the Desk, Trolley had been the eternal 0-0 draw, the endless clean sheet, the perpetual wet blanket. And he would wear that blanket until they buried him in it, no doubt. She shivered. A clean sheet wasn't always good for your health. And who cared if you let a few in, as long as you scored?

Trolley had received the standard letter of complaint from Miss Llidiog of The Almshouses, Feccagafros, Upper Ychafi. Miss Llidiog had purchased a cheap school evening ticket and proceeded to complain about the behaviour of two chatty crisp-crunching Tenth Years – Holly Day and Tatiana Hunt - whom Megan had been trying to introduce to the theatre for the first time. Crisps they'd been sold, as the performance began, by the ushers, and of which a quietly furious Megan had deprived them as swiftly and discreetly as she could, not helped by the fact that Miss Llidiog had kept everybody waiting in the refreshment - and then the toilet - queues for most of the interval. Trolley had asked Megan to put her explanation in writing on a special form that was to be preserved on his records. This serial pain in the arse her reward for giving up an evening's recuperation in favour of hours of organisation, endurance and then Trolley's post mortems. "You're very interested in forms aren't you, Victor?" she smiled sweetly.

"I have to be."

"Well I'm not."

"I beg your pardon?"

"Have you ever actually organised a theatre trip? "

"As a matter of fact I have!"

As a matter of fact, Trolley had. His trip had famously bowled into Stratford, East London, at about the same time that the *Waiting for Godot* he'd taken 57 paying pupils to see was finally getting under way (after an interminable delay and with fifty seven empty seats) several hours away in Stratford-upon-Avon, Warwickshire. A bigger man than Trolley would have accepted the wigging he got on his return - and every time the subject came up thereafter - with at least the appearance of *sangfroid* until the whole thing died down into sympathy, the acceptance that we all make mistakes, even Deputy Heads. But Trolley was not a big man in any sense. He still blamed the lack of cultural bearings in Gwallus Coaches for its sabotage of what would have been the greatest theatre trip of all time. He was so preoccupied by the trivia in his own eye he never glimpsed the magnitude in the vision of others, particularly Megan's, that child of the seditious seventies. He made up for size, however, with a certain metamorphic intensity, the intensity of a career mountain concentrated into five feet two and three quarter inches of frustration. He gave Megan his best stony glare.

"I've organised a theatre trip all right!"

"Then you'll know how much time and energy it takes. Megan pushed by him to the door. "Especially," - she and Angharad were already laughing hysterically before her parting shot - "when you go via London!"

Chapter Two

Troll

I hope I die before I get old...

1

Victor Trolley was back at his immense oak desk, straining furiously against the Times' cryptic crossword. Fifteen down. BED FRAUD IN A & E GETS TO BOTTOM OF WHY CHOPS SLAY A SIN (14) He'd advanced as far as ------ANAL---- and got stuck. Bed fraud getting to the bottom of something was probably that slippery shyster FREUD - a seeming reference to Accident and Emergency really a concealed transposing of the E and A. Was the last section an anagram perhaps? That ANAL stirred something. "Anal and Arg" was an Analysis paper sat every year by the Fifth Form and Arg was short for Argument – that was obvious enough - but what was Anal short for? ANALO-GY? ANAL ORGY? Aghhh, it was on the tip of his- . Pshaw! He let out a blast of pent-up air and thrust the paper away from him. It was no good. His seven minutes of recreation had become fifteen minutes of frustration. He would have to get back to what was really exasperating him: next Monday's sermon.

"And, *eighthly*, I do not expect to find anyone deliberately complicating the perfectly straightforward rooming situation with regard to Metalwork, Woodwork and Technical Drawing. " Some of these newer, lesser pedagogues had bullet points to improvise upon. Not Trolley. He wrote his assemblies out, *verbatim,* like classical music. What was good enough for Beethoven and Wagner and a thousand years of classical tradition was certainly good enough for him. He flourished the fountain pen like a baton and continued. "Until the so-called 'Design Technology' block opens, classes will be held in 'mobiles' near Block H. These 'mobiles' will be numbered as on student timetables. Meanwhile, the new Mathematics Block – formerly rooms 21-27 and 32-35 of the so-called "Craft, Design and Technology" block – is now refurbished and will become rooms 60-69 as numbered on student timetables. Not the timetables issued by Miss Handle last Wednesday – week 1 – which all pupils know quite well have had to be recalled owing to a computer error – nor the replacement timetables Miss Handle sent out via registers, which were in fact an earlier and differently inaccurate draft of the mistaken ones, but those issued last Wednesday – week 2 – by me personally." He rehearsed the next section aloud. " Any new pupils I find, who think it amusing to pretend to look for rooms 28-31 in a 'panic' instead of going straight to their lessons, will find (a) my sense of humour is very different to theirs and (b) themselves reporting for detention in Punishment Room 13 (formerly Room 27) of Block H." He flourished his fountain pen and added, as a concession "(Formerly Block X)" then shook his head impatiently and crossed it out.

"While we're on the point, the nonsense over the deliberate mis-naming of the Punishment Room will cease. Owing to some uncertainty and debate among the staff, not to mention a crisis of conceptual logic in Western Culture, some of you have been taught to call it the "Inclusion" Room while others have been taught to call it the "Exclusion" Room and still others the "Isolation Room". Many of you as a result are now calling it the "Insulation" Room and consequently reporting to the radioactive area currently being cleared by Public Health. This will cease. And, as soon as the current Inspection is over, the Punishment Room will revert to the original name."

"*Ninthly*, pupils travelling on buses will queue as follows. In the North East playground: Buses 1 to 21 inclusive, plus 110 and 111, (except if there is sleet or snow, in which case all these arrangements will remove to the Main Hall). Bus 1 will queue nearest to the fence and the 110 and 111 nearest to the Art Block. The 110 is no longer Bus 14, (there is a separate Bus 14), and the 'Relief' bus is now Bus 8. Bus 8 pupils should no longer queue in their old position by the fence – Bus 8 will now take up a new position between buses 7 and 9 – and should if possible avoid queing too close to the Restricted Area (which is at present having three tons of white asbestos removed by Public Health). Any pupil who IN ANY CIRCUMSTANCES travels on *any* bus for which he does not have a pass will find this extremely injurious to his health and safety. Because I will personally see to it that any pupil so travelling will suffer a rapid, irreversible and permanent breakdown in his health and safety as a consequence!! Do I make myself clear? DO I MAKE MYSELF CLEAR? ... I do not recall the *Acting* Headmaster" (a private sneer) "mentioning *relative* as opposed to absolute silence as your mode of dismissal!" He noted a stage direction in red ink, underlining it several times - *Stony glare.* Now the *coup de theatre.* "That pale little boy muttering to himself over there! Stand up straight! Evidently we need to teach you a lesson! Report to my office at morning recess. You can single-handedly clean up the municipal waste tip your fellow animals have made of the North playground. Berry! You can join him. And if I have to speak to you again, boy, it won't be Berry it'll be Bu*ried!*" Trolley chuckled merrily at the old joke, then stopped himself. Must remember not to do that in front of the boys. "The rest of you, this is your penultimate warning."

"But that was only our first," some barrack room-lawyer schooled by the permissive post-war regime would bleat.

"Make sure it isn't your last!"

"*Tenthly*, girls' knickers." Mr Trolley sighed and paused to consider this undignified item for a moment. It was so intolerably *extra rectum.* He spoke the clenched Latin aloud as if snorting snuff. This entire area –the area between the female knees and waist – was simultaneously Out of Bounds At All Times and yet a chronically unpoliced area of the school uniform. It would be better if the girls left the whole area at home. But Fanny, his traditional ally in these matters, had explained that this wasn't possible. And now that Fanny had finally retired (aged 106), there seemed little hope of grasping the point. Nevertheless it had to be overcome, like Hitler. He fetched his propelling pencil and technical drawing equipment, pinched his nostrils together and, breathing stertorously with the effort, drafted with compasses and T squares a dozen pairs of what seemed to him suitably modest gym knickers. Finally, he grunted with satisfaction and clamped them to a display board. Then, returning to his sermon, he wrote, "Girls' knickers will be congruent with the specifications laid down in the accompanying letter home. Only regulation army-green knickers will be tolerated. (On hot days, these knickers may be rolled up as far as the *rectus femoris*; on very hot days a second fold may occur as far as the *adductor longus*.) Any knickers that fail to conform to these requirements will be removed immediately and their owners will report to my office to collect them at the end of the day. Any girl who is unsure if her knickers are suitable should bring them to me at the end of Period One. Naughty girls delayed by a session in the Punishment Room should convene here immediately afterwards, not keep me waiting. Any naughty girl who comes too late will be reprimanded on the spot and be made to come after school every night this week." Trolley read this through, anxious to eliminate any possible ambiguity or innuendoe, nodded, made a dozen clarifying multiple underlines and finally nodded again. Clear as ice. He placed his entire sermon to one side for the morning assembly, refilled his cigarette case, tucked his copy of "The Times" - with its naggingly unfinished cryptic crossword under his arm - and made his way to his private snug on the second floor. It was while he was there that he realised that 15 across – Scraggy Turkeys (6) - must be PALTRY and so the elusive clue partially filled in as ------ANAL---- must begin, like most of his mornings did, with a capital P.

Carmichael Hunt emerged from under the desk and examined the display board, making copious notes. The dozen drawings of what looked like half-dressed schoolgirls pre-occupied him for some time.

2

A few miles down valley, James Spectre, a local boyo made goodo, arrives outside the Cwmcysgodionmarw Theatre in Penmarw Square, Llansoroti New Town. He knocks at the stage door, rain dripping off his hat and coat, until it opens. He then exits and re-enters carrying bags, trunks and props for a show. A circular drum plaque identifies this as LOVE ME DO: A ONE ACT PLAY ABOUT A ONE MAN SHOW ABOUT THE FAB FOUR. In the doorway stands Mal, a stage manager. Beside the shelter in the middle of a roundabout, a pretty nurse is selling poppies from a tray. Returning to his hometown past in the living present appears to be some kind of hallucinogenic experience for James. He feels as if he's in a play. But he is anyway. The opening chord of A HARD DAY'S NIGHT crashes in followed by the song, varispeeded and echoing in a psychedelic manner, in a psychedelic manner, in a psychedelic manner... James continues to make entrances and reverse-exits in and out. Mal smokes a cigarette and watches, unimpressed and unhelpful. The music fades.

Mal We 'ad Max Boyce yer last month. Now *there* was a show.

Spectre Yeah? Look, I'm on double yellow out there. Can you possibly deal with this lot while I get the rest of the bags?

Mal You can stick 'em in the lift.

Spectre (trying to stay cheerful) Right.

Suzanne was trying to call the Cwmcysgodionmarw Theatre box office from Mountain High reception. She had been asked by Megan to book a Year 10 theatre trip to see LOVE ME DO but instead kept getting through to a looped soundtrack of the Beatles screaming HELP very loudly. The external phone line had become crossed during recent office conversions. It would ring the number you wanted and then transfer you back onto the internal line. So Suzanne was in fact ringing the office next door, formerly the English Department's and now the office of SAMARITUNS - a problem parent (of two of the school's worst-behaved boys) who was allowed to play at being a psychologist using Mountain High pupils as guinea pigs. Suzanne tried again and got the amateur security officer who womanned the school's Behaviour Reassignment Room, formerly the Science Department Office. Megan memoed Dafydd that since the Science and English conversions it was now easier to book an appointment with semi-trained crackpots in confidence at Mountain High than it was for pupils or parents to consult core professionals in private about the thing teachers actually *could* do something about, when they got the chance – their *learning*. And asked - was Mountain High a school, or a welfare centre? Her mistake of course was to assume this was a rhetorical question.

But then, as this memo - and other memoes to Dafydd she'd written never meaning to send - and which had been extracted from her locked desk this morning by the Head of Staff Surveilance on behalf of the Inspection - proved, Megan was biased.

Old Taff sprinted with decreasing speed back to his office. As the Acting Head, he still had one. He crossed the playground where about half a team of latecomers was still playing football. The ball came towards him at the feet of tall blond boy with a shoulder-length corkscrew hairdo and excellent dribbling skills. Dafydd judged the moment, trapped the ball, flicked it up, headed it over the tall boy's head, ran round the other side, beat two others who tried to tackle him, evaded pursuit down towards the Art block, then shot the ball at the wall. It rebounded into his hands. He caught it expertly, turned triumphantly, accepting the grudging applause of the defeated lads, and then presented the blond lad with the ball.

"In your bag, out of sight, do your ties up – and get to lessons."

The boys trooped off. Dafydd felt sick, his lungs stitched to his chest. He staggered office-wards wondering why he could taste blood, rounded the Technology block - felt even sicker as he caught the smell of the Year 9 Food Technology experiment – and subsequently lurched like a wounded cowboy into the Administration Corridor. This, being absolutely out of bounds to pupils, was only three quarters full of them during lesson time.

Canyon Winchester was skirmishing with Cole Hunt and Felicity Buck over some mind-numbingly trivial name-calling that both sets of parents might have avoided with a modicum of thought in the Births Registry thirteen years before. Tommy Jones had hold of Spike Davies in a standing rugby tackle and Dafydd called "Oi, Tommy, let him go. Now. Now! I said NOW!" Tommy usually responded to such exhortations but was unexpectedly contrary here. He gave Dafydd a defiant look. Dafydd raised his voice, "Tommy, I said, LET HIM GO!" "I'm holding him back!" protested Tommy. "If I let him go, he'll kick Canyon's head in." Dafydd looked at the blank animal glare in Spike's eyes and realised that what Tommy said was true. "All right. Where's your lesson?" he demanded. Spike gave him the blank glare. "It's just there. Excuse us, sir, " said Tommy, shepherding Spike in.

Now Cole Hunt was snarling "Say that again fuck features and I'll come over there and smack you one!" and Dafydd was reprimanding him for not following the correct school procedures. He shouldn't 'smack' Winchester after one warning: he should give him at least three warnings, *then* talk to him outside, then re-admit him, then if there was *still* no improvement, issue a 'greener', and only *then* if the name-calling continued, a detention, then an *after* school detention and only *then* – if he *still* persisted – then smack him one....

In spite of all these procedures, though, Shane McCarthy was still leading his gang of spelling mistakes (Mykull Hill, Kriss Tomus, Loo Waters) and rebels without a clause (all of 9NE) into open warfare with half of the tenth year over a hurled pizza, and not only was the correct procedure having no impact but the incorrect procedure of "coming over there and smacking each other one" without all the requisite warnings was having no impact either.

Dafydd called this administrative area of the school The Corridor of Power, largely because it wasn't, or the power was not with him anyway. A blood-curdling Tarzan yell and the sight of a pupil on a flat roof outside took him back out into the playground. "Excuse me. I can't understand why you're there." It sounded like Headmasterly irony but was a bewildered statement of fact.

The kid on the roof locked eyes with him insolently.

Dafydd persisted. "It's not Break and you should be in lessons."

"I'm getting my ball!" whined the boy, clenching a retrieved ball as if he meant to hurl it into Dafydd's face.

Now Dafydd recognised him. Darren 'The Blade' Kelly, in mourning for his mentor 'Bomber' Harris no doubt. Two police cautions for carrying a knife. Two more and he wouldn't be able to go into the army. "You do that at Break," asserted Dafydd, inadvertently sanctioning general roof climbing at Break. "During lessons you should be in lessons." The kid came forward with a vicious glint in his eye. For a moment, the years and the mask of authority slipped and Dafydd was back on teaching practice in Oldport.

"Alkatraz" was a new-brutalist construction of industrial girders, glass and tin, and made a point of showing all its workings – stairs, pillars, kitchens, stores, boilers and the under parts of any girls seated along the sheet glass walls of its second storey – to the passing world. In winter, the joints of its uniform plate glass leaked any heat the boilers managed to waft into its freezing wastes, while the prevailing sleety winds crossed it as freely as the light which above all other considerations (especially safety and practicality) it was designed to admit - while acting as an all-day fridge for any frozen items brought in by cookery students. It would have been more sheltered to teach outside, in a bus stop on the top of a mountain. On a hot summer day, the day of airy idealism and liberation for which it had surely been conceived, it was a giant greenhouse, broiling its occupants first into a morning frenzy and later an afternoon trance. Naturally, it had won an award and was now a listed building enjoying celebrity appearances on BBC 2 and Channel 4 architecture programmes. Just a disaster to teach and learn in, University College had mocked. (But then University College had prepared Dafydd and his fellow PGCE students with nine months of seminars in a room without any windows at all.)

Dafyyd approached 'The Glasshouse', Alkatraz's other nickname, past blocks of new, shiny people-kennels that made up the estate. There were dogs barking constantly and broken glass everywhere. There were used hypodermic needles among the glass for those who looked hard enough. Each house had the same peasant strip of lawn at the front and of vegetable patch at the back. He felt suddenly, unexpectedly homesick for his childhood's stone terrace, with its familiar front view of the disused railway, backing onto its spacious mountainside allotment.

He passed a 'Community' Centre with barbed wire round it and crossed the road through a gang of older kids thumping each other. They turned to stare at him, as if amazed at this invasion of

their territory – their usual teachers stayed resolutely in their cars –
and regarding the flat black briefcase with suspicion.

"Are you the truant officer?"

"No, you're all right."

Mistake number one. The fags came out again.

"Who are you then?"

"I'm uh - a teacher."

The group – a mixture of races unknown up valley – seemed
to find this hugely amusing. Dafydd felt he'd scored an own goal.
A big black kid offered him a cigarette.

"No thank you. You shouldn't be doing that surely at your
age? What's the rule about that here?"

He got his staff handbook out of the briefcase. The group was
now in hysterics. A teacher not even knowing the rules they were
challenging him on! He found the section on smoking and read it
out. " 'Pupils caught smoking are to report to their Pastoral Head."

"Fuck off," yelped a smirking freckled white midget near the
front.

"What?" Dafydd got out a notebook.

"Fuck off," repeated the kid patiently.

"That's a Deputy Head offence," said Dafydd now very flustered, scrabbling through a handbook that recommended 'lifting
an eyebrow' – or 'studiedly dropping a book' - among its pupil-
control procedures. Other kids were now joining in the fun, a ma-
licious joy substitute spreading all over their faces. They'd caught a
student teacher – the chink in the staff armour! The big black kid
was beaming all over his face, large warm eyes seeming almost
sorry for him. "You'll have to see the Deputy Head".

The thin white midget snorted. "Who?"

"The Deputy Head?"

"He can fuck off an' all!"

This creased up the gathering crowd completely.

"Now you're really in trouble!" said Dafydd.

"So who's going to give it to me?" said the midget. Dafydd
met and held the challenge in his eye while all around kids
whooped and started chanting, "Scrap, scrap, scrap, scrap!!…"

What do I do now? thought Dafydd, hoping one of the passing cars would stop and yield someone in authority. It was at this point, almost without knowing it, that he learned his first real lesson about teaching, one that hadn't seemed to come up during training. "You stay there!" he thundered. "Don't you *dare* move!"

Dafydd strode off purposefully towards the school, realising he didn't know which part of the high-surround fence contained an entrance. In a minute he would have to come back and face the gang again. But, by telling the kid to stay put, he of course ensured he wouldn't, thus clearing the scene. "Wayne, get off home quick now," piped a few caring girls. "Aye, get off out of it," advised a boy. And Wayne Rogers, believing such an act to be the ultimate two fingers up at authority, ran off heroically into the back-streets. Dafydd, relieved, but deeply depressed at the start he'd made – he'd doubtless be facing some of these kids in a classroom later – now sought the entrance in confused misery.

The grass verges stretched along roadsides full of cartons and wrappers and other rubbish. The gang was still jeering him. He thought about turning round and leaving now, escaping the whole teaching life sentence as one female member on his course already had done during her first teaching practice – a group of boys had removed most of her clothes behind some cupboards on a stairwell not a hundred metres from the Head's office. The gang yelled something else and exploded in laughter again. He blushed. His youthful gang was years and miles away, chasing each other up the gullies to school in the early sunshine. He missed them, even Ramo the Fist. At least people knew who you were there. Here everything – his whole personality and identity and position of hard-earned approximate respect in the world - had to be established all over again.

He walked through some other kids, yelling moronically at each other and his heart sank. Their voices were dead flat, more like Walsall, or the sharper end of Liverpool, than Wales. Even the serial swearing sounded different. Later, during the Lord's Prayer, he would hear "the power and glory" – so gloriously and powerfully lyrical in a valley accent – recited as 'puwwer' and 'glurry,' with all the vitality of a stale biscuit.

A ball flew past his ear. He swung round, tears of anger springing to his eyes. The original gang was running away laughing. He found the ball in a gutter and was about to fling it back at them but remembered he was a grown-up now and put it in his pocket instead. He heard heavy footsteps behind him.

"Can we 'ave our ball back *please?*"

The big black kid, and a grating grey-porridge piss-taking Old-port dialect that seemed to make no distinction between the sounds of "our" and "ball."

Fuck off, thought Dafydd. "Sure," he said and threw it as far as he could across the road, tearing a bicep-muscle in the process.

The kid laughed. "Childish," he slurred. "Entfromyer, uh? Where you from?"

"Civilisation," snapped Dafydd, his own voice sounding oddly sing-song now, even to himself.

"I'm from town," said the kid, pronouncing "town" as flat as the pavement, "so they all treats me like an outsider. When I comes at all, which en often."

"I see."

"They checks but there's no-one at home so they never catches me."

Dafydd looked at him more sympathetically. No-one at home? So he was alone too. Perhaps everyone was. "What's your name?"

"Carlos Llewellyn. What's yours?"

"Mr Thomas."

"The entrance is over there."

Dafydd looked up to see a cunningly disguised entrance in the high perimeter fence.

"That's kind of you." Dafydd made to move off. "See you later."

The kid gave him a wide grin. "I doubts it."

As Dafydd entered the ruck and maul of the playground, he heard a window open and then what sounded like a banshee shrieking. He noticed everyone getting into line. A witch in a black suit came towards him, wielding a high-pitched, evidently malfunctioning, megaphone. Only it wasn't a megaphone. It was her voice!

Dafydd gaped. He'd never heard anything like it. Later, she would turn out to be his mentor – Miss Shibboleth, the Senior Mistress - and he would ask her how on earth she did that kid-terrifying thing with her mouth, realising too late that she always spoke like that. And the closer she came, the harder she screeched. Dafydd lost the will to think, regressed to primary school age but didn't know which line to join. He put his hands over his ears.

"BOYS," shrieked the voice, "have been losing their balls over the walls of neighbouring gardens. I am NOT prepared to tolerate this any longer. In future ALL BOYS WILL WRITE THEIR NAMES ON THEIR BALLS!"

There was a moment of disbelieving silence and then the assembled school started to rock with laughter. Dafydd joined in, all the tension of the morning, and the previous weekend's worry, rolling out of him. He laughed and laughed and laughed. He cried with laughter, tears rolling down his cheeks. He was still laughing when the voice began again and still laughing when he realised he was doing so in a now-silenced playground. Why did she screech so LOUD? It never stopped, it never got any quieter, and when she spoke to you close up, she seemed to speak at exactly the same volume as when she was shrieking at an entire playground. The girls standing nearby affected not to notice it, and the boys kind of shrugged it off – it was the only way to deal with it, tune it out, ignore it because if you listened to it, even for a moment, you were doomed. But it was certainly effective because when she was screeching at you all you wanted was for it to stop. You just stopped whatever you were doing and stood there until it ended. In lessons, you just waited for the bell, if you could hear it.

But she sorted out the group who'd sworn at him. They all got six of the best on their palms, old-school style. Did it hurt Dafydd more than them? Not really (though it did hurt him). And did it teach them a lesson, one they would never forget, and to never do it again? No. That's capital punishment. They did do it again, frequently, partly in defiance of this assault on their pride and composure, partly because it was simply more interesting than the lessons. Alas, unlike that elusive but palpable classroom atmosphere based on respect rather than habituated punishment, it left only a skin-deep impression on their behaviour. But was there a way of emerging from the classroom with something left of your manhood - and without turning into Miss Shibboleth?

Afterwards, with stinging palms and fingers, they wrote him letters of apology. Even Carlos Llewellyn came in specially from town with the Truant Officer and wrote him a story called No-One At Home, incorporating what seemed to be a description of the River Usk at its mouth in Oldport that was so bluesy and sad that it reminded Dafydd of Ol' Man River. Dafydd still had this description of the primeval, mud-glorious, gull-tongued river mouth upon which Oldport was founded. It was framed on his office wall and it gained him a brief accolade in "The Guardian" when Llewellyn achieved national fame as a rapper. But Wayne's written apology was the funniest. "Deer Mr Tommas. Fuck of. Wayne Rogers. "

6

Dafydd stared down Darren 'The Blade' Kelly's glare with increasing desperation. He didn't have time to set up a permanent exclusion at the moment. And if The Blade hit him, as seemed likely, Dafydd would doubtless defend himself and then his career would be over. "Have I made any progress at all in all these years?" he thought, like a drowning man.

It was like all those heavy industrial 'scraps' he'd had in his youth. There was a definite code. You stood your ground. You didn't look for other more 'mature' ways of solving your conflict, like Jesus or a girl. (And though the Head and teachers always said you should have, you knew they didn't believe it. They regarded your black eye as part of the school badge, a badge of honour). You didn't turn your cheek or tell anybody or rat on your foe. You didn't get counselling before or therapy afterwards. You fought. You took your punishment. You landed some punches, did some damage. You fought like an animal, like a man. And then, at a certain point - when your nose was bleeding or broken and your ear was stinging and roaring and you had some bruises as big as *twmps* (hillocks) on your cheek - and especially if the other guy was bigger than you – then, but only then, was it honourable to put your hands out and say "All right... I've had enough." At that point, the other guy nodded, you shook hands, tried not to bleed too much, made friends for life and it was over.

Well, thought Dafydd, already rehearsing this as his retirement speech. That's been my teaching career. *I've had enough...*

"I've had enough," whined The Blade. "Leave me alone."

"*You've* had enough!" Sheer indignation spurred Dafydd back into the fray. "No you haven't, Darren, you spoilt little brat. You're just a kid! You've had nowhere near enough yet. I'm coming up," Dafydd snapped.

"Why?" sneered The Blade, swaying drunkenly. Partly because the roof wasn't that steady but mostly because he'd been drinking vodka since 8 am that morning.

"Because I'm the Headteacher here, not you!" said Dafydd. "And don't you dare speak to me like that!"

"Fuck off!"

"Fuck off yourself!" Dafydd heard himself yelling.

Unnerved, The Blade suddenly 'fucked' off down the other side of the building to the sanctuary of his own home, where no-one ever challenged his self-esteem like this. In fact, where no-one did anything, even if they were there, which they usually weren't, because The Blade had spent his entire secondary school career drinking and taking drugs like his mum and dad and was now strangely difficult to parent, and almost impossible to love. Unfortunately for The Blade, on this occasion his dad *was* at home. Darren 'The Blade' Senior was off work with a burst blood vessel in his neck – caused by shouting at the television - and having his son join him as he worked his way through a crate of beer was not his idea of convalescence. So there would be trouble before the morning was out, tears before bedtime and a hospital visit before morning.

But even Dafydd's sense of *in loco parentis* had limits. A brief starring role in a thug drama was quite enough. There was, after all, a school to run. A school that was not so much all at sea as in Atlantis. Suzanne needed three hundred forms filling in immediately. Two female staff and Mr Morgan in the music department had all requested immediate maternity leave, despite the impossible cover situation. The Head of RE appeared to be on Eternity Leave. Miss World had run off with John Jones in 9X along with half of the CDT Department's capitation.

On the plus side, one of his Year Heads had not only prevented a road accident on the way in, saved a child from abduction, foiled a gang of terrorists, filled in all the County forms required, completed all her class reports on time, completed all the Exam Board's new paperwork, filled in all the *other* County forms the Government now insisted on, outwitted a gang of international coursework thieves, emptied her In tray, single-handedly put out a fire in W block, rescued three members of her cohort from a mad dog that had got in to school off the mountain – itself running away from a wild horse, which she pacified - but had also managed to get every member of her English GCSE retake class a C or above though sheer bloody-minded brilliant teaching. Dafydd really *must* make two seconds to see her in between all the exclusions he was handling this afternoon. (Alas, gentle reader, but he never would.)

What else? A form tutor drowning in paperwork had lost the key to Davy Jones's locker. Davy Jones Senior was consequently sueing the school. (He needed the money for his court case against his wife). And Dafydd himself was not so much drowning as beached like a blue whale. Or like a last man in, set 173 runs to make off 38 balls, against some of the fiercest bowling since the 1980s West Indian seam quartet, who had been in too much of a rush to to put on his helmet, pads, gloves or box. The sheer impossibility of achieving even one secure over with his incompetent technique meant that he was throwing the bat and scoring boundaries off everything. But he was still 23 short and already two deliveries into the last over. It would almost be a mercy to be dismissed.

Apart from that, everything was fine. And he *had* got 'The Blade' off the roof.

He sought some inner peace, some place in his mind he could go to for absolute sanctuary, if only for a moment. Some Mother-angel who would lend him perspective, excellence and absolution, a wife-madonna who believed in him and whom he in consequence would never let down. All that came into his mind was Inflatable Morfydd, several miles away, homely, easy and familiar as contempt down there in Bridge Street, watching the sun come up over the carboniferous terraces of Trollbridge with the blank gaze of a chapel window.

"Morfydd, give me one good reason to stay here," he prayed.

"O," she replied.

"What?"

"O"...

7

Dafydd cleared the watching crowds in the general direction of their lessons and then made his way wearily to his office door. An even more sickening shock awaited him there. He struggled for breath. "What are you doing here, boy? Pupils aren't allowed- "

"You've done very well for yourself."

"What?"

"'Acting Headteacher'. You've done very well for yourself. Good Progress Made, Sir!"

The boy was in the old Grammar School uniform - complete with grubby Terylene trousers - and this unnerved Dafydd more than he could credit. "Is this some kind of stunt- "

"Man, you don't even recognise me do you?"

"The school's a lot bigger than it used to be! It was a grammar school of 400 when I was here and, yes, before you trot out the old clichés, I know Old Llewellyn-Jones knew everyone by name, even if he occasionally forgot his own. But how can I be expected to know 1,000 pupils by sight and have a word or a joke for each of them? Eh? Those days are long gone. Maybe that old Grammar School Uniform is putting me off." He wiped a sweaty brow with his sleeve and then looked at the damp stain it had made. "Is it something I've forgotten?"

"Oh you've forgotten all right."

Dafydd felt a sudden dispiriting chill of fear but couldn't place it. He'd already semi-dealt with Darren, still had that lesson plan to find, then that Inspector to impress, then something else he'd forgotten - and now this.

"Try checking the name on the door."

"What?"

"Check the name on the door."

Dafydd sidled to the door, filling his lungs in preparation for a huge Yell For Help. He grabbed the handle and lunged out. He was immediately met by several colleagues shouting at him at once.

"Ah Headmaster, about those figures-"

"A word now, Headmaster, please- "

"Unteachable lout, he's just- "

"Mr Thomas, essential that I- "

He slammed the door.

"Something up?"

Dafydd turned to the boy and spoke distractedly. " Nothing out of the ordinary. Except...The Bursar."

"Tell him you're in a meeting."

He called through the keyhole, "I'm in a meeting, Bursar." He listened to the Bursar's curt reply, then looked at the gaunt figure across the desk. "With whom?"

"What?"

"Who with?"

"An Old Boy."

Old Taff lowered his mouth to the keyhole again. "An Old Boy." He straightened and crossed to the phone, sweeping it up and punching the numbers of his personal secretary in one practiced movement. It rang briefly, then - "Suzanne? No appointments, no calls. *Especially* the Bursar. I'm with an Old Boy." He dropped his voice. "A problem Old Boy. I'll have to deal with it, top priority. And you'd better send someone to head the Inspector off. He's supposed to be observing me teach. I'll be along myself as soon as I can." He put the phone down.

"Is a Bursar's visit so bad?"

"Bad! It's the worst two hours of my life, next to the Inspection! I've been putting it off for weeks. But finding a nutcase in an old Grammar School uniform in my office is worse, much worse, if that's what you're after. What exactly do you want? Is this some kind of campaign for Specialist School Status as a Grammar School?"

"I need to talk to you."

"No problem. I'd ask you to sit down but you're in my place already. Who are you?"

"You really don't know?"

"No, unless - is this something to do with Bomber Harris's expulsion."

"Bomber Harris?"

"Obviously not then." Dafydd felt another shiver of semi-recognition but again it passed. He was so preoccupied he hardly knew who he was, too busy even to realise he was too busy. The Krakatoa-resembling In-tray. The probability that Bomber Harris's mother and step-father would appeal against the permanent exclusion, the only way in which either could be described as appealing. The sudden realisation that today was his cleaner's morning and that he hadn't tidied up. Morfydd on his bedroom floor!...

("O," she should doubtless whimper as the cleaner discovered her shame.)

"I'm someone you need to meet, someone you've been putting off meeting for longer than the Bursar and more important than any Bomber Harris. I'm the most urgent meeting of your life."

Old Taff sat down. "Everyone says that. Go on."

"Did you look at the name on the door?"

"Yes."

"What does it say?"

Dafydd couldn't keep the pride from his voice as he spoke the syllables. "Mr Dafydd Ifor Thomas. Headteacher (Acting)."

"Yes I wondered about the 'Acting'. You're not an actor I suppose?"

"Good God no. The Headmistress left suddenly mid term, so I've taken over. 'Acting' just means I'm doing her job."

"Damn."

Old Taff was getting angry now. "Look, the 'Acting' bit is coming off from next term. If everything goes to plan, the Governors will appoint me permanently today." He knocked a glass of water over his papers. "Oh God! That's all I need." He mopped it up frantically with a tissue. "Then it's just the County Inquisitor checking if the school should stay open. I've done well despite a pretty unpromising background."

"Pretty unpromising background?" The boy seemed annoyed.

"You wouldn't understand. My dad was a steelworker – working-class. We don't have a working class anymore. He never really understood the Education system. If it hadn't been for Grammar school - we don't have those anymore either - and a lot of hard work on my part, I wouldn't be sitting here today. Not all Headmasters are born with a silver spoon in their cakehole. Or a golden poker up their ass. A bit of respect might be in order."

"How come you haven't got a photo up on the wall like all the other corpses?"

"It doesn't work like that. First of all I've got to get the job permanently and then I've got to retire. You only get a photo when you retire. Look, wha- "

"Well that shouldn't be long."

"What do you mean?" Dafydd gulped. Time began to race. "You're going to kill me!" Dafydd realised with a start that instead of dread, his heart had leapt with a sudden desire. Death! Relief!

"I don't know what I'm going to do yet." The boy indicated the heads on the wall. "I bet you've already chosen the photo though haven't you?

" Yes, I have. Here."

The boy looked at the heavily posed photos. "Christ!"

"It's going to go *here.*" Dafydd held it up in place, fussing a little, then realised that his captor was totally uninterested, his head hanging in despair. " I uh- "

"What happened to you?"

"I beg your pardon."

The boy gave him an Edvard Munch look. "What have you done to me?"

"What?" Old Taff stared at the boy then recognition clicked painfully in his head. There was a long prickly silence. He sat down. "Oh God!"

"Only if He's here with us. This is down to you and me."

"I *knew* there was something about you I recognised."

"More than I can say for you."

"How dare you! Like I said, I've done really well. I- "

"Done well! You've sold out, man. You're just an inflatable Headmaster."

"Inflatable Headmaster! What does that mean?"

"I mean there are at least three of you in any town, all alike, all following the same dreary County-adopted Government regulations. The inflatable Headmaster in the inflatable school who stabs his inflatable colleagues, stabs the inflatable school wall and then stabs himself."

"What?"

The boy mimicked a more-in-sorrow-than-anger house-masterly voice. "You've let your colleagues down, you've let your school down – and, worst of all, you've let your*self* down!" The boy was choking with laughter now. And every time he met the deflated teacher's disapproving grimace he started laughing again.

Pause. Dafydd wondered if the boy could possibly know about Inflatable Morfydd.

He leant forward. "You need help."

"We both need help."

"I think this has gone on long enough. You don't even exist and I'm arguing with you. It's like having an imaginary friend who not only doesn't like me but says *I* don't exist. It's freaking me out."

"Freaking you out! That's more like it. You're beginning to sound like yourself. *You're beginning to sound like me!* You know, I think I prefer it when you're terrified. It's company for me."

There was a knock at the door. A voice called through, "Mr Thomas? *Dafydd?* It's Suzanne. The Oracy Examiner has just been on the phone."

"Oh God, not her. What about this time?" groaned Dafydd.

"We don't know. None of us could work out what she was saying... And Pantysycham World of Fun Joke Shop have cancelled Darren Jolley's Work Experience placement because he wasn't taking it seriously enough. And there's no-one free to head the Inspector off. What shall I do?"

Before Old Taff could stop him, Young Taff danced to the door, opened it and dropped his trousers revealing ghastly 1970s nylon rainbow Y fronts.

Old Taff yelped, "What are you doing!"

"What's the matter? Don't want your sexy Secretary to see you like this?" He went into his (spectacularly ineffective) Mick Jagger disco mating routine and then whipped down the Y fronts. Even in his panic, Dafydd couldn't help craning forward to check what they revealed. Yep, it was his old friend – the member for Pantysycham South - thirty years younger, as yet unknown to woman, but undoubtedly *his* – dangling there.

Young Taff was pulling back into his Y fronts and refastening those long-forgotten every-day-for-three-years charcoal school trousers complete with the old familiar two and a half year grease spot on the backside. "Don't worry, you old fart. No-one can see me except you. And even you've been ignoring me long enough"

Dafydd had made himself very small behind the door. "Is Suzanne still out there?"

"Oh Yeah."

"Yes, not Yeah. What's she doing?"

Young Taff reported what he could see. "She's talking to some geriatrics. Oh great, it's the British Legion coming to see you."

"What about?"

Young Taff listened. "Something to do with an offer of a long boring speech to assembly this afternoon!"

"Brilliant!"

"Brilliant? And you really think you don't need my help?"

Old Taff became defensive. "While the Lloegrbach British Legion is boring everyone senseless, I can get on with The Development Plan." His heart leapt at the thought! His younger self was looking at him with contempt. "It's not often I have quality time to get on with tedious admin like that, it's a godsend. Also, my next assembly will seem witty, modern and relevant by contrast. Plus afternoon school starts in a quieter fashion than usual because they're all sedated with boredom. What's wrong with that?"

"Everything. Did you really go over to the Dark Side just to run the educational equivalent of a barbiturate while you fill in some Government paperwork? If you're going to be a Headbastard at least do it with some integrity."

"'Integrity'? Where the **** did you learn a word like that?"

Young Taff frowned. "Dunno. From watching and listening to you, I suppose."

Dafydd felt a glow of teacherly satisfaction for a moment, the first that month, then remembered a sea of troubles he needed to oppose. "Look if I keep Major Llewellyn-Jones waiting much longer, he'll change his mind. And I've still got to think of something for Suzanne to do about the Inspector."

"Why not go yourself? You can see me any time you like now. I've waited long enough. Just promise me you'll read some Leonard Cohen out in Assembly or something – anything but the Major."

"I can't read Leonard Cohen! Believe me, ever since Trolley stopped me reading 'Suzanne Takes You Down' – a genuine mystical text - instead of that Prefect's Bible Reading in 1973 – yes, I haven't forgotten - I've wanted to read him but I really can't. I'd have all sorts of complaints from parents, the NSPCC, religious organisations, Born Again Staff, County lawyers, record companies, the Equal Opportunities commission: And Inspector Carmichael Hunt will still be here, remember. I'm not even if sure if it's legal- "

"But you're a grown up – you're the Head. You can do what you like."

"No I can't. I can't do anything. Those dreams we had about changing the world no matter how difficult it might be are absolutely nothing compared to getting Mr Trolley to make the tiniest change to his timetable or the habits of an extended lifetime. Or getting Norman Welch to do his job - or to support anything he hasn't thought up himself, or even to support that once it's up and running. Or getting the Head of Science to start believing again. Or- "

"Why should you want the Head of Science to believe in God?"

"Not to believe in God. I can handle that. Even RE teachers generally don't believe in God now, apart from 'Monsigneur' Riley who also believes that the world is flat and that there are angels around every pin-head. The world's been coping with a religion that's lost faith in itself since the Victorians, or the Enlightenment, or maybe even the Renaissance. No, we're not bothered by faithless vicars and atheist Heads of RE. This is really serious. This is a Head of Science who's lost faith in *science*. And quite frankly, young man, in the absence of a religious vision, science is all we've got in our battle to save the earth."

"D'you mean, like the H bomb?"

"Hmm, I'd forgotten that. No. The apocalypse has moved on to holes in the ozone layer, global warming, climate change, CO_2 emissions, the failure of the Kyoto agreement, deforestation, oil – always oil - and crash and burn burgers along the American Way to dusty death, taxiing down the primrose path to the everlasting bonfire."

"Science sounds a hell of a lot more interesting than the five years of death-notes we had dictated to us."

"Well Mr Green doesn't want to teach it to young people any more. He says it's evil, that it's destroying the planet. Which is all very well but like the best faithless vicar he still wants to be paid for *not* preaching it, which means I can't get anyone else to replace him. Like I said, I can't do anything. Don't be fooled by your pawn's eye view of the empowerment of office: you might dream you're getting the powers of the chess queen and you are – you have the potency of all the other pieces in your repertoire, you're the whole comprehending the sum of all their parts - but you're always tied to that glorified pawn, that figurehead of disablement at the mercy of every other piece's demands, the king. You think you're going to spend your days sweeping majestically up and down and across the board and in reality you spend it trying to keep your pawn-king out of check. Believe me, you're freer now, with the whole of the adult world against you, than you'll ever be in my position."

"You total loser. I'd rather knock the king over and die now than end up like this. In fact- " The boy got out a bulging sock full of some terminal-looking capsules.

"NO! Don't do that. You'll kill us both. I – look, we'll work something out. Look- Please."

"'Suzanne Takes You Down' or the kid gets it." Young Taff's pale despair seemed to be increasing all the time. He started shovelling capsules into his mouth.

Dafydd was shaking. "All right, all right – let me think about it. 'Suzanne takes you down/ To her place near the river/ You can hear the boats go by/ You can spend the night beside her...'" God, no. 'She is wearing rags and feathers/ From Salvation Army counters.' That's not so bad. Unless the Salvation Army offends Islamic Jihad or someone. Tell you what. I'll get the Major to do something short and interesting. Show us his war wounds or something. And then talk about Canadian Jewish culture, the Bible as a sacred text for two – or even three - major religions – not mentioning any actual names - and Leonard Cohen's part in it. Anything you like. Maybe I'll even quote something from that first verse. A bit that doesn't offend anyone."

"I want 'And Jesus was a sailor/ When he walked upon the water...' That verse."

"Might offend the navy. And the Anglican Church. And probably some Muslims as well."

"Why? Because Cohen's a Jew?"

"No, because Jesus was. Or because Muslims regard Jesus as holy. Or both. Who knows? There's so many different types! How about 'All men shall be sailors then until the sea shall free them.' Will that do?"

Young Taff stopped shovelling the multi-coloured capsules. "No – but it's a start."

"Would you mind please putting that sock away? I assure you those capsules won't take you anywhere."

"Really?"

"Really."

"Ok."

"Thank you. Boy, you had me worried there. And I'll talk to you later on about - not being so Inflatable, all right?" Dafydd found The Diary on his desk. "C-can I see you at Break?"

"Like I said, you can see me any time you really want to, man. Though God knows what you can say to get either of us out of this mess."

"Whatever you say." Dafydd scribbled a note in The Diary, then moved to the door. "All right if I just talk to the Major then before he has one of his turns?"

Young Taff shrugged, "It's your school. I would have thought seeing off Inspector Carmichael Hunt is more a priority but what do I kn-?"

"Where did you learn a concept like that?"

"Like what?"

"That word, - 'priority'"

Young Taff looked troubled. "Did I really say that?"

"Yeah."

"It's Yes, not Yeah…. Jesus, what's happening to me, man. I'm turning into you!"

The Major appeared in the doorway. Young Taff gave Old Taff a final look of deep confusion and despair and disappeared.

"No, wait- "

"Now then Headmaster. Not interrupting anything I hope."

"Ah Major!" It was almost a relief to see him. "Nothing out of the ordinary." Dafydd looked ashen. "Just an Inspection to see whether the school stays open, an acute mid-life crisis and a more-than-possible mental breakdown. On top of the Near-Death experience this morning listening to Mr Benson's address in Morning Briefing. And I believe I've just been talking to my own youthful self – who doesn't seem to think much of me. What do you think about all that?"

"Won't keep you five minutes, Old Boy."

" Ah, not wearing the hearing aid? Good thinking, Major. That should speed us along. Come in, come in."

8

The bell rang and kept ringing. It was stuck. Megan felt something prickle along her back as though something extra-terrestrial was interfering with the school's power lines. The bell soared up an ear-splitting octave and then modulated into "Ashes to Ashes" by David Bowie. Pink and puce spots began flashing in front of her eyes in time to the jerks of the music. Megan gulped and looked up. An Inspector was advancing along the corridor towards her like a cyberman. She took a step back, then another, then – after a superhuman struggle - swallowed her fear and held her ground. "Good morning. I'm Megan Morgan. Head of English." The music faded as she held out her hand.

The Inspector took it between finger and thumb and stared at it intently, then looked up - he was about a head shorter than Megan which put her breasts disconcertingly in his line of vision - then wrote something down on his clipboard.

"And you are?" prompted the teacher.

"Carmichael Hunt. No doubt I'm not what you expected!"

This was true. His pin-striped suit looked like it had been bought off a peg designed for a proper man with legs, in a sale, and with a crotch that hung at least six inches below his. He seemed to have no interest in how people on earth were dressing these days. His haircut was a reflection in a cracked and distorting fairground mirror and his miniature beard – miniature even by the standards of his tiny head – seemed to be an attempt to look like George Washington that had ended up looking like George Michael. But all of this dwindled into insignificance beside the fact of the man's eery shortness. Megan would have assumed him to be a Year Seven pupil in fancy dress but for his County clipboard.

"No. I thought you'd be like the Inspector in Gogol."

"Gogol?" enquired the Inspector. He tried the word again, "Go-gol."

"The Russian playwright."

"*Russian.*" Carmichael Hunt frowned and jotted something down on his clipboard.

"Yes, in his play, *The Government Inspector.*"

Carmichael Hunt gave her a hard stare, then let his eyes drop to her hemline – or a couple of inches lower to her knees: it was hard to tell at that height. She tried to remember if there was any staff dress code she was breaking. She was still proud of her youthful legs – indeed had been told by a sixth former that until she took her mask off and revealed her face at an end-of-term banquet that he'd mistaken her for a sixth-former instead of a forty-five-year-old (a somewhat double-edged compliment) but she didn't welcome this County Inspection of them. It was as though Carmichael Hunt's black-eyed gaze was paralysing her powers of thought. So she smoothed her skirt down as far as possible and gabbled on, "You know the one. A whole regime of corrupt bureaucrats in charge of a town try to bribe the Inspector not to notice the wholesale corruption and the joke is that he's not really the Inspector at all but a penniless nobody with just enough wit to ride his luck until his pockets are full. But just when they realise their mistake at the end when the assumed Inspector has gone and all their cover is blown, the real Inspector turns up."

Carmichael Hunt wrote something down on his clipboard.

"It's one of the funniest plays ever written."

"And this is the play we're going to see taught by Mr-"

"Dafydd Thomas."

"For Key Stage Four Geography?"

"No, sorry. You've misunderstood me. Dafydd Thomas is certainly a Renaissance Man but even he couldn't- "

"A what?"

"A Renaissance Man."

There was a pause during which half a millennium of Christendom died.

"A what?"

"A uh - I uh - I was just joking."

"I see." The Inspector frowned and wrote something else down in his clipboard. "Well then, if we could get along and see this 'play' by- ?"

"Gogol. Look you're not going to see a play by Gogol. You're going to see a Geography lesson taught by Acting Headteacher Mr Thomas, Head of Humanities."

"Who doesn't seem to be here!"

"Oh you know, he's probably re-writing the paragraph on punctuality in the Development Plan," quipped Megan before noticing the bleak look on the Inspector's face and wishing she hadn't. "He's not here at the moment. He's - "

A group of tenth years began to mass in the corridor, in danger of jostling the Inspector underfoot.

"He's what?"

"He's on his way."

The Inspector stared meaningfully at the corridor full of teenage wildlife. Oddly enough, this Black Stare, while having such a debilitating effect on Megan had no effect on the children whatsoever. It was hardly surprising. The fourteen-year-old girl at the back in the scruffy uniform hadn't seen her father for six months. He was serving five years in Cardiff prison – the same number of years he had sexually abused her. The deathly-faced girl next to her in the smart middle-class uniform was recovering from the abortion she'd had over half term. Life had already thrown a lot more at them than a Mountain High school sanction could do.

They were learning early from experience that human life was a lot less like the script of *Home and Away*, *Fame Academy* or Football's 'theatre of dreams' and a lot more like David Hume's essay "On Suicide." That Family Life is more *Hamlet* than Hollywood, more *Paradise Lost* than *Paradise Island*. Megan wondered what the Stern Inspector would make of the phone call from a children's home she'd fielded once warning her that a certain boy whom she'd given a lift home was fixated on her and advising her to keep her distance. The phone call was from a woman who represented the Cwmcysgodionmarw ward as councillor as well as providing distinguished care to modern orphans. Megan had of course followed the advice. Only years later had it emerged that the boy, along with countless others, was being systematically abused at the home and the phone call designed to prevent the boy gaining the confidence to talk to Megan about it. Of course, these were extreme cases: the norms of news journalism rather than of normal life, but even so such contexts made a mockery of the frightened little sanctions teachers were still sort of allowed to apply. And even a Mountain High school sanction was more impressive than this little jerk.

"Scott, Jake, Wayne, Darren, Sean, Rhian, Jason, Claire!!!" yelled Megan. Megan wondered to herself (a) why lining up smartly mattered when you knew some of the things that had happened to these kids and (b) why even though her heart bled for what had happened to some of them, it would do absolutely no good to indulge that sympathy here. Lining up might be the only orderly thing in some of their lives. "Be quiet. Line up properly. Single file. Face the front. We'll be with you in a moment." The effect was instantaneous – Darren even managed a "Sorry, Miss" and there was plenty of social and economic as well as educational evidence to make this a remarkable achievement.

If the Inspector had had the appropriate boxes on his sheets for these children, he could have ticked off all of the following. Fathers on heroin, fathers in prison, fathers abusing mothers, mothers living with other fathers or vice versa, single mothers, absent mothers, abusive fathers, itinerant kids following one or other parent and step-parent/girlfriend/boyfriend on their journeys across Britain in search of the perfect holiday they wanted their life to be, hungover, doped up kids in their 'buckets' from last night or even from the bus ride in this morning, and a sprinkling of others displaying all the merely 'normal' pathology of adolescence. Plus Jason and Claire – whom Megan had been asked to seat separately - who were two months on the way to becoming a father and mother themselves. As if seating them separately was going to help now! Carmichael Hunt did not, however, have such boxes on his sheet, nor did he appear to notice Megan's achievement. He was instead noticing the number of pupils who had free school dinners. Megan meanwhile was also organising her own class further down the corridor. They were leading in formally as she came back.

Norman Welch arrived looking like he'd just sat on a spike. "Apparently, I'm supposed to abandon my Key Skills Lecture with the Sixth Form and take *Acting* Headteacher Thomas's Geography class. "

"That's right, Norman." Megan's smile was full of ice. "As of about ten minutes ago. Glad you didn't feel the need to hurry. It's only an Inspection." She handed him Dafydd's lesson plan.

The young deputy smirked. "Oh dear that will look bad won't it. Well, I can't possibly take it, as an inspection lesson I mean – I'm not a Geography teacher."

"No?" Megan met his smirk with a glare. "And what exactly *do* you take around here? Apart from yourself up the ass! You're supposed to be an Assistant Head and the Head's busy."

"I was *trying* to teach Key Skills."

"To a class of five, two of whom are truanting and the other three of whom couldn't care less and who can blame them? And you released them half an hour ago anyway. Now are you going to deal with the Inspector or not?"

"No, I don't believe I am." Norman gave Megan back the plan and called out to the restive line of pupils. "Lead in you misfits! Get out your Practical Geography books and start copying out from page one."

"Great," whispered Rhian, " a whole lesson of copying!"

"Don't be cheeky," drawled Norman with the affected boredom a teacher adopts as a control device.

"I'm not," protested Rhian. " I *love* copying. You don't have to think. Mr Thomas always tries to get us to think and I don't want to. I'm too tired. "

A few other voices concurred and Norman Welch followed them in.

"Can we use felt tips, Sir?"

Norman liked it when they were tired. It meant he could get on with his job applications in peace. "If you've got them, you can use what you like. But you won't be getting anything from me."

"Well thanks a lot." Megan stormed back to the Inspector who was watching the interchange narrowly. "Right. You won't be able to see the Geography lesson. You can see me."

"No. I'm not due to you until Period 3(a.). Year 8. "

"That's right. And so you won't see my Specially Prepared Brilliant Lesson. But it's this or nothing, I'm afraid. Mr Thomas is in an emergency and it would be pointless watching a cover."

"On the contrary, I need to know what quality of cover the school provides."

Megan was now in a quandary. The trade unionist in her was reluctant to expose a colleague to this: an Inspector noticing that a cover lesson consisted of copying out while the teacher applied for Headships. But the company woman in her felt it would be a good idea for Welch to get found out, so why should she protect him? Or was that the other way round? As she tried to decide, another kind of woman in her realised that in fact, deep down, it was Taff she was protecting. They'd been at school together. And even if that didn't mean *quite* as much as it meant to Bertie Wooster challenged by Bingo Little to steal a policeman's helmet or cow creamer – *But Bertie, we were at school together* – it still meant a good deal. They'd sat at the back of some of these very rooms together, though never *quite* as close as Jason and Claire, not even that once in 5B. Taff inspired many things - exasperation, frustration, despair, amusement, affection, resentment and, somehow, loyalty. She wanted the Inspection to reflect well on his Acting Headship, again she wasn't exactly sure why. Why wasn't the blithering idiot here anyway? What was the emergency? Trust him to put himself in the worst possible light.

"Well I take full responsibility. Mr Thomas has prepared this" – she handed Hunt the lesson plan – "but as you can see it's far too ambitious and sophisticated a lesson to be delivered at short notice by a non-specialist." Megan bit her tongue on the word 'short'. "Mr Welch is a Key Skills teacher. So he is getting them to catch up on some urgent Geography revision notes that we have as a contingency for times like these. Meanwhile, I'm offering you the chance to see an English lesson with me until Mr Thomas, who is dealing with an emergency, gets here. As soon as he does, you may of course leave."

Carmichael Hunt was staring at her legs again. He frowned and wrote something down on his clipboard.

"So – shall we begin?"

Carmichael Hunt tilted his head for a different view of what-ever he found interesting about her skirt – perhaps its vaguely Celtic-feminine dragon print offended the St George of his mind set - made a last note on his clipboard, and motioned her to go in. 'Please let Jasper be good," she prayed as she strode in to confront a class now thoroughly unfocused by the delay. And with a skirt-ogling Inspector at her back. 'Whatever Dafydd's emergency was, it had better be good.'

9

Constable Jones was a waiting in reception. He had been there for twenty minutes. He had already been to Mountain High at dawn to release a pupil from a detention that had accidentally gone on all night. The detention teacher made a statement claiming he had checked the room before leaving and locking it. He had added that the pupil concerned had not even turned up for the detention. The detention book corroborated this. The caretaker made a statement claiming he had checked the room before re-locking it and going home, as per the torturous handbook. The torturous handbook corroborated this. The pupil claimed both teacher and caretaker had said, "Right Williams, you little bastard, we're locking you in all night but don't worry the school ghost will keep you company, whoo, whoo…" and then laughed all the way down the stairs. The boy's Year Head, Electra Cummings, suggested that the truth probably lay somewhere between the two, as it usually did with rival claims between children and adults. Constable Jones asked, "What, you mean two professional adults *half*-locked a minor into a public building all night and the other half the boy did himself?" Electra Cummings explained: "Sean's father is in prison and his mother beats him and he sometimes takes refuge in fantasy - but he's not a liar." Constable Jones, getting out his notebook and licking his pencil, asked anxiously what evidence she had of this child- beating and Electra replied that Sean had told her so on frequent occasions, whenever he had been sent to her for misbehaviour. "The stress of being in trouble triggers his need to confide in a sympathetic authority figure, " she explained. "The Grievance Counsellor, for instance – he's benefited a lot from his sessions with her; he gets in touch with his feelings. He generally goes there instead of maths, which antagonises his brain with its pointless puzzles. Or, when the Grievance Counsellor's off with depression, he comes to see me. He can see any authority figure who understands a bit about psychology really." "Are you a psychologist then?" asked the policeman. "No, but I read psychology once. In an 'A' level psychology textbook here at Mountain High – I had to copy it out in the detention room the day I was expelled. You see, the teachers here always hated me because I was so unrepressed. My mother just couldn't accept how beautiful I was. And my father- "

"Any other evidence of the beatings apart from the boy's own claims?" Jones asked.

"N-No."

Despite the Year Head's prevarications, the stricken teacher and caretaker were cleared by the new security cameras which clearly showed Sean breaking in to the school building with his father at about 3 am to "retrieve the boy's pencil case" which had been confiscated by "that bastard persecuting my boy." "Which bastard is that?" Jones had asked.

"All of them," the father replied.

"And your name is?"

"Ponsonby," lied the father automatically.

"Your full name?"

"Ponsonby-Smallpiece. Nigel."

"That's a character in a 1970s children's programme, Sir. Any reason why you don't want to give me your proper name?"

Constable Jones was now supposed to be addressing a Personal Development class about the dangers of drugs – he had some multiple choice work sheets that conveyed how drugs affected your emotions, your levels of tolerance, your sense of time etc - but clearly that rather hippy-dippy teacher in charge of 10 F had problems with her own short-term memory. The constable went once again to reception, waited in the long queue (again) and eventually knocked on the glass frontage. The perfect ex-pupil receptionist – a courteous and intuitive credit to her cohort and secretarial team, who made everything in the school office tick like clockwork – was away with exhaustion. Her replacement, also an ex-pupil, having failed to make her way in the world owing to serial truancy and an enduring obsession with clothes and make-up, combined with semi-literacy and entry-level people skills, carried on typing. She looked up when he knocked again but only to answer the phone. If Constable Jones's mind had been of a philosophical bent, he might have considered whether the Modern Comprehensive School (like its Secondary Modern predecessor) found its apotheosis in producing the school secretary who then returned to serve the institution that had produced her – the variation on this economic incest being that Mountain High (like its Grammar School predecessor) also produced the school teacher who did the same. He might have wondered what other enterprises Mountain High, now the biggest employer in the town, served. Certainly not the local police force because he *was* the local police force and had neither attended Mountain High nor learned anything at all at Millstone Colliery Comprehensive, formerly "The Slagheap". So might a man of philosophy have pondered. But he was not a man of philosophy. He was a man of action (followed by extended paperwork) and as such had no resources to deal with his present enforced inaction. Instead, he eventually caught the eye of the receptionist and pointed to his watch as she put the phone down. She smiled at him and went back to her typing errors. He glared, watching his own glare reflected in the glass, but apart from an absent snort, got no reaction from the receptionist. Eventually he had no option but to sit down again.

Constable Jones's day had begun with an arrest. Now he himself was arrested by the most effective force of all: a large school absorbed in its own minutiae. PC Jones flipped open his notebook and pondered the earlier arrest, the one in which he'd been in charge. A master of events, rather than their victim.

A teenage druggie had woken up walking along a lane in a westerly direction through the posh outskirts of Old Llamidia. He'd asked a policeman if he was going in the right direction to find 'Nirvana' and the policeman had replied, "That is correct", even though it of course had not been so. It comes to something when you can't even trust a policeman to give the correct directions! The teenager looked like he'd been dragged backwards though a hedge. This was because he had in fact been dragged backwards though a hedge the previous night by a fellow druggie whose stash he had posted in a pillar box over three miles away to avoid being apprehended by what turned out to be a split-vision hallucination pretending to be three burly members of the Chilean drug squad. The druggie had been arrested, strip-searched (during which he became extremely shy and ticklish about the condition, size and vulnerability of his private parts) was booked for possession, given most of his clothes back, interrogated by the piggiest constable – whose job he did for him by ruthless self-questioning– and then sent back out into the community. The boy then walked for several miles in the dark trying to find the dumped drugs and by some extraordinary coincidence found them in a sack on the bonnet of a van outside the GPO at five am. He'd then taken a near fatal overdose of ecstasy – containing in its cocktail of amphetamine and hallucinogens almost a *quarter* as much LSD as the average Day Tripper used to take without breaking stride in the 60s and early 70s! – and later been apprehended walking over the roofs and bonnets of a line of police cars he clearly believed were Batmobiles. Giving his name as Robin, the boy was subsequently stowed in the bat-cell with a psychotherapist – whom the boy gigglingly referred to as The Joker - and a doctor with a syringe full of legal narcotics the boy would later become addicted to, whom the boy dubbed Doctor Who.

Constable Jones flipped his notebook shut and sighed. A policeman's lot was not a simple one. He was later due at the prison to teach a First Offender's Open University course in Burglary Skills as part of a new intitiative destined to prepare inmates for a more successful return to work – in preference to re-arrests and a return to prison. Some of his work appeared quite absurd. Some of it appeared really absurd. The rest was absurd. But it was rarely as suicide-inducing as this half hour in Mountain High's reception when there were potential drug victims out there - and potential pupils in here - to be schooled against drugs. Constable Jones got up again, advanced in a westerly direction towards the glass frontage and proceeded to hammer upon the said glass frontage in an agitated manner. It was on the third application of the constable's fist upon the aforementioned frontage that the glass broke.

10

"Thank you, Major. We'll see you this afternoon then. 1 pm sharp."

"Sorry I was delayed. Had to deal with a dead rat. Which reminds me…"

"Goodbye, Major." Dafydd extracted the Major's index claw from his buttonhole, detached himself from the grand old man's pocket watch – running eight minutes (and half a century) slow as usual - and made a break for the door. The conversation had effectively ended ten minutes ago and somewhere an Inspection lesson was occurring without him. Dafydd had of course been a fool to see the blessed Major at all. But seeing his youthful self had clouded his judgement. Or was he just unconsciously avoiding being inspected by Hunt? Dafydd began to run with increasing speed to the lesson. Yes, he had been avoiding the inevitable. He would face it now.

A girl in the wrong uniform approached him down the long corridor, singing "really wanna know you, really wanna go with you..." a song most of the kids had never even heard of. As he got closer, he realised who it was. That slimline walk, that sudden pounding in his heart, those love bites, a neck like Dracula's concubine. She looked through him as they passed, challenging him to rebuke her for lateness.

He took up the challenge. "Why are you late, girl? Why aren't you in lessons?"

"Why are *you* late, man? Why aren't *you* in lessons?"

That mocking voice. Those proto Cerys Matthews consonants and innuendoes. That laugh. That lissom look behind as she disappeared around the corner. That vision of youth and loveliness. Like that girl from Merthwr at Barry that time in the purple maxi-coat, mascara and hotpants - with the Welsh harp-cum-rock-guitar resting in the valley of her thighs, exactly where he himself had always wanted to... rest. Young Megan, the valley ghost he'd never laid, as slender and heart-piercing as life.

And just as dangerous. Dafydd stopped at the water-fountain and drank there as he had done as a pupil, expecting Troll to come out at any moment to tell him to "get to your lessons, boy" in his Cambridge sneer. He was frightened to look up. What would he see next? Sad-eyed loving Jesus? – he didn't have time for God just now. He had an Inspection to run. He ducked into the caretaker's luxury office and phoned Suzanne on the cordless.

"Suzanne. Book me an emergency doctor's appointment. When? Well today if possible, or at least this week. ...All right then this month. No I don't want to go private thank you."

Suzanne's voice – amplified to ear-damaging volume – cut into his ear. "Their receptionist will want to know what's wrong with you."

"That's private."

"You said you didn't want to go priv-"

"I meant the information is private – for the doctor's ears only."

"And the receptionist. She won't give you an appointment at all otherwise."

"I know the receptionist. She's the parent of one of our Year 7s. I don't want my intimate and embarrassing health details broadcast around the lower school playground."

"Well, I'll have to tell her something."

"Oh tell her I've got, you know, that irritable b. thing." Dafydd felt unable to say the word 'bowel' to Suzanne, even over the phone, especially in caretaker Bob Godot's glowering presence.

"What irritable bloody thing?"

"No! Irritable b. syndrome. You know."

"Irritable bastard syndrome?"

"What! When do *I* ever suffer from irritable bastard syndrome? Anyway, that's not a medical condition. That's an occupational condition. Irritable *bowel* syndrome."

"Irritable BOWEL syndrome!" Suzanne exploded in guffaws, then stopped. "Sorry." Suzanne's telephone voice could carry a long way. Everyone in the corridor looked in.

"Why not say it a bit louder, Suzanne? I think there might still be someone in Aberdisllythyr who hasn't heard you yet."

"I didn't know you had an irritable BOWEL?"

"I haven't!" Dafydd's blood pressure was now 140 over 100 and rising. "I just don't want half the County to know the Head-teacher of Llewellyn the Last Mountain High is having stress-related hallucinations!" Suzanne screeched the last three words back down the phone in astonished wonder. Dafydd grimaced at a crowd of truants who had gathered in the doorway to watch.

"Are you having stress-related hallucinations, Sir?" said a truant.

"Let's put it this way, Morris. If you are an hallucination, you can stay there because you won't be needing any qualifications. If you're not - get to your lessons – *all of you - now!!*"

Suzanne's voice cut through the air again. "I'll tell him you've got high blood pressure brought on by smoking and fatness. That's all the rage at the moment. You'll get an appointment almost immediately."

"Suzanne, you're a marvel."

"While you're there, Headmaster. The Inspector is- "

"Not now, Suzanne. I have an Inspection to run." He slammed the phone down and then he did indeed run. He did not allow anything to distract him from his running, not even the surely hallucinatory impression of a uniformed policeman vandalising the glass frontage in reception. He stayed focused and ran all the way back to his classroom. He ran as if his whole life, armed and lipped like Young Megan, was following after.

11

The Inspector was droning at three quarters speed. "I've already seen Double Literacy with Mr Norman, Swiss and Austrian with Mr Grossfarter and Double Dutch with Mrs Probert. But I might as well see a bit of English before recharging my batteries."

"Very generous of you," said Megan. "Please take a seat anywhere you wish."

Mr Carmichael Hunt took the seat she'd borrowed from Dafydd earlier and placed it on a special platform near the back of the room but directly in her line of vision, bearing down on her, fixing his gaze on her skirt as before. She tried to look past it at the class.

"English," sniffed the Inspector, writing it down. Megan noticed that he spelled it wrong. "Do you teach anything else?"

"Literature, naturally."

"Literacy," repeated the Inspector.

"Literature."

"Literature," he sniffed." He wrote it down. 'Literacy.'

"And Listening," she said ironically. "List-en-ing."

He wrote again. 'Literacy'. Later he would wonder why he'd written 'Literacy' three times.

She made to begin.

"How much do you get paid?"

Not wishing to expose her salary in front of children, she resorted to the professional codes. "Management 4." The Inspector sniffed. Megan felt desperate for some respect. "Plus all three Threshold allowances. For outstanding classroom teaching."

He wrote it all down as if the sums offended him. "Shall we begin?"

Megan looked up. "Where's Rhiannon?"

"She saw an alien in the corridor, Miss. It cloned itself and then the double walked off across the playground. She fainted. She's gone to the sick room."

The sick room, like the Work House after the 1834 Poor Law Amendment Act, was made so deliberately unwelcoming by office staff that Rhiannon must have been really ill to want to go *there*. Similarly, the rooms where hard working and/or bright, motivated pupils sat exams that would determine their futures were cold, damp, noisy and distracting Dungeons of Little Ease. This was in marked contrast to the Punishment Room (aka the 'Inclusion' Room, the room to which behaviourally Excluded pupils were sent) which was as pleasant, airy and welcoming for those in need of punishment as a good deal of educational funding and all the genius of modern educational theory could devise.

"It wasn't an alien. It was Mr Trolley. The lights were off, that's all."

"It was too small for Mr Trolley."

"Don't be daft! How could it be?"

"It was moving past the toilets. It was horrible."

"Why were the lights off?"

"Mr Thomas said that it was like the Crystal Palace with all the lights blazing."

"I'm sure Mr Thomas wouldn't say that."

"He did, Miss. He said we're not millionaires and that anyway we had to be seen to be cutting costs when the Inspector gets here."

"The Inspector IS here, Jasper. He's sitting at the back listening to you now. Or hadn't you noticed?"

For anyone other than Jasper, this question would have been rhetorical.

Megan resumed. "You'll be telling me that the alien was sucking away all our energy and electricity as part of its invasion next. The trouble with you lot is that you watch too much science fiction and don't read enough books."

"Books," mutttered the Inspector, unsure how to pronounce all these new sounds.

Megan tried again. "Now then, if you'll just turn to – "

Rhiannon entered. "Sorry Miss. I've been in the sick room."

There was nowhere to sit. Megan hurriedly gave Rhiannon her own chair, a padded one. The Inspector made a note on his clipboard. "Can we get started now?" he snapped. He needed a cell, a padded one.

"Right, please turn to page 86," said Megan.

"Miss, I haven't got a book."

"Great. Go and get one from the stock cupboard. Rhiannon start reading."

"I haven't got that page."

"Barry."

"Where from, Miss?"

"From 'You delighted in literature as some might in torture'…"

"That's page 84, Miss."

"Great! Turn to page 84 then. Can we please get on with it?"

The pupil without a book came back in. "It's not there, Miss."

"What isn't there? The stock cupboard? "

"The book you sent me for."

"Oh I see." Megan's normally calm classroom voice began to acquire shades of frustration. "I thought that perhaps you meant that the stock cupboard wasn't there. That it had decided there was no point coming in today as it didn't have its books with it!" She took a sharp breath then hissed. "If you hadn't forgotten your book, Sian, we wouldn't be having this conversation would we?"

"You never gave her one, Miss. There wasn't enough to go round. She can share mine."

"Brilliant! Brilliant! Why didn't I think of that? Katie."

"What?"

"READ!"

Katie read. Sort of. Leaving torturous gaps in what otherwise was rendered approximately as - "you delighted in literature as some might in torture we were forbidden to write i liked the poem we read by wordsworth you'd reduce i liked to lashes scald three solid bars across the poem grill a word as emotive and colloquial as we and with arrows and scrawls that stabbed and blushed their brand amid the acne add in your slap round the face standard english red-ant stinging the page simon lee the old huntsman by wandsworth is an admirable poem can i stop reading now miss..."

Mr Carmichael Hunt's Eye now seemed to be entering Megan's mind's eye like a blade. She turned away to the white-board in an effort to keep focused and began writing. As soon as she did so, his glare transferred itself to her skirt again. And, as a result, mortifyingly, she – an expert speller for over two decades - had unaccountably forgotten how to spell. Anything. She stood in front of the nonsense she'd written to conceal it. And noticed the appeal in Katie's eyes.

"Not bad, Katie. Not bad at all. But what's the poet *feeling* when he says all that?"

A forest of eager hands went up. Even the Inspector's sudden opening up of filing cabinets, rummaging among papers (and old cigarette cartons) and subsequent frenzy of note-taking didn't quite put them off.

"Simon?"

"Anger, Miss."

"Anger. He's furious isn't he? Show us Alice."

Alice read with passion, precision and punctuation, going on to complete the part Kate hadn't even attempted, " The twenty second time you repeated that lesson, our Fifth Year bulks crammed through the legs of our Third Year desks, I stopped writing altogether, could only parrot your shrieked corrections, but you wounded even those..."

The lesson was going well at last, the whole class getting involved and enthused, even Wayne. Megan sneaked a look at the Inspector.

The Inspector was stony-faced. This extract was going on so long; it was in danger of becoming a Whole Text. There had been no ten minute starter, no twenty minute reading task, no twenty minute writing task and it looked very much like there was going to be no plenary. The Government formula had been flagrantly flouted. Megan received no ticks in any of the four boxes. And then something very odd happened. Megan's eyes took on a possessed look, a dragon-red fire seemed to descend upon her and she began speaking in Welsh.

12

Troll poked the coal fire in his office. He switched on the Hacker and tuned the gathering hum to the Home Service. It soon began to boom out, vowels rolling around in the large wood and leather cabinet. Although the service had long since changed its name to Radio 4, Troll would never demean the set by calling it that. His oak and grey leather Hacker had the solidity and *gravitas* of Churchill and listening to it, Troll often fancied he was back in the army. He'd reached the rank of temporary Lieutenant and had managed to get an accelerated military back passage into Cambridge for an engineering degree at just the right time afterwards and then a deputy Headship on the back of his army record. Many said he had never left, just transferred his authoritarianism from squaddies to schoolboys. He knew how to Handle Chaps, or so the Chaps of the Old School said. But from this propitious start under Llewellyn-Jones, he'd never made the Headship. It was a perpetual gall to him.

He had a point. Pansy 'Calamity' Handle, The Curriculum Deputy appointed just before Dafydd's infamous takeover - in a desperate effort to get some of 'Assistant' Headteacher Norman Welch's tasks actually done - was paid a large salary like Trolley. And there the similarity ended. Trolley still produced a timetable *as well* as managing the school's punishment systems – to Trolley punishment and the curriculum were in any case the same thing – and he could remember the days when a Deputy did everything. By contrast, Miss Handle still seemed unclear six months later whether she had a job description at all. She would still be unclear six years later. She would, alas, always be unclear. She did *something* – unlike Welch for instance – but neither she nor anyone else knew what it was. Like the messenger from Eli, she had a mind that multiplied the smallest matter. The 'job' she performed – single-handedly causing a busy staff enormous amounts of extra work every time she got into the data systems on the school computer, or picked up a telephone, or passed an in-tray, or a pigeonhole - blithely scattering their contents with the air-torrents of her flailing blouse and skirts - had certainly never been described in any County document or indeed anywhere outside the pages of absurdist fiction. When a teaching assistant turned up in her lesson at the start of the year with a message from a frantic teacher asking for help with a class list which had mysteriously grown - under Miss Handle's green fingers - to 39, Miss Handle had smiled and co-opted the classroom assistant into her own class of seven. When she finally grasped that there was a problem, and was told how to solve it, she got swiftly to work, increased the numbers to 47 and took away the class assistant. Dafydd, in the middle of a year assembly, had to drag her away from the computer and do it himself.

Trolley couldn't exactly blame Dafydd for Miss Handle's appointment but he would never have put up with her as Dafydd did. "I'd give her a timetable so heavy with hard classes she'd disappear within the first half term like a puff of wind up the pastel pink hole of her uselessness!" he snarled. (Privately. Troll would never allow the public the slightest hint of what he really thought about anything and had never broken a confidence nor confirmed a piece of gossip in his entire professional life. And he would rather an entire cohort lost its life-chances – he would rather allow a pupil to walk around the lower quad in the forbidden direction!- than peach on a fellow manager, even Pansy. Even if she couldn't *manage* a satin bow in a drapery shop let alone a curriculum.)

Perhaps Trolley had settled for too little. He could never turn on the Hacker without imagining what might have been if he'd continued in the Intelligence corps, sending radio messages home on a set like this from some battleship-grey East German night. Some said he was still employed by an espionage unit in the more obscure regions of the F.O. (There was also Trolley's Cambridge connection – which could of course mean he was really working for the other side as well). Some said it would explain his longevity – the authorities' evident reluctance to get rid of him – and also the fact that for long periods of every day no one knew where he was or what he did. Others like Union Rep Megan Morgan said, as this was standard practice for the Senior Leadership Team, how could you tell?

However sound as a general principle, this assessment of the school's senior leaders was as unfair in Trolley's case as it was in Dafydd's. Trolley never stopped working –he worked like the pro-verbial clappers. The proverbial clappers (like the satanic mills) had long since been replaced by electronic and digital equivalents but it was still a matter of genuine doubt whether Trolley's clappers had been superseded. When the time saved by the latest *Computer Says No* hardware had been subtracted from the time lost in its perpet-ual updating, malfunction and endless convergence technology trivilialisation facilities, there remained Trolley's tried and trusted clappers. Even now as he invited two newly qualified teachers into his Private Orifice for their weekly debriefing, he was actually mentally elsewhere producing a contingency timetable for when Miss Handle's computerised one disappeared up its own data bank. Again. He was producing this timetable on what looked like a giant crib board extended across his Orifice wall. The only other object against this wall was the filing cabinet in which Trolley kept all the dog-eared hand-written files in manilla folders representing an administrative regime stretching back to the time of Metternich, each file containing traditional solutions to problems the computer couldn't read. The fattest folder was labelled "Our Finest Hour" and recorded the brief time in which Trolley had himself run the school while another of these young whippersnappers was being recruited to do so.

The two newly qualified teachers waited in trepidation as Trolley shared these reveries of an alternative regime prior to giving them the 'feedback' ('Judgements') they were supposed to get from his observations ('Invigilations'.) Then his face appeared to explode. "PSYCHOANALYSIS!" he cried. The warted eyelid of his left, and most obviously cast, eye flew out like a shaggy moth towards some invisible light. The other eye turned upside down. He upset the small table and with it two ashtrays and a cup of coffee. The table was so upset it would probably need counselling before it could get back on its feet again, but this was nothing to the effect it had on the two young people present. The shy but incredibly conscientious, and now coffee-splattered, new Psychology mistress, Miss Bond, stood up nervously, unsure how much more of Trolley's pastoral care she could take. The hideously fat, carbuncular new chemistry Master, Mr Barry Hunter, dropped his bun and farted with elephant copiousness. He jumped up as if to do so might avoid detection and turned towards the trembling Psychology teacher. Their eyes met. Trolley appeared to have gone mad.

"Why! – that was Y – chops slay a sin. Y chops slay a sin! It *was* an anagram!"

His charges giggled nervously. "What was, sir?" farted the hideously fat, carbuncular new chemistry master.

"Freud gets to the bottom of why chops slay a sin! It's so ridiculously simple!"

"What is, Sir?" persisted the chubby young chemist.

"THE CRYPTIC CROSSWORD, BUNTER! Why chops slay a sin!" He laughed like a light-hearted girl in love. "Why, it's almost *too* easy."

The two youngsters agreed and edged towards the door. "I think he's talking about the crossword," farted Bunter.

Trolley filled in the offending spaces on the crossword with fierce energy, set it aside and took a deep puff from his cigar. "All right, you two. Here's fourteen simple points to work on for next lesson."

He scribbled them down in crabbed strokes of his fountain pen, covering eight pages of foolscap. They waited in terrified silence. At last, he stopped. "That should do the trick with those little brats. And remember, Bunter, familiarity breeds contempt. And fear, Miss Usher, breeds rabbits."

"Bond," she corrected him. Then lost her nerve. "Sorry."

Trolley chortled at a joke no-one else understood and pushed the young people out with as close to jocundity as he'd been for forty years. "Psychoanalysis. Not my discipline of course though doubtless young Napoleon here could give us a lesson in it. Eh Bunter?"

"Hunter."

"What?"

"My name's Hunter, not Bunter. Barry Hunter. Sorry."

"Not at all. Not at all! PSYCHOANALYSIS!! Of course!"

"But I'm the Psychology teacher anyway," hissed the young woman. "I'm sure he doesn't even know what I teach."

"And my name's not Bunter," whispered the chemist. "Or Napoleon." Trolley slammed the door. "*Cripes!* He's caught my backside in the hinge!"

Trolley opened the door to release the impediment and then waved the youngsters away. "Same time next week, even – in fact especially - if I've got something more important to do." The most conscientious deputy ever to have walked a school corridor placed his wave hand into his blazer front. "Off you go. I've got a school to run you know."

'Miss Usher' burst into tears – and 'Bunter' into blood, tears, toil and sweat - as Trolley slammed the door on his backside for a second time.

Left alone at last, Troll took another deep puff of his cigar and tried to avoid the panoramic view of Greater Pantysycham, Garnlloegr, a blue-distanced Trollbridge, the entire Lloegrbach valley and its entrance into the mighty Cwmcysgodionmarw valley, from his window. The view showed him 21st century Wales and he didn't like it. He had arranged for a large painting in a Victorian realist style to be placed adjacent to the window and liked to pretend this was the actual view.

The painting was called *Lloegrbach Memories* and captured the whole of the industrial Lloegrbach valley spread out along its polluted industrial river. The painting was in colour but was nevertheless mainly black and grey, the claustrophobic air it evoked a speckled smog of rust and dust. A piece of anachronistic graffiti on a disused railway bridge still spelled out FREE WALES AMY in shaggy white paint, a reflection on the local dialect pronunciation of "Army" without the 'r' or perhaps a jibe at the mid twentieth century standard of spelling. Some people forgot very quickly that despite proofreaders on newspapers in the 'good old days' and even on some shop signs, not very many of the newly literate masses even then had ever been able to avoid the misused apostrophe or spell Grammar without an e. Not even a very high percentage of elite Grammar School Boys, one of whom had mispelled the advert for the Brynbuga Public School in the *Lloegrbach Herald* recently in its bid to cream off the brightest boys of Mountain High. Troll smirked contemptuously. Some people who saw the painting pronounced it like a girl's name, Amy, believing it to be a hint of Trolley's prehistoric love life! Ha! Too many Females in education already, without making up nonsense like that. Well, "The Boyhood of Raleigh" was still up in the Hall of *his* school and no-one was moving it while he was in charge.

However accurate or otherwise Troll's art criticism was, the artist already knew, as Alexander Cordell knew and Richard Llewellyn probably guessed, and Troll apparently still didn't, that the world *Lloegrbach Memories* commemorated was over. The general atmosphere of the painting was of a few last iron foundries and coalmines distilling toil and noisome slag into the air as a great heavy metal age passed into history. The Council Waste Tip – pictured near the top of the painting- had been the biggest in South East Wales then (and there had been literally miles of pre-ecological dumpings along the quieter streams) and thus a matter of great pride to Trolley, but alas was now in decline. How Green Was The Valley? Not very, though Trolley's constant contention was that it had certainly been more alive than this Green-livered age was. The valley had seethed and grumbled with energy in those days, with as many new enterprises as there were toxic effluents in the river – a Nineteenth century melting pot, with men thronging from every county of England and the world beyond (except Huntingdonshire) to work the seams of the Workshop of the World.

This was a point many more progressive than Troll argued, along with questioning the wisdom of closing down a coal industry which the Germans, for instance, (no slouches they) still subsidised. Troll's own view (which never changed) was that the engineering workshops and technical drawing classes he'd overseen like a Victorian mill owner in his heyday had been the most advanced period in Welsh and British history, never to be surpassed or equalled. Everything else was a footnote, a heritage postcard of Lloegrbach memories amid the manic thumping of plastic Third World radios.

He patted his Hacker, puffed his cigar and purred, temporarily content.

13

Dafydd burst into his classroom to find it occupied by Norman Welch and thirty-three silenced children. "Where's the Inspector?"

Norman Welch was already on his way out with his pile of application forms. "Next door, old boy, inspecting Ms Morgan."

"Wait a minute. Why?"

"Not much point watching your lesson when you aren't here, old boy."

"It's *Mr Thomas*, as we're in front of pupils. I'm still talking to you actually."

"I have a lesson of my own to teach, actually."

"Three students. They've gone. Which reminds me I think we need to talk through some of your timetabling: I'm not sure we're using you properly."

"Is that a threat?"

"Oh no. A promise. Of what's to come when I take over properly."

"Don't think I'll fret too much about that, Dafydd. Not looking too likely at the moment, is it?" Norman smiled sweetly and made to leave.

"Will you STOP walking away when I try to talk to you!"

"Temper *temper,* old boy. You'll give yourself high blood pressure."

"And you no doubt will give yourself a handful of tiny and undemanding classes while the rest of us cope with that pressure. I thought the point of your fancy computer programme was that we improved on the Trolley-Llewellyn model."

"By the Trolley-Llewellyn model I take it you mean turning up on the first day of term, dreaming up a timetable and moving a few pins around a wall-board. And then when only three classes turn up for a third of the staff, the rest have to pick who they want from the crowd in the hall, making a few 'practical' adjustments, a bit of 'fine tuning', before settling back to read Baden Powell's "Pig Sticking" in the study? I understand from the old folk who linger in the staff room that things were invariably clear by the end of the first term but unfortunately a modern school can't afford to muddle by with a thousand students on a score of sophisticated courses."

"Precisely. The school has trebled in size and everything else has dwindled into torturous minutiae. It was the tedious torturousness of it that convinced me – wrongly it now appears – that you were the man for the job."

"Thank you," mocked Welch.

"But, unlike you, I admit my mistakes. Appointing you as timetabler - number one. Agreeing to your Key Skills mission – number two. Assuming senior management responsibilities would stop you being such a tight-assed self-centred little shit - number three."

"Thank you. Now if I may…?"

The Young Pretender left, well pleased with his morning's work. Apart from exposing Dafydd several times now as too emotionally unstable to be a Headteacher, Welch had avoided all the interruptions – that is, all the requests for help and attention from every pupil or colleague he'd come across - to his important and necessary work as a senior leader. Soon, he thought with satisfaction, he would be running the school in the same way, on what he hoped would become known as the Welch System. Then, who knows, he could revolutionise other institutions along the same sharp lines. The Norman Welch Joint Education Committee. The English and Norman Welch Cricket Board. The Norman Welch F- The list would have continued but Norman cannoned into an open cupboard door, sustaining the excruciating trauma to his thigh known as a 'dead leg'.

Dafydd watched this happen, remembering how the entire cohort had found it hilarious when one of their number – a singularly unpopular boy known as Pariah - had slid twenty yards down to the bottom of School Hill and into a busy main road on a slide they'd made - before breaking his leg in two places while they broke into laughter in twenty more. He felt a tinge of guilt for the darkness of man's heart – both for Pariah then and for his lack of much sympathy for Welch now - and then noticed the class were watching him, open-mouthed. "Yes?" he snapped. "What do you lot want?"

"A Geography lesson?"

Dafydd laughed. "Very well." He looked lost for a moment. "Anyone seen my lesson plan?"

"On your desk, Sir, " said Tommy. "It was there all the time. Under Mr Welch's Disposable Information Bulletin."

A rosy sunrise finally peeped over the grey moor and in through the recently polished windows of the classroom. Dafydd felt momentarily cheered. He had wondered whether the extra-cost cleaners he'd especially got in to prepare the school for the Inspection last week were actually under-cover Inspectors from County but it was looking definitely as though Carmichael Hunt was the one they needed to worry about. Ha ha ha, it's all beginning to come together. Then a horrible thought struck him. "Where did Mr Welch say the Inspector was?"

"Next door with Ms Morgan, Sir."

"I see. You'd better go and get him then. Tommy." Tommy got up. "Hang on. Why are there three of you still standing at the back without chairs? We need three chairs. Ms Morgan took one, damn her eyes. Where are the others? Tommy, you'd better ask Ms Morgan for some chairs as well."

14

Ms Morgan had taken off her skirt and handed it to the Inspector. "As you seem fascinated by this garment, I thought you might like a closer look."

The boys at the back were gaping in astonishment. A masturbation fantasy had come to life before their eyes: shapely-legged Ms Morgan in Agent Provacateur panties. Teaching poetry.

Carmichael Hunt made a note on his clipboard.

15

"Brilliant, lad," said Dafydd. A few more answers like that and we'll have you applying to do a PE degree at Lunn Poly."

Beverley Hancock snorted, "It's not called PE anymore. It's called Sports Studies."

"Is it? Good old National Curriculum. Now all we need to do is change the name of the World Cup to the Welsh Cup and Wales might actually win it!"

Beverley pursed her lips. Tommy re-entered looking pale.

Dafydd looked up, "Where's the chairs? Where's The Inspector?"

"He's… examining Ms Morgan's skirt, Sir." The class gasped. *"What?"*

"May I speak to you in private, Sir?"

"This had better be good." Dafydd followed Tommy into the lobby, pausing to address the three standing pupils. "There's no chairs for you, I'm afraid and you can't stand up for an Inspection. Go to my office. If anyone asks anything, say you've been sent for punishment." He turned round on the others, raising his voice. The rest of you – you shouldn't be talking, you should be getting on."

"What with, Sir?"

Dafydd ignored them and turned his attention to Tommy. "Well?"

"It's about Ms Morgan, Sir."

"Yes?"

Tommy told him.

Dafydd entered Ms Morgan's class, averting his eyes from the blur of pink he noticed poised on the front desk, and explained to the Inspector that he should follow him next door. He retrieved Megan's skirt, handed it back to her with a reassuring smile, looked away while she put it back on, (receiving a mumbled and distracted 'thanks'), frowned at the white board which was covered in a bewildering matrix of what looked like Welsh rather than English, ordered the class to 'get on' and left. The Inspector followed.

"Everything ok?" squeaked Dafydd.

"42," said the Inspector. He gave Dafydd a piercing stare.

Dafydd smiled and nodded.

Then turned away and frowned. 42? What the hell did it mean? The meaning of life, the Universe and everything? Some obscure new grading system from The Ministry of Educational Statistics and Standardisation (MESS) in association with the Committee of Revolutionary Educationalists and Evangelising Parents (previously the Crusade of Reactionary Educationalists and Enthusiastic Preachers) (still CREEP) as regulated by the new Bureaucratic Office of Learning Levels, Organisation, Classification, Knowledge and Shibboleths (BOLLOCKS) and the previous Government's Shoppers' and Homeowners' Independent Tribunal for Education (SHITE)? A rather un-gallant reference to Megan's age? (She was in fact 45, the same as Dafydd but perhaps she'd been a little ladylike with the truth?). "42?" Dafydd was about to ask for clarification when the Inspector became absorbed in arranging his clipboard for the Acting Head's own inspection lesson.

Dafydd tried to focus on the task in hand. He looked up. The class went into instant Inspection mode. He thanked them silently from his heart.

"Rather an oversized class," observed the Inspector.

"What d'you mean, *oversized?!* I've just sent the extra ones at the back to my office to get them out of the way!"

Tommy groaned. Carmichael Hunt wrote something down on his clipboard.

Dafydd cursed himself for his schoolboy error and decided it was the poisonous dwarf's black-eyed Stare that was doing it, putting him off, making it seemingly impossible to think straight. The man's hyperbolic shortness – shorter by some distance even than that king of little hitlerdom Victor Trolley (and that was saying something) – was surely unique. He was just rallying with a better explanation when a knock came at the door and *another* equally impossibly short man entered the room. Dafydd did a double take. How could this be? If ever it was possible for a County Inspector to be cloned, this was it. Mr Carmichael Hunt's double had joined them in the classroom!

"O" said Dafydd, looking very like Morfydd had earlier that morning. (And as she did still, unbeknownst to Dafydd or indeed anyone, except possibly his cleaner. Morfydd was lying peacefully and undisturbed in the corner of his bedroom, the Napoleon chiming clock ticking comfortably away in the next room from the living-room mantelpiece, the first rays of March sunlight just reaching her trouble-free cheek over the bedroom window sill). If only I could be there like her instead of having to face all this…

"Yes, what is it?" snapped Carmichael Hunt.

The newcomer turned a tiny face to Dafydd so like his interlocutor as to be terrifying but with an expression of respectful cheerfulness he had never seen on its counterpart. "Do excuse me. I'm fully aware that you have an Inspection going on, Mr uh…"

"*Thomas,*" whimpered Dafydd.

"Ah Thomas. The Acting Head. How do you do? Good to meet you." The newcomer shook Dafydd's barely sensible hand lightly but firmly, avoiding both the limp flutteriness of Mr Power the supply music teacher and the killer crush of Troll and the Major. "I realise that this is the last thing you need at the moment but my brother Carmichael here is needed by the Inspectorate for a moment." The tiny man put his hand up to his forehead in amused deprecation. "Sorry, I forgot to say who *I* am didn't I? Robin Hunt from Personnel at County Hall. I deal with issues like Equal Opportunities, equitable distribution of capitation based on amount of periods taught rather than on shall we say 'traditional' methods of what some prehistoric deputy believes is a proper subject or whom he plays golf with, fair distribution of classroom space, size of classes and the like. Equal Opportunities is rather our thing. It all started with us – Carmichael and I – not being able to get work merely on the basis of our height and so on. Can you believe that?"

Dafydd nodded. Yes he could believe it. His first thought on seeing Carmichael had been, 'How can that shortass be a County Inspector. He's four feet tall!' He thought it best not to extrapolate on this at present though.

"Anyway, Carmichael was particularly incensed at the treatment we got, ever since the playground, at the hands of bullies and so forth, so we came into Equal Opportunities and then Inspection. Equal Opportunities is routinely misunderstood of course. People see it as a threat, a front for paranoid minorities to persecute the majority, or shock troops of the female revolution – because of course women aren't a minority are they? - but in fact it's about each individual being recognised as an individual. Even you and me, eh?"

Dafydd tried to see the tiny twin as an individual, guiltily failing to do so, but also attracted by the man's respect for Dafydd's own individuality – a characteristic so completely lacking in his brother. "People are too afraid of Government and County. We're just modernisers, that's all," Robin Hunt went on. "But I'm gabbling. I'm the talkative one, I'm afraid. Carmichael just glares at you. He has perfected a technique for glaring people into submission. He wants to get to the top so that he can see what's going on as he never could as a boy, you see? But he's not a bad man, deep down." Robin Hunt stood on tiptoe on his neat highly-polished size four shoes and whispered in Dafydd's ear. "Let's just say that faced with our diminutive size and vulnerability to insult, I took the Gandhi and Mother Theresa route to salvation and poor old Carmichael here has gone down the Napoleon and Little Hitler world domination path to the everlasting bonfire. Still we're all individuals. Now, if I may borrow him for a moment, there's a discrepancy we need to look at in the timetabling. I'm afraid Mr..." Robin Hunt consulted some jottings in a diary.

"Welch?" guessed Dafydd mechanically.

"That's right! You'd spotted it! Well it won't do, I'm afraid, though I'm sure you mean well. He's doing practically no work at all for a deputy's salary and the rest of the staff is by and large working its socks off. You'll have to look into it."

Dafydd felt a bit better. "Oh? Yes, I had actually begun to uncover something to that effect myself. Mr Welch, to be fair, has a lot of application forms to fill in."

"Quite so. But meanwhile he is being paid a large salary by County to do a job here. So sorry to interrupt and I'm sure Carmichael will be back with you soon. Carmichael." County Inspector Carmichael Hunt duly clamped his lips tightly shut, snapped his clipboard, muttering something about having to quit just as he had his man on the ropes, and followed his brother out. "I shall return."

"Very well. We'll see you shortly."

The tiny head reappeared looking very cross. "Did you just call me 'shorty'?"

Robin's cheery face joined it. "Carmichael, you're being over-sensitive - and anyway, unless we can laugh at ourselves, how are we ever going to be able to laugh at others? Carmichael's head disappeared leaving his brother's to add, "Perhaps you can regroup your forces during the ceasefire, Mr Thomas, eh? I'm sure you can still show us what you're worth." Then he was gone.

Dafydd, humbled by the magnitude and magnanimity of this, stared at the closed door and then at the class, who stared back at him. "Where were we?" he asked after a moment.

"An Inspection lesson, Sir."

"Ah yes. How was I doing?"

"Hopeless, Sir," said Tommy kindly. But that first twin didn't show you any respect. We didn't like him."

"Yeah he was dissing you, Sir."

A murmur of agreement went round the class.

"It's 'Yes' not 'Yeah'. The other one was ok though wasn't he? He was bigging me up." The class laughed at their Headmaster's adoption of street slang, then at the paradoxical reference to size, then got the giggles, passing them on in turn to Dafydd.

Dafydd, with tears still in his eyes from all the laughter, tried to balance what had happened so far. A row with Welch in front of kids, even with certain important points made. Not good. Having to leave a class (to deal with crises). It went with the territory, true, but on an Inspection day? – not good. Part of these crises being hallucinations and/or hauntings by his younger self and (briefly) Young Megan complicated by pains in the chest and down the left arm. Not good. Megan – one of his best classroom teachers, a gold medal hope for the day - teaching in her knickers, in front of Carmichael Hunt. Disaster. She had looked bloody good though. (Maybe he could start what was going to be a tricky debrief of her by saying so?) He schooled himself sternly. That's enough of that. Now, the plus side. He thought for a moment. Robin Hunt seemed to be rumbling Welch without necessarily holding Dafydd responsible, and he seemed – surely – to be on Dafydd's side? What else? Dafydd strained to remember. Couldn't. Clutched at straws. The Major taking Afternoon Assembly? His younger self didn't see that as a plus but that's because his younger self needed to grow up a bit, see how the world worked. Dafydd sighed. He wasn't even convincing himself.

His eye caught Beverley Hancock, still pouting about his put-down earlier, gazing pointedly out of the window at the wooded hillside. The one Dafydd still used to point out seasonal variations and plot terrestrial rotation by where the sun rose over the mountain. Being March now, it was about halfway between the golden high summer solstice and its piercing red low winter equivalent. The equinox. He sighed. That old valley side with all its geographical features still got mentioned in his lessons one way and another almost weekly, after all this time. And yet he hadn't actually *been* up there for years....

16

February 1971. After a steep climb through wild and increasingly hostile trees, and then up beyond the tree line, Young Dafydd looked back in triumph at the height he'd scaled. The school, perched on the hilltop dizzily far below him, lay dull red and copper green in the winter drizzle. He gave it a Pantysycham salute (both fingers).

He approached the star-bitten lintel of the signal box of the old mountain railway. He inhaled the thin green air and fragrant dried sheep-shit of home. Far below, the valley's workaday world fretted and fumed, worrying the carcase of a disposable song. He felt he had somehow passed into the landscape and eternal verities of The Old Testament. An old grey-green ewe 'started' on the edge of the mountain, sending shale scattering hundreds of feet below and panicking the flock.

It reminded Dafydd of a rare occasion when he'd come up here with a gang of slightly older boys bearing pellet guns and sniping at birds, who had found it amusing to surround and try to force just such a ewe off into the abyss. He'd lacked the courage to indict the act at first, insecure as he was back then about challenging the mores of the Welsh Male. All he did was aim and deliberately miss the achingly alive sparrows they'd pointed out to him in the trees on the lower slopes. Negative capability, like Keats. But as they ascended into hawkish heights, the gang's brutality began to run wild and so at last did his revulsion. "Very brave, lads. Pushing a fucking dumb animal off a fucking mountain. What's the fucking matter with you?"

Shamed by this 14-year-old upstart's outburst but nastily affronted by it, they'd let the sheep go and turned on him instead. He'd snarled himself into a heavy industrial scrap with Rhys. He'd lost of course but given a decent enough account of himself, scrabbling in the shale and scree and trying to avoid ridicule if not blame. He'd stopped coming up here with the gang after that. And they evidently had stopped coming at all, less a tribute to his winning the territory for mystical romanticism than their getting jobs and outgrowing such jaunts. Then Dafydd supposed their slightly younger peers stopped coming up the mountain at all, finding less natural amusements in the towns, because he had the place to himself ever after.

In some ways he missed them: they'd had a laugh and a lot of cut and graze rough and tumble adventures when they weren't torturing dumb beasts. Wordsworth – whom he was studying at present – was only right up to a point: nature taught the heart some very healthy lessons, some healthy toughening of the skin so that it grew like the bark on a mountain tree, a real man for all seasons, but hawks and dogs also taught ripping the weak to shreds. Not many lads other than Wordsworth and his idealised farmers learned to bring themselves into accord with "the spirit of the woods" while they were raiding birds' nests. Most of them at best just fought like spirited young animals. Dafydd, haunted by a sensitivity that could have become cowardice if he hadn't been hurt into empathy and defence of the weak, oversaw the old ewe struggling to safety now as he imagined biblical shepherds had done since before the time of David.

Dafydd turned and entered his truant's bolt-hole, the signal box on the edge of the moor, then froze. He noticed new dog-ends underfoot, smelt recent smoke, heard someone breathing.

Heard a transistor radio playing "The Green Manalishi" by Fleetwood Mac. Someone was in there. He moved forward uncertainly. Then checked himself, unbelieving. Young Megan! – a lonely fantasy come true before his eyes - propped up on her school satchel, alone. She was absolutely still. Asleep...

He gazed at her, the school dragon crest thrilling red against the white blouse and, as her chest rose and fell with her breathing, rippling to life across her breast pocket. She dropped a sleeping arm and the dragon seemed to leap out and be ready to consume him. Her skirt was so far up her leg it could have got a part time job as a vest.

She opened her eyes wide, startled at first. Then amusement was shining in them like sunshine over a morning tide. "Dafydd! Is that a packet of fags in your pocket or are you just pleased to see me?"

"What are you doing here Megan? You should be in English with Mr Edwards."

She laughed. "You sound like a Headmaster! Or a truant officer. Come down by yer and 'ave a cwch."

He scrambled back down the mountainside instead, hearing her amused calls to come back, getting scratched and torn by gorse and stone, almost crying with frustration. Why had he run away? A Real Man would have stayed, taken control. He could have woken her, offered to share his last fag, traded it for the usual going rate (a kiss). Up there, no-one would have laughed at him, noticed he didn't know how to kiss properly. She might even have taught him how to.

There was nothing else to do but keep running – maybe forever - nowhere else to go now but back across the teenage wasteland to school in time for the next lesson. Dad was on Earlies so home was out of bounds and the mountain was out of the question to him now. He'd failed to rise to whatever occasion it had offered him.

He sprinted past the old abattoir at the foot of Pantsycham Hill at considerable pace and was faced with a snarling Two Headed Dog that emerged from a doorway. He stood petrified. He couldn't go by and it was too far to go round the other way. One of its heads was a ewe's, the other a collie's. There was something deeply Welsh about it.

Was it really just a dog who had run off with a sheep's head from the abbatoir? Or was Something showing him his own deeply divided self, part healthy animal, part panic-stricken sheep? The dog growled deep in its throat and came nearer, slavering over his shoes, which brought further speculation to a halt. Dafydd was hammering for help at the nearest door-

17

He lurched back into the present. The class exploded into laughter as the door thundered to the floor, like some mighty tree in a Canadian forest. Tim-ber! The laughter was immediately defused. Dafydd's famous cynical grin, or what they took to be that grin. (In fact, it was a rictus of terror). They had learned not at any cost to return this grin with one of their own, however engaging it appeared. "Tommy Jones!" Dafydd grinned.

"Ye-es?"

"The Inspector will be back at any moment. You unhinged this door." Dafydd was looking as unhinged as the door. "GET IT FIXED NOW."

"B-but I-"

"NOW!"

A messenger arrived in the doorway. Dafydd's Personal Secretary, Suzanne, had impressed this messenger so fiercely to follow the correct procedure of knocking on the door before delivering his note that the absence of a door to knock, and the evident unhinged state of the Headteacher within, temporarily unmanned him.

Dafydd turned on him in fury. "YES?"

The messenger handed him the note. It was scrawled, complete with mistakes and punctuation errors, in Suzanne's schoolgirl hand. It read *maths have'nt taken very kindly to the inspectors criticism's youd better come and sort it out qwik*

Dafydd ran out through the doorway, snarling encouragement (and imploring for increased speed) at Tommy's efforts to raise the door, and ran across to the main building in search of a phone. He got the engaged signal several times then heard a panicky voice. "Suzanne? What's happening with maths?"

"This isn't Suzanne. It's Dora." Assistant Secretary Dora screeched hysterically for a moment, then – after something hit her very hard - cried out in pain, then started sobbing. Suzanne's voice came over the phone. "Mr Thomas."

"Suzanne? What's happened? You haven't for God's sake let Dora speak to the Press!"

"Of course not. Her phone's been disconnected for just that reason which is why she's trying to use mine."

"Make sure she doesn't get anywhere near any kind of communication device for the rest of the day. Give her that literacy filing to do. Now. Tell me straight. What happened with maths?"

"Nothing really. Mr Hunt did say they were stuck in the 70s."

"I TOLD Umbrage and the rest to put up the new numeracy strategy charts. Why don't they effin well listen? Why can't that vicious bastard fall into line just once in his conceited bloody-"

"Sir?" Tommy's anxious face appeared.

"Fuck! Where did you spring from? I mean blast it. What?"

"Do you want the good news or the bad news?"

"The bad news."

Mr Carmichael Hunt's back."

"O great. I'll be right there! Suzanne. He's coming now. I'll do what I can. Keep Dora out of his way." He replaced the phone and followed Tommy back to mobile.

"What was the good news?"

Tommy grinned cheerfully. "The door's back on."

Dafydd opened the said door carefully to find Carmichael Hunt back in his crevice at the back of the room, scribbling a furious inventory of the contents of Dafydd's drawers. He was holding an empty bottle of brandy between finger and thumb and regarding it quizzically. He did not appear to be a man who had much time for cakes or ale. He returned it to its place between fat files full of compromising documents Dafydd was sure he'd locked away out of sight. Inadequately minuted (because unnecessary and distracting) meetings, skimped (because pointless and distracting) paperwork, jocular notes and doodles to Suzanne during Full Governors' meetings etc.

"I understand you've ratified Ms Morgan's third threshold allowance," said the Inspector.

"Naturally. She's a gifted classroom teacher."

"How often does she take off her clothes during lessons?"

"Ah, I can explain that."

"Well?"

"Sgert dileu. Staff dress code."

"Not in any of the documentation I've seen."

"It's in the new Development Plan. Megan's always been ahead of the game."

"Game?" Carmichael Hunt made a note. "And what is this staff dress code?"

Dafydd thought quickly. "No skirts. Distracts the boys when female members of staff expose their legs to observation."

"And you think exposing her underwear is an improvement?"

Dafydd affected a laugh. "Very good, Mr Hunt. You are referring of course to Megan's preferred wear for drama lessons. Leggings and pink leotard. The class was about to do drama when you left."

Mr Hunt made another note.

"Right then. Shall we proceed? The lesson title is Isostatic Response To Denudation. The objectives are, as you see, written out on the board." Dafydd was grateful to see that most of them hadn't been rubbed off in the various confusions and longeurs the lesson had suffered.

Mr Carmichael Hunt studied them, pleased to see that the rivers Dafydd was talking about were willing to obey the rules the Government now laid down for rivers to follow. He made a note on his clipboard. *Follows the strategy.*

"That's mine!" snapped Dafydd, whip-cracking out his customary phrase as he confiscated the packet of cheesey crackers a little group was munching together behind the back desk. He interned it in an overflowing drawer. "You can collect it at the end of term." The Inspector made a note.

Dafydd proceeded with Phase One of the Government Improvement of Teaching Strategy (GITS). He decided not to point out that a *strategy* allowed room for professional manoeuvre. What Hunt called a strategy was in fact a mind-forged manacle, a string of tactics, the result of some young theorist in Westminster not trusting the veteran geography teacher to come up with any of his own. Still, this was not the time for quibbling: he'd got his first ball in the net.

There was a knock on the door. Myfanwy came in looking pale. "Sorry I'm late Sir."

"Ah Myfanwy. Good of you to pop in!" quipped Dafydd. "Can you stay long?"

"I've been ill."

"Hmm. Have you got a note?"

"No."

She moved towards a chair that Tommy had mysteriously concealed next to him. Tommy's feigned reluctance to give it up fooled nobody. Dafydd was deciding whether to risk the brewing outburst Myfanwy was evidently sitting on in the cause of demonstrating clear late note procedure to the Inspector and the rest of the class (who tended to be irritated by Myfanwy's ability to get away with this sort of thing in any case) when there was another knock. The door jerked open.

"WAIT UNTIL I SAY COME IN!" yelled Dafyyd.

The door slammed shut again.

Myfanwy was still waiting to be dealt with. Something else caught his eye. "Top off, please."

Everyone stared at Myfanwy's shapely torso. "What?" asked Myfanwy.

"Not you!" Dafydd blushed as everyone laughed. He indicated the target. "You, Daniel. That's not a school top. Take it off please."

"Jesus!" protested Daniel. "God!!"

"I told you not to call me that at work," quipped Dafydd.

"What?"

"I told you not to give away my secret identity at work. Apart from the gratuitous blasphemy of taking the Lord's Name in vain, now the whole class knows who I really am."

"Mr Riley says we're *all* God," protested Tommy.

"We are, Tommy. We are. Potentially. But I'm the nearest you'll get to it in this school…. And I *told* you not to give away our secret identity!" A couple of the quicker kids laughed, the rest wondered what the hell Dafydd was going on about. Dafydd sighed, returning to Myfanwy. "Sit down, Myfanwy." He turned back to the door. "COME IN!!

The door jerked open again and again began to come away from its hinges. Dafydd drew in his breath sharply, willing it to stay up. A girl entered.

"Well, girl?"

"Ms Morgan says- " The girl exchanged a grin with several of her mates in the back row.

"Ms Morgan says what?"

The girl now waved to someone passing outside. Dafydd began to see black spots in front of his eyes. "I'm waiting!"

The girl glared. A growing din began to penetrate from the sound box that was Megan's mobile classroom.

"Right. You've already disturbed my lesson-"

"I was sent yer by Ms Morgan!"

"Yes. You've had a little chat with your mates, and now you've waved to some others outside who shouldn't be there anyway." He broke off. "Myfanwy, will you please go next door now and tell Ms Morgan to keep the noise down. Tell her I have an Inspector in here!"

"I'm ill!"

"NOT AS ILL AS YOU'RE GOING TO BE IN A MOMENT."

Myfanwy flounced out. Jordan and Jericho Jenkins, daughters of the notorious communist freethinker Jeremiah Jenkins, whose letters in the local newspaper chastised the school almost as regularly as they were a thorn in the side of the Government and local council, were comparing bust sizes. Jordan, naturally much more interested in her own version of Personal Development than anything Dafydd could teach her, was admiring under mascara-lashed and solemnly shadowed eyelids the way her new scarlet bra frothed up over the non-regulation low top, the whole business concealed under a frilly pink scarf pretending to be a school tie. Old school ties aren't what they used to be, sighed Dafydd. Jericho, jaundiced to the hue of a glowing amber traffic-light with fake tan, was applying lip gloss. "That's mine!" barked Dafydd, his routine confiscation phrase having an unfortunate comic effect on this occasion. Dafydd added the lip-gloss to a drawer full of Jezebelia and tried to recover his lesson. It had all been going so well. "Now you, girl. The correct way is to come in here and quietly tell me that you have a message, not disturb the whole class. Understand?"

The girl pouted, "I was only- "

"DO YOU UNDERSTAND?"

The girl shrugged, "Yeah"

"Yes. The word is Yes."

"Yes."

"Sir."

"Sir."

"Yes, Sir."

A sardonic frown. "Yessir."

"Now get back to your lesson."

"But I've got a message."

"*Sir.*"

"What?"

"I've got a message. *Sir.*"

"I've got a message. *Sir.*"

The girl's small but growing audience of admirers was now rocking back on its chairs. Dafydd glanced nervously at the Inspector. The Inspector, however, wasn't on task. He appeared to be trying to work out why his powerball pen wasn't working and then realised it was because the ceiling was leaking rainwater onto his page. One pupil who had forgotten there was an Inspection on until Dafydd mentioned it looked round curiously at the coconut headed Carmichael Hunt. Dafydd was finding it difficult to breathe. "Right. I've got a message. *Sir*. That's better. YOU LOT SHUT UP. Now. What was the message?"

Another girl's – prohibited - mobile rang in the front row.

The messenger looked incredulous. "Can Ms Morgan borrow another chair please?"

Dafydd felt his hands reaching out for her neck. He recovered them with an effort. "Another chair?"

"Yeah. Yes. *Sir*."

A boy farted briefly. Silence. "It's taken us a million years to evolve from the beast, Jones. You have just reversed the process."

"Sorry, Sir." The boy blushed.

"Anything to add?"

"No, Sir."

"Good, I- "

"Can Ms Morgan borrow another chair please?" interrupted the girl sardonically, in an effort to regain her audience.

The class recoiled. She shouldn't have done that. Dafydd turned to face her.

"Sir," she added weakly, unnerved.

Dafydd grinned. "Would she like to borrow my filing cabinet as well? And perhaps a couple of desks? And a whiteboard? And how's she doing for pupils? WOULD SHE LIKE TO BORROW SOME OF MY PUPILS?"

The girl backed away. The class was silent now. She whispered. "No, Sir. She just wants a chair."

At this point, Myfanwy returned, unaware of the change in atmosphere. "Ms Morgan says it's not noise, it's drama, Sir. Her class and a few others are putting on a production of *Romeo and*

130

Juliet tonight for the Eisteddfod. And she asked would Tommy and me be able to come in and do our love scene now- "

"Never mind love scenes. Tommy and you are busy doing the National Curriculum in here with me!"

The Inspector made a note.

"As if I haven't got enough drama on my hands as it is! She's been doing that damned play for months. Surely it's ready now!" Dafydd grimaced, the grimace of a man who had lost the will to teach. Trust Megan to complicate everything at exactly the wrong moment. His off-white collar was now blue with moisture. "Thank you Megan. Thank you very much." The banned mobile phone went off again. "Give me that - phone!!" Dafydd seized it and rang Megan.

"Samaritans," quipped Megan's voice, then became suspicious. "Alice, what are you doing using a mobile phone during lessons?"

"It's not Alice. Nor is it Samaritans," said Dafydd testily. "It's your Headteacher. Remember me? I'm not sure how aware you are of the situation in school this week but could I remind you I'VE GOT AN INSPECTOR IN HERE AND WE KEEP BEING INTERRUPTED. AND I CAN HARDLY HEAR MYSELF THINK! - SO I'D REALLY APPRECIATE IT YOU COULD KEEP THE WRETCHED NOISE DOWN!"

Mr Hunt's Black Stare sought and held Dafydd's (which was flexing like the lens of a Hughsian eye) then wrote *Unsatisfactory* down on his clipboard. The bell shattered the silence. The kids immediately started to put their books away.

Dafydd made one last desperate effort to win the game. "Did I say put your books away?"

"No," said Myfanwy.

"Has the bell gone?"

"Yes," said Beverley Hancock.

"Anyone know where?"

The class groaned.

"Ok. Off you go." He lifted his voice above the stampede. "Except Myfanwy. Could I, uh, see you for a moment, please?"

18

The door of Trolley's office creaked slowly, and melodramatically, open. The man himself emerged with the green-ghoulish glint of a Hammer Horror vampire from a coffin. Unlike the rest of the staff, the Inspector held no fear for him. Inspectors had come and Inspectors had gone and he himself had remained. Troll was as old and cruel, and as jealous of his school's reputation, as the grave. He was so old he could remember when Archaeology was a new subject. His old wartime-scholarship mentor Griffith "The Bastard" Jenkins up at Oxford had once said that although he, Griffith "The Bastard" Jenkins, taught Archaeology (what would in these service economy days be called 'delivered' Archaeology), Trolley *was* archaeology. Trolley took that as a compliment. Indeed, he was so old he could remember Old Labour. He was so old he could remember when The *Kinnock Arms* was called The *Labour In Vain* and had a sign depicting a big black mama washing her babies. He remembered the political correctors insisting this be taken down and blamed the EEC bureaucrats, although the latter organisation had in fact been responsible for funding the transformation of Trollbridge town centre after eighties market values had reduced it to a wasteland. It was the Commission For Racial Equality that had done for the sign. But to Trolley they all came out of the same post-50s decadence.

Robin Hunt met him in the corridor. "Ah, Mr Trolley."

Here was one of them now. And the bounder had the temerity to undermine Trolley's lifelong Napoleonic height offensive by being a short head shorter even than himself. He sneered, "Yes?"

"I believe you're in charge of school archives?"

"That is so."

"I'm just on my way to inform the Head."

"Acting Head," sneered Trolley.

"It's about the statue of Prince Llewellyn the Last."

The blood drained from Trolley's face. Or it would have done if his face had contained any. The statue of Prince Llewellyn, dated in the school prospectus as 1282 though actually made in 1746, was a locus of all the remaining passions that could shake the walls of Trolley's heart. Trolley owed spiritual allegiance solely to his thirteenth century Welsh Prince. And he cherished the hold this relic evidently retained over parents and grandparents who had come to the school themselves in its Grammar school heyday – whatever their attitude to what the relic actually represented. The statue was worth 200 pupils a year quite apart from the material value of its bronze furnishings (or thinly coated wrought iron depending on whether you read the school prospectus or the insurance policy). And 200 pupils was a lot of money. With the stringent per capita rules now applying, to expel a pupil was to throw away £3,000 and whatever damage a pupil might be inflicting on the minds, bodies and souls of staff & scholars had to be balanced against this loss. If the pupil was inflicting damage on the actual *building* itself, however, that was different! Trolley waited in mounting fear to hear what had befallen his icon.

"Mr Trolley are you all right?"

"Of course I'm not all right. Has it...?" Trolley was unable at first to go on. Then he pulled himself together. "What is it? Chalked with Nationalist slogans? Hatted with a police cone? Endowed with auxiliary parts? For God's sake, man, what? - Put me out of my misery." He thought of the worst that could have happened and dared to whisper its name. "*Damaged?*"

"Stolen, Mr Trolley."

"*Stolen!*"

"Yes, Mr Trolley."

"In broad daylight? From its plinth in front of the school? In full view of the public? How on earth- ?" Trolley's face was lengthening by the minute. His skull began to appear through the parchment skin. A death pallor spread itself across his cheek. It was the face of a man who had lost the will to undie.

Robin Hunt tried to look sympathetic. He followed the procedure used by surgeons reporting the fatal failure of an operation to next of kin. Stay factual, stay calm, give the details, however apparently futile. "It was stolen sometime between the arrival of the

County Inspectorate and second period, Mr Trolley. I'm very sorry."

"And nobody *saw*?" Trolley swooned but steadied himself. "Has the County Constabulary been informed?"

"Apparently the theft was reported by a witness. Mrs Owain the School Shop. She saw the statue being lowered down a ladder onto a grocer's van and rang immediately."

"But it must have taken the best part of an hour, Hunt. Why didn't the constables catch them in the act?"

"The Police didn't believe her. They rang the Caretaker for confirmation…"

"And?"

"The Caretaker was on a not-to-be disturbed priority action."

"What priority action?"

"Washing my brother's car."

"*What!* On whose authority?"

"The Acting Head's – naturally. He left specific instructions."

"Thomas! I knew it!" Trolley's knees weakened. "And what about the Assistant caretaker?"

"He was teaching RE. The Rev Shepherd is apparently still sick."

Victor Trolley smiled weakly and sat down on one of the Main Hall's genuine Tudor pews. The Assistant Caretaker, an Enthusiastic lay preacher, was often to be seen leafing through English department stock during the school holidays and so Connie had used him to teach Literacy Progress Units and to solve her RE teaching crisis. He also occasionally did caretaking jobs. Trolley leaned his head back against the oaken panelling and repeated the name of Dafydd Thomas and some Old Testament phrases about The Work Of Mine Enemy Hath Undone Me. Above him, the names of all Head Boys since 1284 were glorified in gold lettering, his own and his father's and his father's fathers among them. The roll of Headmasters' names – his own name conspicuously absent – seemed to mock him from the opposite wall.

"But this is catastrophic, Hunt. If your brother finds out he will assume it's a deliberate show of Welshness."

Robin Hunt bristled slightly. "There's nothing inherently Welsh about incompetence, Trolley."

"Not incompetence, man. TREASON."

"Treason? But surely, it's a statue – a very valuable one, granted, but – even in the eyes of the school's distinguished Archives Officer (Trolley received this title with a Metternichian bow) there's nothing treasonable in losing an antique!" He smiled.

Trolley gave him a withering look. "An antique! Do you think Wales stopped like a sun dial the day Edward the Conqueror marched in with his castles? The Saxons and their new-fangled ideas never conquered here, you know. We had the ancient mores of Britain in our care in 1284, not a few hundred years of German knick-knacks. There's a thousand years of Welsh culture and heritage embodied in that Stone. My Prince, my lost Prince Llewellyn, my poor dead Welsh Prince..." Trolley began to wail, a wail of harrowing intensity not heard in those parts since the invincible Welsh went down to Bill Beaumont's 1980 grand slammers. Robin Hunt stood awkwardly by. Trolley's wails seemed in due course to be calming into rational discourse but this was merely the next stage of his delirium. Words began to form on his foaming lips. "Remove! Remove! Remove all other statues, sculptures, standing foliage, rugby posts, cupboards, filing cabinets and all other movables into the traditional locked underground storage until the danger is past- "

Robin Hunt decided he must act. "Chin up, man. Tragic, I know, but this theft does make the next item a little easier to broach. Now I just need to talk to you about a corresponding change to the school name. We shouldn't fossilise our young charges' fifteen thousand formative hours with a defeatist name like 'The Llewellyn The Last Mountain High School.' And I have convinced the committee that 'The King Edward The First Mountain High' (my brother's choice) - though *apparently* much more progressive - and of course inviting excellent sponsorship deals with British Potatoes – is only the other side of the same old coin. And there's nothing so certain to retard progress as an attempt to modernise too quickly, so we wondered how you would feel about – The King Edward The *Seventh* Mountain High School?..."

Trolley emitted a shriek.

Robin Hunt back-pedalled three hundred and fifty years to another royal educational pioneer with quasi-Welsh connections. "Or uh, the *Henry* the Eighth Mountain High School?"

Another shriek and a strangled reference to what Robin Hunt could do with all his syphilitic English kings. Victor Trolley loved his statue and what it named more than life itself. Indeed so much of his love was absorbed into that carved block of millstone grit that none was left for any human being – not even himself, with whom the statue shared many qualities. Endurance, rigor, firmness of principle, unshakeable convictions, deeply-grounded old school traditions, the tyranny of dead forms.

Mountain High's Head of Pastoral Care certainly wasted none of his love on something as mutable as the school's pupils and he regarded "Uncle" Joe Benson – who cared for nothing else - as an idiot. The relationship - Trolley was after all Joe Benson's line manager – might be expected to cause a certain everyday friction and it did indeed, but only the kind of wear and tear a long wet April causes concrete. Trolley's real enemy was of course Dafydd, who had not only changed and grown up but who was now his superior. Until Dafydd, Trolley had always consoled himself with the dictum that Heads come and go and make silly changes and then other Heads come and change them all back again (Trolley regarded them with the withering contempt that Senior Civil Servants regard elected British politicians) while with Victor Trolley you got what you paid for: continuity - the kind of continuity maintained throughout the sprawling Austrio-Hungarian Empire against those fanciful French-Revolutionary decades around the turn of the eighteenth century. But Dafydd was different. Dafydd was beginning to oversee – or allow in – or actively embody - something that might eventually erode the very foundations of the Old School itself. This atrocity, allowing the statue to be stolen because of the passing distraction of an Inspection – Trolley had seen off more of these than his old adversaries the Children of

Israel had seen off the plagues of Egypt – was only the worst example of some dreadful sea change, some youthful erosion of the valley floor of Trolley's existence, which every new generation of pupils had sounded and chattered in Trolley's stone-deaf ears.

"Mr Trolley, can you hear me?"

19

But Trolley was years away in a much better place. The past. And not even David Bowie could spoil it. "Starman" may have been playing through a housewife's open window but Trolley could block that out by shutting the Punishment Room door. Young Dafydd was copying Leviticus and Dueteronomy (in the special issue Punishment Room fountain pen) for not wearing his Grammar-Technical Old School Tie properly. Trolley had allowed him to miss out one verse of Leviticus, as a special concession, because Dafydd had hurt his hand copying out Genesis, Exodus, Numbers and Chronicles the week before. Trolley accepted that the hurt hand *may* have made knotting the Old School Tie difficult and so allowed him to leave out the verse (famously quoted by Our Lord in the New Testament) about loving one's neighbours as oneself (He wasn't a complete monster). But he wasn't going to let him off any of the others.

At her desk on the other side of the room, Young Megan – an eye-corner blur of long dark hair and shining blouse - was copying out Logarithms. That would teach her - Troll checked the Punishment Book – to stand "at the top of the stairs over the boys' cloakrooms *showing off*". Miss Winterbottom, who had entered her in the Punishment Book, had not recorded exactly *what* she had been showing off to the boys' cloakroom but, judging by the abbreviated hemline of Megan's uniform gymslip, Senior Mistress Fanny Williams (who set, in column three, the sentences to be served) had not found it difficult to guess.

"I trust this session has been an *education* for you both!" Trolley snarled with a twitch of his fossilised lip. He enjoyed his little jokes all the more for the pupils not getting them. "Morgan, you may go. Now." Megan collected her stuff, got up and left, lingering by the door for Young Dafydd. But Trolley had no intention of allowing them to enjoy each other's company on the way to the bus stop. "On your way, girl." He smiled- a truly frightening sight. "Thomas will be a while yet."

Dafydd's heart sank. He was aware of Megan's retreating shadow and then of Trolley's face in his. "Let me tell you about the Old School Tie, Thomas. When parents see a pupil wearing a tie like ours, firmly knotted in the proper fashion, they know its wearer goes to a Good School."

Why? wondered Dafydd.

"Why?" asked Trolley, and Dafydd was about to say, 'That's just what I was thinking!' when Trolley revealed it was a rhetorical question and then answered it: "Because it's *firm*, Thomas, firm as an RAF handshake. None of this limp-wristed poncing your generation goes in for. Firm for principle, firm against fads."

Trolley certainly resisted 'fads'. When 'the Beatles pop group' was awarded the MBE in 1965, he sent back his bronze Duke of Edinburgh medal in protest at the devaluing of the public awards system and never believed the said Duke's vacillating 'correction' of a statement in 1964 that the Beatles were 'away' (his original statement that they were 'on the wane' showed to Trolley a finger much more pulled out and on the pulse). 1968 and its revolting students had tested Trolley's endurance to breaking point but 1970-1974 had restored his steadfast doubt in human nature. His adherence to enduring principles extended to his continued teaching of School Certificate instead of 'O' level more than a decade after it had changed. He got away with it, somehow, and would not *actually* have to adapt until the 1988 Education Act - two and a half decades later. And when he did so he found to his delight that the changes were largely reversions to his 1950s type. He even found that translating the school's Latin motto into Welsh in 1988 largely preserved the spirit of the original, because this spirit was the one pathologists use to keep corpses 'fresh'. But oh he found Young Dafydd's ardour, like all youthful energy, wearing. And he spent the next ten minutes trying to extinguish it.

Dafydd left the room almost in tears at missing his chance to walk to the bus stop with Megan. He slammed out of the Main Entrance reaching for his fags and was overjoyed to see Young Megan waiting there for him.

"What did Troll want? Was he warning you about me?"

"No." Young Dafydd passed her his cigarette and tore off the tie again in his excitement. "He was trying to strangle me with this."

They walked to the bus stop, smoking like the Trollbridge factory chimneys, down the 1 in 4 gradient of School Hill. They reached the bus stop along New Road - a carriageway that had been surveyed and partly-levelled in the early days of the Industrial Revolution when Trolley drove up it to take his first Metalwork class — by way of a shortcut down Old Lane, a 1 in 3 gradient that predated even Troll. It was a beautiful spring evening and their walk was bathed in primrose sunlight and the occasional flutterings of blossom from the overhanging trees. It made Megan feel even more romantic than usual and Dafydd, though terrified of any actual bodily contact, was close to erupting like a spring bud himself at any moment.

But something was clearly wrong. Megan kept asking inviting questions but Dafydd remained awkwardly silent, partly out of acute shyness, partly total inexperience of what to say after some brief observations on the weather but mostly because of a 'gentleman's problem', locked at a 45 degree angle to his pelvis and seriously compromising his Prince Charming persona. So he tried to make a grimace convey a variety of wry acknowledgements of what she was saying.

"Are you shy of me or something?" she eventually asked.

Dafydd tightened his lips even further. His dream of walking to the bus stop alone with Megan — of even going into the park on a fragrant spring evening snowed on by petals and blossoms and into who knows what earthly paradise of discoveries — had turned into a nightmare of tortured hip manoeuvres. Happily, he was saved at that moment by some older boys yelling.

"Oi Megan! You prossy! Get 'em off!"

"Scrubber!!"

"Phooooaaaar!"

As Megan's attention was taken by these courtly salutations, Dafydd hoiked his trousers into a missionary position and then, liberated, charged off to defend his lady's honour. His lady, meanwhile, was winning her own battle in a torrent of sexual abuse, most of it directed at the inability of her accusers' members to perform. Dafydd, oblivious to this, was just yelling himself – via some eccentrically applied Biblical quotations about "let he who is without sin cast the first stone!" - into an ill-advised knightly combat with two of their assailants at once, while a fourth boy sneered that what's the point of fighting about a *girl*. What else was worth fighting about? cried the chivalric Dafydd, now preparing to fight a third older boy as well. And then, a saviour knight manqué, along came Mountain High's very own scale-plated dragon.

Mr Trolley stopped the car, wrenched open the door, and saw not a boy defending the honour of beauty but one disgracing the Old School Tie he was *once again* refusing to wear.

Megan, seeing Trolley, disappeared swiftly into the park - along with the three older boys, united in their reluctance to discuss the matter with Troll – and Dafydd did not see her or any of them again that evening. Trolley meanwhile informed Dafydd, at some length, that he, Dafydd, had about as much chance of ever achieving anything in life as Nelson Mandela had of becoming President of South Africa, promised the boy hadn't heard the last of this incident and then drove off to his coffin evening carrying the glow of a job well done. And, after finally escaping from Troll (until the next time), Dafydd waited at Megan's up-valley bus stop for over an hour, before finally crossing the road to his own down-valley one, catching an empty bus and feeling very strongly that he'd missed it. He continued to feel so for the next thirty years.

20

In the lull before the breaktime storm, a flyer was blowing across the playground. Nathan the Cleaner picked it up and read it. "No taste? Awful gaudy clothes? Can't hold your drink or queue at a bar without shouting? Can't even hold a glass of piss-yellow lagerpop without spilling it over your trainers? Can't even hold a glass? Can't even see the 'A' list authentic away-day curry houses lining your way to the Kentucky fried junk trough at the bin end of the street? Unable to distinguish between natural colours and day-glo? No interests? No abilities? Stupid? Obese? Graceless? Nothing better to do on a Tuesday night or a Saturday but to travel up to Hartlepool to yell obscenities and abuse in unison with a crowd of drunken oafs who boo the ref *before* the game? Devoid of all individual discrimination or logic? Wouldn't know a good film, play, painting or newspaper if it punched you in the face? No real understanding even of sport or its place in a healthily balanced lifestyle?...

Then you're exactly the sort of person we need on the terraces of the Purgatory Stand down at Dis Park, week in week out, man and boy, rain and shine, decade after decade, through thin and thin. You're not one of these flash git fickle supporters. You're a *real* fan."

Nathan looked in vain for somewhere to put the flyer. He didn't want rubbish like that in his bin.

As he dithered, the long-awaited and incredibly loud school bell went for break. (Where it went is anybody's guess but probably to that quaint little elevenses tea roome in the shadow of the Abbey Church at Castell-y-amerchislawerech, just outside Ugh). The break bell had been checked and rehearsed throughout the week before the inspection, and now – exactly as programmed, 11.03 recurring – and very loudly indeed - it went. Unlike the snack-menu boards of hot and bothered school canteens all over the country, it had no choice.

Chapter Three

Home For Lunch

Doncha know
They're gonna kill
Kill your sons,
Doncha know they're gonna kill;
Kill your sons,
Doncha know they're gonna kill
Kill your sons
Until they run run run run run run run
Run away

1

Aftermath. Or Geography anyway. The yells of escaping pupils faded into the distance as a moment of calm descended on the classroom. Old Taff looked in dismay at his desk. Somehow it was back to the mess it had been in before Tommy tidied it. He shifted a few things around, uncertain how to begin. "You used to help me with this," he said at last.

Myfanwy hoisted her bag impatiently, "I used to do it for you!"

"What?"

"Ms Morgan says you should tidy you own desk."

"You've grown up, I suppose. Different hair, different clothes."

"What's wrong with my hair?"

"Nothing. It suits you. I was just remembering- "

"A girl who used to think nothing was more important than your praise and rewards. I'm afraid I've rather grown out of being your slave. Ms Morgan says-"

"MS MORGAN SAYS THIS! MS MORGAN SAYS THAT! MS MORGAN SAYS LIE ON THE CLASSROOM FLOOR AND SHAKE YOUR LEGS IN THE AIR!"

Silence.

Dafydd rolled his eye heavenwards. "Sorry. I didn't mean that. I shouldn't take it out on you. It's been a tough lesson, that's all."

"It wasn't so bad. It was getting quite good at the end."

"The bell cut me off in my prime. And the Inspector wasn't watching then anyway. And your precious Ms Morgan didn't exactly help my case by sending in for chairs."

"You were explaining it quite well. It was really interesting. At the end."

"I wasn't supposed to explain it or make it interesting. I was supposed to hit an attainment target."

"What's an attainment target?"

Dafydd almost cried with laughter. "Something Governments can shoot me by!"

"Well you're still my best lesson. You and Ms Morgan. I used to hate Geography at my old school. And English – well, it was called Literacy for Life there."

"More like Literacy for Lice."

"Ms Morgan says…"

"No, go on. It might do me some good to hear what Ms Morgan has to say."

"You're wrong about her, Sir. She's always saying what a good teacher you are. She says you teach Geography like it should be taught, as a *humanity*. She says you 'awaken enthusiasm'".

"Does she?" Dafydd couldn't prevent his heart glowing for a moment. Then - "She's just being professional."

"You don't like her do you?"

Silence. Dafydd's looked absently through the window and up at the Western mountain.

"Sir?"

"Sorry. Yes?"

"What did you want to see me about?"

"Tommy came to see me. He said you were upset about what I said in front of the class.... I wanted to apologise."

"Oh."

"No I don't."

"No?"

"No. I do. Duw, English is such a ridiculous language. I *want* to apologise.

Myfanwy gave him a look of unbearable sweetness for a moment. Then her face crumpled into tears.

"Oh God, what have I done now? Myfanwy, don't, please- " Dafydd looked round helplessly, "Myfanwy?"

Carmichael Hunt appeared in the doorway, examining the hinges. He frowned at the sight of Dafydd comforting a sobbing girl and made a note.

"She's uh- " But Dafydd realised that explanation – like resistance in Nazi Germany - was useless.

In the distance, Trolley's voice was already calling through his duty megaphone across the sports field - warning pupils that the warning bell for the end of break bell would be going shortly. Carmichael Hunt went out to investigate.

"It's just – I just don't care about any of it, Sir. I don't care."

"But Myfanwy- "

"And no-one listens when I say so. They just keep telling me I'm bright, doing well, Head girl material. World my oyster. Exam marks. Form prizes. Approval Certificates. Credit to the school, a League Table Tip Topper."

"So – that's good isn't it?"

"No. Nothing means anything."

"I don't think it means anything to Tommy either."

"But it wouldn't. He's a boy. I'm supposed to like school."

"Tommy is very concerned about you. It's nice to see. I'm glad someone appreciates you."

Myfanwy brushed aside a tear. "I like him too."

The warning bell for the end of break sounded.

"Well, look after each other. I think that was the warning bell. What's your next lesson?"

"Life Skills. With Ms Morgan."

Myfanwy didn't move.

"I'll explain to her why you're late. Don't worry."

"Sir?"

Dafydd was writing Myfanwy a late-to-lesson note. As he finished it – and no-one could say they hadn't been warned - the end-of-break bell sounded.

"Sir?"

"Yes?"

"Why don't you like Ms Morgan?"

Silence.

2

"Time" by Pink Floyd was thumping out of the record player and walls of Young Dafydd's late-Victorian bedroom record player in the 1970s. He air-guitared his way to a climax, then gratefully received the rapturous applause offered by his fans. He addressed his bedroom wall, glowing. "Thank you. Thank you. We're gonna do one more for you then we gotta go. It's a song I wrote way back when I was sixteen and it's dedicated to a girl who taught me everything. And if you're out there Megan drop by the dressing room after the show and we can chew the fat about the old times." Young Dafydd dropped the false voice. "And maybe we could go for a walk together. Up the mountain…." He was being kept in – he had been seen on School Hill talking to a girl after a detention instead of hurrying home to his homework – and Pink Floyd at full volume was his response.

"Dafydd!! DAFYDD!!! That's a bloody NUFF!"

"Let me out! I've got things to do. Megan won't wait for ever."

Silence.

"How dare you talk to your mother like that!"

"Unlock the door. My life's out there."

"Aye and who's paying for it?"

"Why don't you get a job? Your father and I were both working at your age. Younger!"

"How can I? I'm doing O levels."

"So get on with your homework."

"Yeah."

"And why don't you ever watch telly with us?"

"Yeah- why don't you ever watch telly?"

"I WANT TO SEE MEGAN!"

Silence. The father's neck cricked out of place.

"Dirty little devil," hissed Mum.

"Sat there playing records with himself!"

"Supposedly doing his homework."

"I'VE DONE MY BLOODY HOMEWORK."

"DON'T YOU SWEAR AT ME YOU FUCKING LITTLE CUNT!" His father tore open the door, sledgehammered the boy's cowering head, tore the record off the deck - scarring it forever across "Time" - and hurled it at the bedroom wall, then came out again, turning the key in the door. "Records full of drugs!"

"And sex!"

"LET ME OUT!"

3

A bell to end all bells rang and kept ringing. Alarm clock, school bell, telephone bell, warning bell, knell, fire drill, curfew, invasion and calamity bell, burglar alarm: all bells in one. Dafydd wasn't sure if the bells were ringing inside his head or out. It was the 'early' lunch bell, introduced ten minutes into period 3 as a way of getting the first wave of school lunches over before the main lunch period – the lunch 'hour' proper (45 minutes) - that incorporated the second, third and fourth wave of school lunches. It was also the 'late' break bell for that substantial section of the school's increased population that couldn't buy their snacks in 'normal' break time.

In the broom cupboard Mr Quasimodo The Cleaner, wrote Chapter 57, of his autobiography - *The Bells, the Bells* - an epic he had begun writing at Dafydd's request after the Acting Head-teacher had been accosted once too often in the middle of urgent trivia by Mr Q's detailed self-narratives. Now Dafydd skim-read the narratives at home in the evenings and gave their driven and copious narrator a monthly written response. It saved time.

"How long before you get your fifty years' back pay and lump sum, then Mr Q?"

"I've got another chapter for you here and you'll never guess-"

Dafydd locked the door of the classroom behind him and cleared a crowd of 'late breaktime' reprobates from the corridor. One threatened to contact his lawyer over this blatant infringe-ment of his human rights. Gladstone White wouldn't stop whack-ing his tennis ball into the display boards so had his racquet con-fiscated. Gladstone White's mother would be seeing Dafydd about this, Dafydd was informed, the boy already tapping the number into his banned mobile phone, then realising that in fact he'd brought his family's home phone into school by mistake, thus ef-fectively cutting off himself, his family - and an entire network of litigation - from a grateful nation for hours. The other twenty-six pupils lingering off limits merely threatened Dafydd with physical violence. One refused to move five times and on being told he was now in serious trouble responded with "I'll live". Dafydd added this in writing to the boy's Permanent Exclusion Case Papers, now into their third volume, eventually got the corridor clear and stepped out into the playground.

Llewellyn The Last Mountain High had, since the teachers' strikes of the 1980s, followed a continental day. A day in Nurem-berg in 1936. Staggered breaks were reduced to ten minutes; stag-gered lunches to fifteen minutes each (three times) and afternoon break to nothing at all. The net effect was to turn the school day into a gerbil wheel. And that was undeniably more comfortable than the previous model, as long as you weren't one of the gerbils.

He was glad that the time he had here on 'late' break duty was so restricted: the kids got wilder and wilder as the breaks went on. As with horses made secure by open fields and clear fences, the teenage jungle needed some order, if only so that teenagers themselves could negotiate it safely. But this routine restriction of time and freedom to its minimum was neither principled nor effective. Play taught kids who they were - and recreation aided the formal learning to come after 'break' – and he had inherited instead a Trolley-like path between a rock and hard place. And the kids were actually made wilder by the relentless pace, the constant drive to performance, the remorseless lack of breathing space in the day. It needed changing certainly – but it was writ into the millstone of a mountain that even Mohammed might find hard to shift. And Dafydd's energy was sapped so comprehensively by national 'targets', County 'initiatives' and mountainous molehills, he doubted he could survive at all, let alone bring some radical force to bear on the real problem.

Do we all turn into Trolleys in the end, he wondered? Dafydd knew that Trolley had not enjoyed the early '80s managing nine hundred pupils through the ninety minute lunch hour, effectively on his own. That would make anybody hard and cynical. In those days (Dafydd was a keen young Geography teacher elsewhere then) the staff body of Mountain High was off site every lunchtime, withdrawing its 'goodwill' when it wasn't actually striking. Which was a bit like the Welsh dragon threatening to withdraw from the Union flag in most cases. And Trolley's nominal colleagues – Ted Floyd, Norman's predecessor as Second Deputy (known as 'Teflon': nothing stuck), along with Connie 'the Con' Francis - were as much use as a literacy adviser in an English classroom. Connie was generally in photogenic locations speaking to the media about how results were not at all affected by lessons without staff. And Ted Floyd could never be found, not even – for all his commando and espionage experience - by Trolley. Especially when Trolley looked for him in his office opposite the 'Behaviour Reassignment Room.' But even when not out on his interminable Headship training, Ted was never seen anywhere else either. He held the school record for missed substitutions, making a gracious acceptance speech by phone from one of his courses, and while he was undoubtedly a man of absolute principle, this principle (alas) was: maximum work for colleagues, minimum for self. He would end his career addressing conferences of Senior Managers about how to run schools. (He would end his life confessing on a lido deathbed in the South of France that he found everything too difficult so just kept escaping through promotion loopholes to 'safety').

His lasting bequest to the school was its motto STRIVING FOR COMPETENCE. Various staff sub-committees working on a change to STRIVING FOR EXCELLENCE felt 'STRIVING' was "too challenging to be realistic" (though one, led by Norman Welch, had agreed on 'EXCELENSE'). Dafydd – wanting something less worthily plodding –suggested AIM HIGHER.

Meanwhile, another bell sounded and continued to resonate in a thousand skulls. Students made their way to various Life Skills lessons and a lifetime of stimulus-response wailed like an electric shock treatment through Dafydd, their Acting Headteacher's, inner wasteland.

He needed somewhere to get away from it all and nowhere in the present offered anything except more of the same. Future holidays were just something else he hadn't got organised yet, a deferred headache, another sequence of worrying unknowns conducted in some new technological language he had still not quite mastered. So, as he had begun increasingly to do of late, he sought a Troll-like solace in the past. At least you knew who/where you were, then.

4

A year to the day after providing the soundtrack to the Thomas household's epic row about Young Dafydd speaking to Young Megan instead of coming home to his homework, Pink

Floyd were again performing 'Time' on vinyl in the youngster's bedroom. Dafydd's parents left the house – late - accompanied by unseen Peace Off signs from behind their son's curtains. Young Dafydd immediately turned the sound up until the walls vibrated. Mrs Thomas looked back uneasily. Various letters were filed away with the Embassy Regal and car keys in her handbag. "Dear Mr and Mrs Thomas, I regret Dafydd has been seen smoking on the way home from school." "Dear Mr and Mrs Thomas, I regret that Dafydd was seen in a public house at lunchtime." (No doubt, Dafydd joked, there would soon be one that read. "Dear Mr and Mrs Thomas, I regret that Dafydd has just fed LSD into the school water supply and set purple flames at the heart of the examination hall just before 'O' levels. Imagine the clouds dripping one by one. Looking through a glass onion....") Mrs Thomas snapped her handbag shut. As her husband drove her up the valley to the school, past various 'males' in pastel variants on drag, she wondered what had happened to her son's generation. She intended asking the school that very question.

The Thomases entered the main hall at a gallop and found their 6.30 appointment, with Miss Winterbottom, in the nick of time. But they were still waiting for it forty-five minutes later.

"Hello," said the teacher at last. They all shook hands with each other nervously, including Mr and Mrs Thomas. "I think we missed each other at the last Parents' Evening."

"I couldn't get away," sniffed the mother.

"I was on the night shift," snapped the father.

Miss Winterbottom smiled. But her heart sank. She foresaw herself sitting here thirty years on, and no way out. It was a terrifyingly accurate vision, though what she could not forsee was that she would be sitting here in a wholly new climate of teacher terror and parent 'power' - a climate in which parents would be able, without rebuke, to name their children with a spelling mistake - like Mykull or Rachil - and where a colleague behind Miss Winterbottom would be giving his routine anti-litigation defence to each parent he saw, irrespective of the conduct and attainment of that pupil, and of any attempt by the parent to speak, while beside her, another colleague would be presenting a bewildered couple with an impregnably defensive sequence of graphs and tables analysing their daughter's progress in relation to school, county and national norms. Meanwhile, 30 years before all this progress, in Miss Winterbottom's young and frightened present, Mr Thomas's medical support collar was making him appear even more rigid in discourse than usual, and she wasn't looking forward to the notorious Mrs Thomas getting her pound of flesh either. Plus Miss Winterbottom had just realised that she'd spent ten minutes talking to the mystified and increasingly annoyed parents of Rebecca Eastern 5A about Rachael Eastham in 5C.

"Please do sit down."

Even before she did so, the mother opened fire. "On his report it says he has great potential. He never seems to get enough homework. I can't help him much but I do try. I don't really approve of some of the books he has to read."

The father looked up from a sheet. "Is this English?"

"If his spelling is poor he gets it from his father. Or doesn't spelling matter anymore? The Government's always going on about it. I was always good at spelling."

The father glared, "Is he top of the class?"

"Apparently he sits next to a girl in your lessons - Megan Morgan. Is she a nice girl? He talks about her a lot."

"He's not queer is he?" demanded the father.

"What do you mean by potential? I don't really approve of all these universities. I never needed drugs to enjoy myself."

"Or sex," added the father.

"He's doing well then? We left him doing his homework." The mother got up.

"I'll keep him at it, don't worry," growled the father. "If he plays up just clout the bugger."

5

Dafydd unlocked his classroom again. He had forgotten his car keys which were somewhere on his desk. His head was *tamping*. "This is all I bloody need. I– "

Someone was huddled in a chair. He stared, thinking it was his young self again, but it was Tommy. His relief recoiled into a different kind of anxiety. The police had been in today about staff locking pupils into schoolrooms overnight and he himself had once incarcerated a reprobate until seven o clock (the end of a senior management meeting) having forgotten the thirteen year old's simpler verities in the minutiae of his own torturous agenda. He didn't relish those sorts of recriminations again.

"Did I lock you in?"

Tommy indicated the open window.

"You got in there? Why?"

"I am a doppelganger."

"What?"

"I am a doppelganger."

Dafydd paused. "Where did you learn a word like that?"

"You."

"I don't think so, Tommy. Are you feeling ok?"

"Fine."

"Good. Why don't you go to lunch?"

Tommy shrugged. In Dafydd's own day, this would have been a stupid question. But these days school lunches were, if not always so good for you, at least as *tasty* as the chip shop.

"I don't have school lunch. I only live over the road. There. The terraced house facing the entrance. With the red door and green railings."

"I remember it well. Why don't you go home then? You're not in detention."

"I can't."

"Why not?"

Silence. The boy stared at the teacher. Dafydd frowned back, bewildered by what the boy was saying, bewildered by where he'd put his keys, bewildered.

"Sir, do you know who won the 1927 FA Cup?"

"What? No." Dafydd shifted a few precarious piles of junk and found a fiver.

"Cardiff City did. They beat Arsenal 1-0. It's the only time the cup has ever been won by a foreign club. I can't go home."

"Why not?"

"It's not there anymore."

"It is. I parked the car outside it this morning."

"Oh aye. It's there physically. Just like Myfanwy is there physically when she walks by with someone else. But it's not there for me."

"Oh. I see." He didn't. " Why not?"

"My old man tried to beat me up. He said I wasn't the son he knew. He said I'd changed. He tried to strangle me."

Old Taff went silent. "He tried to *strangle* you?"

"Well – he pushed me."

"Listen, Tom, some dads really do stuff like that. Bomber Harris's dad for instance. They're the ones who make the front pages of the papers. I sometimes wonder if that's why they do it. But the vast majority of fathers, the ones we never hear about, would rather lose an arm than lay it on their children. So did he actually try to strangle you or not?

"Well, he grabbed me a bit – here."

"He's just desperate for some contact that's all. You're his son. He loves you. Tommy, have you seen my keys?"

"No. He's been in a strop with me about something or other for years – ever since he lost his job at the steelworks. I stood up to him. Man to man. I told him to get his bloody hands off my thro- arm."

"That's not so bad. He'll respect you for it."

"I don't want his respect. I want him to stop strangling me."

"He might be redundant, Tommy, but he's still your father. Go home. He'll be pleased to see you."

"No. He really did go for me that once. I thought, this is it. Man to man. He punched and swore at me. Called me a cunt."

"Tommy! Language!"

" I didn't hit him back. I was scared."

"I know," said Dafydd quietly. He went through the desk once again, methodically. He found some vital papers he'd lost earlier and a pile of field trip letters he should have given out last week but still no sign of the keys.

"Scared I might have killed him."

'Bollocks,' thought Dafydd.

"What Sir?".

"I didn't say anything."

"I said - I was scared I might have killed him."

"And I thought- 'Crap'."

Dafydd closed and secured the window.

"You shouldn't swear, Sir. What do you mean?"

"I mean - 'Crap'. You weren't scared you'd kill him. You were just scared."

"You were there were you?"

"Yes I was. We all were. Once. It's an old story, son. Oedipus versus Lauis. In your case, New Valley Boy versus The Original Heavy Metal Industrial Male, now largely extinct. A testosterone brute dispersing his old body spice up your nostrils like a Henry Cooper advert. And no European court of children's rights stopping him. And you- you were scared you might have killed him! Ha! Look, I know all you want to do is get older. But there's a bit more to growing up than killing your old man. You want some kind of rite of passage, and hitting him now he's down probably would kill him, but not in the way you mean. The poor sod's lost his job and he doesn't know who he is anymore. You're not the only one who has a hard day now and then. Go home. He'll be pleased to see you.

"Bollocks," muttered Tommy.

"In a word, Tommy. Those are doubtless the source of the problem, just as in Brendan Behan's happy phrase they were the foundation stones of the Protestant Church in the days of King

Henry VIII. Nevertheless, one day you'll be pleased to see him and he won't be there anymore. He'll be lying there in a casket. Go and talk to him now while you've got the chance. He just wants to be your father."

"He wants to be my murderer!"

"Run away from this now and you'll spend the rest of your life running. Believe me. Growing up isn't a place you run away to. Growing up is the time and place and the state of mind you learn to accept your parents. Or at least learn to accept what they tried and failed to be. That they loved you in their way- There they are!" Dafydd pounced on the keys. "Right Tommy. Shift yourself. I've got to lock the room. All on my own without any Key Skills qualifications. Then I've got to be in two places at once. Then I've got a Union meeting to face. And then something else I can't even remember. Go *home*."

6

"Not forgetting our duty are we, 'comrade'?" sneered Norman Welch.

"Why do we feel 'we' have to remind 'us'?" answered Dafydd

"Because 'we're' late."

" 'We' are not late."

Norman brandished his watch. " 'We' are – one minute late."

"'We're' late *now* but only because some tosser got in 'our' way. You, in fact. Anyway, *I've* got to be somewhere else. The Union meeting. Remember?"

"Are you refusing to do your duty?"

"I'm refusing to be ordered about by you, yes."

"Then I shall have to report you to the Head."

"I am the Head, Norman. Remember? And you're *supposed* to be my Assistant. And isn't the word 'Union' something to do with team-work?" Dafydd pushed past Norman and into the staffroom.

Gathered around were various members of staff including Megan. Norman pushed past Dafydd and just beat him to the same seat that caused their argument earlier. Dafydd fired him a look and sat in the other vacant chair next to him. "Comfy?"

"Very, thank you. Does that bother you?"

"No. I'm beginning to think it doesn't" He was watching Megan as she organised herself to speak. "But old habits die hard."

"Dai Hard? I preferred Dai Hard 2 'One move - and the Taffy gets it.'" Norman was holding a subversive two-finger gun at Dafydd's temple. He laughed.

Dafydd felt his fist clench. "Norman you've been an Assistant Head too long."

"Couldn't agree with you, more, old boy."

"You know the price of everything and the value of nothing."

"What?"

"Voltaire. Sorry. I forgot you've never read anything except briefing papers. You know the time and the place everything happens and you have no idea at all about what *should* happen. It's time you applied for a genuine Deputy Headship."

"Why, thank you."

"Somewhere else."

"I've been an Assistant Head for eighteen months. If I'm not a Head here by the end of the day, I will be in a rival school within two terms. My journey up the career mountain seems to have a pretty damn good sense of time and place, actually, particularly in comparison to the Long March of your so-called career- "

"You'll never be a Head, Norman, because you don't believe in anything. You think a school is something you can assemble out of County directives and interview babble, when you stop thinking about your own career mountain long enough to consider it at all." Dafydd moved his face very close to Norman's. "And don't ever talk to me like that in front of my staff again."

Megan spoke. "Gentlemen, please! Ladies and gentlemen. If I could call this meeting to order – gentlemen - please."

Attention was focused on her. Sort of.

"Before we get underway with the agenda, Norman has something to tell you."

Dafydd looked round like a naughty boy caught fighting and blushed. Norman Welch rose. Dafydd regarded his old chair carefully. Norman seemed indecently pleased with himself as he spoke. "Thank you Megan. It has fallen to me, uh comrades, to announce that this will be the last time Megan will chair this Union." Several staff looked up at this shock. Norman basked in the attention. "The reason for this is that she has decided to resign at the end of the present term, and considers that with the interests of us all in mind it would be best if she gave up her chair now. A chair, may I add, to which I will be standing for election. I am very sad to have to announce this news to you, as I'm sure you agree she has been both a valued member of staff and a strong Union voice."

The new Art teacher stifled a yawn, born of late nights preparing lessons on Norman Welch's interminably opaque proformas. A teenage science teacher began clapping, then stopped, embarrassed by her mistake. Norman continued, his smile glowing, the tanned seat of his trousers – an exact copy of those worn by Connie, the woman who had appointed him - all but wagging. "I remember my first term here at the school when the Head was bawling me out in the staff-room for having talked openly to the press about the dilapidated state of my teaching room and Megan told her in no uncertain terms that if she wished to discuss an item of school business with one of the members she must make an appointment with Megan first and allow her to be present during the discussion. Those were the days."

Dafydd shook his head. "'Those' days, Norman, if they ever existed, disappeared in the late eighties, when you were still a schoolboy."

"I'm talking actually," said Norman. He attempted to make an Old Labour clenched fist but had never been really sure how to do it. He went on. "I'm sure you all have such memories of the good work Megan has done and will be generous when called upon to contribute to her leaving present fund. I like to think of Megan not only as a colleague and a staunch comrade but also as a valued personal friend. I for one will be very sorry to see her go."

There were murmurs of agreement and stunned applause as Norman sat down, checking first that Dafydd had not taken his place. Several members of staff, exhausted and ravenous, began to take their sandwiches out.

Megan rose. The sandwiches were put back with a stifled cry. "Thank you for your kind words Mr Welch. Naturally though, I believe nothing of what you have just said."

Sandwiches were forgotten now.

Megan cleared her throat and went on, her voice made husky by thirty years of smoking, or perhaps something else. "I am aware that all of you are either totally indifferent or, certainly in your case, Mr Welch, very pleased indeed to see the back of me. And believe me, the feeling is largely mutual. But that is not to say that I am not grateful for your words, because I am. When I hear someone making a speech like that, I feel a glow of satisfaction inside of me, a glow that is fired by the knowledge of how right I am to resign. And as I have no intention whatsoever of discussing the reasons behind that decision with any of you, let us proceed with today's meeting."

"Excuse me." Dafydd who throughout all of the above had been getting more and more agitated, vacated his chair and walked out.

A shock passed through the room. Megan watched Dafydd go, another decision flickering across her face, to leave now or to go on.... "Well, ladies and gentleman, as we remain a quorum, and as I know several of you are desperate for your pungent tupperware diet-pasta, I suggest we press on. I have here- " Megan took a photocopied bundle of papers from her file. "- a typed up sheet for you all, that contains the outcome of this meeting. I have not taken the liberty of actually putting the words into people's mouths, but have outlined the general discussion we will have and have minuted the conclusions that the meeting comes to."

She handed out the sheets, uncertain a moment what to do with Dafydd's then leaving it on his vacated chair.

"Norman, should you wish to maintain the façade of grass-roots democracy, feel free, but I assure you, you will stand a much better chance of your customary double helping of chocolate crunch and pink custard if you follow my lead. As you can see, the main item on the agenda is the Governors' decision to restructure my Head of English post to which I was appointed two years ago as a result of Rhiannon's nervous breakdown.

"The County's proposal and recommendation is that this post is 'restructured' as Head of Literacy for Life. Such a post is cheaper to run, needs only cuttings taken from any old kind of writing to achieve –sales leaflets, unemployment benefit application forms, instructions about how to assemble and operate another state of the art music-acquisition device, briefing papers for divorce and litigation, all our various service economy texts- instead of whole works of Literature - and eliminates the tiresome distractions involved in the education of thought and feeling.

"It rebrands English teaching so that it can be 'delivered' – in a battery of bullet points - by classroom assistants, civil servants, woodenheads and the various supply teachers that have to be brought in to replace the old fashioned awkward-bugger believers now occupying the psychiatric wings of our decaying hospitals. Some government apologists will tell you this is simply the situation they inherited and a heroic response to the wholesale skills-decline in the recruitable teacher-workforce - but this apology never considers that alienating anyone of sensitivity and education from 'teaching' is what caused the workforce-skills relegation in the first place.

"The new curriculum *buys in* as completely as the Iron Lady with her parsimonious handbag ever did to the notion that education is *solely* about the economy - though as someone once said man does not live by bread alone - and as someone else added -if he does, a lot of people don't even get bread. I probably need to spell that out these days don't I? - If all you teach is literacy, you don't even get literacy. Even the employers are saying so.

"It also doesn't work - so it will keep the County's expanding army of Advisers and bureaucrats in gainful employment for the foreseeable future, or until such time as these industrious *Animal Farm* Boxers are also delivered up on the altar of the next Five

Year Plan. (Now Only Three Years!) It is only a recommendation of course but the recommendation comes from the Government so if you don't accept it, you can expect the agents of the cultural revolution to be around your house - with re-education programmes and a warehouse full of County box files crammed with rush-release videos starring shiny twenty somethings from Stepford showing us how to do your job better than we've been doing it for twenty years – in real comprehensives with real pupils and as often as not against real parents.

"I read somewhere that Literacy is not education; education is not culture and all these together do not constitute knowledge, but as all we seem interested in now is producing willing tools in the hands of the exploiters, don't let that worry you. Should you want to discuss all this and vote, feel free, and if anyone wants to vote against it, they of course always have the option of leaving the Union."

Silence. She surveyed them.

Then, slowly, "Ladies and gentlemen. Brothers and sisters as we used to say. Never 'comrades' by the way, Norman, that was the Communist Party. Brothers and sisters, in resigning my post on this Union and my job in this school, I leave you with the following thoughts: What is *National* Union policy at present on getting back the lifetime we sold for money?

"What is National Union Policy on a Lost Property Cupboard overflowing with clothes, trainers, sports kit, watches and even mobile phones because parents have more money to buy new ones than time to get them back?

"What is National Union policy on our campaign for the rebirth of an effective state education service?

"What is National Union policy on getting back the job I used to love, the most important work in the world?

"I suggest to you that in each case, National Union Policy remains what it always has been - through a succession of 'opposed' Governments - clear, vigorous and unambiguous. Take the money, pay the mortgage, hide your head in the bullshit and shut up."

Exit Megan. Silence. The new Art teacher wondered whether she should applaud now. Megan, walking down the corridor of freedom suddenly realised she had nowhere to go.

7

She wanders into her old form room. Young Megan, aged 15, puts down her pen and turns a heightened glance up at her. Her naked eyes are made up, their nakedness thereby underlined in bold. "Hello, Miss. Where are you off tonight then?"

"Parents' Evening. You?"

"I've got a date. Ramo. He's got a car now. His dad's been a bit flusher since the strike."

Megan sighed, "I wouldn't bank on any long term prospects."

"Who cares about long term prospects?"

"Why Ramo and not Dafydd?"

Young Megan laughs, "Dafydd!"

Dafydd.

Young Megan returns to her work. "Dear Francoise. Howbe. Miss said that we've got to have penfriends. She said it'll help us with our composition. Mam said 'I hope it's not a boy'."

Megan answers, "The trouble with Mam is she's got a dirty mind."

Young Megan looks at her. "I said 'you mind your own business. It's my life. You've had yours.' And she says ...

'Yes, and look where it got me.'"

Young Megan goes back to her letter. She writes, "Why is it called 'French kissing'? Do French people do that all the time?"

She sucks the end of her pen thoughtfully.

Old Megan leaves her to it, moves back into the corridor. For some reason she is crying. She is a strong woman, a match for any man. She's been fighting all her life. At school they dismissed her with reports. In her job as a teacher, Government Inspectors and County Advisers have dismissed her with a grown up version of the same. Why couldn't someone just once appreciate her for what she did?

For what she *was*?

8

Old Dafydd watched her from the Hall. He turned away towards a crowd of pupils and then noticed a boy out of uniform.

"You boy!"

"Yeah?"

"Yes. And it's Sir."

"Yes. Sir."

"What's your name? Where's you uniform."

"Dafydd Thomas. This is my uniform."

Oh God not again.

Dafydd threw a look at the herd of pupils massing around him. They looked no less astonished at Dafydd's daring to harangue them than usual. "You need to be outside. Come on. Clear this area." Dafydd was trembling. "Not you," he said to the boy in the old Grammar-Technical school uniform. "I want a word with you."

"OK."

"OK, 'Sir'," said Dafydd testily. For God's sake, set an example."

"An example?" asked Young Dafydd.

"You'll be a prefect soon."

"Really? Cool."

"Really. Despite the Head's last minute attempt to defy democracy and have you left off the elected list. The staff protested on your behalf."

"I thought they hated me."

"O they do. You unnerve them, but you shouldn't take it personally. It doesn't mean they aren't principled."

"What?"

"Hating you is just business. It's just...keeping order. For all our benefits."

"For all your benefits, you mean. Still, cheers Sir. Prefect!" Young Dafydd paused. "Will I be any good at it? I've always rebelled against authority. I can't imagine *being* it."

"Frankly, you'll be hopeless. It's maybe why I'm still doing it, because you couldn't. But look – can we discuss this in private? That rather intense little boy in year 8 is giving me curious looks. I know he can't see you but he can certainly see me and that means he's seeing his Headteacher talking to a pillar. Not good for discipline."

Young Dafydd flexed his muscles. "Shall I tell him to clear off?"

"No," said Dafydd. "You need a certain presence. You haven't got it - yet."

Young Dafydd tried anyway. "Oi, squirt. Piss off outside!"

"Oh very good! You're not allowed to swear at them. - Dan. Outside, please."

Dan looked up at Dafydd through owlish spectacles. "But Sir – it's cold. And I want to read my book."

"What's the book?"

Dan came alive. "*Wholly Babble Part One*. It's about Jesus reincarnating in Wales. The Virgin's not allowed into the story unless she sleeps with the author, The Whore can only be in chapters set in the bedroom and Martha can only be in chapters set in the kitchen. When they all try to turn the world upside down, the authorities crucify the Boyo Jesus on Cardiff Bridge. It's brilliant."

"Does it have a pub in it - where people aren't allowed to drink?"

"Yes!"

"That'll be the Lost Agnostic Gospel Mr Coleridge was writing during the last Heads of Departments meeting. He's been looking for that."

"Has he?"

"Yes, he's lost more visions than you and I have had school dinners. He'll be thrilled."

"So - can I read it?"

"No."

Dan limped sorrowfully out onto the Games Field, pocketing the dog-eared, hare-breadthed exercise book. Outside the cold and the bullies waited to pounce on him.

"You cold-hearted bastard!"

Old Dafydd sighed, "You know, when I trained four years for this job I thought I was going to be a liberator of young minds? Instead, I'm the tedious whistle-blowing referee cramping the flow of your game because otherwise I wouldn't be able to keep up with play. All right, teenage wildlife is a jungle, but it's a jungle of such glorious colour, heat and excitement that nothing I'm going to teach you is ever going to beat it. Shakespeare? Ha! Young love triumphs over all odds. Young love gets married. What then? The play ends. Romance dies. The lovers grow up into old farts who in their turn also try to make Juliet marry Paris instead of Romeo and kill everybody in the process. That's why Romeo and Juliet have got to die because otherwise they'd do exactly the same to their own children wouldn't they! Ever wondered why Frank Sinatra at seventy something was still trying to look like Sinatra at 'thirty something'– singing songs for Swingin' Lovers?"

"Frankly, no."   -

"Just ask the Man Who Used To Be Mick Jagger. Because no-one in his right mind wants to be old. I went to see a band called the Counterfeit Stones recently and guess what. It was the Stones. What can I possibly teach you except that? While we're both at home fantasising about Megan Morgan, you at least have the hope that one day she'll come true. You can still dream of that wonderful first grope around in the knicker elastic behind the bus shelter after youth club even if it hardly ever happens. But she's gone for me now, disappeared under twenty years of chalk dust. I can't think like you anymore."

Young Dafydd snorted. "You bastard. Can't think like me? You can't even remember me! Is your memory so bad? Or is it just that you're so far away from it you can flirt with the past anyway you choose? Just remember that flirting is fun, even flirting with danger, but I can't buzz away from it like a bee away from pollen. I'm in it, right up to my nostrils and at this range it stinks. I've spent every lunchtime for three years in the gym watching Megan vault over the horse box. Time and time again I've watched her heavenly thighs thump onto the leather, but do I go up to her and say 'Megan I want to go out with you.' No. For three years I just stand and watch. I don't even speak to her. And yet I spend three years of nights fantasising about being that horse box! Don't you see? She was showing me the Earthly Paradise, the garden of delights, offering to share Eden with me, and I couldn't move! *That's* what it's all about." Young Dafydd laughed mirthlessly. "And even if I did take her out, I'd only spend the whole evening panicking that I wasn't doing it right. And I wouldn't be. I'd spend the whole time worrying that she was laughing at me. And she would be. Instead of feeling wonderful, I'd spend the whole time feeling sick." He turned on Old Dafydd angrily. "You're right. You can't think like me. You're safe on the other side. Why not just stick to being a teacher? Don't try and 'empathise' or whatever it is you call it. Don't say you can 'help' when a kid breaks down because you went through it all yourself..."

Old Dafydd shook his head sadly.

"They don't want a big brother or a Funky Uncle, I don't want a big buddy. I want a teacher, someone who can get me out of this stinking place."

"What, like I did? Oh great."

"Just teach us what we need to know. So we can do better."

"That is all I'm trying to do! That's why I've got to have this job. I can't do anything without power."

"That's what they all say, man."

"Who?"

"All the sell outs. Throughout history. All the rebels who've ridden to power on the back of rebellion."

"I'm still a rebel. Compared to Trolley, I'm bloody Che Guevara.

"At least we know where we stand with Trolley. He doesn't pretend to be on our side. He doesn't pretend to be cool by throwing a few pieces of fashion and a few hip words around the class. You're old."

"I'm 45."

"That's ok. Just don't try to be young."

"I'm not trying to be young. I'm just trying not to be dead before I'm 60. That's why I want to retire now."

Young Dafydd began to roll another cigarette.

"*Another* cigarette!"

Young Dafydd responded negatively and continued to roll and then to light it.

Old Dafydd sighed. "Do you know the worst thing about being a Headteacher?"

Young Dafydd inhaled luxuriously. "The country mansion? The football manager's coat? The reserved place in the car park? The enormous captive audience for Monday morning assembly?"

"The loneliness." Old Dafydd also inhaled, getting a passive hit off Young Dafydd's roll up and still missing it after all these years. "The meetings. The budget deficit. The Government *initiatives*. The County 'recommendations'. The League Tables. The Headline Hunters. The Union reps manipulating me up the backside with their Members. The Inspectors demanding an Act of Christian Awe and Wonder from a multicultural generation whose capacity for awe and wonder is largely confined to 'aw, I wonder when the old git is going to shut up.' The Problem Parents. The middle-class parents. The Parents. The parents who really want the school to be the independent one they couldn't afford or to which their Guardian consciences won't allow them to send their kids. The minority parents who want to know why the school's results, class sizes and Oxbridge entrance figures aren't better than Eton's. The majority parents who want everyone else's child disciplined except their own. The lumpenprole-parents who think you make an appointment by yelling "Oi, you, ya four eyed git" in the foyer. The governors who run local shops offering 95% adverts and 0% service but who want to know why *you* haven't fulfilled all the targets they set for you, targets which will be replaced just before the next exam results fiasco with a new contradictory set of utopian balderdash. Again. The Torygraph parents who want all the old names for the subjects back, along with capital punishment, gym knickers, spats, plus fours, leadership trainin', huntin', shootin', cookin' n' Sex Education through rabbits. The new School Sign back from County manufacturers with the slogan EVERY CHILD COUNTS on it, minus the 'O'. The copymaster of my Staff Handbook with the question 'is this rubbish? scrawled over it by the cleaner because I left it within three feet of my office waste bin. The fact that the average member of QCA is like the Judges used to be – mumbling 'And what, pray, is a *teenager*?' into his Victorian beard." Old Dafydd wondered if he could just steal *one* puff at Young Dafydd's fag without re-igniting the addiction but decided against it. "Like I keep telling you, the time I was your side of the desk still only feels like yesterday. But you can still ride that bike home after a punch up on the Games field or out to a blind date, your lungs bursting with the unbearable lightness of being. All I've got is the Cycling Proficiency Guidelines and a letter home emphasising that the school cannot be held responsible for an unsecured bike. I want to be free again - like you."

"Free! How many times do I have to tell you? I'm a prisoner. Get me out of here."

"I'm trying."

"Well - try harder then."

"Listen to yourself! I'm already trying harder, harder than you ever did."

"Listen to *you!* Have you actually done any of the homework you set lately, met deadlines, met word limits, tried to understand really difficult new concepts, put up with idiots monopolising class discussion and your teacher's attention even though they haven't read the books; revised those books night after night, scribbled them out from memory in high pressure exams."

"All right. All right. I'm already trying *as* hard as you did, but in a different way, a way you couldn't dream of. That's why I went for this job in the first place. I'm fighting the system for you aren't I?"

"Fighting the system! You are the system."

"No, no, no. Believe me, young Dafydd, old son. Mr Carmichael Hunt with his host of clerks, his Government health warning and his County photocopier – he's the system. What if he gets County to take over? What then?"

"It makes a big difference to you, maybe, but how does it affect us? You know as well as we do that you're in it for the mortgage and the nameplate in the door, and The Kids calling you *Sir* in the street. And the neighbours thinking you're Somebody even if you do walk round in clown-size chinos during the vacations. You say I'm not answering you but it's you - you're not listening to me. Just shut up and listen. Stop trying to amuse the sleepers in assembly with your embarrassing references to a youth culture that died twenty years ago. Take it from me, Playstation 2 is unlikely to be a kiddies' train set. Stop mentioning your teenage niece as evidence of street cred, especially as she goes to a school with a much snobbier reputation than this one. And despises you for it, as it happens. Don't worry if your tie isn't up to date. Just make sure it isn't poking out through your zip fastener. And stop using words like 'groovy.' It isn't doing either of us any good."

Silence.

"I can't win with you, can I?"

The bell rang, having no alternative, on the nothing new. There was a roar like the African jungle when a kill has occurred. An explosive device was let off in the only metal refuse bin not yet replaced by a plastic one. The reverberations shook the entire south side of the school. It was the third wave of Lunchtime.

Dafydd went out into the corridor to bellow at a few pupils, then wearily re-entered to find Young Dafydd with his feet up on the desk, lighting another roll up

"You still here?"

"No."

"Look, you're not supposed to smoke in here. Landslide Labour governments are even persecuting adults for smoking now, let alone minors"

"Yeah, I wanted to ask you about that. Mr Llewellyn-Jones always used to smoke. The room was like a bonfire. You could smell it half way down School Hill. So what's happened?"

"New County regulations. No smoking anywhere on school premises. Staff and pupils alike."

"But that's Big Brother! What are they going to do next? Stop people smoking in pubs?"

"Yes."

"Bollocks!"

"No, it's true."

"That was actually in their manifesto and the workers voted for it?"

"No-ot exactly. What was in the manifesto was to ban fox hunting."

"Didn't anyone notice?"

"Only a few fanatics. And the *Daily Mail*. When it comes to cleansing the world, it's a lot easier if the people you're trying to change don't actually own most of it. The last time Puritans were in power - in the seventeenth century, I mean - they found the same. *These* Puritans haven't cancelled Christmas yet – it makes too much money. But they've cancelled a lot of other things. Of course, it's still perfectly all right to pollute the atmosphere with cars and wars but like I said you have to take on the people who actually own the world to stop that. However, much as I hate siding with the Malvolios, it wouldn't hurt to curb that habit a bit. You'll be smoking crushed aspirins next."

"Will I?"

"'Fraid so."

"What are they supposed to do?"

"Kill the pain. Ease the boredom. Clear the confusion. Make you feel like you're where it's at."

"Does it work?"

"Of course not."

"I'll stick to baccy then." Young Dafydd glanced at the packs of King Sized cigarettes Old Dafydd had confiscated from pupils, each of them tombed with King Sized WARNINGS in death black. "They're still treating us like kids. When are we going to grow up!"

"O don't worry. Winston Smith is alive and ill and teaching at Mountain High. He says you've got to take all these Government Health guidelines with a pound of salt. Mr Hoskin smokes in his stock room among the violins and tambourines. Mr Sotherby and every other Head of Department - except the Head of Resistant Materials - joins Year 10 behind the Sports hall. He says it's a choice between dying of cancer there or going to the staff room and dying of boredom. Madame Guillotine — our chic French assistant - sits fogging her car with Galloise in the staff car park. Mr Trembath sparks up among the chemicals in the remotest Science Lab. Miss Lucinda Williams Senior favours the staff toilets. Troll smokes in *class*. And I of course don't know about any of this."

"And where do you smoke?"

"I gave up."

"You bastard! When? Why?"

Old Dafydd indicated his inhaler. "I took up asthma instead."

"Does it give you a buzz?"

"It's a bronchial disease."

The man and the boy inhaled together, the boy on his ciggy, the man on his Ventolin.

" So how many years of the blessed weed have I got left?"

Old Dafyyd exhaled, his voice thin with the effort. " How old are you now?"

"Sixteen."

"Seven years next Easter. Minus a year when you take up transcendental meditation and give up everything except organic rice." Old Dafydd inhaled again. "That's the nearest you and I ever get to Resistant Materials. Enjoy the weed while you can."

"What *is* Resistant Materials?"

Old Dafydd laughed. "Metalwork."

"You'll be telling me cookery's called Food Technology next!"

Old Taff made a face.

"You're joking!"

He wasn't.

Young Dafydd, looked for an non-existent ashtray and then stubbed the fag out in a school cup. Old Dafydd tutted fussily.

"I'd rather you didn't put it in the Good Endeavour Cup." He retrieved it. "I'll put it here. This is called a waste bin." Another explosion occurred in a waste bin on the south side of the school.

Who was on duty? Dafydd wondered. He checked a list then rang Suzanne. "Suzanne? Could you remind Mr Welch he's on duty. What? I see. All right, I'll get down there myself in a minute." He replaced the phone, then frowned at his young self. "Could you excuse me?"

"No."

Pause.

"Now you're joking."

Young Dafydd shook his head. The smile on his face faded. "No. I mean I can't excuse you. If you go now you might never see me again. I don't mean I'm going to overdose again or anything. I can't now. Just before I bumped into you again, I was hitching down to hippieland and the Pigs pulled up so I had to throw the sock of delights over a hedge. And when I went back, several very stoned sheep had devoured it."

"I'd forgotten that day. That was the morning you woke up already walking along and couldn't remember how you'd got there or why. Or who you were. Like being a Head in fact."

"Will the Pigs find anything on me? I can't remember."

"There'll be a bit of a fuss when an Inspector Price contacts Mum and Dad about you standing naked in someone's garden thinking you're a sock. You apparently had traces of something illegal up your backside. Enough to kill me several times over these days no doubt."

Young Dafydd blushed. "I'd forgotten that. I tried to hide the sock up the only available place before I threw it."

"I always thought the pig sergeant tried to plant it on you during the strip search?"

"No, no. It's all coming back to me. *Mr Thomas, my name is Detective Inspector Price. Can you explain why your son has traces of amphetamine sulphate up his backside?*"

Old Dafydd looked round nervously. "Shh. I've repressed that memory for thirty years, this is hardly the time or place- "

"Or was it anal nitrate?"

"Amyl nitrate you daft sod. Shhh!"

"But even without the sock, I can't excuse you for much longer. Something's happening since we've been having these talks. I think I'm beginning to die."

"What?"

"You've got to release me."

Dafydd felt a cold sweat on his brow. On both of his brows. "Have I? *How?*"

"I don't know. You're the grown-up."

"Aye – and I've got a thousand other problems to sort out."

"More important than this?! Like what?"

There was another explosion from the metal bin. "Like that boys' 'prank' you can hear for instance, which no-one else is dealing with because they're probably in a union meeting or just being Norman Welch. Like an assembly in front of a thousand people – observed by Mr Carmichael Hunt of County Hall – attempting to prove the school has firm leadership..."

In spite of himself, the boy felt sympathetic. "All right, I'll hang on – but hurry. And, well, good luck with the interview and assembly and stuff." The boy started to disappear.

Now Dafydd was impressed. Teenagers rarely hung on beyond the split second of their attention span or their immediate gratification reflex. To 'hang on' like Jesus on Cohen's "lonely wooden tower" for an unspecified period was remarkable. "Thanks. Though that was a terrible thing to say."

"What was?"

" 'Good luck.' "

"Why?"

"I don't need luck."

"No?"

"No. I need a bloody miracle."

9

Dolly Jones entered Megan's classroom for a sixth-form lesson that (owing to a sophisticated computer system invented to solve all timetable problems) could only be timetabled during sixth-form lunch. She was an elegantly slender, exceptionally tall and even more exceptionally dim girl, the tallest and dimmest of Megan's career by some distance. Inevitably, her parents, both equally tall and of exceptionally slender intelligence themselves, were convinced that Dolly was some kind of genius. They wanted her on the county Gifted and Talented register, believing that this was a large book kept in a room at County Hall where she could report for registration with other privileged intelligences. "Not a lot going on in the top pasture," one hill-farmer governor commented as the case for Dolly's gifted and talented classification came up once again at Governors' meetings – though whether he was referring to the girl or her parents - or even absent-mindedly to his own worrying under-use of the upper paddock that spring - remained as unclear as the look in Dolly's eye during her lessons. So dim was Dolly that she had just recorded in her 'A' level Science folder Darwin's belief that "the human race had in fact descended from monks." (In another context – Satire, say - her notes may have been a work of genius: In Science, alas, her target Grade of U was beginning to look optimistic). "Sorry I'm late Ms Morgan. I've been making myself up in the toilets- "

"She's not here yet, Dolly," said Passion. "Or hadn't you noticed?"

"And you're not late," said Magdalene Price, "For once. Miss is though."

"Ms Morgan's never late," said Clytaemestra Philips. "And there's two pieces of paper out of place on her desk. It'll get like Mr Thomas's if she's not careful."

A bellicose Mancunian voice floated in from next door. "DON'T MAKE ME ANGRY! YOU WOULDN'T LIKE ME WHEN I'M ANGRY!"

"Who's that?"

"The new English teacher."

"Blimey," said Magdalene.

"What happened in Psychology?" asked Dolly.

"But you were there," said Passion.

"Yeah but I didn't understand it."

"We did Penis Envy."

"What's that?"

"Dolly, we've been doing it for weeks."

"I know. What *is* it?"

"Penis envy is Freud's definition of the clitoris," said Clytaemestra. "A disappointed penis."

Dolly wrote that down. "Thanks."

Clytaemestra giggled. "Mind you there's nothing disappointed about my-"

Megan came in flustered. "Sorry I'm late, girls. Inspection business. Dolly put that mirror away. This is a poetry lesson, not a beauty salon." Dolly paused then carried on regardless. "What are you all laughing at?"

"Nothing, Miss, nothing. Are we going on with the Thomas?"

"That's right. Turn to page 99 please. *Welsh Landscape.*"

"THE NEXT PERSON WHO SO MUCH AS BREATHES GETS THIS WINDOW POLE UP HIS BACKSIDE"

"What on earth's that?" asked Megan.

"Mr English. The new English teacher."

"Oh yes of course."

Dolly came up to the desk with some papers from her Science folder. "Miss, have you got a stapler?"

"But why are you doing that now?"

Dolly smiled sweetly and helplessly. Megan began absently looking for a stapler.

"WHO FARTED? COME ON, WHO FARTED?"

"Right, read the poem through silently first and make notes on anything that interests you." She eventually found and handed Dolly the stapler.

"Oh I didn't want one, Miss. I just wanted to know if you'd got one. I'm doing my Christmas list soon."

"Great. Right, Passion, could you read the poem aloud to us, please?"

Passion brought out RS Thomas's Biblical consonants and cadences as only a Welsh accent can.

"To live in Wales is to be conscious
At dusk of the spilled blood
That went to the making of the still sky..."

The room went very quiet, listening to her.

"...You cannot live in the present.
At least, not in Wales..."

Megan shook her head at Dolly who was turning her notes into a birthday card for "Mr Tomus"...

"There is no present in Wales,
And no future;
There is only the past,
Brittle with relics,
Wind bitten towers and castles
With sham ghosts;
Mouldering quarries and mines;
And an impotent people,
Sick with inbreeding,
Worrying the carcase of an old song."

"Beautifully read, Passion," said Megan, blowing her nose and wondering whether to find an excuse to go into the cupboard. She was rarely moved to *actual* tears by poetry now, apart from First World War poetry and its generation of Owens cut short. What's the matter with me today? "Any comments?"

Clytaemestra spoke up, "Doesn't Thomas like the Welsh, Miss?"

"I'm not sure. I do know he *is* Welsh."

"Blimey."

Dolly wrote "RS Thomas. Not Welsh" and then underlined it carefully. Clytaemestra shook her head and guided her through an excision of the word "not".

"DROP THE KNIFE SONNY OR THE BITCH GETS IT."

There was an awkward silence. Megan hoped the Inspector wasn't anywhere within hearing distance, but as that could be anywhere between here and Port Talbot she wasn't sanguine.

Emmanuel Evans came in. "Sorry I'm late, Miss. One of the Inspectors wanted to interview me."

"Did you get the job?"

"No, Miss. Too tall." He could always make Megan laugh. "What we doing, Miss? Ah. *Welsh Landscape*. Great."

"Yes, we were discussing whether RS actually dislikes Wales."

"I think he loves it," said Emmanuel.

"TAKE THAT YOU NIGGER-LOVING BASTARD!"

"What's *that?*" asked Emmanuel.

"Edward. I mean Mr English. The new supply English teacher," said Megan, realizing she couldn't ignore it any longer. She was already on her feet and on her way next door when Carmichael Hunt came in. She returned to her place, praying that Mr English would not yell anything else, especially something so flagrantly against the grain of the school's Equal Opportunities and Corporal Punishments policies. She was finding it hard to concentrate. The students' intense method acting of themselves being good – except drama student Dolly, who could no more act than she could do anything else - was putting her off. Megan called the register from the list in her neat planner and wished they wouldn't all so studiedly avoid sniggering when she called Dick Longstaff's name.

"There's no need to be *quite* so good, you lot. I'm sure the Inspector realises you are real human beings!"

The Inspector counted the number of people in the room, calculated the proportion of girls to boys and measured one of the students' craniums.

"The question of whether Thomas liked Wales is like the question of whether or not Dante liked Florence," said Emmanuel.

"Really?" asked Megan, forgetting in her interest that most of the class wouldn't have the foggiest-

"Yes!" enthused Emmanuel. "Florence exiled him and yet in a way he *was* Florence, the poet-conscience of her narrow streets and surrounding hills. Her better self. And now he's everywhere you go there."

"Yeah but is he as grumpy about her as RS Thomas is about Wales?" asked Passion.

"O I think so," said Megan, defending the higher ground being staked out by Emmanuel.

She didn't need to. Emmanuel continued. "Yeah- I think RS has an ideal Wales in his vision that he's criticising the 'real' Wales from. Or rather his vision of Wales is the real one and he's criticising the apparently real Wales from the really real Wales."

Megan tried to contribute the right terms to distinguish Emmanuel's 'real' from the Platonic 'Real' – guiding their enthusiastic and independent engagement as a teacher ought - but was distracted by the Inspector's uniform check.

"O I get it – like those happy endings Miss was going on about that are a critique of real life and a spur to change it rather than a escapist cop out."

"Yes!" said Megan delighted with this application of ideas. "Only you will use the word 'evasion' rather than 'cop out' in your essay of course." Megan stopped feeling like the spinsters you saw leading classes of bright young things in the cities of Europe, spreading illumination across their faces – upturned to view the arts and sculptures of a millennium – and yet doing so mechanically, tired with a lifetime of passing on the meticulous sacred knowledge by rote to successive generations of sub-adults.

Passion was alight with enthusiasm, young eyes flashing. "But wasn't that Beatrice rather than Florence?"

"Ah…" Emmanuel thought about it. He knew the answer – it was both, equally – but the flame of beauty and youth on Passion's face was giving him a new insight into what Dante must have seen in the radiant Beatrice. "Oh…"

Megan tried to open the discussion to the rest of the class. "Beatrice was a girl of fourteen loved by the poet Dante–"

"That's disgusting!" said Dolly.

"No no no. Remember Juliet was only thirteen and lives were shorter and more intense then – girls married young, had large families very young, and died very young as often as not. Love and childbirth was your best bet of avoiding extinction, even if it killed you."

The Inspector looked bewildered.

Megan pushed on. "*He who saves himself loses himself,* that text from St Matthew we did as context to Shakespeare's sonnets. Like Rosamunde, so in love with her own beauty that she disappears up her... er. There was a horror of self-love then, of keeping love and beauty to yourself ..." Megan looked around and felt she was going steeply uphill.

Passion and Emmanuel were still talking. "The ideal Florence was like the City of God – it was a potential heaven - but the 'real' one was on its way to being the City of Dis. Florence naturally didn't like being told that - so they exiled him. But Dante loved the heart of her, the city that contained Beatrice. And Michaelangelo and the rest painted and sculpted in that spirit."

"So Michaelangelo's David is a kind of ideal Florence? The perfect Florentine man?" said Passion.

"Excellent, Passion," said Megan.

"Yeah." Emmanuel was pleased to hear his thought reflected back so cogently by Passion. It vindicated it. Most of the class, sensing Megan's approval of Emmanuel's, but more able to retain this succinct version of Passion's, was writing Passion's version down.

"How can Florence be a man?" demanded Dolly.

"No, Dolly. Florence is the city. Beatrice is the man." The class laughed. Megan corrected herself. "Sorry, Beatrice is the ideal *woman* – a kind of Virgin Mary – that Dante *saw* in the girl Beatrice, whom he loved with such fervour."

"So who's the man?"

The class was getting impatient. Clytaemestra snapped. "Michaelangelo's *David.*"

"You can see it for yourself in Florence today, Dolly," said Megan breezily. "A statue of perfect manhood. He's gorgeous. Go to the Galleria Academia and fight your way through the hordes of snappy tourists from America and China and Japan and ask for Michaelangelo's *David*. He'll be the one posing patiently in the middle of all the camera flashes, sending his image out through space and time and into photo albums and onto computer screens and mobile phones all over the world." Megan cast an uneasy eye on the Inspector, the clock and at the set text. "And you could say that RS Thomas's poems about the Cyndyllans and Davieses of Wales record a similar protest on behalf of the ideal, religiously *saved* Welshman that RS loves and protects and serves in his work - as a poet as well as a priest. That somewhere behind these real fallen sick crumbling Davieses that RS evokes and criticises with such passion stands the noble redeemed *Davies* of his ideal beloved Wales."

Dolly wrote her notes and when the exam came would be able to copy them out word for word. But as she misread the rubric and answered a question on Dafydd ap Griffyth instead, a period they hadn't studied, all her effort (not to mention the long-suffering Megan's) was wasted. Or was it? In fact, on her Italian Cities coach tour honeymoon some two years later – to a wealthy banker twice her age – Dolly spent a contented afternoon armed with her A level notes, interrogating the locals and searching the streets - of Rome - for a statue of a squat mediaeval Welshman called Michaelangelo's *Davies*.

Meanwhile back in the eternally tormented present Megan was keeping the tense silence of a teacher who knows the class hasn't recorded the essential notes dictated and who needs now to 'press on'. She drew a breath to speak. Dolly came up with the card.

"What's this?"

"Birthday card, Miss."

"It's not my birthday."

"No, it's Mr Thomas's", called Clytaemestra, trying to save the situation with humour. "We thought you might like to see what one looks like."

Megan took the card. "Thank you, Dolly. I'd rather you read the poem."

"She can't, Miss," joked Clytaemestra, as Dolly sat down.

"Why not?" said Megan.

"She can't read."

The Inspector made a note. Clytaemestra felt her jokes going wrong and wished she could take them back. Megan noted the maternal instinct in Clytaemestra's assumption that her lesson needed help and wasn't altogether flattered.

Dolly put her hand up.

"Yes, Dolly?"

"Miss, can you spell what you said before - about Florence?"

"Which bit?"

"All of it."

Carmichael Hunt looked at the 'notes' Dolly had made, and recorded his own. He naturally looked at no-one else's, especially not Passion's nor Emmanuel's, whose notes were excellent.

Megan thought she'd better finish the register. Justin Smith sneaked in late and sat down without explanation. It put Megan off. "See me at the end, please, Justin."

"Justin Time, Miss. " said Passion. "Or not on this occasion."

"What?"

" 'Justin Time', Miss," said Clytaemestra and Passion together. "You usually have a joke there."

Megan knew that of course. But she cursed them for being a bit too helpful.

"Justin whom?" asked the Inspector, making to write it down.

"Who," corrected Megan mechanically.

The Inspector wrote down HOO.

"No. Time," said Justin helpfully. "T.H.Y.M.E. Who's this?"

"He's an Inspector," said Megan. "But don't let that hurry you."

"Cool," said Justin, sitting down to the long process of getting out his 'work'.

The Inspector was trying to find 'Thyme' among his list of names. "His name's Smith, " said Megan dully, wondering where RS Thomas, the divine Beatrice and Florence had gone.

Dolly put her hand up.

"Yes?"

"What does Smith actually mean by 'There are the cries in the dark at night?/As owls answer the moon/ And thick ambush of shadows/ Hushed at the fields' corners.' I don't get it. Dolly sat with her pen poised, ready to copy out word for word what Megan would say.

"Thomas, Dolly. Not Smith. What does he mean? Well…"

"IS ANYONE LISTENING TO ME OR AM IN HERE ON MY OWN?!"

Megan could ignore it no more. "Excuse me, everyone. I'm just going to check on Mr English who of course is new to the department and doubtless nervous about being inspected so early in his time here." She thought on her feet, her mind already somewhere else. "Could you, in pairs, list words and phrases which show a positive attitude to Wales – 'relics' for example, 'immaculate', often Biblical words – and also list words and phrases which show a negative attitude to Wales – 'inbreeding' for example, 'carcase' – and finally any examples where the Biblical cadences create a positive music even where the words themselves are negative. Passion, work with Dolly, please." Dolly had already twisted round to copy out a version of Rosemary's easy-read notes. "I won't be long."

The Inspector made a note that she had left her class unsupervised, then followed her into Mr English's room. Edward English was, of course, alone, shaggily bearded, attired as a pirate and rehearsing enthusiastic extracts from "Nigger of the Narcissus" for his difficult Period 8 with Year 11 …

10

Edward English had got the job (a) because Megan was desperate and there was no-one else and (b) on the measured and precise recommendation of his wife, Miss Clark, an outstandingly successful Head of English at what Megan would always call "The Slagheap." Miss Clark used to teach with Megan at Mountain High. She had been very well organised, an absolute whizz with the paperwork, though wary of those aspects of the subject, like poetry - and all those wild and shaggy glories germane to The English language since its pirating into these islands off the intrepid Saxon boats - that she couldn't reduce to the ignoble art of tick boxing. A glittering career lay ahead of her. The same could not be said, on any of these points, of Edward English.

The bell for the start of the fourth wave of lunch rang like the end of round thirteen. Mr English hurried off. Megan returned to her classroom groggy with all the punishment to find everyone gone and her lesson notes all over the floor. Passion had left early, picked up by a policeman who was currently screwing her – along with her University chances if she got pregnant - and with whose flash car a despondent Emmanuel could not possibly compete. If Megan's metaphorical towel hadn't been confiscated by Trolley earlier, for not meeting obscure regulations, she'd have thrown it in now...

Chapter Four

Sex Education

Do I love you? My oh my -
River deep, mountain high

1

Dafydd hurried down the corridor and into the fresh air. Then he followed the reek of cordite, tobacco, urine and something vaguely worse to the outside boys' toilets. (The inside toilets had been closed since 1964 pending an improvement in behaviour). Outside, a metal bin was disgorging smoke and the ruins of someone's school bag. The torn up exercise books and questions it had contained were, like Bob Dylan's original answer, blowing in the wind. Dafydd advanced into the urinal, past the whitewashed wall under which his own schoolboy depictions of Troll in compromising positions with Mr Hacker the Head of Metalwork still faintly showed and towards the cubicle full of smoke. He knocked on the door. It opened. "What the f- . Oh, hello Sir."

"You again, Tommy!"

"Aye. Sorry, Sir." Tommy nipped his dog-end and slipped it into his pocket for later. "When's the detention?"

"It's not as simple as that, son." Dafydd patted his pockets for a 'greener' – a green Disapproval Slip – but could only find a packet of Exeats, a grubby Lem Sip, a pad of lemon Approval Slips and a confiscated filthy but curiously naïve sex-note. Tommy handed him a greener already filled in. "Here you are, Sir. I brought one just in case. I don't do Mondays, Wednesdays or Fridays because I'm in with Troll then for fighting."

"*Mr* Trolley to you," said Dafydd.

'Troll' to you, said Tommy absent-mindedly and Dafydd struggled not to laugh. "I've numbered it up, Sir. That's my twenty-eighth so I'll have to see Mr Loblolly, the educational psych, if I get two more."

"The slip isn't really the point, Tommy, and besides – " He broke off. He didn't want any of his pupils seeing *that* nutcase, but could hardly tell Tommy that. "The point, Tommy, is not this whole game we play with slips. It's your life. Disapproval Slips only record behaviour in various ways. The point, however, is to change it."

"That's very good, Sir. Catchy. That ought to go in the Staff Handbook."

"How do you know about the Staff Handbook?"

"I have to copy the Behaviour Policy out a lot in detention, Sir. Most of it isn't as punchy as what you just said though."

"Thank you, Tommy. It's not exactly my own thought. I've adapted it from the original Marx brother, Karl. *The philosophers have interpreted the world, in various ways. The point, however, is to change it.* Well, what say I rip up this slip now and you give up smoking? I'll do better than that. If you can give it up, now, today, I'll cancel all your slips."

Tommy thought about it. "Nah. I'm better off with the slips, Sir. You can 'ave these though." He handed over the fags. "It's only fair."

Dafydd sighed. "Tuesday after school then. Don't bring your fags. Now GO HOME!"

Dafydd followed the pupils racing – like liberated animals – to the last wave of lunch, the first thing many of them had really understood all morning. He carried out his job – teaching manners as a foreign language – in as many of Norman Welch's abdicated flashpoints as possible, then pushed near the front of the queue to inspect the economy burgers, fatty meats, low grade fruit, full fat cheese and other junk sanctioned (against the dinner ladies' wishes) since the Milk Snatcher's Education Act. This, sighed Dafydd, was the great liberal Act of 1980, the one that among other things 'liberated' schools from the need to provide nutrition rather than to make money, just as they had been liberated from the need to supply free milk in its architect's earlier career. The eighth most obese boy in Year 8 ate four moon-bunned beef burgers in succession and returned Dafyyd's stare aggressively.

As Dafydd waited, he glanced at Carmichael Hunt's list of suggested promotees. Two of them dumpy old women under five feet tall! And that was just the males. He glanced out of the window through the ancient rusty over-wrought railings Connie should have replaced for Health and Safety reasons a decade ago, railings he could himself remember scaling as a boy on the run. He had a sudden urge to cut and run again now from all the responsibilities and shabby compromises of adult life, play truant from everything up the mountain.... Then an unemployed ex-miner lumbered by en route to the Ex-Miner's Arms and a soft-palmed pint of forgetfulness. Was that freedom? Na. Dafydd looked at the small selection of good food the dinner ladies were pleased to produce - and most kids didn't want – and wondered (as he did with so many other aspects of school life) how he and the cooks were going to combine the good intentions of the old-fashioned (if stodgy) state with the instant post-70s market-led gratification of the kids' taste-buds - to produce a school lunch everyone was happy with. Meanwhile, a dinner lady gave him his new no chip diet bacon-and-chicken-with-tomato-and-rocket filled-to-bursting baguette and a morale-boosting smile....

He remembered telling his father about his appointment as Acting Head. They were down at the St Margaret's Home for Redundant Men. Ifor was lined up for tea in the Limbo Room with all the other industrial-strength ex-males and they were taking all day: it was a bit like being behind Angharad in the photocopier queue. Everything there seemed redundant. The poster advertising the Counterfeit Carpenters' tour date at the Marquis de Sade in Ychafi the previous Wednesday. The plastic electric fireplace disguised as a coal fire, the neo-70s chimney, the plastic hearthside implements painted to look like heavy wrought iron.

A young man in a Cwmcysgodionmarw Folk Club T shirt with MAKE TEA NOT WAR on it eventually handed him three polystyrene cups of weak dishwater. Dafydd felt sick at the memory. "You'll have to beef that up," he'd said. "My father was a steelworker. And Jim was a miner. Heavy industrial males. They needed *tea* in those days. Something to keep them going."

It still moved Dafydd that the Welsh miners had gone down, solid as anthracite, unscabbed, flags flying, as a *union*, to the total defeat of their last historic strike in 1985. After a year fighting on territory – and through long coal-unrequiring summer months – chosen carefully in advance by the enemy. Lions led by donkeys said Kinnock. Class collaborators led by revisionists squirmed Scargill, in his ideological donkey-jacket - who hadn't been able to hold the Yorkshire miners back from wholesale breaking of ranks but didn't let that stop him dissing the Welsh. But where were those lions now?

But Dafydd's father was brightening as he took the beefed-up tea back: "It's good news, boy. This job of yours. It's socialism in office." The old trade unionist and his old butty raised their teacups. "To the new manager!" then swigged. Ifor asked, "*Can* you manage?"

"Not in the way they do, no. But could the Tower colliery co-operative manage until they had to?"

"So why did they offer you the job?"

"Dunno. Maybe they finally called Norman Welch's bluff."

"Is it a Permanent Contract?"

"Six months. Contingent on me improving results by an amount difficult enough to discredit me and bring in an external candidate if one becomes available. Don't worry. I'll make it work."

Ifor Thomas blinked round at the Limbo room. "I used to make things too, Son. Real things. Things that drove things that drove other things. When they talked about *saving* jobs, we thought they meant keeping us in work, but they meant the opposite. Now the Government's got to keep us all! Brilliant…"

"Get that bloody suit off," interrupted a visitor Dafydd remembered like yesterday from a holiday job on the council.

"Percy? Percy! How are you? It must be twenty years."

"And the rest. I see you've joined the middle classes."

"Aye." Dafydd flicked his cuffs. "Delayed gratification. But it's not all it's cracked up to be, believe me."

"Delayed what?"

"Gratification," said Dafydd. "Delayed gratification – having to wait for your pleasures – it's meant to be the emblem of the middle classes."

"I thought that was olive oil and garlic, and wearing a white collar to work and real coffee. And what's the emblem of the working classes then?"

"Instant coffee. A wage at the end of the week instead of a salary at the end of the month. Wages at sixteen instead of a student loan until you're forty. Music you can kick back to without having to study it first. A heavy industrial male like Brian Butcher taking out all the girls I fancied in the sixth form just because he had a car and I didn't." He was thinking of Megan now. Just how delayed did gratification have to be? "The emblem of the working class is Immediate Gratification - on the never never. So the sociologists tell us anyway."

Ifor snorted. "Immediate gratification? Waiting fifty factory weeks for your two weeks holiday at Barry Island? Forty-eight hours of dead time for your ninety minutes of live wire footy at the week end? Counting down every toiling minute of your eight-hour day towards your pint of oblivion?"

"Fair point," said Dafydd, a little uncomfortable under his white collar. "Not that Percy used to wait that long. Nor did he ever stop at one- "

Percy growled. "Those were the days. Friday pub at noon, drink until four, work another hour, book overtime until six, then fuck off home."

Ifor pointed at his son. "I knew you wasn't doing a proper job that summer. Jim and me never got that at the steelworks."

"You got *paid* real money at the steelworks," growled Percy.

"It wasn't like that with the other charge-hand. Percy got through the work quicker because he wasn't stupid or slow or trying to show off to the men all the time."

"There are two ways to do things," confided Percy, making the old joke. "There's the wrong way – and there's my way."

"Well Percy," said Ifor, pride drowning his banter. "It looks like young Dafydd's finally learned the right way now. They've just made him an Acting Headmaster."

Dafydd looked at his father. The fierce pride he saw now in Ifor's eyes – like a light that had finally set liberating fire to its bushel – was so bright it made everything else in the room recede into shadow for a moment. Like the steelworker's hand-me-down overcoats that had kept Dafydd warm like an all-over hug through many a teenage Welsh winter, Dafydd was suddenly aware the old man was clasping his hand. He returned the clasp.

Percy's mock-courtly bow now made Dafydd smile but a pleasant atmosphere of congratulation overcame Dafydd's worries about the job and everything else for a moment. Percy said "Well, be seeing you," and tipped Dafydd a click-wink. Ifor, seeing this, gave Dafydd a thumbs-up. Dafydd returned Percy's wink. Percy departed. Father and son click-winked at each other. Working-class semiotics.

A restricted but very real code. As real as real coffee anyway.

The conversation turned to the future in general. Dafydd saw not his father for a moment but a working-class boy brought up to drive railway engines: a heavy industrial male lost in a new 'middle-class' world which began with the premise that there is no society except the market place - and swiftly redefined that market place as - not a place where you sold what you made (because nothing was made) but where you sold adverts. The school too had shrunk into first an examination - and then a PR - factory. He'd taken the Headship at least partly for his parents' sake, he knew. To restore - in the teeth of this - their view of human progress, of the forward march of history. The Triumph of the Thomases!

Maybe it was time to stop saving his father's dream and settle for one of his own....

"Anything else with that, Mr Thomas?" asked the dinner lady.

Dafydd came back to the present. Delayed gratification was all very well but a besieged Headteacher needs some comfort. "Twelve chips, please. And a cup of that cardboard coffee."

2

Megan crossed Channel View and parked outside 29 Mawr-fach, the Victorian terrace she'd inherited from her mother. The channel only actually came into view on such clear days as came to Upper Garnloger in the dry season (the last week of July and the first week of August) but, on such days, the 20-mile prospect was breathtaking. It was then possible to imagine characters from Celtic mythology – Artos, the original Welsh Arthur, say, and his sister-goddess Morgan, his wizard Myrddin and his knights Cei, Bedwyr and Gwalchmei - distilling on the still air. But today the disused Viaduct – a glory of Victorian Great Western Railway engineering – was casting its long-legged shadow over the house-front, leaving only the bedroom window glowing in contrast. And overlooking all, even the Viaduct, crouched the Marw, like a giant beast-of-prey in the March quiet. In August, it could get so hot up there that the bracken would set itself alight, driving scores of snakes down into Upper Garnloger. In the five-month winter it could freeze the tail off a glacier. Today, a deceptive thaw was winking in the sun, and the air it sent down was sweet as a mountain stream. But it was still winter at heart.

Megan left the front door open and raced upstairs. As she ran towards her bedroom door – a ghastly modern affair of ply painted with brown gloss (which she had still not got round to 'restoring' with something more authentically Victorian) – she nearly died to see a woman charging out at her. She screamed. But at the moment of impact, she saw it was only her own reflection in the gloss.

Her documents drawer was in a chest she'd inherited from her grandmother. It stuck as usual and in her haste she split the joint that held one of its flimsy corners together. She shook away her hand and dislodged a packet of old letters from her teenage penfriend Claudette. How odd to find them there! She felt instantly transported back through decades but at the same time had only seconds to spare, needing to get back to school in time for the bell, so she put the letters carefully aside to rediscover later. It was time to have a clear out. She sighed. Then she found what she was looking for. A cutting.

She put it into her bag, her eye caught by an old school photograph, cherished by her mother and retained for her sake by Megan though never a particular favourite of her own. She picked this up, blowing off the dust. Too much lipstick and make-up, yes, but the layers of make-up somehow emphasised the nakedness. She was smiling a little guiltily from the bed in that bright red blazer, her tartan skirt carefully too short, her school tie carelessly discarded over the bedpost. She was writing to someone and her mother's appearance with a camera had caught her at a guilty moment. She was doing her best to look innocent there but the naked eyes gave her away. Guilty as the hell her father joked she was going to....

She bagged the photo next to the cutting and locked the house quickly, glancing at her watch. She drove, very fast, back down the old mountain road, a steep narrow descent near the very top of the valley side. The construction of roads in South Wales seemed to occur in inverse proportion to the economic decline of the coalfield, and to the gradual disappearance of all those mountain-cut railway systems and canal banks they previously used as walking shortcuts everywhere. But of course more cars kept appearing to fill the new roads. The mountain road avoided the traffic that still bottlenecked the narrow nineteenth century streets of the town and also the new traffic-littered by-passes. In Megan's case, this was not a traditional Welsh capitulation into the mountains of retreat but the quickest way back to something she should have done years ago. She drove like Fate, like the furies. She was going back to school to have it out with him, there and now, once and for all-

A Lada – Dafydd's? - emerged out of the bend. She thrust her red shoes well-nigh through the brakes. The driver of the Lada also braked. He swerved on the gravel, a full forty yards up to the bonnet of her little white sports. There was a moment of silence. The dust began to disperse. She could hear "The Boys Are Back In Town" thumping from the Lada's speakers. She waited for the unreconstructed abuse of a male driver whose left and right balls have been simultaneously activated by danger-adrenalin and the sight of a woman in the driver's seat of a car (having the same Kick Me Hard connotation as an L plate.) However, he grimaced at her instead in companionable relief and then just sat there. He didn't try to thrust on past her, nor did he aggressively point out the obvious escape lay-by just behind into which she could reverse so that he could pass on his way, though very narrowly. He just sat there, like a lemon.

She glared at him, willing him into some action. He was fiddling about with something under the dashboard. Wanker. Eventually, a roar arose from the Lada, a crunch from a rusty gearbox, and then - nothing. Pathetic. Had he stalled then? Some penis-substitute!

Was he scared of driving round her in that narrow space? Or was he just some old fashioned gentleman being chivalrous, treating her Like A Lady, waiting for her to go first? Or was he one of these New Welsh Men scared of taking the initiative in case he offended against feminism? Better than being abused by a Dick in a white van or a silver Mondeo, certainly, but Megan wasn't sure all this pussy-footing was getting them anywhere

An early incident in her career at the school flashed across her mind. Trolley had reduced Angharad to tears again with a nasty reprimand about leaving the drama studio light on (at the end of a long week in which she'd broken the school record for extra-curricular hours on a school play). Dafydd had been on his way to Trolley's office with a baseball bat until Megan had stopped him.

"You can't do that, Dafydd. It's like you're saying Angharad can't fend for herself because she's a woman."

"Well she can't fend for herself at the moment can she!"

"That's patronising."

"It's friendship. But don't worry, sister. I won't ever offer it to you!"

That had hurt.

She tossed her head impatiently now, scorched round the Lada driver – it wasn't Dafydd – and exploded into the distances of his rearview mirror.

3

Dafydd was biting into his sandwich when a familiar knock came at his office door. He bit his lip instead. He gnashed his teeth in frustration and this caused him to bite the fleshy inside of his mouth. Another two nine-day ulcers to nurse. The knock came again.

He gave up. "Come in."

Dafydd had been dreading his younger self but instead Emmanuel Evans stood in the doorway.

"Well?"

"You were supposed to take us for Extension level in the Geography room half an hour ago, Sir."

Dafydd's heart sank. "Oh God! Sorry!– I forgot. I've had a lot on."

"You said that last week, Sir. And Ms Morgan missed Extension English yesterday as well."

"It's this Inspection. We're all run off our feet."

"So are we, Sir. The exams never stop. And there always seems to be some Inspection or other. I'd have thought you were fully Inspected by now."

"Very perceptive, Evans. And precisely why I've told you not to waste your potential by becoming a teacher."

"That's what Ms Morgan says, Sir."

"Does she indeed. I shall have to have a word with her about morale. What else does she say to you in these famous Extension sessions you have together."

"She gives me the come on, Sir. And then we have sex."

"*What!* What did you say?"

"I said she hears my poems, Sir. And then we deconstruct the text."

Dafydd's world stopped spinning. "Is that really what you just said?"

Evans looked at him curiously. "Yes of course. What did you think I said?"

"Nothing. My hearing must be playing tricks on me – along with everything else today. Uh, does she think your poems are any good?"

"She's says I'm the best shag she's ever had and that I make her feel like a woman again." Emmanuel shrugged. "She says I send her into shivering orgastic ecstasy..."

"Say that again," said Dafydd in a strangled voice.

Emmanuel shot him a worried look. "Are you sure you're all right, Sir? She says I'm the best bard she's ever had and that I make her feel like a teacher again. She says it's fantastic poetry. It's a bit embarrassing."

"Oh – good."

"She might just be getting me into vice but she says she wants some bondage magazine to punish me."

"Vice?" asked Dafydd faintly.

"She might just be being *nice* but she says she wants some Cambridge magazine to publish me."

"Oh." Dafydd remembered something about a poetry evening at the Eisteddfod that Emmanuel had qualified for last year. A real Headmaster – or did he mean the kind of Headmaster he himself had had in the days when schools weren't the size of small towns? – would know all about it and ask the boy all about it in an avuncular way now. He did his best. "How did your poet's evening at the Eisteddfod go last year, by the way? What was it called?"

"Nos yr bard."

195

"Don't be so diffident! You did the school proud. Miss Morgan's delighted with you."

"I really get into her knickers, that's all."

"Really, Emmanuel! I'm not sure it's appropriate for you to-"

"It's an expression, Sir. Christ! Did you really think I... Jeesus. It's a *metaphor*. It means-"

"Yes, yes, I know what it means." Dafydd blushed and hemmed. "And stop saying Jesus and Christ all the time. There's no need for blasphemy on top of ... on top of ... on top of everything else. *I* meant I'm not sure it's appropriate for you to describe to me your inter, uh interactions with M- Metaphor as-"

"Can you give her this?"

Dadfydd registered the fist and flexed forearm being brandished suggestively before him and then realised it contained an essay. He took it. "What is it?" Dafydd read the title, "Appreciation of 'Welsh Landscape' by RS Thomas."

"Hang on. No. Damn. I've given you today's notes as well." Emmanuel took the pile of papers back, then selected a bulky essay from them. "It's the essay on 'Purgatorio' she set us before. It's my third go."

"What did she say about the first two?"

"*Must Try Harder.*"

"Like the rest of us then. Practice makes perfect."

"Hmm. It's a bit hard to fit in with all these exams."

"That's what exams are. Practice."

"No they're not, Sir. Not anymore. Exams are the real thing and they never stop."

Dafydd knew this was true and that Evans was intelligent enough to see through a system that judged him. But-

"On top of which I've got to earn money and learn to drive. In fact, Sir, I think I'll...." His voice trailed off.

"Go on."

"I've got 4 A2s on as it is. I might as well drop 'Geogers' Extension if we're not having any lessons and, well, do I need English Extension when..."

"When what?"

"Well, you did all this grind too didn't you Sir? And in the tenth year your lessons about Florence and all those visions of Paradise they built made me really want to go there." Emmanuel gestured vaguely at some purgatory that seemed to tower around him. "Look, Sir. Will all this grind actually get me out – of this?"

"This is just exam nerves, Emmanuel."

"No it isn't. *You* passed all your S levels. You've gone all the way up to Headmaster. And yet you're still here in the Circles of Troll, toasting Morfydd the Mascot at the Clwb Bar with the boyos every Friday night. And any time they want, the boyos can get to Florence with money or because their grandfather made a success of a pizza shop." Emmanuel opened the door to go.

Dafydd stopped him in the doorway. He felt he'd lost the argument so he stopped looking for it and spoke from the heart instead. "Ok maybe you're right. You look at a sad old git like me and think maybe he's fallen from grace a bit, not achieved his potential. Must try harder. Maybe he'll never get out of the pit he's settled for. But never mind me, Evans. *You* keep your nose and that wonderful intelligence of yours to the grindstone for a bit longer and I *promise* you I can help get you out of purgatory and into a good University. Your future's more important to me than almost everything I've done in my capacity as Head today, believe me. I don't know where I'll find the time but I will. I *will*... Whether you stay out of the proverbial pit is another matter. That's up to you." He laughed, indicating the essays Emmanuel had given him. "I'll be like Virgil in that poem Ms Morgan's teaching you. I can guide you out of the pit and through purgatory but I can't give you Paradise. You have to do that. And to do it, you'll need a Beatrice."

"A what?"

Dafydd sighed. "A very feisty, Pennant-gritty, Welsh, cool, modern Beatrice, paradoxically hard and vulnerable, a woman who rocks as good as a Welsh mountain range..."

"Sir?"

"Sorry, Emmanuel. I drifted off there. I said, school can guide you out of the pit and through purgatory but it can't give you Paradise. For Paradise, you need a Beatrice."

Myfanwy Madoc passed at that moment. A shaft of sunlight kindled her blue cardigan and long blonde hair and Emmanuel watched her go by like the sky and beach of some perfect holiday. He drifted into her slipstream, oblivious to Dafydd now. Dafydd rubbed his chest ruefully. He'd have given his Biology O level to be 18-year-old Emmanuel at that moment, following Myfanwy, willing her to turn round into a conversation. How come it had never been like that for him?

But it had. He *had* been 18-year-old Emmanuel, and he'd blown his chance to do exactly that a hundred times a term. Even that special once Megan had thanked him for his help with her Biology project on the Alimentary Canal – she confused it with the canal along whose bank she conducted Biology practicals with Ramo and other remnants of heavy metal masculinity – and she'd pecked his cheek and said, "Thanks, my lovely, you're a star." And for once, he'd had the spunk to answer.

"Alimentary, my dear Megan."

And she'd frowned and said, "What?"

Did his heart ache now because Myfanwy was so young, warm and beautiful, and the world that would take her was so old, cold and ugly? Or because *he* would never possess that youth and beauty now, had never done so, even when it had been offered to him? Or did it just ache because he was getting into the queue for an NHS coronary?

4

"And does anyone know what this is?" Ms Morgan held up what seemed to be a stallion's condom.

"*Ch*rist!" ejaculated a boy in the back row.

"No need for blasphemy, Darren, please. Remember where you are!"

"Sorry Miss." Darren had turned red with embarrassment. "Our usual Sex Education teacher doesn't show us condoms that - big."

"She just goes on about male B.O.," said Robert.

"She's boring," said Jezza.

"She did tell us to get a good look at a woman breast-feeding a baby the next time we get a chance."

"What? Did she?"

"Yeah. You weren't listening as usual."

"What?"

"Nurse Watkins is on maternity leave so you'll have to make do with me," said Megan. The boys didn't seem to mind. "So – any offers?

Silence.

"Anytime, Miss."

"Thank you, Wayne. A 3.30 detention for you, I think. I meant any offers to answer my question." She held up the stallion's condom again.

Silence.

"It's a Femidon," she said briskly. "It gets placed inside the vagina like this." She demonstrated on the model. The model bore the same pleasured expression as Morfydd, and several of the boys shuffled prudishly. The girls of course took notes.

A pale boy in the back row fainted. It was unlikely he would feature in any future wife's labour support plan. Megan looked for help. "Tommy."

"NO! Please don't send me out, Miss. This is brilliant. I know we got taught masturbation last week but I want to learn about the real thing."

"I thought masturbation *was* the real thing," said Darren Williams.

"You and the rest of your sex, Darren, more's the pity, " sighed Megan. "I believe Woody Allen defined masturbation as sex with someone you really love. I suggest you join Wayne in detention and copy out Lord Justice Cockburn's 1868 gloss on the Obscene Publications Act of 1857. Fifty times. Tommy, could you take Karl to the office for me," she smiled, "please?"

"But, Miss!"

Tommy took Karl to the office and by the time he'd returned Megan had moved on to something even more amazing. "Now I'm going to pass some silicone breasts and genitalia around the room. I want you to caress them – not like that Darren - and try to find the lumps."

Angharad came in soon after and tried to make her voice heard above the pandemonium. "10 AH's contraception box has a missing femidon. Can we borrow yours?" Receiving no response in the general bedlam – Darren had managed to break one of the breasts with his manipulations - she shouted even louder. "I NEED A FEMIDON QUICK!" Naturally this time all the class stopped to hear what she was saying. Dafydd came into the wall of noise with the Inspector shortly afterwards. The Inspector picked up a model penis and studied it in extreme close up. Megan tried to keep a straight face. She looked up to see Dafydd looking past her very solemnly.

"Megan. Could I see you please - after registration?"

"Fine." Megan tried not to sound worried. "Your office?"

Standing replicas of erect penises, complete with helmets, were having condoms manipulated over them by female hands all over the room. Dafydd looked away and found himself gazing into Megan's eyes instead. "…No. Mr Welch is there this afternoon… The staff workroom."

The bell went for registration drowning out her reply.

"What?" asked Dafydd tensely.

" I said 'fine'."

5

Constable Jones looked up wearily. It was the end of a very long and very trying shift and the very last thing he needed was Billy. "Billy Liar" – real name Waldo Watkins (though when asked he went under any number of pseudonyms, William Mendacity,

Walter Mitty, Richard Nixon etc etc, as the mood took him) - was reporting his third 'incident' of the day.

"What happened this time, Wald?"

"Well as you know, as a result of all the Emergency Fireman call outs and fights with killer snakes the bush fires have sent down off the mountain I've only had two hours sleep in six weeks."

"Two hours – in six weeks. That's not possible, Wald."

"Thanks. *Miracles we can do straight away. The Impossible takes a bit longer,* as we say in the Service. At least you appreciate me. Anyway, I was just driving the double-decker down the lane from Old Llamidia when a driver in a blue two door Citroen registration NWY B665 exceeds the speed limit by fourteen mph and causes an accident involving a cat, a schoolgirl and a bicycle. He also yells abuse at me through a window. My bus conductor, Wes Griffith, also saw the incident and may be reporting it also-"

"May be?"

"Yeah. He didn't seem convinced. He's new. I had a row with him about it."

"How long has he been your conductor?"

"Three weeks. The other conductors keep swapping over with him for some reason."

"Could that be because the other conductors then don't have to work with you?"

"Not sure what you mean. When I was in the SAS, that sort of swap over often happened. You could have incompatible personality configurations. You could be dating the same sex worker. You could have flown the same missions over Saigon and not want to risk your cover stories being compromised. There's any number of reasons."

"I see. How many incidents have your reported this week, Wald?"

Wald checked his sheet. "Fifteen."

"And this new conductor has supported how many?"

"Just the first four. He seemed to lose interest after that."

"I know the feeling." Constable Jones yawned. "All right, Wald. I'll look into it."

"Check. I've got some snap shots, recordings and video tape footage if you need them."

"I'll let you know."

"Check." Waldo Mitt was on his way to the door. Constable Jones looked and called. "Oh, Wald?"

Waldo looked round. "Yes?"

"Doesn't the route from Old Lamidia go under a low bridge?"

"That's right."

"And you said you were driving a double-decker?"

"Yes."

"Wouldn't that have wiped out the people on the top deck?"

Such a tragedy had indeed happened in days gone by. Even Waldo's blood ran cold for a moment. "I meant single-decker."

"Ah."

"I'll be off then."

"Right you are."

"Check." Wald made for the outside.

" Oh and Wald?"

He turned again. "Officer?"

"Didn't your employers stop using conductors in 1979?"

6

Dafydd sat on the hard public seat pretending not to notice the pupils, ex-pupils (as unable to queue, socially inept and offensive here as they'd been in school) and parents who recognised him. He'd raced against time all the way here and his shirt was sodden through. The imminent embarrassment of being seen in a sweaty shirt made him get even hotter under the collar - and the sight of a nurse with an enormous syringe entering a room with a man belly down on a table brought him out in cataracts. But Megan's Personal Development lesson had been the last straw. This was an emergency. He tried to stop hyperventilating but the fact that there were eight walls to the room did not help.

"*Dafydd Thomas.*"

A snooty intercom voice summoned him, as if resenting his right to be there. Dafydd got up, hearing sniggers from pupils at his first name, and pushed forward to the consulting room. A sign on the door read Dr. Faustus. Duty Doctor. He knocked and entered.

"Thanks for seeing me," said Dafydd, looking at three faces and not sure where the real one was. "Sorry about the shirt."

Dr. F. said nothing. The nostrils of her enormous hooked nose flared in a clear signal that she felt Dafydd was a malingerer who should be at his post rather than wasting her time. After all, she had a job to do.

She thrust a thermometer into his ear, hard. This is what I would do with malingerers, she implied, doing it. "Slight temperature," she snapped.

"Is it possible to see my own doctor?" asked Dafydd.

"He's busy with his patients," said the duty doctor.

"I'm one of his patients," said Dafydd.

"You can see him in two or three weeks."

I could be dead by then. This is an emergency."

"I see the emergencies," she snapped. "Strip down to your underpants."

Dafydd did so, unpeeling the wet shirt and tired trousers, then blinking in horror to find himself wearing his underpants back to front. He gaped at the doctor to gauge her reaction. I know I was in a rush this morning, he thought, but this is ridiculous. Dr. F. didn't seem to register anything. He gaped again and found he had in fact removed his underpants altogether and was wearing nothing. He went brick red with embarrassment, shook his head a second time and noticed with acute alarm that his pants had in fact been on properly the whole time.

"Earlier on today doctor, I saw my own privates on a fifteen year old boy."

"Breathe in," she snapped. "Tch. Harder. Now out. OUT."

"I said I saw my own privates on a boy of fifteen."

"Quite normal."

"Normal! How is that normal?"

"Your breathing is normal – a chronic cold on your chest. Nothing serious." By this she meant he was wasting time that she ought to be spent on 'patients'. "Scales please."

He stepped onto the scales.

"Fifteen stone five pounds minus whatever your pants weigh."

Dafydd was secretly pleased. He'd lost four pounds since his last weigh- in at the motorway service station.

"Your BMI indicates you should be no more than thirteen stone."

"I've got heavy bones. A big head. These scales are wrong."

"Bones weigh very little more than feathers. Think about it."

"These M&S pants weigh a ton. You should try them."

"Tch. Bend forward."

He did so. She massaged her hands into his kidneys feeling around for something.

"Ouch. This boy of fifteen. Listen, doctor, it was me."

"Up. Mouth please. *Open.* Tongue out. Say Ah."

"Ahhhggggggggggggggh."

The doctor tossed the stick into the bin contemptuously.

"I keep seeing things. A girl I loved when I was kid. My younger self - the boy I was at fifteen, the one who loved that girl - keeps turning up in my office and talking to me. And I've got an inspection in school. I keep getting panic attacks. Ouch."

The doctor thumped him between his shoulder blades with a stethescope. "We also have Government targets to hit. We also are at breaking point," she snapped. She grabbed hold of a fistful of his waist. "Face it. You're overweight. Look at this. You need to lose at least two stones. Do you smoke?"

"No. I get asthma."

"Drink?"

"Not while I'm on duty thanks."

"I've got plenty of *patients* to see if you're going to waste my time."

"Only at weekends."

"Hmm. How much?"

"Four or five each weekend evening. Listen none of this is the problem. The *problem* is I'm talking to the walls. The problem is the impossible targets the Government wants you to hit are stopping me hitting the impossible targets they're setting for me. Perhaps I should book an appointment with the *pathologist* now so they'll have time to cut me up before I decompose? Eh? Would that help? Knock knock. Who's there? NHS Doctor. NHS Doctor who? NHS Doctor who turns up so late he might as well be a pathologist."

"Four or five glasses each weekend evening," said Dr. F., writing it down. "That's all right. But you are still much too fat. Cut out the comfort eating, the crisps, the sweets, the cakes. How old are you?"

"Old enough to eat crisps… Forty-five," he said. "And I meant four bottles."

"Of spirits!"

"What do you take me for, an alcoholic?" Dafydd got a guilty flashback to the previous night's alcoholic blur. True, he didn't usually drink during the week for the simple reason that even one small drink turned into one massive hangover with flickering eye spots if he mixed it with the alarm clock, school routines and the uneasy night anticipating the same – whereas a weekend of pure unmixed alcohol had no apparent ill effect whatsoever. But last night had been the exception that proved the rule. He'd mixed a weekend into the week. And he'd mixed beer, champagne, rough cider, wine and spirits, a takeaway and several packets of health-food flavour crisps, too - he remembered that much. His frowned on his returning headache. "Spirits! Of course not. Wine."

"Four bottles of wine every weekend! That's too much."

Dafydd decided to keep quiet about the two half-gallons of weekend lunchtime beer.

"Cut down. Better to drink a glass or two a day than binge like that."

"I'm too busy to relax during the week."

"So how exactly do you organise this drinking?"

"On Fridays, I drink to drown the week just gone. On Sundays, I drink to stave off the next one."

"What about Saturdays?"

"I drink to celebrate – or to blot out - the sports results. And before you ask, I'm watching the sport – the unreliable opium of the masses - to avoid thinking about work."

"Opium!"

"Only metaphorically – and only if they win. And they usually don't. Never mind all that. The weekend is fine. It's the week without end that's the problem. You can have no idea how exhausted I feel all the time. It never lets up, doctor, and now I keep seeing this kid- "

Dr F. considered her two-trick pony. Antibiotics now being more or less illegal substances, she defaulted to the other trick, the modern GP's one remaining option- tranquillisers. After all, she had public health targets to hit. "Any particular stress in your life? Any generic erosions to your self esteem?"

"Apart from being called 'fatso' by 'my' doctor? No."

"No stress." She wrote it down. Now what?

"You said any *particular* stress. My stress is generic. It's ubiquitous. It's omnipresent and eternal. We've got an inspection. I'm forty-five. My wind's broken. I come home after work and conk out for two hours and then go to bed early, solving nightmare-school problems in my own over-bedtime (without pay) and then waking up from them at about four am to lie in churning anticipation of the next day. Once in a blue moon, like on my birthday, I escape from this routine and try to get my life back and as a result usually end up with a murderous hangover. I'm not up to the job but I'm better than anyone else they'd get. I work with teenagers who want me dead and who also with touching childlike faith depend on me to secure them a future in spite of all their efforts to the contrary. Every day is a winding minefield and at the far end of it is death. And I keep seeing this kid- "

The doctor was pumping something onto his arm. It felt like it was going to burst it. She bent over him, twisting his arm in what felt like a half nelson and pushing him down into a chair. Her

Amazon bosom behind the white coat pressed into his back. He felt exposed in his pants and worried for a moment that he might get a rush of blood to the groin but luckily manhood-diminishing fear – and his sturdy M&S faithfuls - triumphed. The pressure on his arm became unbearable.

"What are you doing?"

"I'm taking your blood pressure. Relax."

"How can I relax? You're crushing my arm without telling me what you're doing. You've been attacking me since I came in here for taking up your time. On top of that, you ignore everything I'm telling you."

"I've got plenty of other p– "

"Targets to hit, I know. Perhaps I should tell your daughter the next time she asks me for a lesson that I can't teach her because I've got a school to run! You're a public servant just like I am and it's your job to get me back into shape so that I can do it properly. Instead, you tell me I'm two stones overweight and you want me to stop drinking. And that I've got to relax. Everything I do to relax you've just banned. What unwinding strategy do you suggest? A Special K party?"

Dr Faustus wrote 160 over 140 down on a sheet. "It's a very high score."

Dafydd cheered up. "Oh – great." This spot of good news encouraged him to finally take the plunge and pop the vital question that he'd been sitting on since he came in. He was screwing up the courage to ask her to have a look at that *growth* "or it's more like a recurring *swelling* on my groin" when-

"160 over 140 is dangerously high. Heart attack high. Stroke high. You need to cut out salt, lose two to three stones, get some daily exercise – some sport perhaps - and yes, relax. If there's no improvement, we'll have to put you on blood pressure tablets. Once you're on them, you won't be able to come off again. Come back in a month."

"Meanwhile, what happens to your daughter's education?"

"My daughter goes to a private school."

"Exactly. And what if she didn't- "

"Have a 20 minute walk before and after work. Don't fret about it so much. It's not going to kill you-"

Dafydd became hysterical. "I'm overseeing the most examined generation in the history of British education, doctor, and there are more measures of how I'm doing it than there are instruments in your city hospital. Heart Attack High is where I work. It *is* going to kill me. I keep seeing double, treble. I'm dizzy, I can't do my job at the moment. I keep seeing myself as this kid. I keep seeing this *girl-* "

Dafydd found himself outside the door, saying all this aloud to several intrigued members of the public. An old woman pushed him aside. She glared back at him as if a young fit man like him had no business occupying her duty doctor rights.

"I pay – through the nose - for that doctor and I haven't got all the time in the world to see her like you," he snapped. "You pensioners are always queueing for lunch out during my rush hour when you've got all day and I haven't even got ten minutes. So stop looking at me like that."

"I've got arthritis!" trumpeted the pensioner.

Dafydd felt a little shamefaced. "Well, I've got 160 over 140 on my blood pressure," he mumbled.

"That *is* high," said the old woman, impressed. "That's dangerously high."

Dafydd stood taller. He walked back through the waiting room with a bit of a swagger.

7

Megan waited in the staff workroom, tapping her fingers on the contraception box. She was nervous and resented being so. Also, Suzanne had turned up half an hour ago to say Dafydd would be late.

"He's already late. Fifteen minutes."

"Something's come up," Suzanne 'explained' haughtily.

"Tch."

Ten more minutes passed. Megan, exhausted and heat-stifled, fought off the urge to fall asleep, eyelids drooping, then finally gave in to it. Almost immediately, she snapped awake in a panic. But no-one was there. She waited again for a further five minutes, eyes strained wide.

Dafydd entered like a man who meant business.

"Where have you been?"

"Doctor's. Emergency appointment."

"Oh."

"Sorry."

"Right."

Megan's earlier determination to have it out with him quailed. Was he ill in some serious way – or just man-ill? What was he going to say to her? Was he going to bawl her out for destroying his Inspection lesson by sending, of all people, Kelly Harpy with that message? What on earth had she been thinking? Had she gone too far with the Sex Education class? Was he going to talk to her about taking her skirt off earlier and presenting it to the Inspector? That would be it, of course. She would explain that she was under too much pressure. He was pretty supportive of staff, after all, on the whole. And, anyway, what did it matter now? She was leaving.

He didn't sit down. He was all serious and formal and it rather thrilled her, despite the flutterings in her stomach. He frowned. "So what was that all about at the meeting?"

"The meeting? What?"

"You're pregnant aren't you? "

"What!"

"You heard me. Whose is it? Welch's?"

Pause.

She looked away in astonishment and then back. *"What?"*

"You haven't changed a bit have you? Once a slag, always-"

Megan gasped. "WHAT!"

Dafydd scowled at a point about three millimetres left of her ear. Had he really just said what he'd just said? It was political incorrectness gone mad. "I'm sorry … it's none of my business." He made to leave.

"You're damned right it's none of your business. Of all the bloody nerve, you treat me like some kind of stranger for ten years and then …"

Dafydd shouted her down. "I SAID I was sorry."

Silence. They confronted each other across the male-female divide. He could see the pain under the broken eyeliner in her eyes. You could drown in those eyes, he thought. He sat down. He said softly, "I …"

"I'm not pregnant. Not for lack of trying. Usually with men who move me about as much as the *Trollbridge Morning News* does when it plops through the letterbox at 6.00 am. But honestly, you! You're as naïve about women now as you were in the sixth form." She got up, paced the room. "I'm not a chair for any man to park his affections on. Least of all Welch." She made for the door.

"Megan …" He bit his lip.

"Yes?" Her hand was on the door-handle.

"Why then?"

Megan came back into the room and sat on the edge of the chair for a moment. "Yesterday I finally got a girl who's never been able to string two words together to write her first sentence. Capital letter – subject – verb – object – full stop. She was *thinking*, Dafydd, her first complete thought. Not a thought to challenge the world, but it was like watching a poet. Like watching Yeats make new sense out of chaos. It was like watching 'that dolphin torn, that gong tormented sea' come heaving out onto the paper. You should have seen her face."

Dafydd thought he could. He was thinking. *This teacher mustn't leave.*

"And where were the photographers? Where was our PR man?"

Dafydd became the professional headmaster again for a moment. "Covering a feature about my Oxbridge candidate, the last-gasp victory of the school rugby team, Geography's famous prize winner, and your latest star at the Eisteddfod…"

She picked up the *Aberdisllythyr Advertiser*. "I'm all for that, Dafydd, but actually, no. Read how well *our* 'A' level results com-

pete with somebody else's. Read how well *our* school fosters caring, co-operation, mutual respect and a love of the finer things in
life. Unlike 'theirs'. None of it has anything at all to do with learning, at any level. It's just league tables. But do you know what?
After that lesson yesterday, I could even have kissed a deputy head
I felt so happy. And guess what, large as death in the doorway of
the staffroom shortly afterwards, stood a deputy head. And what
did Troll do? He told me I'd left the heater on in my classroom at
break!"

"He's under a lot of pressure he never trained for. And it
can't be easy walking round with a poker up his arse."

Pause. She didn't laugh.

"Hang on, the heater in your classroom doesn't work anyway!"

Years of black woe began to slide off the mountain of griev-
ances her career had become. "English used to be the heart of the
curriculum, now it's the pacemaker. When was it exactly we
stopped teaching them how to learn by their mistakes? When was
it exactly that we stopped letting them get things wrong, stopped
teaching them how to think and feel? What's the point of setting
the authors of our 'great tradition' for A level and then treating
what they actually *say* about education as a joke? 'How little that to
which alone we give/The name of education hath to do/With real
feeling and just sense.' That was true when Wordsworth wrote it in
1805 and it's true now. My A2s have just been memorising Jane
Austen on the impact of poor education. 'Principle, active principle, had been wanting...they had never been properly taught to
govern their inclinations and tempers by that sense of duty which
can alone suffice. They had been instructed theoretically in their
religion, but never required to bring it into daily practice.' Is all that
just a memory exercise or are all these books we teach supposed to
mean something? And if they don't mean anything even to the
educators who set the specifications who else is going to make
them meaningful? Not us. This isn't a temple of learning anymore,
this is a dry run of the lean mean market place. The kids that leave
here are so loaded down with targets that you can see their shoulders sagging with the weight of the next sixty years. It's a plot, I'm

211

sure of it. A plot to turn out a huge semi-skilled work force who have just enough training to get work, just enough money to waste, but not a single idea between them."

"All that's exactly why I think you should stay."

"Nice deployment of the oxymoronic rhetorical gesture, Socrates. Shame about the facts."

"You should stand and fight your corner. Make a difference. "

"What corner? County's knocked me down and put a coke machine in my corner." And shall I tell you why 'Make A Difference' isn't the school motto it ought to be? Because there's no league table to measure the *only* difference that counts – the look on that girl's face yesterday. O Dafydd, you've still got about as much grasp of anything concrete as you did when..." She looked up at the clock. The moment for confronting him seemed to have gone. "What have you got next?"

"Assembly. Then Sixth."

The bell went. It hurt their ears. They responded frantically, robotically, collecting books, checking bags. Her next words were drowned.

"What?"

"I said, 'good luck with this afternoon'."

They were in the corridor now. "What for?"

"The job! Headship. You hadn't forgotten?"

"Not quite. But I meant the question philosophically. *What for?* What's the point of you wishing me luck when (a) you're leaving and (b)- "

Norman Welch passed them *en route* to Dafydd's office, grinning sarcastically. That there was no time or place to have this conversation seemed oddly appropriate. "Are you free now?" Dafydd asked her.

"And everywhere in chains," she said. "I've got a tricky cover in twenty minutes – fifteen minutes now - and I haven't done my marking for the period after but as it's you. What did you have in mind?"

Dafydd was making a speech at the Local Labour Club in the early 90s. He was trying to avoid sounding too much like Kinnock, whom he loved dearly but whom he thought inclined to be too soundbite-happy, too concise, too anti-elliptical, flat, weary, stale, unprofitable, too ungrandiloquently rhetorical, too shorn of music, soul, spirit, hywl, dynamic emotionalism drive, heart and passion, too Biblical parallelism-light. He tried to rise above Brother Kinnock's prosaic tendencies. "Exactly. *Exactly*. Capitalism. Look at the *ffacs.*" His audience looked for a fax, but there was none. Dafydd evidently meant 'the facts'. 'Look at the *ffacts*. Wales had the best coal, the best iron, some of the best steel too. Our coalfield drove the empire, built the American and Russian rail systems, forged international communities in the valleys. But it was pretty much English-owned. The ordinary Welsh people got very little out of it."

"The ordinary English people got very little out of it either. I thought that was why we all vote Labour," called some clever dick female spoilsport in the crowd. There were a few growls of agreement.

Dafydd's Welsh blood began to boil up into his brain. He tried to win back the meeting with party political poetry - an appeal to the ritual emotionalism of the left. "The English attitude to Wales, to Cymru, is the same as their attitude to King Arthur. They call him the hero-king of the English. He was a Welsh hero who *fought* the English! He was king of *Logres,* Lloegr, the Lost Lands, our Welsh word for England still! A hero the English have appropriated. But a *Welsh* hero nevertheless. " Cheers and applause moved into a crescendo as he perorated. " You start with the absurdity of settling for deputy leadership of our own land and end with the grotesque chaos of a Welsh assembly – a *Welsh* assembly! – hiring taxis to scuttle round the city handing out redundancy notices to its own workers..."

The thunder of the applause here disguised the fact that Dafydd seemed somehow to have wandered smack bang into a

Neil Kinnock speech from the 1980s. He rode the applause just long enough, raised his arms, then lowered his voice slow and deadly for the master stroke, right fist into left palm: "And we're playing them this afternoon, boys!" Wild cheers!

" 'And we're playing them this afternoon, boys…' " mocked the woman, despite the intimidating presence of two such Boys coming loyally to their friend Dafydd's aid at each of her elbows. "Except politics isn't a Rugby match, boys. And if ever Holy Writ was quoted out of context, Comrade Thomas has done it here with his mangling of Kinnock's conference demolition of the deputy leader of Liverpool council. If I remember rightly, Kinnock on that occasion was arguing *against* utopianism."

Megan Morgan! Dafydd thought. He met her in the bar afterwards. "All right," grinned Dafydd. "Put your carving knife away. I lost the dragon a bit in there. But never mind the oval shaped balls of the heavy industrial male for a minute. You've got to admit that it's time the Fellowhip, the Cymru, got their Lost lands back. Like Barry John said, our Rugby had become boring and predictable. It's all systems and grind and no *music*. Well, that's Tory England for you. "

"All systems and grind and no music is hardly the way to describe a country that produced The Beatles."

"They're not English. They're Liverpool-Irish. Celts. Dreamers, innocents, love children of the sixties, writing the otherworldly soundtrack for a lost Eden. Even the label – Apple - is more Avalon than Granny Smith – as, I might add, their gargantuan lack of business acumen showed."

"Dafydd! They were always measuring success in money until they had so much it didn't matter any more and even then they never stopped moaning about taxes. But all right, say they were Celtic dreamers and fools with money, despite earning more than almost anyone else in music history. You've still left out the greatest English visionary of them all. Shakespeare. *The* Bard."

"Tch. Not according to the heritage *Daily Mail* readers who set him for SWATS."

"Tch. You can't blame Shakespeare for the Heritage Brigade any more than you can blame Jesus for the Inquisition. Even if we assume this *ridiculous* argument of yours is true. What then? What are you going to do with all your allegedly barbarian soulless Saxon English businessmen inhabiting Maidenhead and Harrogate and Leamington Spa and all the other places that used to be Logres? Send them back to Germany?"

"Of course not. That's uh no longer practical." Dafydd trotted out the Welsh Labour line, partly against his own finer feelings. "England exists as a neighbouring foreign state now but our Parliament shouldn't be there and we need to re-connect with our own history. People living in Wales, wherever they're from, would be able to vote whether they wanted to become Welsh or not. I'm not a Fascist."

"Oh, Dafydd, I know, but you're very muddled. Nothing you're saying is wrong, exactly. Cymru may well be the oldest and most conquered English colony. The wild sky made out of spilled blood and all that, the "strife in the strung woods vibrant with sped arrows", the mausoleums of derelict industry haunted by the ghost of sacrificed labour. It's wrong. It's wrong to grow up in a 'conquered' culture with a chip on your shoulder - but if you really value the future, if you really value *education*, you'd better think about the children you're teaching now, rather than excavating Welsh defeats of 700 or 1500 years ago. And the Rugby variations on the same. Calling a toilet a toiletdau doesn't make it a Celtic shrine. I'm sure Nelson Mandela never thought like that."

There was something in her face, the familiar jut of her chin, that irritated him then. Dafydd had just been about to suggest another drink to chat over when Megan's cocksure preaching about his own profession stopped him. He'd been in the game a bit longer than her and here she was telling him what to do, on the basis of one year into her first post, somewhere cushy, no doubt, some place he hadn't heard of on the other side of England. Wait until you've got a few more difficult Year Tens under your sexy belt, madam, was what he thought. Wait until you've dealt with a few more bureaucratic advisers and hoary Heads. And he remembered, sharply now, how she had just very nearly ruined his speech in the meeting, with her naïve hubris. That could have cost him a lot; on home ground it could have cost him everything. She was at it again! She had always seduced him into confidences and then left him feeling like this, as plucked and gutted as a chicken. Well, not anymore. He got up suddenly. "Ah well, Megan. Good to see you again anyway. And the best of luck in the career. While it lasts...."

9

Fifteen years further on – during which that career and the luck wished on it had indeed lasted, though not it seemed for much longer - the sometime heckler and her sometime hecklee looked at each other. The issues hadn't changed exactly. But they looked very different. "So what *is* the Welsh for capitalism then? 'Preiddin'? "

"That's 'booty'. It's *Priflythyrenaeth*. Like Slytherin in Harry Potter – but starting with a *Prif* - and with an *aeth* on the end."

"You've just made that up."

"What else can I do in a country whose language stopped regenerating itself seven hundred years ago? "

"Start by asking why the most beautiful flag in the world - the red dragon on its green and white field — is still about as present in the flag of 'Union' as a Norman Welch Key Skills class?"

"Maybe it's time to stop living in the past-." Dafydd faltered.

"I will always love you and above you there's no other," laughed Megan quoting the Jethro Tull song from what felt the Stone Age.

Once again, they seemed to have come to a tide in their affair, which needed to be taken at the flood, as in *Julius Caesar*. Instead there was a Hamletian silence. Besides, as Megan said *Priflythyrenaeth*, Angharad had entered the room like a ray of sunshine trying to penetrate the Aberfan valley, not sure if she was entirely welcome. She watched them curiously and then broke the silence. "Oh good. A Wenglish Lesson! My turn? Which of you clever scholars can tell me the Welsh for *Chutspah*?

"Caerphilly," muttered Megan, "but it doesn't quite carry the full sense of crippling diffidence. Your go, Dafydd. Practice for your interview. What's Welsh for diffidence?

" 'is it possible to 'ave a little more milk, please' over a fourth rate breakfast in a fifth rate bed and breakfast in the Forest of Dean," whined Dafydd.

They laughed. Silence.

"What do you catch on a fishing holiday in Tenby?"

"Pollock."

"I only asked an innocent question!"

They laughed again. "Which side of Hadrian's Wall is Newcastle on?"

"The Welsh side. Unlike the rest of Northumberland which is on the chilly side. Which was the first foreign team to win the Welsh Cup?"

"Bristol City. The organisers made a big boob that year!"

They laughed again. Then stopped laughing.

Megan sighed, addressing Dafydd alone. "What time are you up?"

"Three."

"Well," she paused, seemed about to say something, then stopped. "Well- good luck."

"Thanks, Megan. I- "

But she had suddenly gone. And as she did so, he realised he wouldn't be able to bear the Llewellyn The Last Mountain High School – whatever syphilitic English king or glorified grocer they were going to rename it after – without her.

"Thanks," he said absently, "I think I'll need it."

"Do you think so?" chirruped Angharad. "I thought the Governors were rooting for you?"

He recovered himself. "Oh, Llewellyn-Jones likes me all right. We're both Cardiff University Old Boys. I've still got the slim volume he presented me with in the 70s for getting the best 'A' level results. *The Comic Poems of Milton and Wordsworth*. But Troll will see me promoted over his dead body and Welch is as sharp as a knife on the new SWATS."

"A boys' pen-knife, then. What will staff meetings be like under him?"

"A lot simpler, a lot quicker and a lot more efficient."

"But he can't get on with people."

"I'm not sure it's a requirement. He certainly gets on! He knows where he's going, and he'll take us with him. It's like being up against a career mountaineer who thinks Macbeth was only trying to streamline an uncompetitive society. 'A few judicious cuts never did an organisation any harm, Dafydd.' Besides, I can't get on with some people either."

"Don't you know where you're going?"

"I just follow my intuitions and usually end up in a field."

"I like fields."

Dafydd felt suddenly awkward. "Aye. Well, we'd better be going."

"Oh, good luck, then."

"Thanks."

They left. Inspector Carmichael Hunt emerged from behind a loaded table as they did so, making copious notes. He noticed a pile of lost property that Miss Handle – the mistress in charge of lost property - had lost there earlier (she'd carried off the school's rugby kit instead, thereby sabotaging the afternoon's away leg at Mountain Ash.) A brace of cap guns attracted his attention. He drew them out slowly, looked round to check for spies, then pointed them at the ceiling. "Git them wagons rolling! Yee hah!!" He let them off, then yelped and dropped them. He hadn't expected them to be loaded.

10

Outside in the Staff Car Parc, Dafydd turned the keys in his Lada for the umpteenth time and cursed. The motor still wouldn't start. "I must be the unluckiest bastard on God's earth! A handful of Anadin Extra from the local chemist so that I'm in some kind of shape for the assembly! Is that too much to ask? " He glared up at the mountain-halved sky that was Wales' heaven.

He checked the fuel gauge and tried again. Nothing. He punched the windscreen and cracked it. "AHHGGGGGHH…"

Trolley's gargoyle face filled Dafydd's rearview mirror, like the face of a red dragon in close up drained of all red, a truly terrifying sight. Terrifying at the best of times and this was not the best of times for Dafydd. Nor indeed for Victor. Victor had just realised that *Bed Fraud in A & E gets to bottom of why chops slay a sin* <u>couldn't</u> be PSYCHOANALYSIS because it didn't fit with 13 across, *Red saint drops H and introduces hell* (6). *6. 6.* Can't be LEN*IN. To a Marxist-Leninist that would be standard false consciousness, of course, peddled by the bourgeois crossword press. He repeated the thought processes furiously. Don't be distracted by the spurious cold war reference to a hydrogen bomb. Rearrange SAINT and introduce hell without the H - 'ell. L. STALIN? It had to be. So then 13 down couldn't be PSYCHOANALYSIS after all. Damn. DAMN. If *Bed Fraud in A & E gets to bottom of why chops slay a sin* wasn't PSYCHOANALYSIS could the anagram at the end be THE CYCLOPS? Too short. POLYPHEMUS? Still too short, too short! KALEIDOSCOPE? ENCYCLOPAEDIA? No, something to do with hollow-hearted one-eyed fanaticism. No, he was mixing it up with the other red saint clue now.

Trolley had his timetable face on, that summer-term face in which one wrinkled eye was permanently closed in a problem-solving effort of concentration, a god-like sustained vision of congruent possibilities. The other eye was always half closed anyway. The last but one thing he needed was any interruption at all from any living creature on God's earth. The *very* last thing he needed was Dafydd's comic hysteria. So that's what he got.

"Great news from the Education Ministry, Comrade deputy! The October building will be opened a month early to give teaching comrades the glorious opportunity of completing the Five Year School Development Plan in five months and all syllabuses are going to be reconditioned – again - to make them run on time. And hopefully not over pupils this time. A matter for great rejoicing, comrade. The revolution could be here by Christmas."

No answer.

Dafydd gabbled on. "The red fox is flying south for the Leningrad winter. And your brief case is remarkably like mine. It would be easy to mistake the two would it not?"

Dafydd didn't expect Trolley to laugh and Trolley did not laugh. Trolley never liked Dafydd's allusions to his supposed Cambridge spy work. Probably because his mechanism for laughing at himself had seized up – but also, possibly, because the rumours about him were true. And if so, now the cold war was over, his alleged and much discussed weekly meetings with Boris 'the Spy' Williams were 'obsolete' like everything else that mattered. "I remember a time when we were very glad of the Red Army, Thomas. Neither the British nor the Americans *ever* faced more than one fifth of the Nazi war machine. The rest of that monster was absorbed – and broken- between 1941-1945 by the Soviets, at the cost of sixteen million comrades. So check your facts before you mock the saviours of your country."

If this was a surprising remark coming from the arch conservative Trolley, it also fitted his stony habit of living in the past, a place where the fatal cement of extreme conservatism can mix all too comfortably with the rubble and sand of gritty Stalinism and, on any contact with the wildly unpredictable running waters of life, set like concrete. Whether Trolley was simply one of those Conservatives who (faced by the 'new' threat of Islamic Jihad or Korean nuclear weaponry or nouvelle cuisine) long for the comforting familiar uncertainties of the Cold War – the Iron Curtain certainties and excitements and twists of the spy thrillers - or whether Trolley actually *was* an agent caught, like John Le Carré in the early 90s, in the spotlight of an espionage that no longer mattered, wasn't clear. But he was certainly touchy as hell about any reference to it.

Dafydd looked at Trolley's impenetrable scowl. If all the jokes were true and he was just possibly an agent, how did his life's work appear to him now? As ultimately disappointed as the teaching career and never-quite Headship it used as a cover?

Dafydd realised that he *wanted* Trolley to be an undercover agent rather than just an old school Tory because being in a spy narrative was a lot more exciting – not to mention more ideologically heroic and engaged - than being in a comprehensive school story with an old bore. Trolley's car, unlike Dafydd's, did not come out of the old Soviet Union: in the paradoxical logic of a spy novel that would confirm that Trolley *was* working for the Reds. In a spy story, Dafydd's own Lada would not just be a combination of outdated engineering and personal tastelessness. No. It would be a *symbol* of an enduring solidarity by a Westerner with a lost vision of an international community now replaced by the shiny market 'opportunities' and 'choices' of New Labour. A bit like retaining his student account with the Co-operative Bank.

His Lada would also represent a repayment of his debt to a system that had put working-class boys like himself through University on a Government grant and paid his tuition fees. And sent him back, crippled with guilt, to do the same for others like him. That's what the Lada would be in a spy novel, a Western working-class Old Labour counterpoint to Trolley's Cambridge Tory public school marxism.

In a comprehensive school novel, alas, the situation was much less romantic. Trolley's capitalist starting motor worked. And Dafydd's 'communist' one didn't. He was going to have to ask Trolley for a lift down into Lower Pantysycham now. He sighed, swore and wound down the window - just in time to see Trolley disappear into his car, like a thief in the night. Dafydd was about to curse the deputy's inhuman efficiency but saved his energy for a physical attack on his own over-engineered Marxist-revisionist Russian rust bucket. He removed the rearview mirror with a neat right hook and pulled off the door handle with his left. The lead-heavy door was almost immoveable at the best of times but now he had no handle on it at all. He kicked at the fiercely blowing heater levers – the heater was so powerful it could drown out a Wagnerian opera on the radio and turn the coldest Welsh winter morning into a Siberian summer noon at the same time, and that was on the lowest setting – broke one of them off along with his sole and then hunkered over to the passenger side. He lunged out of the car and slammed the door, his head tamping.

He only heard the ticking as he turned the corner up the steep hill towards Big Bill's garage. And then - BOOM.

"Christ," he recanted, immediately seeking heaven.

"HOLY ASSASSIN" exploded Trolley in visionary triumph, adding a rogue S and losing a C, the other Y and a P in the blast. His car was blown into the lane and he himself hit the windscreen as the crossword's apparent solution hit his brain, rendering him a temporarily happy (if as it turned out deluded) man. The shock invited him to give in. He shook his head once, Pulled Himself Together, and carried on driving. When the police interviewed him about it later, he had absolutely no recollection of the incident and no perceptible ill effects beyond a stiff upper lip.

Dafydd meanwhile had a vision of himself at the wheel of an all-red, and *yet* also paradoxically all-green, sweet-running, dragon-roaring Welsh Llada received into the mist of massed angel-winged Methodist deacons playing Welsh harps - and smaller immigrant groups of Catholic saints, still gaunt from the Potato Famine, playing Irish harps. They were all welcoming him home in an epic Heavy Metal Male Voice Chorus, while the Cymru-consonanted cardigan-cuddly catatonically-Celtic Cerys Matthews (and all the maternal saints) descanted in excelsis.

"From the wilds of Broncaeau,
To the vineyeards of Bordeaux,
From Nantyglo to Idaho
Move your body to and fro.
Hit me with your rhythm stick. Hit me. Hit me...
In the deserts of Sudan,
In the gardens of Cwmbran.
From Milan - to Aberfan.
Everywoman's everyman.
Hit me with your rhythm stick... Hit me. Hit me...
Das ist gut. Ich liebe dich. Hit me. Hit me..."

But the early and explosive end to Dafydd's story that 'Bomber' Harris had prepared for him on the chassis of his Lada had been foiled by a non-firing Stalinist ignition motor...

"Well at least this gets me a courtesy Lada – one that works – and puts paid to any hope Bomber's parents had of returning him from Permanent Exclusion on Appeal," concluded Dafydd with grim satisfaction as Constable Jones took down details. They were either side of a table at the part time police station in Pantysoch.

"Yes, on this evidence I think we'll be putting young Harris away for a very long time. You're a lucky devil, though - lucky to be alive. Have I said something funny, Sir?"

"No, no. I'm not sure I am."

"What – lucky?"

"Alive. Tell me, Jones, have you ever read Gogol?"

"The Russian playwright, Sir? Yes we did 'The Government Inspector' for Drama GCSE. I enjoyed it."

"I meant his civil service novel, 'Dead Souls'. Everyone in it is dead and in hell and don't realise it. They just think they're at work."

"Sounds a bit depressing, Sir. I get enough of that at the station. I like to read something that takes me out of myself."

Dafydd laughed again.

"I assure you you're in Nowhere Lane, Pantysycham, Sir. Half a mile down valley from Garnlloegr. Not far from from Lloegrbach. About two miles up valley from Trollbridge. But nowhere near hell. It's probably the shock."

"No, no. This is hell right enough."

"Driving might not be such a good idea, Sir. Shall I give you a lift back up the hill?"

"Thank you, Jeeves."

11

Megan looked again at her schooldays photograph. Thirty years ago. How beautiful she'd been without knowing it. How discontented she'd been with that beauty!

But the photograph had been a distraction. She discarded it now and examined the cutting, checking the date. Ten years ago. The day she'd nearly escaped – into another future. Beyond the contempt of familiarity and the safety of all the devils you knew. And yet...the whole business still spooked her, whenever she let herself remember it. It was one of the reasons she'd stayed put. Not the only reason, perhaps not even the main reason, but a reason. Some things can't be explained. Many times, she had wondered if the whole thing had even happened, but here, yes, here was the cutting. Here was that Somerset county logo and heraldic wyvern, savage two-legged twin to their own dear familiar four-legged pet Welsh worm.

It had been a perfect day in a perfect school set among lush green pastures and golden wheatfields. The 'Summer Country' indeed. Even the May sunshine weather had been perfect. The kids – wearing blazers and immaculate uniforms - were polite, unusually bright, articulate, engaged; the GCSE and A level percentages were impossibly above the national average. The school sign had the simplicity of real elegance, its lettering *Cromcruach Comprehensive (Voluntary Aided)* laid on in gold leaf. The school buildings, sports fields, specialist resources and general educational riches glowed like a chest of treasure promising to fall into her lap. The school motto – AIM HIGH – avoided the negatively 'striving' connotations of the vandalised school signs she'd known in all her other posts. The Head had clearly loved her and she'd interviewed like a dream. She was *finally* getting on in her career, really going places, *realising* the potential her 'O' level teachers had purred over – amid the claws and catty remarks about her hemlines – before she'd lost all interest in school that first Christmas term in the sixth form. And yet when the smiling panel had looked on complacently as the Head offered her the job, she found herself asking for the weekend to think about it.

Book Two

Chapter One

Afternoon Assembly

There's a kind of Welsh
All over the shop
Tonight.

1

Per corer migliori acquae alza le vele. It was purgatory, only without the hope. Purgatorio without purgation.

Extreme Unction – Mountain High's answer to punk rock -
had just performed "Californication".

An upwardly yearning *Miserere Nobis* it was not. It toiled but it
did not spin. It began with an expletive not in the original and was
neither God nor with God, nor did it have the light of men in it,
though it did blow one of the stage lights.

Dafydd sighed. This then was Nobob's idea of an assembly
with religious content- as had been his last Christmas concert offering versions of Beethoven's "Erotica", Tallis's "Sperm in Alien"
and "Fire" (by The Crazy World of Arthur Brown) to a church full
of bemused if only vaguely Christian parents.

This remained Mr Nobob's contribution to the two-thousand-
year tradition of Western religious music. The band's four young
performers had come out as shy and fresh as evening stars in a hot
moony, powder-blue July dusk, promising a moment of awe and
wonder. And then a kind of moral night sky had fallen, in which all

four blazed like lucifers in the spotlights. Burning out their immortal souls for fifteen seconds of celebrity. Not so much Paradise Postponed as Unimagined In the First Place.

But "Californication" was kids' stuff, albeit kids whose only striving appeared to be for self-destruction. It had been followed by something genuinely Godless: Norman Welch's "Key Skills Attendunce Prize Prezentation."

The school had a policy of Overcelebration of Underachievement (Michael Unbrage's phrase) and Norman's presentation enacted it in full. His IT'S COOL TO 'SUCEED' banner tableau, for instance - photographed by an Old Boy from the *Trollbridge Morning News* wearing the old red and green Grammar School tie – had gone badly wrong when the banner collapsed, when the two students up for 100% attendance had been absent and when the three receiving Most Improved Behaviour Awards (ie they hadn't set off the Fire Alarm yet this term) had been throttled by Trolley's tie check.

Trolley was now tightening the Old Boy's tie as well. The emotional temperature of the Hall was at boiling point. And, thanks to the massed ranks of pupil and parent bodies therein, and the proximity of the post-lunch kitchens, the actual temperature wasn't far off either. Stan Whoreson was talking loudly to a parent, with detailed evidence, about how incompetent every single employee in the school was – with the illustrious exception of himself. A boy attempting to escape from The Inclusion Room had been mistakenly – and successfully – interviewed for the post of Site Manager in the room next door. And, to make matters worse, Trolley had suffered one of his action cramps while seizing the Old Boy's tie and now had the Old Boy's neck in a grip-like vice. Fearing a media Incident, Dafydd gave up his forlorn attempt to chase up the late Major Llewellyn-Jones by telephone and leapt, cloak wings flapping, from his office onto the stage to rescue the fallen assembly. Meanwhile, a garlic-faced Norman Welch was cursing his luck that the Inspector was seeing this instead of his maiden assembly as the new Head of Special Foundation Areas the day before...

2

Norman's winged jacket was poised stage-right on the chair-back and lots of laminated display trivia had been prepared for him earlier by overworked office staff. He had studied the effect for half an hour before school, while 'Sheep Dip' (Winston Jeremiah) and 'Tickbird' (Trevor Moses), his usual detainees, put out chairs. Welch's personal presentation showed that he had understood from his numerous training courses that, while some actions speak louder than words, nothing speaks louder than a shirt.

He whistled. "Tickbird, you moron. That row goes over there!"

'RESPECT' by Aretha Franklin blared out of the speakers. Welch stepped up to the rostrum and stood smirking over the sullen pupils. "Today's assembly today is about RELATIONSHIPS. Relationships is one of the Special Foundation Areas that the Government has decreed is necessary for educational success. And *I*, ladies and gentlemen, boys and girls, am now in charge of these Special Foundation Areas in this school. The tickbird ...and elephant" - a picture of each in succcession appeared, in the wrong order, on a giant screen – "seem to have no use for each other, but in fact they have a very positive relationship. The tickbird rides safely and royally on the elephant's back and the elephant gets all the ticks that burrow into its hide picked out and eaten. Relationships are like that." Norman ticked off a bullet point on his Inspection rehearsal sheet. Then ticked off a boy at the front who asked his neighbour what a tick was.

"You have many relationships in the course of the day. Relationships with PEERS– " He flicked out his wrist. The screen screamed PEERS in capitals. "Relationships with PEERS have been poor here of late, particularly in my recent absence on interviews and I will *certainly* be dealing with these on Tuesday when I get back from my course."

Another flick of the shirt. The screen screamed FAMILY in capitals- "How many of you actually work at these?" Silence. The powerpoint whirred. "Absentee fatherhood is so common it's almost the norm and absentee motherhood – an unfortunate bi-product of the Government drive to get women out to work, as I could have told them if only they'd asked me - is becoming so. But now so is absentee childhood. How many of you actually go home and then straight up the stairs to your computer games?"

'RESPECT' faded. The wrist flicked. A giant TEECHER in capitals filled the screen. "Teecher-pupil. This is an unequal relationship based on respect." The bell went apologetically. Welch ignored it. He whistled "Hamid! Get back in your place!"

"It's Ahmed."

"Hamid. Sorry. Get back in your place. Pupils are expected to respect teechers. Teechers are trying to train you to suceed." He bobbed on his trainers. The shirtsleeves twitched for the last time. IT'S COOL TO SUCEED filled the screen. "An increasing number of pupils here at Mountain High think it's trendy to truant. It is not trendy to truant and if you are truanting we will be comming round your house with a Truant Officer. We've got to get these Attendunce figures returned back up to Ninety Percent."

Welch glowed with the memory of that big match performance. It was his best since that unforgettable September kick off, pride-in-the-shirt, hail-the-school-uniform brand-merchandising half-time-team-talk assembly (filmed by bemused exchange visitors from Germany) in which he'd team-stripped down to his sponsored and initialled school PE top beside identically-topped-and-trainer-shod Sports Studies Students. NW. LLMHS. His finest hour. (Even if it should have been twenty minutes.)

He sipped the water he'd brought with him off stage grimly.

He believed in the will of the elephant, the wit and individuality of the tickbird. He had seen a placard on display in the history room and had asked the Head of History to copy it for him, after getting the secretaries to laminate it for him in their 'spare' time. It would make an excellent mission statement in bold black capitals under NORMAN WELCH, HEAD OF SFA, on his new office door:

"THE MASSES NEED SOMETHING TO GIVE THEM THE THRILL OF POWER. A NEW AGE OF MAGICAL

INTERPRETATION OF THE WORLD IS AT HAND, OF INTERPRETATION IN TERMS OF THE WILL AND NOT OF THE INTELLIGENCE"

Until this morning, that is. The Head of the PE Department had even asked him for a copy for his own departmental board, believing that it said some vital things for his students about the triumph of the will over weakness, until the Head of History told him that it was actually a quote from Adolf Hitler. Shocked, he had binned it and advised Welch to do the same.

Welch had done so, not wishing of course to associate himself with Hitler. But he could run an assembly, and he was a natural leader. A natural Head.

He drained the last of the filched water noisily. And instead of that triumph of the will – his smile faded – the Inspector had seen him humiliated by the failure of his Key Skills assembly, by which he meant of the other people involved. The wreckers who had failed to attach the banner correctly, for example, the delinquents who had failed to turn up for their 100% attendunce prize, Trolley's ridiculous tie inspection, the parents and pupils in the audience who had somehow created the pressure that had sabatagued what would have been the greatest assembly ever seen. And Dafydd Thomas – his presence, a catalyst somehow (Welch wasn't sure exactly how) for all the other failures. Alas, the Inspector had therefore witnessed, on this day of days, Welch's worst humiliation since driving a minibus of Year 11 boys to a spring sports event under strict instructions - "Now then boys, I get hay fever so if you see any pollen-heavy crops, oil seed rape and the like, close the windows and the fans and give us a shout."

He had spent the entire journey enduring yells of RAPE! RAPE! from delighted Year 11 boys – at first whenever anything yellow came anywhere in sight in the country and later, in the middle of towns, when any passer by could be treated to Mountain High seniors in full cry, with more and more graphic gestures to go with them, as the afternoon wore on. "Rape! Rape! RAPE!"...

3

The rock concert whistles and yells of Mr Nobob's 'religious' assembly eventually subsided, no thanks to Bob's exchange of hip hop fist whirling with the 'kids' nor to the assistance of any of the deputies (Troll was expressing his disapproval of the assembly's post-mediaeval content by for once refusing to deal with the consequences. Pansy didn't seem to notice there was an atomic fart explosion followed by a Year 11 riot occurring right under her 1950s loafers and a slightly cheered Norman was smiling approvingly at the general catastrophe). No thanks either to 'Radical' Joe Benson, who was still gambolling at the back with several of his Year 7s. Until Megan silenced him with the kind of slap you gave hysterical women in films in the 50s.

Dafydd said, "Thank you Extreme Unction. What all that was about see, is that all religions are one, and we've all got to try and overcome our differences and get on together."

"No it wasn't," protested the band's lead singer. The rest of the fab four was high-fiving with Year 8 groupies and ignoring their Year Head's demands to be quiet. "It was- "

"Well it damn well should have been," declared Dafydd. "Now SHUT UP!"

Mr Nobob's 'religious' assembly angel- EU's lead singer - shook his head in disbelief. The guitarist continued whining about this assault on his self-esteem until 'taken out' – feet not touching the floor - by Michael Umbrage. Angharad and several other members of staff felt encouraged enough by Dafydd's stance to look a bit stern and say Shhh a few times. Megan silenced some latecomers with a castration gesture. Norman Welch chatted idly and audibly at the side with Bob. Joe mimed Dafydd looking cross as a kiddies' amusement and several members of Year 7 ran to him to play. Carmichael Hunt made notes.

"Thank you. I'm ready to start," declared Dafydd.And at last there was silence.

Dafydd glanced down at the lectern at the blank sheet of paper before him and realised that in fact he *wasn't* ready to start - because all he had prepared was a careful introduction to the conspicuously absent Major Llewellyn and another sheet Megan had given him about an Eisteddfod Poetry Competition. He looked at the thousand waiting faces and swallowed the blank that was coming over his mind. "Today is March 1ˢᵗ, St David's Day, the day we celebrate the patron saint of Wales. It is a very important date, perhaps *the* most important date, in the national calendar of Wales. And we are a part of Wales, are we not, everyone here? Now Wales is a minor country in world terms and if the country were a football team it would probably not be in the Premiership - or maybe not even in whatever they are calling the League these days." A glimmer of inspiration began to come to him. "Wales might well, however, be one of those little clubs that take on the big boys going into the third round of the FA Cup to emerge from it as giant-killing heroes." The school of course was listening now, mostly because they thought he was talking about football, the national alternative to meaning. He sensed the Inspector making a note, imagining the invisible host of critics and bureaucrats, judges and little-empire kings that marched with him. "In the Book of Samuel, there is an almighty clash between a boy named David and an awesome nine-foot giant – complete with bronze armour, spear, sword and shield carrier - the champion of the Philistines, named Goliath." The Inspector raised himself to his full height, rather pleased at the turn the assembly was taking. And the school was also still listening - with some pleasure - to the eternal story because each pupil identified immediately with the child against the adult. And Trolley was pleased because Dafydd was quoting from the Old Testament, which he probably remembered being published when it was still new. And Dafydd was pleased because he thought he'd scored a point against institutional bullying. So everyone was happy. "And David said to Saul, let no man's heart fail because of him; thy servant will go and fight with this Philistine…" - a meaningful sideways glare at the Inspector - "Then said David to the Philistine, Thou comest to me with a sword and with a spear, and with a shield: but I come to thee in the name of the LORD of hosts, the God of the armies of Israel, whom thou hast defied." The school looked at Dafydd blankly. "In other words, it doesn't matter how gigantic the Goliath you face, as long as you believe in what you're doing."

"Ha!" snapped Trolley.

"Mr Trolley?"

Trolley hadn't realised he had spoken. "There's a bit more to it that that!" he growled.

"Not at the moment there isn't, Mr Trolley. If you could reserve your points until the end of the assembly?" Dafydd stepped back into his core beliefs and glanced at the Inspector. He loaded his metaphorical sling, lifted his voice an octave, raised a finger and went on the attack. "The Member – the *Member!* - for North West Clwyd once told us that Wales has achieved little in a century but to leave people with low self-esteem, poor education, no expectation and little sense of self-worth. He naturally blamed this on what he called the (quote) 'short, fat, slimy, fundamentally corrupt *Labour* politicians' who have been in power all that time!"

Suzanne mounted the stage with a menu. "Headmaster, could you *please* select your Christmas meal choices now. I've been asking you for weeks."

"Suzanne, it is the first mild day of March. The daffodils are barely in bloom. We have almost nine months before us for Christmas menus. And you may not have noticed but I am addressing Full School Assembly *at this very moment*" - he lowered his voice to a hiss - "with an Inspector watching."

"Oh very well!" Suzanne descended the stage again in a huff, watched by a thousand fascinated children and seventy gaping adults.

"Where was I?"

"Wales, Sir," called Tommy. Trolley glared at him and wrote *Tommy Jones* (again) in his detention diary.

"Wales, yes. *Wales*. But what is Wales?" Dafydd adopted the pose of a man for whom all mere words have failed. This was because all words had failed. His mind was as blank as the sheet of paper before him. He coughed... Paused. Coughed again. Choked. Went into a choking fit. Paused. Looked in despair for his water. Noticed Norman Welch sipping from it complacently at the side of the Hall. Choked even more. Took in a series of rasping breaths feeling each might be his last. Appealed to the Inspector in desperation to *pat me on the back quick please pat me on the back* – it came out as – Pghhhhh mhhhhhheeeeeeeeqckkkhheeeessqkkk. (The Inspector made a note). Received an Inspectorial glare as blank (and indifferent) as his paper in return. Took another series of Last Breaths, the very last of which appeared to contain some air. Felt the world come partly back into focus. Wiped his brow. Croaked. Thought of a word. Had an idea. Spoke, very gingerly, in fear and dread of The Return Of The Dry Bokes, gained confidence, gained strength, gained volume. Lifted his voice. The relief! I'm alive! I'm speaking! I'm – oh dear – I'm speaking to an Assembly. What about? I don't know. About Wales! Wales! *Wales!*

"The word 'Wales' is Saxon for *foreigner*, synonymous with slave. A bit of a cheek really when you consider whose country it was. Right, Tom?" Tommy looked up solemnly and called "Yes Sir." Then, in a marvellous rhetorical flourish, Dafydd switched to the mother tongue - or what little of it he could remember. *'Mae hen wlad fy nhadau yn annwyl i mi Gwlad beirdd a chantorion enwogion o fri Ei gwrol ryfelwyr Gwladgarwyr tra mad tros rhyddid collasant eu gwaed...Gwlad, gwlad, pleidol wyf I'm gwlad tra mor yn fur, I'r bur hoff bau, O bydded I'r heniaith barhau.'* The sounds licked around his consciousness like a tongue of fire, and if the reaction was anything to go by almost set light to a few pupils in the front row as well. *'There is an ancient land of my fathers that is dear to me, a land of famous olden time poets and singers, a land whose warriors have fought to make it free. For freedom blood was shed. My country, my country, I offer you my strength. Though I wander far from home in lands beyond the sea, even beyond the grave the ancient mother calls.'*

Silence.

The entire hall wondered what he would say next. Including, of course, Dafydd.

He licked his lips. "That's a half decent translation of the lines - but what do they actually *mean?*"

The entire hall, in spite of itself, wanted to know. Especially Dafydd. But alas, Megan, whom he was unconsciously addressing most, suddenly walked out, throwing him completely. He couldn't know she was in fact just asking the dinner ladies to lay off the naughty jokes and dirty laughter – all spectacularly audible at the back of the hall – while the Acting Headteacher finished his performance. The vast sea of blue uniforms swayed slightly under his eyes. He gripped the lectern. His beautifully judged rhetorical silence, initially perfect, had now gone on about ten seconds too long. And he couldn't remember if he'd brought in any religious content yet to satisfy that bloody irritating little Hitler of an Inspector he could still always just see out of the corner of his neuralgic eye. "I - Where was I?"

"The lines - what they actually mean," called Tommy. Trolley took his name *again*.

"Aye, the lines. The lines. The *lines*. What they *actually* mean." The hall agreed and gaped at him. His existence gaped at him, like the gap through the Red Sea - the essential void of his life, his work, his existence, his immortal *soul*. "The lines, my friends, mean the same as the name of the country itself, 'Cymru' – The Fellowship. What a great name for a country. Not Angle-land – the land owned – in fact stolen - by the Angles. Or 'Wales-land.' – the rump retained by the slaves. Or Pays de Galles. Region of the 'Galles'. Nor any other partial noun. No. 'Cymrodoriaeth' - Comradeship. I put it to you that what we often mean by Wales is *not so much a place as that human need for community or fellowship...*"

And just as he dried up in every sense – he couldn't lick any more moisture onto his lips and neither the old rhetorical silence nor a coughing fit would save him again – Dafydd saw Megan coaxing a familiar figure up onto the stage and towards his Chair. He brightened. "And on that note I am very happy indeed to introduce to you our guest speaker for thith afternoon."

The school craned its neck to see who it might be. Surely not that unkempt woman on the end who looked like a tramp (but was in fact a member of the maths department)? Nor that badged bearded visitor who had helped lead the day's UFA Conference (University of the First Age, though that was not how the acronym was translated in the staffroom) - and thoroughly enjoyed the refreshments and an excellent lunch as well as being in out of the rain- but was in fact a tramp? No. An ancient white-haired man with a handlebar moustache and the ghost of a military bearing now turned and held up a Bible. Some of the seventh years at the front thought he might be God and cowered away.

It was The Major. And he was fumbling with his papers as only an old man can, signalling that he was not – yet - quite - ready. Dafydd panic-improvised one more time. He tried to suck some moisture back into his mouth, bursting a blood blister in the process. "A gentleman to whom everyone in this Hall owes thankth. Not only because he was part of the heroic army which helped turn the tide of the Second World War against the Nazis at El Alamein, but because he returned to become Headmathter of thith thchool from 1945 until 1970 establishing it as one of the finest grammar-technical schoolth in Waleth in the proceth."

The school – apart from Victor Trolley - was unimpressed. All they saw was a sad old git from the irrelevant Past, a Past that contemporaneously included black-and-white television, the World Wars and dinosaurs. Speaking of which, Trolley stood to attention and saluted, privately believing that the school had never, after Llewellyn-Jones been so effective or relevant again. So the boy Thomas had learned that, if nothing else.

The Major continued fumbling. Dafydd tried thrice to lick his lips and went on. "A man whose religiouth faith not only carried him through the war and several near-death experienceth – including an actual bullet which lodged in his heart-pocket Bible on May 4 1944 - but also through what he callth the *'greater* dangerth' of running a thchool!'" The old man smiled indulgently. Dafydd sucked at his mouth. "Boys and girls, please welcome - our ex-headteacher, local champion, chief fundraiser, benefactor and Senior Governor, Major Tudor Llewellyn-Jones. Welcome, Major – Welcome. And May The Forth Be With You!"

Dafydd clapped enthusiastically and continued doing so - on his own - for about thirty seconds. Trolley would have joined in but his saluting arm seemed to have got stuck. Dafydd, looking round in vain again for water, casting a look at the glass Welch had drained such as a soldier in the desert casts on a mirage, collapsed into his seat. And Major Llewellyn-Jones wandered off stage again.

Megan came to the rescue, tore the second sheet she'd given Dafydd out of his wilting hand, turned it the right side up and waved it. "While we're waiting a moment for Major Llewellyn-Jones, I want to remind the school about this year's Total Bardom Award at the Eisteddfod." She read from the sheet. "The theme this year is Making The Best Of Things and it is part of an exciting initiative in national self re-identification, a *New* Poetry for a New Wales. Entries should be addressed to Nos Yr Bard, c/o the Rev Rectus Nickwhistle, The Old Buggery, Hiraeth Gardens, Mount Pleasant, Pentrehedron, Upper Pant Road, Ychafi...."

At this point, Major Llewellyn-Jones re-entered, accidentally barged Megan offstage, placed his giant black Bible on the lectern and looked up in the old headmasterly way. Megan suppressed a curse, smiling at the silenced school as though her humiliating ejection off the stage had been all part of a much-rehearsed plan and wondered - not for the first time - why she bothered. Dafydd was lisping his thanks but, as soon as Major Llewellyn-Jones began, became instantly a boy again, looking up from schoolboy memories of a filth-blackened canvas assembly floor at the man he would always call "The Boss." ...

3

Luke Seer (26), clear-eyed harbinger of the Morning News, filed his Mountain High story – Brian said he'd trim it for the Splash or leave it as it was for the local boyo makes goodo feature, on page 29 – filed his review for the Argus and then pushed off into Trollbridge to get Friday blind.

4

"Well all right! Well *all right!*" Neil Kinnock faced the Labour movement assembled at Sheffield in 1992 as a decade of defeat and despair came to a triumphant end. A spotlight blinded him as he grinned into a future of power, peace, parity, plenty and two or three more Ps than were strictly necessary. He picked up the microphone stand and twirled it playfully. He let a shoulder jut forward. He let his pelvis slide. He was Rod Stewart, Mick Jagger, Elvis Presley. He was Roger Daltrey and Robert Plant. He was The King.

"Well *all right!*"

The drums unrolled in a playful false start behind him. The bassist ran his fingers over an auditory *hors d'oeuvres* as the atmosphere built. Kinnock leered into the thousands of gaping faces. They were waiting for his usual oratory. They wanted rhetoric, analysis, commonsense, sustained metaphors of decency and discrimination, Miltonic grandiloquence breaking like a spring tide over the Thatcherite wasteland, the liturgical lilt of the left. They wanted *truth*. They held their breath for Neil, their much-loved and much-maligned prophet of the proletariat. They wanted his reassuring bass voice riding the surf of its Bible-trained music, in long lithe lines of golden parallelism and grandeur.

"I fink I bust a button on my trousers, hope they don't fall dahn... You don't want my trousers to fall dahn now DOO YOU?"

There was a shocked silence. The guitarist started tapping his feet, finding time with the rhythm section. He whispered, *One, two, three, FAW!* Kinnock began to gyrate, his ginger hair became dishevelled and his freckled face contorted in a grin of ecstasy. The band found the rhythm. The rhythm began to spurt outwards from a bristling core of sound. Kinnock strutted like a cockerel from one side of the stage to the other.

"You don't want my trousers to fall dahn now DOO YOU?"

"YEEEEEEEEEEEEEEEEEEEEEEEEEEEEEEEEEEEEE EEEEEEESSSS!!!" answered the liturgical crowd.

Kinnock Babes began hurling themselves against security guards, one or two of them getting through to a sublimely patient Kinnock. Knickers covered the stage like every shade of confetti.

"Paint it red, you devils!" shrieked a woman from Rhymney.

"Peacock! Peacock!" screamed the groupies. Glenys and the Half-Clad Hookers began cooing the doo-whop backing vocals. "Ooo- Ooo…"

Kinnock beamed complacently as the band moved lazily but with awesome power into the opening bars of *Honky Tonk Women….*

5

"*My* text this afternoon, " thundered the Major, "is from the Book of Revelation. It's not a book you will have heard of. Jenkins, you're whispering boy, see me after this assembly. It's not a book you will have heard of but it's the last, and Most Important, Book of the Bible."

The Inspector nodded.

"Some of you, at least, may have heard of the Bible."

The Inspector made a note on his clipboard.

"Even though the Bible is not, of course, a book prescribed by the National Curriculum!"

The Inspector looked puzzled.

"Any more than speaking in tongues is part of the Modern Foreign Languages syllabus! …What *is* prescribed by the Law – at least the last time I looked - is that we must all participate in some kind of assembled 'Act of Worship' *every* day… Most *Headmasters* have decided, in the interests of cultural and racial harmony, to obsewrve this in the same way Our Lord obsewrved the Sabbath. And how did our Lord obsewrve the Sabbath? That's right, our Lord did not obsewrve the Sabbath. He explained that 'The Sabbath was made for Man not Man for the Sabbath' He obeyed the spirit not the letter of the Law!"

The Inspector looked horrified.

"THAT DOES NOT MEAN THAT *YOU* CAN DO THE SAME!"

The Inspector nodded.

"You will be wondering why not. The answer to that can be found in the Book from which today's text is taken: the Book of Revelation. Tommy Juns! I'm speaking English boy, yoour language - at least do me the couwrtesy of *pretending* to listen! See me after this assembly."

The Major opened his giant Bible and in top revivalist gear announced, "'Behold! He is coming with the clouds … and all tribes will wail on account of him …' Revelation Chapter 1 vewrse 7. A-men." He slammed the Book shut.

Silence.

"Is this a vision of meekness? Of Permissive tolerance? Of 'Oh well try not to do it again?' of 'Boys will be boys and girls will be girls?' Of 'They're only growing children once, you can't expect them to always do their homework?' NO! It is a vision of JUDGEMENT!"

The Inspector nodded.

"JUDGEMENT! Rachael and Rebekha Rhondda, you are SMILING at me while I am talking. I have told you time and time again, NEVER smile at me when I am talking. See me after this assembly! 'Behold he is coming. Coming to what? Coming to JUDGE! Coming to carry out RETRIBUTION. Coming to open up your exercise books and say WHERE'S YOUR HOMEWORK GIRL? WHY HAVEN'T YOU COPIED UP THE CLASSWORK YOU MISSED WHEN YOU WERE ILL BOY?

WHERE ARE YOUR LINES? WHERE IS YOUR REVISION FOR THE TEST?"

The Inspector nearly shouted "Amen!"

The Major swept the audience with his eyes and with his cane. He repeated in a whisper.

"Where ...is your revision ...for the test?"

Silence.

"And not just one test! A multitude of tests. Tests at five, seven, leven, fourteen, sixteen, seventeen, eighteen. *Mock* tests at 1, 2, 3, 4, 6, 8, 9, 10, 12, 13, and 15. Generation upon generation of tests. As it was in the Old Days so shall it be again, week without end. Amen. He is coming to FIND YOU OUT!"

The Inspector yelled, "YES!"

"Coming to ask: *'WHERE'S* YOUR GREY SHIRT?' *'WHY* ARE YOU WEARNING EARRINGS?' *'WHAT* WERE YOU DOING BEHIND THE BIOLOGY LABS?' He is coming, coming today and tomorrow and tomorrow and EVERY day next week, coming in all his glory, coming to demand an EXPLANATION OF YOUR BE*HAVI*OUR!!!"

"YES!"

Silence. The bell rang and rang and rang.

The Major allowed it to finish. "Stay where you are. Thomas see me at the end of this Assembly. I have instructed the staff to draw up a programme of toil, wailing and gnashing of teeth. The results of these tests will be of considerabwle pewrsonal int-er-est to me in each indi-vid-uwal case. And I am not talking about unfathomable subjective learning, I am talking about" - he caned his hand on each word- "DEFINITE, MEASURABLE, RESULTS!"

The Inspector screamed, "TAKE ME NOW!"

"These results will decide yoour fate for the rest of yoour lives, and quite possibly beyond. This is a school. We are responsible for your growth to maturity. I DO NOT EXPECT TO FIND ANYONE ENJOYING THEMSELVES AND WILL PEWRSONALLY COME DOWN LIKE A TONGUE OF BRICKS ON ANYONE WHO DOES!" The Major made a clenched fist salute. "Aberllanfairpwllgwyngyllgogerychwyndrobw llllantisiliogogogoch!"

Silence.

"I trust I make myself - abundantly - clear."

6

Dafydd rose to his feet and began applauding. This time he was joined with a thousand pairs of hands. The Major acknowledged the enthusiasm with a stiff bow and marched swiftly off. Dafydd persuaded to come back on for a swift second bow, applauded again, then suddenly remembered he had been going to spend the assembly time working on the relative minutiae of his Development Plan. He turned his eyes to follow the Major and in a rebellious moment felt rather pleased he'd stayed for the assembly instead. He joined him in the wings. "An absolute triumph, Major. Just like the Old Days. Well done. Well done."

The Inspector added his congratulations. "An outstanding assembly, Sir. Who needs the Cane when you can SWAT the little bastards into submission like that?"

"What?" yelled the Major, cupping his bucket-ear.

They left the hall in a swirl of black gown, dust and pentecostal fire. The glow of the Major's performance would untypically last Dafydd until afternoon break - when he met Young Dafydd again and remembered his forgotten promise to mention Leonard Cohen.

Mr Trolley replaced Dafydd at the lectern like a top of the bill act kept waiting by an over-enthusiastic warm up man. You could only just see the top of his head. He sneered. "SILENCE!" Megan handed him the Poetry Announcement that she'd been butted off the stage before completing. He glared at it. "One message. Mr Publicity Stunt, the performance poet, and Bard Pitt, with his 'Rap of the Fair Country Valley Inheritance Show', will be in room 101, Miss Morgan's room, as part of the continuing Eisteddfod celebrations, after school on Monday." He added his own rider. "Anyone who has *not* returned the correct forms, signed and dated, will *not* be able to attend that event and will also be in detention. One warning: boys and girls must remain at least nine inches apart at all times. No talking, no smiling, no looking at each other. One announcement. Ceri Jones in Year 7 has managed to lose a microscopic screw from her spectacles somewhere on the rugby field, she *thinks*" (a cynical sneer) "sometime between break and lunchtime yesterday. Could any member of staff who for any reason sent a pupil out of lessons during those four periods who might therefore have seen it, send those pupils to my office immediately after this assembly. Beech, Bexley, Bond, Chamberlain, Cooke, Cole, Emmanuel, Fackerell, Harrison, Hewrbert, Hodson, Howells, Ives, James, Lasota, Leaman, Kemp, Milling, Morgan, Morris, Nelson, Nicholls, Nicholas, Peploe, Pritchard, Rafferty, Reed, Thomas, Jones, Jones, Jones, Jones, Preece, Preece-Jones, Preece-Rice-Jones, Price, Hymen, Cutler, Grey, Rickards, Hawkins, Thorn, Tudgay, Pearce, Mogford, Hill, Skinner, Chilvers, Ballinger, Bishop, Bartlett, Bridges, Gould, Tapper, Traherne, Flynn, Fleet, Cochrane, Monroe, Watkins, Worsell, Seer, Jones, Hope, Crosby, Stills, Nash, Young, Gifted and Black. See me after this assembly. The rest of dismiss quickly and quietly, you're already *five* minutes late for afternoon school!"

7

"Thomas! Take the names of anyone who talks. My bronchitis is playing up so I'm going to the staff room for a fag and a sit down." The teacher raised his snarl to the others. "Anyone on Thomas's list gets sent for the detention book. Understand?"

The class understood. Satisfied, their Biology teacher, 'Colonic Irrigation Ken', the biggest hypochondriac on the staff, left them to it.

The atmosphere lightened. 'All The Young Dudes" by Mott the Hoople played through a nearby window from a workman's paint-spattered radio. It was very pleasant in the sun-shafted room. Young Megan and Young Dafydd were, as always, sitting next to each other. (Ramo, like the rest of the boys, had taken Physics instead.)

Megan moved her hips in time to the music. Her bare legs seemed to brush his brain like pollen. She read from the worksheet.

" What's this? 'Corn ear?'"

"Cornea."

"What did Colon say we had to do?"

Young Dafydd read from her worksheet. "Copy out the diagram, copy out the headings, copy out the notes..."

"And then?"

"And then, if there's time, look into your partner's eyes and see if you can see the cornea ..."

"Oh."

"... but he said we didn't have to do that bit."

"But we can if we want? Come on then."

But there were too many nights with Ramo, too many bigfisted fuckers, between them.

"Honestly. Is that the best you can do? Look. Like this."

She turned his head tenderly in her hands to face her: Young Dafydd endured her gaze with helpless longing then pulled away and returned his attention to the worksheet.

"What's the matter? Don't you like me?"

"I did it didn't I?"

"Look at Trish and Ramo mooching off Physics down there behind the tennis courts. That's what I call doing it."

Young Dafydd followed the line of her gaze, then said, almost angrily, "Do you know what he called you at break?"

"Who?"

"Ramo."

"What?"

"I'm not saying."

"Dafydd!"

"He called you his slag."

"His slag, or a slag?"

Dafydd paused. "His."

Young Megan looked away again, out of the window. "Oh."
Silence

Her eyes were fixed outside. His were fixed on her averted face.

"Dafydd."

"Yeah?"

"Would you take Trish out?"

"God ... Yeah ... Not that she'd ..."

"Would you take me out?"

He dropped his pen. "Uh ... Yeah ... of course I would ... but ..."

"But what? Don't you like my perfume?"

She sprayed some on.

"It's gorgeous."

"My lipstick?"

"It's lovely."

"Eyeshadow?"

"Megan, I really love you."

"And would you take me out?"

Dafydd was embarrassed. "Yeah. But..."

"But what?"

A heartbeat.

"You wouldn't ask me."

Her eyes swivelled back into the room, fixed on Dafydd. He had removed his eyes from her face and was eyeballing his work-sheet.

"Dafydd. Look at me."

He tried to.

She laughed incredulously. "Are you wearing eye shadow?"

"Course not!"

"What's all that black around your eye?"

Silence.

"Dafydd!"

"I had a scrap at break."

"Who with?"

Silence

"Who...with?" She placed her hand on his leg.

He picked up his ruler. "Ramo."

Silence.

"What about?"

Dafydd stuffed the work sheet into his bag, kicked over his chair and stormed out.

8

The clock on the exam room wall said five past two. It had learned to tell the time and was rather proud of itself. The candidates, all sixth formers, were restless. Norman Welch hadn't noticed that they were five minutes past the time allowed. Some stared with that look of knowing that they have failed, others with quiet satisfaction, others with the grim helplessness of hope, still others with the misplaced complacency of certain failure. Colin Boffin was the most restless. He put his hand up.

"The exam's over Sir," he said. "It's five past two."

"You've always been a little smartass haven't you Boffin?"

There was a shocked silence. "Sir?"

Norman Welch glanced out of the window to make sure Inspector Carmichael Hunt - or an inspector from the Exam Board - wasn't about to discover his error. He would be in deep trouble, particularly today. He was sweating profusely under his cotton-rich and nylon-richer white shirt, purchased earlier during one his free periods from 'The British Shop' in Lower Pantysycham. He rearranged his British Shop tweed sports jacket with leather patches on the elbows and loosened the sensible sturdy plastic belt of his cavalry twill British Shop trousers. The crotch was intolerably tight and the British Shop Y-fronts, with their over-starched over-tight Vas Deferens moulding and heavily stitched Peter Groyne 'Y', didn't help. He wiggled his British Shop wool-rich and air-poor stockinged toes in their sturdy British Shop brogues. He tried to remember why he bothered shopping at the The British Shop. Everything was too stiff and/or too understated. He remembered he shopped there because he had a Discount loyalty account that he'd arranged after mis-hearing 'Bunny' Warrington, a fellow golf player at the Llansoroti Sports Club recommend what sounded like 'The British Shop'. He was in fact recommending The Brush It Up, a 'traditional' massage parlour in Upper Pantysycham High St.

Norman peeled his thermal vest away from his hairless chest and squirmed under the uncustomary work-pressure. He loosened his British Shop knitted tie whose Windsor knot had had his neck imprisoned in its white-collared tower for the entire morning. He quickly concealed his Headship Interview notes and called time. "All right everybody. Put your pens down. The examination is over." He started collecting the scripts. Alice Rhys started to talk. "No talking until all the scripts are in. Anyone who talks will be disqualified."

He collected everybody's script except Boffin's.

"Ok everybody. You may go."

The candidates filed out. Boffin looked anxious. "You haven't collected mine, Sir."

"No Boffin, I haven't."

"Here you are then, Sir. I've got to go home to revise for my physics."

"Oh? We're actually revising for our physics are we? That's a bit different to your attitude to *my* examination."

"This is different, Sir. This is 'A' level."

"Exactly. And without this 'A' level, your application to where is it … *Maudlin* College won't proceed will it?"

"Magdalene. You can't do that!"

"*Maudlin,* actually. Yes I can. Do you know what happened to me over your decision not to even bother to come in and sit the GCSE for which I had entered you?"

"I had too much other revision to do. And I didn't need Key Skills. I'm a scientist."

"I was summoned to Mrs Constance Francis the Comedy Headmistress and asked to explain why Mr God Almighty Boffin – 'one of our berightest prospects, Mr Welch!' – had lost all motivation in my subject."

"But it was so arbitrary, Sir. None of it had any constants or discipline. It didn't make sense. It didn't matter. It was boring."

"As boring as it will be for you to come back and resit *this* exam eh?"

"You... can't do that. It's not fair."

"I'll tell you what's fair. And what you can expect a lot more of once I'm in charge here. Me ripping this script into as many strips as the Head tore off me the day you decided not to grace my GCSE exam with your luminous presence."

"What are you talking about? She told me I had disgraced the school and her personally. And she threatened to get all my other results cancelled. She went berserk. This school has always had it in for me."

"You really want to get out of it, don't you? Get away to University. 'Find yourself'."

"Yes!"

"Take it from me, Boffin. The University will have it in for you too. It's not the school, it's not even the teachers, it's *you*. You'll never escape that. Not even in the postgrad laboratory." He took Boffin's script contemptuously, filing it with the others. "Go on, get out."

Exit Boffin, heading for a nervous breakdown.

It wasn't Norman's fault. Norman was under intense pressure too. Below his smooth surface, Norman had more stresses than the rich unworked seams of the ex-coalfield: a father who never spoke and a mother who worshipped her son, faults and all, whose house was a photographic shrine to her departed darling, who would have worshipped him even if he'd been Hitler. It wasn't his fault. Norman went back to his Interview preparations.

But it wasn't Boffin's fault either.

9

Dafydd looked at the shortlisted applications – actually the *application* - for the Head of Music job. Although Dafydd would be very glad indeed to see the back of Giles Nobob, Nobob was going to be a devil to replace. There had been four applications in all. Twenty years ago, it would have been fifty. Two of the discarded applicants were on the County blacklist. One was a defrocked clergyman, with the emphasis on 'frock'. The other was a clergyman who had not been defrocked – who on the contrary had a testimonial from his bishop declaring him to be a wonderful, if tormented soul, and a gifted violin teacher. A third was not on the County blacklist but should have been. He was certainly a religious nut – naming Jesus as his second referee - and possibly just a nut. He was not going to be allowed anywhere Mountain High at any rate. Which left Mr Pugh, whose violet writing paper with a rose motif was a challenge to place in the comprehensive school mainstream of Mountain High, and whose letter included the following:

"I am active in the local music scene and am known humorously as a bit of a Scheidt fan. Indeed, the Pantygasseg Wind band, which I conduct from the second horn, will be playing Complete Scheidt throughout the forthcoming Pontyhedron Wind and Bras Festival. My article, 'Why is there never enough Scheidt on Radio 3?' was published twelve years ago in the *Western Mail* - and also later in *Private Eye*. In addition to the horn, I am also a keen fiddler and can think of few things I would enjoy more than fiddling with the little boys and girls of Mountain High. I was at your School Eisteddfod last year but was unimpressed with the children's playing –particularly the Finale which everyone knows should be played like Kreutzer. Alas, they played it like Kuntz."

10

Carmichael Hunt attacked another room. It was very dark in there and if it hadn't been for the control lights on a disabled pupil's chair, Hunt wouldn't have been able to see his way in at all. The Cambridge-educated, Edwardian-moustached and rather donnish Head of History currently dictating notes was known as 'The Dictator.' As were two of his moustached mainstays, Hitler and Stalin, who were very bad men for the planet but very good for history: they had saved many a history syllabus. There would doubtless come a time when Sadaam Hussein, another moustached dictator, would join them among the racier narratives of school history.

The Dictator's class of eleven-year-olds was dutifully scribbling everything down at impressive speed. Hunt, losing interest, inspected the wall displays and the bookshelves. He was pleased to see that the *Bad King John/Good King Richard* interpretation of history had been replaced by the more sophisticated *Inadequate King John/Inadequate With Elements of Satisfactory King Richard* interpretation now in vogue with the Inspection agency. A *From Alfred The Satisfactory To Ethelred The Serious Issues With Elements of Harrowing* wallchart (freshly put up that morning for the first time since the last Inspection) received particular approbation - and a recommendation for a mention in the Report. (The even more praiseworthy *Ethelred The Unready For Anything* wallcharts had arrived too late for Hunt.) The Dictator meanwhile was approaching the last in a serial parenthesis.

"And, *sixthly*, Labour – then an unreconstructed socialist party dedicated to the nationalisation of the means of production, distribution and exchange - had won a landslide, inexplicably defeating the saviour of Europe, Winston Churchill, by an humiliating margin in 1945." The children struggled to keep pace. One moaned and shook an arm. "Shape up, Sian – you're British aren't you!" urged her partner in a jolly voice. The dictation got even quicker as the teacher got more and more excited. "Labour had of course proceeded to set up the National Health Service, to nationalise heavy industry and oversee the 1944 Education Act. In short, Labour had demolished the Empire and built a modern – smaller – humbler – more worker-friendly Britain. And by 1951, after a feeble re-election by a whisker in 1950, everybody hated them. New paragraph.

"Sub-heading. Austerity, rationing and George Orwell's *1984*, perhaps a version of the Labour England of 1948? Question mark. Underline. No matter how and when they were elected, and by what name they called themselves, Labour would in many people's minds always destroy itself in this way. They would always resort to a Well-Meaning Dictatorship, the Nanny State, the Namby Pamby Pandering to the Weak and Parasitic. Sterling values would 'succeed' to the British Army complaining about the culture of targets and bullets and the Navy behaving as described in a poem published in *The Daily Telegraph,* as follows. New line. Heading.

Sterling Values: A Statement
What concerns Her Majesty's Government
Is not the loss of face,
The decline of British Sea Power,
The copybook headline disgrace,
The selling tales to the tabloids
But this – and we're not joking-
That Nelson's heir in the tv age
Was caught *smoking.*
Full stop. New paragraph…"

The Inspector nodded benignly and left. History was in safe hands.

"Ok kids, the nasty gnome has gone now," said the Dictator, sparking up a coffin nail. "Get your Manics albums out." *Libraries give us power…*

11

The bell went for break. It certainly needed one. In the corridor, pupils passed in both directions, like flotsam and jetsam hurled around in the flood tide of the rock-breaking Afon Marw river in the fast twenty mile section between Bryn Marw and Aber Marw. Dafydd met Boffin. "How did the exam go Colin?"

Boffin ignored him, disappearing under a sea of troubles.

"Colin? Are you all right?"

Dafydd tried to follow him but met too much pressure coming the other way. It was as if the silt which accompanies the flow of a river had built up into its own river and changed the original course and direction: the original course and direction being the education of young people. In spite of which, against the shark-filled current, as if onto a beach, Tommy was swept up against Myfanwy.

"Tommy!"

"Myfanwy!"

"Tommy…"

"Yeah?"

"Thanks for what you said to Mr Thomas this morning."

"What?"

Myfanwy smiled. "About tidying his desk and that."

"That's ok."

"I've got something for you."

"What is it?"

"Piece of chewing gum."

"Someone's been chewing it."

"Only me. Well do you want it or not?"

Tommy took it.

"Well, chew it then."

Tommy put the warm pink gum into his mouth and chewed.

"God you're disgusting!"

"I'm not am I? No one else has chewed it have they? Only you?"

"Only me."

"You and me."

"You're a headcase. What are you doing at afternoon break?"

"Nothing."

"I'll meet you. Behind the biology lab." She moved off into the flood, her mobile phone ringing.

"YES!" Tommy punched the air with a clenched fist.

Dafydd spotted him "Tommy! Are you eating in the corridor?"

"No Sir."

"That's a detention. See me at afternoon break."

12

Myfanwy's mother chatted inconsequentially down the line to her daughter, repeating the same sentiments and platitudes over and over again and taking the exit sequences at a spectacularly slow pace. She appeared to be rehearsing the lines of an entire episode of a soap opera too pedantically faithful to real life to be of any interest and 'feeling' it all too convincingly. Finally, she closed the call. She looked up at the customer she'd kept waiting for fifteen minutes. "Yes. Can I 'elp yew?"

"That would be nice. I'm looking for 1970s copies of The New Oxford History of Music? Volumes 6 and 9?"

"'ave yew looked at the Music Section?"

"Is that the one over there, by the Customer Is Always Right sign?"

"The one marked MUSIC yes."

"There was only The Ladybird Guide to the Orchestra and The George Michael Story there. I wondered if you had any Music?"

"I'll ask Mr Vanderbilt." She called, "Mr Vanderbilt, 'ave we got Volume 6 and Volume 8 of the 1980s New Music History of Oxford for this gentleman?"

"1970s copies of volumes 6 and 9 The New Oxford History of Music," corrected the gentleman.

Mr Davies came in from the back room. "Mr Vanderbilt's not yer at the moment. Can I 'elp?"

"Ah, Mr Davies," said Myfanwy's mum. "'ave we got Volume 6 and Volume 8 of the 1940s New Music History of Oxford?"

"1970s copies of volumes 6 and 9 The New Oxford History of Music," corrected the gentleman again.

Mr Davies was furious. "Irene, where are the till pens and pencils?"

"The what?"

"There should be two pens – a red one and a green one - and two HB pencils. They need to be here by the till at all times. Have you taken them?"

"No, I don't think so."

"Well, there should be two of each." Mr Davies separated the remaining one pen and two pencils fussily into their correct compartments. "One of the pens is missing."

"I'll 'ave a look upstairs."

"No, I'll do it and *then* I know it's done. You look after the customer."

"Mr Davies," said the customer, "before you do, would you have any 1970s copies of volumes 6 and 9 of The New Oxford History of Music anywhere?"

"'ave you tried the Music Section?"

"I've tried the toddlers' book and pop star fanzine, if that's what you mean," explained the customer patiently, "only I'd read the advert claiming that the Welsh for Booktown is *Mynyddmorynmarwrhol* but there seems little evidence of it here, in Mynyddmorynmarwrhol Books."

"You could try Llewellyn's, Cordell's, Mynyddmorynmarwrhol Music or Preedle's – they're all music book specialists." Mr Davies disappeared upstairs.

"I have done. I've also tried the Continental Wine Bar on the top of the hill."

Myfanwy's mum looked interested. "The one that used to be a Miners' Pub?"

"The one that still is a Miners' Pub only now it has a row of wine bottles along the top shelf and a traditional Welsh menu partly duplicated in inaccurate French."

"It's got French people in it! I 'eard them myself just this lunchtime."

"Were they actually eating the food?"

"Aye!"

"Good God. Anyway, I think I'll leave it now and resume my search for those books in Blaenafon."

"All right then, my lovely. Good luck."

"You'll let me know if you ever get those books in?"

"No. We don't do that."

"Thought so. Ok. *Thanks.*"

"Bye bye."

Mr Davies came down with the missing pencil and Volumes 6 and 9 of the The New Oxford History of Music, which he placed on the extensive section devoted to Oxford. "That chap gone?"

"Aye."

"Nice chap."

"Very"

"A pity we can't attract a few more like him to this god-forsaken place."

"Aye," mused Myfanwy's mum absently

13

Megan and Angharad came down the corridor towards the la-dies. Dafydd saw them check their bags and go in together– why did women do that when men did everything they could to avoid it? - and it reminded him he had missed afternoon duty in the girls' cloakroom. No doubt Welch had his absence on security camera for showing to the interview panel.

He heard Angharad's piercing voice above the drying machine through the window. And then Megan's.

"How old is Pansy now. Eighty-five?"

"Thirty-one."

"You're joking."

"Sadly not. But you never seem to age."

"Thanks. Misery and a deeply unfulfilled love-life keep me young."

"Aye - and the curse of a magic ring."

Dafydd tried not to listen and lost what they said anyway in the giggles that followed. It sounded to him like -

"I wouldn't want to let the panties down. We should screw and dangle and suck."

But it was actually –

"It must get Pansy down."

"That's the usual way! Unless she does it standing up."

Outside the ladies, Dafydd was wondering – a little feverishly - if the fact that in Welsh one of the words for 'woman' (*merch*) was independent from one of the words for 'man' (*dyn*) unlike English where 'woman' 'came out' of 'man' in a piece of biology-defying Biblical nonsense, meant that in Welsh-speaking communities the whole relationship was thought of differently. Or whether the other words for woman and man (*gwraig and gwr*) represented the sexes' connected and dialectical relationship in exactly the same unequal, exploiting way? Or not? Whether, for example, that feminist 70s mutation 'wymmen' invented by sisters - who preached *a woman needs a man like a fish needs a bicycle* in a denial of all relationship altogether - would be unnecessary in Welsh? Thinking of the Welsh-speaking couple he knew, he rather doubted it. And ladies remained a mystery behind a closed door to the vast majority of Boyos with whom he spent his Friday nights at the Clwb, that was for sure. He wondered, as with so many developments since feudalism, whether Welsh in fact had a living word for 'feminism' at all or whether it just used English with a lilt, as usual. Perhaps the New Welsh Assembly should invent a proper *Welsh* word for feminist discourse now as part of its independence. The Boyos would doubtless suggest something like *pantygas* and listening to Megan and Angharad's muffled chatter within it was difficult to disagree. But the feminine of 'Cymru' ('the fellowhip') would be better, if there was such a thing.

Unless 'Cymru' *was* the feminine?

Meanwhile, back in the real world, or inside the Ladies at any rate, Angharad had gone very quiet, thinking of Llewellyn the Last High School without a Megan in it to cheer her up. "I think you're mad to resign now, Meg. Won't you always resent never being a Head yourself?"

"Na. This career mountaineer thing. Men make too much of it. What's on the top of that mountain: a pile of money and no time to spend it? Yes. Power and glory? I doubt it and anyway I want something more: a great love. Money can't buy you love, Angharad."

"No, but it can rent it!"

They laughed again. (A little bitterly though.)

Dafydd blundered away, wishing he'd not listened. That four letter word, uttered and overheard so casually, had ruined his day, changed everything. "Love." The one thing in the world that increased when you shared it. The one thing that two people could even *lack* together, could suffer the tragic loss of, a lifetime's longing for, a wasted youth and advancing middle age of, *together*. What had his life and his career been without *her* after all? Nothing. A poor joke. Auden's Ascent Of F6 - only without the approving 'mother' figure - or in his case, the love of his life – at the long-delayed peak. He accepted that delayed gratification was the emblem of the middle classes but this amount of delay in proportion to that amount of gratification seemed ridiculous.

An old-school exam desk had been placed nearby for pupils excluded from the Inclusion room to sit at during lessons. Dafydd sat there now, utterly deflated, and cast his eye over the graffiti, appalled at its sexual crudity and its gross abuse of peers. Not so much a tainted exam desk as a toilet wall. Better clear this up, he thought. He stopped. Very faintly, near the old ink well, a familiar teenage heart was scratched deep and desperate in dead biro.

DT Loves MM. True For Ever.

DT Loves MM. True For Ever.

DT Loves MM. True For Ever.

He covered it up quickly before anyone could see.

Chapter Two

No Future

Yours was the kiss that awoke my heart.
It lingers still though we're far apart.

1

Christmas 1973. 'Merry Christmas Everybody' by Slade hung
like cheap 'n' cheerful tinsel in the air. Young Megan came in to
the sixth form common room wearing a short, fashionable winter
shirt and a mohair cardigan. She got up on a chair to fix up mistletoe. Young Dafydd sat nearby in a scruffy jacket and flared trousers, his hair as hippily long as he could get his parents to accept:
never long enough though actually much longer than he realised.
His Lennon specs glinted as he pored over some history books.

"I knew there was something missing when I put this lot up,"
said Young Megan. "Dafydd?" Dafydd was absorbed in his books.
"Dafydd! Are you going to give me a hand or not?"

"Sorry – yeah."

"Well come on!"

He joined her on the chair. Giggling, they eventually managed
to attach the mistletoe she held up.

He coughed. "Megan, *are you coming to the school Christmas dance?*"

It had taken him three years but he had finally asked her.

She looked at him. A teacher came in. Miss Winterbottom.

"What *on earth* are you doing?" The teacher kicked at the mess on the floor.

"Christmas decorations, Miss Winterbottom!"

"Get down at once the pair of you! Megan, you're to see the Head of Sixth immediately. About your appalling exam results."

Megan made for the door. "See you later ... gorgeous."

The teacher frowned, "What?

"I wasn't talking to *you*, Miss."

Miss Winterbottom followed her out. Over her shoulder she rasped, "Dafydd, I want these decorations taken down immediately."

"But it's Christmas!"

"It is also the last day of term. Clear them."

Young Dafydd, left alone, rebelled briefly, by doing nothing. Then petulantly started to tear down the decorations. He paused under the mistletoe. It was one of those moments when time seems to stand still...

"You again! The new boy from the Taff valley is it? Has anyone shown you the ropes?"

"Sir?"

"You showed him before, Sir."

"I mean, has a pupil?

"No sir."

"Ramo."

"I'm in detention."

"Megan."

"Yeah?"

"Yeah what?"

"Yeah, I'll show him the ropes-"

Young Megan came back in. She walked angrily to her desk and packed the decorations that Dafydd had taken down into her bag.

"What's the matter Megan?"

"I'm leaving."

The world shuddered on its axis. "No!"

"What are you so bothered about?"

"You *can't* go!"

"Why not?"

"Because … It's not a matter of 'Why not?' It's a matter of *why* for God's sake."

"Because I'm 'not academically suited and I have the wrong attitude'."

"What?"

Young Megan translated. "I'm thick and I'm rude."

"Yeah, but …"

"Oh Dafydd, I did well to get this far. My old man says I'd never even have passed the 11 plus in his day. And here I am trying to do 'A' levels. Even Miss Millington said yesterday that I would be better advised to concentrate on schoolwork instead of 'Other Activities'".

"Other Activities?"

"Sex. And I'm so fed up with not having any money. Brian says, I could be a manageress in a year or two, instead of doing checkout shifts for sod all."

Dafydd stopped clearing the decorations. "Who's Brian?"

"The Personnel Manager."

"That's the one who got me the sack. Called me a moron."

"They don't give you the sack here though, do they? And they say I'm a bad influence on you. You, so they tell me, are University material."

"That's what they tell me too. If I 'apply myself' and if I make my application to a Welsh University. Sod that."

"Why?"

"Because you can get into a Welsh University easier if you're Welsh, so they say."

"No. Why 'sod it'."

"Because I am going to apply to a University that is as far away from here as possible."

"Oh." It wasn't the answer she wanted. She picked up her bag and purse. "I've got to go. Brian's picking me up at one o'clock. Here's that pound you wanted to borrow for lunch. Don't spend it on fags again."

He panicked. "You can't go yet." They looked at each other for a reason why not. "What about these decorations?"

They began removing the decorations. Dafydd laughed wryly. "Do you remember when you used to sell snogs for fags?"

"Yeah! I didn't have *any* money then."

"I never had any fags either." He paused. "You did that for love, not money!"

She stroked his cheek. "Maybe."

"When shall I give you this quid back? Will you be at the school dance?"

"Give it back to me when you're rich."

"Do you really have to go? You might do well at 'A' level?"

"No Dafydd. It's Sainsbury's for me. The clubs. The lads. Chance of making a bit of money. You've got your sights on higher things. University History, Geography. That is what you want isn't it?"

He sighed, "I suppose so."

Pause

"Well, are you going to take that mistletoe down?"

"No."

"Good." She got up. "Come over here."

He crossed to her, suddenly terrified. "Ok, but look, I won't be able to do this as good as usual. I've got a crick in me neck."

She kissed him skilfully, her hair redolent of last night's perfume. His arms appeared bolted to his sides. And Time stood still again….

"Don't worry. I came here late too. From the rough school on the valley estate. And look at me!"

"The rough school?"

"Millstone Colliery Secondary Modern. I'm a Modern Girl." Megan smiled at Dafydd again….

"Something to remember me by," she murmured, and was gone.

Because time never does stand still really. Dafydd came to, looking around, still feeling her back under the soft cardigan in his fingertips. And still feeling the spines of the Edwardian radiator in his back. The winter sunset was turning the room red." Megan?" He started towards the door.

Ramo came in. "What's up?"

"Nothing. I was just ... looking for someone."

"Well, here he is! And look what he's got!"

He held aloft a small package.

There was a silence.

"You're joking!"

" No. Genuine. Hewn from the deep mines of the Misty Mountain. Processed in a laboratory somewhere in Reading. State of the art."

"I'll not take that in this dump."

"We'll go out. Onto The Mountain."

"It's got to be a fake. Let me have a look."

"Give me a quid first."

Young Dafydd did so. "Listen, Ramo, if this turns out to be a rum deal..."

"*Bum* deal, you daft sledge. I thought *you'd* be able to tell just by looking."

Dafydd bluffed. "The stuff I've had before has always been red."

"Twat. That's Kriptonite. The Dragon is green, man."

"We'll see." While Ramo checked the corridor for teachers, Dafydd swallowed the lot.

Ramo came back too late to stop him. "Taff?"

"Just make sure you've got that pound ready to give me back when nothing happens."

A mask fell from Ramo's face and smashed. "Dafydd! You've swallowed it all at once!"

"Never do things by halves."

"Dafydd, I'm not bullshitting. Honest now. You've just taken an overdose." Ramo looked frightened to death.

"Yeah, yeah." Oh God.

"Listen, I've seen what that stuff can do. It was a nightmare and I only had half of what you've just taken. I was in the boys' bogs. All that filth on the walls – Trolley and the Geography teacher - came to *life*. You've got to get out of school quick."

"Nice try. You know the new tutor boyo wants me to recite that Welsh about Arthur and Cei in assembly. *Cei had these gifts: he could hold his breath under water for nine nights and nine days; a wound inflicted by Cei no doctor could heal; victorious was Cei; he could be as tall as the tallest tree in the forest when it pleased him...* I'm shitting myself enough as it is." Dafydd laughed. *Very* loudly.

"Shh, Taff."

From the assembly hall, they could hear Trolley's end of term knees-up rendition of the Gloria Gaynor classic floating up. Every year, just to prove he was human, Trolley would let himself go in this way, like the Lord of Misrule reversals he had doubtless enjoyed as a boy about the time King Henry VIII had originally funded the school. *'I will survive, I will survive!'* Letting his old grey hair – and indeed his old grey school - down while his knees jerked up, and with his turkey-neck stretching like a suspender, he managed the near impossible task of appearing even *less* human than usual.

"Remember that Druid stuff we did in history? About the Great Bard who would return and lead Wales out of captivity?"

"Yeah. The nutter never came down from the mountain when we needed him, Sir says." Dafydd laughed – very loudly again - and again. And again.

"Shh, Taff. What d'you fink took him up the mountain in the first place?"

"The Council refuse lorry?"

"No, Taff, The Green Dragon!"

"Cut it out Ramo. You're freaking me out." Dafydd reached out an arm to steady himself and it appeared to float into mid-air. "Your eyes have gone funny..." Dafydd clutched at a passing psychedelic straw. "Hey! Hey! I know who you are! You're Cei in the Mabinogion! You're Cei in the Mabinogion! You're Cei in the Mabinogion! And I'm King Arthur!"

"No you're not. Taff, listen to me. They say that anyone who eats too much of that stuff will ride the dragon for eternity, pursued by living nightmares, without ever finding what they seek."

"That's not funny." Dafydd paused. "Ramo. I can't feel my legs. You're not being serious are you?"

"Deadly. Let's get up the mountain before anyone comes."

Young Dafydd tried to follow Ramo then stopped dead. "Look at that big green tree in the window. In the Garden. In Avalon. In Eden. I can't tell whether I'm the tree out there looking in at me or whether I'm in here looking out at the tree."

"You're in here all right, but you're out of your head. We've got to get you up The Mountain. You'll be all right up on top, the world is big enough."

"But can't you see? I *am* The Mountain. You can climb me! Woooo!!" Dafydd broke down. "Oh Jesus I'm scared. What's happening? This isn't funny, Ramo. Make it stop Ramo, make it stop."

"I can't."

Mr Trolley came in in a Gloria Gaynor wig to investigate. "Thomas, I've been looking for you. Major Llewellyn-Jones needs you for assembly."

"You can't do that! Oh God I'm scared."

"I'm sorry?" said Trolley.

"What are you playing at? Acting like I am your creation to do with as you please. You are not God. Christ what's happening to me?"

Ramo was looking really worried now. "Taff, let's go."

Trolley went on: "The Head insists... What did you just say to me?"

"And who *says* it's not Christmas? It *is* Christmas. I've just said so. And do you know who I am? I am - the Great Bard. The Total Bard... Ramo, make it stop now. Please."

Troll stared. "Have you two boys been drinking?"

Dafydd considered whether this was a way out. "No that was someone else. It could have been if you want though. Yeah. Ok. It was us. Oh God. Oh God."

Ramo explained, rather unnecessarily, "He's not very well, Mr Trolley."

"You boys stay here. I'm going to get the Head. Right now. With any luck this will be the last time I have the pleasure of your unsettling company Thomas." He strode out.

Ramo grabbed Dafydd's arm. "Come on Taff."

"I don't understand this. I want to get off the Dragon. Get me off the Dragon please Ramo. I think I'm going mad." The thought struck him suddenly, like a missile "Go mad? Ha ha Yes! That's what I'll do. That's *it*. I'll go mad."

"Taff. Come on!! Trolley's gone to get the Head!"

Young Dafydd had a momentary vision of Major Llewellyn-Jones's severed head in Trolley's cormorant claws. Ramo grabbed his arm again. Dafydd roared, "Let go of my wings or I'll burn your scales off!!" Then he saw himself reflected in the window, not the god or angel he expected to see there, but just a pimply kid. "Who said that? Who said that? That's what a madman would say."

"It's the Dragon talking. Listen! They're coming back. Come on, follow me."

"I don't trust you."

"Neither do I but I'm all you've got, Taff. God, your eyes are as big as your head. The Head's bound to suss."

Young Dafydd covered his eyes in horror. He slowly lowered them again. "I want Megan."

"Ok," said Ramo, seizing his chance. "We'll go and look for her shall we, where all the heads hang out? Up The Mountain."

Ramo pointed. A dragon-red sun was sinking onto the dragon-green Earth, whole and perfect and beautiful. Ramo, hearing voices along the corridor, yelled, "Taff! if you don't want Trolley's tender Pastoral Care on your back, you've got to run. Now, Dafydd! Quick, Dafydd! Run. Run!" Ramo ran.

Dafydd stayed rooted to the spot. "I want Megan..."

2

Megan entered the staff-room, utterly fed up. She threw her books down and sat. Norman Welch came in complacently.

"Ah! There you are, Megan." She glared and he became less sure of himself. "You've, um, left your eighth years unattended."

"Quite possibly. Yes."

"I was looking for you in your room. Two of your year 11 lads have apparently taken some... *wheeze* is it?"

"*My* year eleven lads! When pray, did they become *my* year eleven lads?"

"Well, you are responsible for them."

"Am I? Since when?"

"Since they made you acting deputy head of year."

"Not good enough I'm afraid. You see, in these days of money-wealth and time-poverty, when they bestowed that extra title upon me for the princely sum of twenty-five extra pounds a month, they decided that because I was only acting deputy and not the real thing, they would only pretend to give some extra time to carry it out, but not really do so. I therefore decided that if I was that highly thought of, it was only right that I take on responsibilities commensurate with the time allowed. So, if you want some Year 11 lads sorting out, go and see Steve Riley - he's the one with all the free periods."

"I can't find him. Anyway, you know pastoral care is not his strong point."

"You mean because he's a man?"

"No. Because he's halfway round the twist. He hasn't even noticed that the kids have changed the title on his door from Pastoral Care to Past All Caring."

"You go and sort them out then. You're not doing anything."

"They're not my responsibility."

Norman paused, hoping that Megan would soften and he would not be forced to say what he did not want to say. But she took a Union magazine from her bag and started to read. Norman got increasingly uncomfortable.

"Megan. I – I don't know what to do."

3

'My Little Town' by Simon and Garfunkel was playing at full volume out of the sunlit shopfront of *Pantysycham Pants*. *Pantysycham Pants* was a new fashion shop for 'young persons' with a wild psychedelic frontage based on the Stars and Stripes. Its windows were filled with similarly striped bri-nylon 'loon' pants in heliotrope, powder blue, rainbow-pink and scarlet – tailored evidently for young men without genitals. Being Sunday, the shop was of course closed but this had little impact on the number of customers. The latest customer had left, without purchase, on the previous Friday. He was an American visitor in search of his roots up at Pen Marw colliery and ironworks (source of his "lit'l old town's first iron railway in the 1840s") who had dropped in for a casual "vest and pants". He needed them, he said, for a 'show' in Cardiff. Not what he really wanted to wear on holiday, naturally, but he needed to "please the ladies". After an awkward pause, he had been sent down on the bus to check out *Fanny's Foundations* in Trollbridge. ("A shop called *ass* – you're kiddin, me. Oh, that's the proprietor's name? It doesn't mean *ass* here in England. Wales. It means *what?*") Like the occasional attempt to provide the coalfield young with a disco - despite the inevitable closure through vandalism and violence - *Pantysycham Pants* would last about three weeks.

Young Megan waited at the bus stop for the bus to Oldport, looking at the manikin in the window. The manikin was also wearing crushed velevet hot pants and, like Megan, looked stunning, though not quite as stunning as Megan. Megan in fact looked and felt so beautiful, poised and potent that *anything* in the world seemed possible. It was the finest hour – though but an hour – of the valley girl. She felt as Boudicca might have felt during her brilliant triple triumph over the grey-souled concrete pedestrian Romans. She felt her hair falling onto her shoulders like sunshine. Then she looked at rings in the adjacent jewellers' window.

Ramo came by carrying a black Evangelical Bible, and wearing his Sunday best.

"Hiya sexy!" she hailed him. "Where have you been all my life?

"Hello Megan." Ramo raised his hand. " Jesus!"

"Pardon?"

Ramo raised his hand again. "I said, 'Jesus!'"

"That's what I thought you said. Why are you dressed like that? You look like you're going to church."

"Chapel."

"Chapel? You've never been inside a Chapel in your life."

"That's right. Until I discovered what a sinner I was."

"This has got to be a joke."

"No Megan. My life has been a joke. But now, thanks to the Lord and The Rev Canon, I am saved. You ought to come along to the meeting after the sermon. Lots of the other girls do."

She put her hand on her hip. "I think I'm a bit too naughty for the Lord."

"No you're not Megan. No one is."

"What do you do?"

"We confess to the group and to God what we used to do before."

"What! Say all that! In front of other people?" She looked aghast. "You haven't told them about us have you?"

"Yes."

"*All* of it?"

"Yes. But don't worry. We hear far worse. Even Dildo Dora's been in lately."

"No!"

"But I've done much worse that that Megan."

"*Worse?* Like what?"

" There's a whole gang of us who have confessed in front of the Lord that we used to do... drugs. I was miserable Megan. Pathetic. I just couldn't stop."

"And what on earth does the Lord have to say about that?"

"Why not come and find out for yourself?"

"I've got a date." An old protective instinct made her add, "No one you know."

"It's not like you think, Megan. You'd really enjoy it after a while. Maybe you could even Join."

"Join what?"

"Spreading the word to other young sinners."

"And wash my minxy linen in public? No thank you."

Ramo seized her arm. "Megan! Listen to me. You are lost. I can save you."

Megan shrugged him off. "Have you heard the joke about the Welshman marooned on a desert island, Ramo? He built two chapels. When they came to rescue him they asked him why."

"Why?"

"He said, 'That's the one I go to, and that's the one I *don't* go to.'" She laughed.

"I don't get it."

Young Megan sighed. "I got sick of you beating up other boys Ramo, but I think I prefer even that to Bible bashing. If it lasts, and keeps you off drugs, then I'm pleased. But don't try and get me on it. Find someone else to save. Here's my bus." She jumped on.

Ramo chased after her, alarmed for her soul in the Gomorrah of Oldport on a Sunday night. "Megan! *In that day the Lord with his sore and great and strong sword shall punish leviathan the piercing serpent, even leviathan that crooked serpent; and he shall slay the dragon that is in the sea.* Isaiah chapter 27 verse1. Megan. MEGAN!"

The bus sped out of sight down valley. Nothing remained but the smoke of a thousand chimneys. Ramo turned away and thumped the Book in frustration. Another pleasant valley Sunday.

Chapter Three

Tommy

I was a lonely teenage rocking buck
With a pink carnation and a pick up truck
But I knew that I was out of luck
The day
The music
Died

1

Angharad tapped her feet impatiently. "Are you the boy who's in detention with Mr Thomas? Tommy Jones?"

Tommy nodded.

"Right come with me."

"Miss, can I be excused this detto until Monday? I have to meet somebody."

"You should have thought of that before you got yourself a detention. Who - whom have you to meet?"

"Myfanwy Madoc."

"I don't think Mr Thomas would allow that. Come on, I haven't got all day."

"But Miss, this is important. It's - about the play. Myfanwy will wonder where I am."

"I won't ask you again."

"I can't, Miss."

A silent power struggle occurred, which neither could afford to lose.

The tension was broken at last by Tommy leading into the classroom, exhaling a Napoleonic sigh of defeat. He slammed into a seat.

Angharad ignored the affront, magnaminous in victory. "Thank you, Tommy. Take this down, please. 'I must refrain from the regurgitant activity of the bovine quadruped.' Fifty times." She made a face. "What on earth have you been doing?"

Tommy wrote feverishly, watching out through the window for Myfanwy. "Can I just get on with it, Miss?"

Angharad watched him for a few minutes. "How many have you done?"

"Ten."

"I'm too soft-hearted see? Behind every incompetent man is a competent woman on a fifth of his salary. I do his detention while he sails upstairs to get himself promoted! Tell me honestly, who-whom do you think makes the school tick? I don't mean whom does all the glory boy stuff at the top end and in the Press. Whom actually keeps the wheels turning?"

Another boy approached Myfanwy.

"Twenty. I dunno. The secretaries?"

Myfanwy and the other boy started talking.

"Exactly. The sec…. No! Not the secretaries - female members of st- "

"Miss can I go now?"

"How many have you done?"

Tommy became frantic, "Twenty-four."

"Have you learned your lesson?"

"Yes Miss!"

"What is it?"

Tommy was distracted by Myfanwy moving away with the other boy. "Uh, ...behind every incompetent man is a competent woman on a fifth of his salary."

Angharad swooped up the page. "What! What have you written that for?"

Tommy watched Myfanwy go and the tension went out of him. "I don't know. It doesn't matter now anyway."

The bell rang.

Angharad read his lines. "You had me going for a minute there. Go on, you'll be late for Non-Literary Texts."

"It's Non-Litera*cy* Texts."

"Only because of a typing error in the office. Go on. I'll let you off the rest."

Tommy pushed his face into hers. "I can do better... I can do better ... I must try harder ... Only fair progress made ... Too easily distracted..."

Angharad was shaken. "What?"

"I really do agree with all that stuff about women, Miss. And I know I shouldn't have been chewing in the corridor. But between you, you and Old Taff have just wrecked the only real crack I was ever going to get at Myfanwy Madoc. Excuse me."

"Tommy Jones! Come back at once! Tommy! Come back here! Tommy. TOMMY!... You've forgotten your lines!"

2

Old Dafydd was in the Interview waiting room in a dark suit, running through his answers.

"How do I see the role of a Headteacher in a modern High school? Well if I could split that question into seventeen parts, Mr Carmichael Hunt ... If I could split that question into seventeen parts..." Dafydd became whimsical. "If I could just get over the fact for a moment that you are a surreally bearded four foot dwarf wearing pixie shoes and a pair of 12 year old boy's trousers, and remove all words connected with brevity, downsizing or the prefix 'mini' from my interview vocabulary..." He glanced at his briefing paper. "A Headteacher must, in short, have a vision for the school. A short Headteacher must. A Headteacher must brief his deputies to *lead* while getting on with their subordinates as well as possible. He must, however, not be afraid to give short shrift to his detractors where necessa... Oh it's hopeless."

Young Dafydd stood watching Old Dafydd ramble on.

"A Headteacher must make draconian decisions that unite a blood-hungry staff against him... A Headteacher must organise work-socials like an army officer issuing orders to 'volunteers'. ("You will enjoy yourselves.") A Headteacher must remember that class sizes should be as high and staff salaries as low as possible. A Headteacher must attempt to cram every moment of every day with as many good *intentions* as possible, even if (1.a) they diametrically contradict each other and (1.b) nothing of consequence ever actually gets *done* and (1.c-500.z inclusive) they continuously enter the school for a Guinness Book of Records attempt on List Futility, Laser Bullet Suicide and White Collar Slavery. A Headteacher must remember that the percentage of GCSE exam grade passes at A to C takes precedence over exciting, life-changing but otherwise non-exam grade enhancing lessons, school play performances or extra-curricular activities. A Headteacher must present to his school a clear and lucid understanding of National Curriculum Attainment Targets and all the subsequent recommendations, revisions, denials and reversals of the same. A Headteacher must begin each and every sentence with 'A Headteacher must' in the hope that the Governors at least will be fooled by a flashy display of Welsh rhetoric. To conceal the complete lack of cogency underneath."

Dafydd addressed a noble bust of Major Llewellyn-Jones, that outdated hero who had taken the school from a pre-war Mining and Technical Institute to a post-war cutting edge bilateral Grammar-Technical school. "But sadly, old boyo, this is not the Eisteddfod, and the prize is not a temporary Bardship but a job I am totally unsuited for. The Governors are in the bag anyway. Except that ancient hill farmer you probably taught who still thinks that wisdom and self-knowledge are in some way related to teaching. I

274

don't suppose he'll last long in Education." Dafydd paused. "If I could split that question into seventeen parts, Mr Carmichael Hunt..."

Young Taff stepped forward.

Old Taff shied like a Beatnik confronted with the coloured cover of Leonard Cohen's 'New Skin For The Old Ceremony' after wall-to-wall monochrome in the previous three albums. "What are you doing here?"

"I wanted to ask you about University- "

"Look, I know I forgot to mention Leonard Cohen in the Assembly – I got distracted by the Major being late - and I know he said some terrible things but he was just doing his bit for the old school tie in the post-education era. I...Sorry, did you say University?"

"Yes. Look. Maybe I was a bit hard on you before. About being no different whether it's Trolley or you. I do appreciate the semi-personal approach. At least you try."

"You were no harder on me than I deserved. You made your points. They were sharp ones and they hurt. But, despite being a teacher, and despite wondering from moment to moment whether I believe in a single thing this institution stands for, I am still a human being and I really do have your best interests at heart. Yes, it's easy to romanticise teenage angst. It's also easy to forget how much of it I have to soak up as part of the daily grind. Believe it or not, there is more to Old Taff here than your image of me throwing fish into your piranha pool. I'm in there with you, son, five hours a day and I have the fang marks to prove it. It might be difficult to believe when you look at me but I still see myself in you. I got stuck there and I never really moved on." Old Dafydd paused. "Look this really isn't a good time. I'm trying to swot up for an interview."

"It won't take a moment. I just wondered whether University will turn out to be all it's cracked up to be."

"University is like that walk of ours up the mountain. Up past the hilltop semis and terraces and then onto the country lane and up the old pit railway with the disused signal building full of sheep-shit. Up the higher slopes to the moors. Then the highest peak of all with nothing but thin air all around you. You see everything in perspective – through the breaks in the mist – in a way you've never seen before or will again. But you're too high and too far away to do anything with it. In the end you have to come down again. I don't go up anymore. It's too lonely."

"But if someone were with you. If she were with you...."

"Waiting for me? By the Druidstone of the Ancients. Mine for a Bardic song? Listen. Before much longer you'll be coming back here to confront me with your undergraduate uniform of student scruff and when I say 'Have you found her yet?' you'll suck in your pale undernourished cheeks and your drippy Celtic moustache and say it's a betrayal of The Struggle to go out with women who aren't in the Communist party. After which you'll doubtless take on capitalism by selling The Big Issue, the Standard Issue, the Extra-Large Issue with and/or without cream and all the other 'choices' that issue out of gutters to demand the spare change of our inflated salary-slavery. Now, I really must- "

"So what am I going for?"

"What am I going to this interview for?"

Young Dafydd started to shout, "You're the teacher! You tell me!

3

The end-of-school bell went apeshit, releasing a thousand souls from their misery. The corridors flooded with homeward bounders. Myfanwy and Tommy's courses crossed.

"So what happened to you at break?" snapped Myfanwy.

Tommy snapped back. "I changed my mind."

"Listen, creep. No one stands me up. Least of all you."

"I just did."

Dafydd entered the corridor en route to bus duty, going over his lines silently. Myfanwy and Tommy's argument drew his attention. He stopped and stared.

Myfanwy was getting crosser. "Really? As a matter of fact I didn't even go. I went to the shop with someone else."

Tommy forced the chewing gum back into her hand. "That's your chewing gum back. I hope you choke on it."

"It wasn't even mine. I found it under the desk."

"Slut."

"Loser."

They glared at each other. Dafydd approached them.

"Hello you two. Have you forgotten there's a noise exclusion zone around here this afternoon?"

"What's it for Sir?" asked Myfanwy.

"Sshh. Keep your voice down. Interviews. Headship. Me or Mr Welch as it happens. What's going on between you two? You were yelling at each other like an old married couple."

There was a difficult silence.

"He stood me up."

"I didn't. I wanted to be there, but I had a detention. With *you*, Sir. Remember?"

"Don't start again. Why don't you walk each other home? Look, I can't be getting involved in all this. I've got a future to sort out in a minute."

Tommy and Myfanwy moved away, exchanging a nod as they went. They looked back. Myfanwy called. "Good luck Sir!"

Dafydd went off to bus duty, once again engrossed in his lines.

"He's got about as much chance of getting that job as a space-ship has of landing on Mars."

"There's already been a space ship on Mars, Tommy. And at least he's better than Welch. Why didn't you tell me you had a detention?"

"You didn't really give me chance."

"The thing is, though," she paused awkwardly. " I don't really want to go out with you...I'd just like to have you as a friend. To talk to. We are friends aren't we?"

"What you mean is, I'm all right to have around to listen to you talking about other boys. But you don't fancy me."

"It's not like that."

"Do you fancy me?"

"You're very nice."

"Do you fancy me?"

"You've got … You're not bad looking. Really."

"Do you fancy me?"

"What do you want me to say?"

"I want you to say 'Yes, I fancy you'. I want you to tell me that I drive you crazy, that you can't stop thinking about me."

"Tommy, you're gorgeous. You're Gavin Henson. You've got the best legs in the tenth year. I dream about them in gold and scarlet. Will that do?"

"No it will not. You don't mean it."

"I mean it - when I say you're a great friend."

"I don't just want to be your friend. I want a girlfriend. I want you."

"You do now, but in six weeks time you'll be bored, looking around for the next beauty that comes along, a new peak to conquer. I know, believe me. I'll just be a photo tucked away at the bottom of a drawer with 'first love' scrawled on the back."

"You won't. Honestly. Just give me a chance. Please!"

"You fall in love too easily."

"No I don't. I've never felt like this before. This is the real thing."

"I'm sick of the real thing Tommy. I want someone to talk to."

"I'll get a better haircut. I'll get a leather jacket. Anything. Just don't say 'No'."

Myfanwy turned away. There was nothing to say because 'No' was the only thing she wanted to say. She sucked the bridge in her mouth absently.

"Maybe you're right."

"I know I'm right Tommy."

"Tina was everything until we met you and Rhys in the park that night."

"I've finished with Rhys."

"Where is he anyway?"

"Looking for me I expect."

Tommy picked up his bag and looked round fearfully.

"Don't worry we're not doing anything wrong."

"Tina's told him to kick my head in."

"She misses you."

"I want to get out of this dump, Myfanwy. Tina's idea of a classy night out is a trip to the chip shop, a walk round the block and a grope in the bus shelter on the way home. I just thought you could do a bit better than Rhys, that's all."

Silence

Myfanwy shrugged. "I'd best be going. I told Tina I'd go round her house tonight to start revising for those new tests. Shall I tell her you'll text her?"

Silence. Tommy looked up at a high window spilling with sunlight.

"This would have happened anyway Tommy."

"What would?"

"Even if we had spent the next six weeks proclaiming our undying love for each other, it still would have ended like this. Sooner or later. Probably sooner. Nothing lasts, Tommy."

He adopted a tragic look that he hoped would appeal to her maternal side and stop her leaving. Her mobile phone peeped. She left.

Tommy watched her walk away. How exciting she looked in that shaft of sunlight. Too good, alas, for this world. He shouted, "What new tests?" but she didn't hear him. Someone tapped him on the shoulder and he turned round, expecting Old Taff again. He opened his mouth to protest. His adam's apple disappeared.

It was Rhys.

4

Myfanwy's father, Evan Madoc, was in a swanky new bar in Cardiff.

"Myfanwy! Can you hear me?"

"Loud and clear, Dadboss. Cool music."

"Oh, that's music is it? I thought it was some spoilt doggerel-yelling brat who needs a good hiding."

Myfanwy laughed. "Where are you?"

"Uh- *The Beer Chest*. I needed to wind down after the interview and it was supposed to be within staggering distance. But the locals kept directing me to BHS instead. I think it's the Cardiff accent."

"How did it go?"

He took a sip of the large glass of icy white liquid that the ultra cool and ultra-pimply teenaged barman had placed before him and wondered if he was speaking too loudly into the mobile phone as several heads turned to look. He lowered his voice. "I think I got the job. They'll confirm in writing next week."

"So it's all basically kicking off. Mental!"

"Yeah? Hope so." He lowered his voice again as heads were still staring at him - in apparent astonished amusement. He sipped nervously at his drink. "Could you tell Mum when you get home? Only her mobile seems to be turned off."

"Why don't you text her?"

"I can't send texts on this phone." More heads turned in amusement. He took another sip, affecting the stylish boredom that seemed to be *de rigeur* in here and noticing absently that for all its posh glass and serviette on a tray, the drink was a bitter, taste-less fizz. More like sparkling iced water. If this was New Wine, they could keep it.

"Yes you can! All you do is- "

"I can't. Not now."

"I can teach you."

"I'm too old to learn. Look – can you just tell her for me."

Myfanwy laughed. "All right. So what's it like in Cardiff?"

"It's changed a lot. There's lots of new wine bars and stuff – like this one." He said this rather proudly. He had asked for beer to begin with but the barman hadn't known it under that name, so Evan had opted for a very expensive glass of house white, appar-ently only available in a very expensive giant glass. He took an-other wincing sip, lowering his voice still further. "Mind you, there's plenty of the old Cardiff here too. Last night as I was walking down Duke St back to the hotel, there was a man relieving himself in the middle of the main road."

"Really?" Myfanwy didn't appear to be as shocked as she should be. Mr Madoc had been shocked to his core.

"And then I got propositioned by a prostitute!"

"There you are, Dad. You may be fifty nine but you can still pull the birds."

"I'm forty two! I've always said that Italy is the only place in the world where just sitting down at a table makes a person look cool. But maybe your mother and I can do it in Cardiff now as well."

Myfanwy's voice became slightly anxious. "Did you get your hair cut before the interview?"

"Oh yes. A girl from Mutt-Town Dressed As Lamé snipped at a couple of strands for fifteen minutes and then charged me twenty nine pounds."

"That's probably what attracted the prossy. Was it worth it?"

"Myfanwy I would never- !"

"The haircut, I mean!"

"I can't tell any difference. But the latte and lifestyle advice was probably better value than anywhere else in Card- ."

"Sir?" The barman interrupted.

"Sorry am I talking too loud?"

"No – but you're drinking the glass coolant. I need to pour your Sauvignon Blanc."

5

Dafydd was back walking with his father at St Fagan's on a blistering hot day the previous summer. They'd been there an hour or so. Now they were crossing a replica of a nineteenth-century Welsh village, every building and every lump of heritage coal brought faithfully from the 'real' Wales outside. The authenticity was undeniable, it was a work of genius and imagination rivalling the Victorian period it commemorated. But Dafydd was frowning.

"I don't like it, Dad. It feels wrong."

Redundant Ifor was worried his Day Out had failed and he was desperate to have a function these days. "What d'you mean? Nothing's wrong. They've even put the Lloegrbach Working Men's Clwb over there complete with library, social club and theatre, brick for brick, just like it is in Loger."

"But that's what I mean. Why isn't it in Lloegrbach? Why aren't the workmen in Lloegrbach using it?"

Ifor made a face. "They only ever used the bar anyway."

"Well, why aren't they using it now?"

"You know why. There aren't any workers left. Don't you remember that ice-cream round I tried to get going after I got made redundant and the mafia had threatened me out of Oldport? You were there with me. I sold about six cones all morning and when we knocked off for a bite: the café was Closed for Lunch. There's no point the Clwb being in Lloegrbach any more. Never mind that now. Look how realistic this village is. Victorian tea-room, Edwardian post-office. This is really how it was."

"But can't we do anything better than conduct tours of what we used do? The country's a living bloody museum."

Ifor looked glum. Dafydd changed the subject. "Let's check out the Photograph Emporium." He smiled reassuringly at his father as they posed for the photo until told by the leggy modern photographer that "they didn't smile though, the Victorians." Dafydd instantly adopted a grave expression next to his father's false-whiskered one.

But he continued to brood. Other 'spots of time' had imposed their different realities during the visit. The eighteenth-century gentry dwelling, for instance, with its mountain ash and walls painted red against evil spirits: the one a lilting West Walian visitor described with obscure Celtic logic as "quite a big house for a small cottage". But the reality faded as soon as he and Ifor passed on to another, or back to the burger-and-chips present. Even the Pentref Celtaid – the Celtic village – enormously powerful in its appeal to Dafydd's root identity – took its place as a redundant past as soon as he moved on to something else. But this reproduced Nineteenth Century seemed more present than the 'real' post-60s twentieth-century toy Wales outside, all industry-light processing, tourist or information technology units that used to be pitheads and steelworks. He noticed how handsome and striking his father looked in the Victorian hat and greatcoat compared to the emasculated scruff he appeared in his ex-worker's sports clothes and baseball cap - and decided that this too was evidence that the great days were over. But Ifor was nudging him to look at the women being prepared next to them, climbing into the suffocating layers of Victorian femininity. Short-skirted modern girls, whose attire would have shamed a prostitute then, transformed into starchy Victorian frights.

"Don't fancy yours much," laughed Ifor.

But Dafydd was lost in his gloomy thoughts. Travellers on the very edges of science, constitutional progress and belief, though, the women then. This was when Wales *was*. Maybe everywhere has its moment – and stays there. Norwich essentially still in the Middle Ages; Bristol in the eighteenth century; the North of England in the industrial revolution, like Wales. This living museum *is* the real Wales....

"Come and see this," urged Ifor. "Dafydd?"

Dafydd came back to the 'present.' It was a row of two up, two down houses furnished as they would have been in 1800, 1850, 1914, present day. Ifor enthused. "Look. It ends with *now*, IMF furniture, DVDs, computers. It makes you feel part of history."

"That's the trouble, " muttered Dafydd. "I want to feel part of the present."

He went and sat in the cockpit, a beautifully crafted miniature stone theatre devoted to the destruction of one cock by another, and the money that could be lost or won on the bloody result. Three boys were running around around the tiers of spectator terrace, a mother calling to them in mountain-stream clear North Walian English. "The only one behaving himself is Dafydd!" she concluded, startling Dafydd with the correct pronounciation of the second syllable of his name for once. He looked to see which boy was his namesake and noticed that the other two were giving the praised one a Criccieth wave – one finger - and a mimed thumping behind their mother's back.

A sudden shock and yet somehow not a surprise: Norman Welch, then a thrusting new appointment, came in, sneering at something on the wall. Their eyes met across the pit.

"Hello, Dafydd. Here with the Retired Gents?"

"No that's the *toiletdau* you left your personality on," Dafydd riposted wearily, then nodded towards Ifor through the doorway. "I'm here with my father."

"I thought that was your brother, poor sod. He looks younger than you."

"Maybe that's because he doesn't have to work with you, Norman." Dafydd looked at the woman Norman was with and waited to be introduced but Welch ignored her and, presumably bored with the banter, she drifted off.

"Your partner?"

"Not really."

"Very chivalrous."

Norman shrugged with all the complacent arrogance of the spoilt male brat. Dafydd was all for the unstinting charity of maternal affection – he could have done with a bit more of it himself – but some mothers needed to offer their sons a bit less unconditional love and a bit more stinging criticism, he thought.

"I don't hear her complain. Not much of a set-up here is it?"

"It's probably the best Living Museum in the world!" snapped Dafydd. He nearly added "next to Llamidia" but decided even the pretentious end of Llansoroti New Town couldn't be held responsible for Norman Welch. "And I'm not saying you're an anal retentive, up-your-own-arse twat or anything but you do realise that organ between your girlfriend's legs is different from your own anus don't you?"

"You calling me gay?" Norman really didn't know.

"No, that might mean you loved a man other than yourself, Norman. I'm calling you anal, you anus."

Well that was mature, thought Dafydd to himself. He cringed at his own flash of temper. He wanted to go and had seen enough of the cockpit anyway but now felt he couldn't surrender the position to his adversary. It was ridiculous. He had already been through the baptism of coalfield manhood, learning the faith partly in the school playground, partly at the hands of his oil-grained tattoo-bruised father, partly in the romantic pages of Cordell's "The Rape of the Fair Country", and all so long ago that it felt like another life. There was no need to go through it again. Yet here he still was, middle-aged, middle-class, Middle Welsh, educated, a deputy head, clenching his fists like some crude Celtic warrior, every sinew strained for death.

"Excuse me, Dafydd. I'm trying to get by."

Dafydd stayed put. As boys, they would have pushed each other around a bit now and then brawled ineffectually until someone landed a decisive punch. And then – maybe – things would have settled down. But if he swung his fist at that sneering face now – and he certainly wanted to – his career would be the immediate and permanent loser. The New Welsh Male had somehow become the hero of its own defeat. Maybe it was never as simple as that anyway, even for boys, but the urgent satisfaction of punching the smooth superiority off Welch's face now was certainly no real solution. And yet what was the alternative – let this interloper walk all over him?

They were interrupted unexpectedly by a larger-than-life figure in a denim jacket. Dafydd did a double-take. "Ramo?" He couldn't believe it.

"Taff! Howbe butt!"

So there *are* ghosts! "How you doing?"

"Cool. Just back from Spain."

"Working?" Dafydd bit his lip. Were they far enough away from the wilderness years when this would have been a tactless question in a coalfield?

"Working? Aye!" said Ramo. A sly smile. " A bit of this, a bit of that." He offered Dafydd a King Size, raised his eyebrows at the refusal, then lit one himself. He glanced at Welch without interest. "Three months working every hour God sends, then a month on the Costa del Sol doing sod all in the sun. Paradise. Teaching en you?" Ramo's deep voice was unexpectedly pleasant, nothing like the hectoring bully Dafydd remembered.

"Yeah."

"Married?"

"Divorced. You?"

"Separated," said Ramo, inhaling sharply. "Remember Trish?"

"I certainly do."

"She wants a divorce so that she can marry John Masters. I 'ope to Christ she doesn't insist on another double-barrelled married name like she did with me."

"Why not?"

"Trish *Bates*." Ramo waited for the penny to drop.

"She wouldn't!"

"She bloody well would. Masters-Bates. Can you imagine the stick their poor bastards would get at school?"

It wouldn't be the first – or even the most – tactless name given out, Dafydd knew that. In a novel no-one would believe parents could be so stupid but he really *had* once taught a (very plump) little girl named Fatima Bastard. And only today he'd received an application from a seaside town pupil named Sandy Beech. He'd probably find out that the parents were called Naturist and Private. He'd probably find out that the three Chelsies (of variant spellings) he taught in one Year Eleven class would all have changed their names to Manchester United by five pm on Saturday. He told Ramo all this knowing Ramo would think he was making it up. But truth really was stranger than fiction. The truant officer really did have a son in the school with the worst attendance record in any year group. The Lost property room key really had been lost along with the whereabouts of the room. And the Careers Teacher really had never done anything else except teach in this same school, the school he had himself attended. You couldn't ever put all this in a novel because real school life kept suspending your belief.

The two old antagonists laughed then eyed each other uneasily. Both he and Ramo were a lot bigger than their teenage-sylph selves, but Ramo was a giant. He was evidently no longer working for The God-Botherers and his wine-eyed machismo and big biceps under the black T-shirt were a subtle threat – a return to the fray - that Dafydd couldn't help measuring against his own, and made him reluctant to mention Megan.

Ramo nudged Dafydd in the ribs, damn near breaking them. "Seeing anyone?"

"Na. What do I want another ring through my nose for?"

Ramo growled approval at this. "Listen Taff, some dozy beggar's parked his rust bucket without the handbrake on properly and it's got wedged under my boot. Give us a hand out would you?"

Dafydd felt absurdly flattered by this Real Man request and also now able to leave the cockpit to Welch without dishonour. Welch had somehow been made redundant by Ramo anyway – his waspish ironies emasculated and laughable. It would be even more wonderful if the car concerned should turn out to be Welch's tight-arsed little Merc.

When they got to the 'Parc Cerbyd', of course, it was Dafydd's Lada.

The two men lifted Ramo's glossy car free of Dafydd's rusty one. Dafydd was brick-red with embarrassment, praying that Ramo wouldn't find out it was his car, and to make matters worse Ramo junior, a pupil, in his Washington redskins cap and a Coca Cola T-shirt, was eyeing him coldly from the back seat. It was a good moment, though, the cheerful sharing of a task and its results. The up-side of machismo.

"No damage," grinned Ramo.

"Ramo, it's my car."

"I wasn't going to mention it if you didn't. Get that bloody handbrake sorted. See ya!"

They could have been brothers. Maybe they should have been. Ramo drove off in his futuristic chariot past the nineteenth-century museum and with Ramo Junior moodily fiddling with his laptop in the back. Who was the better role model for the lad after all, Dafydd wondered: himself, the successful academic with a dodgy handbrake, or his heavy ex-industrial (neo?) male (post?)

working-class hero dad? That Old Grammar School propaganda needed some interrogation, maybe. It certainly gave Dafydd a windfall of unconstrained satisfaction to see Ramo accelerating past Norman Welch on the way out.

A busload of baseball-capped North Walians came by now talking excitedly in Welsh. Their monolingual destination board read CAERDYDD. Ifor mistook them for foreigners. It got a bit wearing to his Welsh-less ears, all the impenetrable sing-song. Dafydd decided that in a way they *were* foreigners here, though foreigners of time rather than place. Dafydd's Wales was the nineteenth-century coalfield kind, the world-shaping heavy metal valleys. Now instead of that rust-red South East Wales – which this lot would doubtless call English Wales (whereas everyone knew that was Tenby)- here on a day's holiday from the north was 'real' Green Welly Wales, Picture Postcard Wales, Starchy Teatowel Wales, Witch's Hat Wales: in short, 'Welsh' Wales. Who says? Dafydd imagined a middle-class and relatively-claused conversation about holidays. 'Oh we're going to *German* Germany this year, which everyone knows is so much more real than *French* France nowadays, which was nice. How about you?' 'Oh we thought we'd try *English* England.' Which would of course be somewhere like Leamington Spa or Kirkby Lonsdale, rather than the England most English people actually lived in, which was nice. It was like that Aussie he'd met on a course at the Gordon Knott Insititute. "You mike your own luck, mite" the Aussie had chirped when Dafydd had, he thought neutrally, suggested that some Australian sports team had had the rub of the green against England. Then he saw his name-tag. "Norman English."

"Crikey, cobber, your mother must have hated you."

"Norms are different down under," glowered Norm.

He must send Norman a tea towel "With Sympathy from Wales - the first, oldest and most shoulder-chipped English colony of all."

But now he noticed that some of these shoulder-chipped *Welsh* Walians today were speaking *English*, albeit an English that had the cadences and grammatical structures of mother-tongue Welsh. It just sounded like Welsh.

"Is it possible to 'ave a little bit more milk, please?" moaned one such voice in the Heritage café later. The national anthem of self-pity.

"Oh for God's sake," fumed Dafydd at them. "Stop bleating like a sheep and *demand* some decent service."

The entire café looked at him. Even Ifor wanted an explanation of his mouthburst.

"You mike your own luck, mite!" he roared.

Chapter Four

The Interview

May you build a ladder to the stars
And climb on every rung
And may you stay...
Forever young.

1

Outside the interview room, Dafydd was going through his lines. Inside, Head of Staff Surveillance Mike Crowsoft, (staff nickname Jabba the Hutt), was typing in his password (Jabba The Hutt) on the school's intranet. He then went through Dafydd's recent internet history with the interview panel.

Dafydd had returned to Oval Balls Up, the official website of Trollbridge Rugby Club, fifty-three times yesterday, like the Biblical dog to its vomit. There had been no appreciable impact on Trolbridge's trademark result – a heavy home defeat - later that evening. There was a repeat visit to the complaints section of Interflora, presumably a dispute over Mother's Day Flowers, followed by further visits to Oval Balls Up and the online sports pages of South Wales newspapers including the *Trollbridge Morning News* and the *Cwmcysgodionmarw Argus*. There was a hit on a discipline link that the panel was at first reluctant to attribute to Dafydd's search for a coherent sanctions and rewards policy for the school on www.educational discipline.com rather than to any wish for the attentions of Miss Whiplash. One member of the panel took down Miss Whiplash's contact details and promised to investigate further though. There was a despairing hit on a Modern Foreign Languages Situations Wanted chatroom searching for keen young newly qualified modern foreign languages teachers who turned out to be old, expensive or blacklisted staff who had lost the will to teach but still wanted to paid for it...

There followed a dozen hits on Weekend Escape Travel sites, a single hit on the site devoted to St Jude, the patron saint of Lost Causes, several hits on religious sites – presumably for assemblies - and then a prolonged visit to marksandspencers.com, where Dafydd had an account, for extensive clothes and food shopping, the shopping trolley of which Dafydd had painstakingly got all the way into the electronic checkout and all of which he then presumably lost in a frantic and timed out search for his credit card at the key moment. The entire process was then repeated, though restricted to basic groceries and with errors evidently caused by fury and food-deprivation, and ultimately brought to a conclusion partially resembling the original trolley.

Temporary Internet Files then recorded a full hour spent by Dafydd gazing at pages of beautifully proportioned men standing in sculpted briefs. The interview panel agreed in the end that it was related to Dafydd's subsequent credit card purchase of a triple pack of STRETCH AUTHENTIC HIPSTERS (BUY ONE, GET ONE FREE.)

What had happened to *Marks and Spencer*, the foundation and fabric of British life? the panel wondered, shifting wistfully in their Y fronts and old lady slips. Alas, what had happened to us all?

Dafydd had then spent over four minutes on a screen showing a beautiful model in an M&S bathing costume. The Dyslexia governor said she didn't realise you could get S&M swimwear and how much did it cost? Carmichael Hunt said the bathing lady looked suspiciously like the school's Head of English. In fact, on reflection, she *was* the school's Head of English! Everyone crowded round the computer, and Trolley even put on his blurred and cracked spectacles to check. (He normally averted his eyes from computer screens). "If it is Megan Morgan, he said, she'll never work in this town again." He studied the picture at close range and then took off his spectacles, disappointed. "No – it's like her but it's not," he said. "I'd know that cheeky young madam, anywhere."

After four minutes with the Megan lookalike, Dafydd made various online purchases of classic early 1970s vinyl albums and then a sustained use of the Radio 2 Listen Again facility, mainly the post 10 pm stuff he was evidently unable to stay awake for these days.

More visits to Oval Balls Up followed and then a long list of Geography websites that had the interval panel longing for the sight of drying paint.

Dafydd's visit to the Personal Development Website (soon to be the Citizenship Website, formerly Values, formerly Religious Instruction) was standard county training for the delivery of Personal Development. Its hideous full frontal pictures of sexual organs devoured by warts, self/other-abuse and disease passed without comment. After all, PD (like the media) was supposed to make life out to be even less innocent, and even more corrupt and debauched than it actually was.

The Personal Development Curriculum, being of least interest or examination-value to pupils and staff, was the one that the Governors were most interested in. "Alcohol Awareness! Splendid! " exclaimed the Science Governor, leafing through the Personal Development Syllabus. "It's about time State school pupils were taught to appreciate fine wines." Then he read the actual lesson content – it began with a fifteen minute video showing how *particularly* repulsive and yet how vulnerable to sexual tragedy a drunken woman is.

"Economic Awareness!" exclaimed the retired bank manager who was the Maths link governor. "Excellent! Give the chap who thought that up an OBE!"

"Other Buggers' Efforts!" barked the Literacy Governor, otherwise known by the English Department as The Bed and Breakfast Star in honour of her 'Valley View' Hotel business. She proudly announced at every English department meeting that she'd "never read a book in her life."

"Economic Awareness!" spat a teacher governor whose theatrical manner and cavalier apparel proclaimed a drama teacher. "I'll be expected to put on 'A Midsummer Night's Economic Awareness' as the school play next!"

"*I* put it on in 1951," snapped Trolley. "It was the best school play we ever had. Simpkins revived it, with partial success, in 1983"

Dafydd had finished his day with thirty-six official school emails which Mike Crowsoft insisted on reading out verbatim followed by another quick survey of Oval Balls Up (three visits) and the sports pages of the national press, again without any posthumous influence on the Trollbridge RFC result.

Jabba The Hutt had discovered how to access colleagues' internet use as a result of some hacking into the school's hard disks by gifted sixth formers. These sixth formers (now banned) would have been much cheaper and more effective in charge of the school's ICT systems than Crowsoft, but no-one ever said so. (The draft of the previous Inspection Report had mentioned "A hideous, complacent brass-necked slug of a person who has clearly sat on a salary for decades evading accountability by slithering off into new 'job' descriptions every couple of minutes," but this had been redrafted for the official version - by the only employee then able to use the software – Jabba- as follows: 'A committed and versatile professional who has mastered every post in the school before moving on to others.' In his present new capacity as Head of Staff Surveillance, Jabba concluded with some satisfaction that, *apart* from the absence of hard-core porn, Dafydd's internet history seemed normal usage for a male member of Mountain High staff.

"Thank you, Crowsoft," said a rather tight-lipped Major. Shall we continue?...

In her tidy classroom on the storey below, soothed by Radio 2 playing very quietly, Megan was clearing out her filing cabinet. She would have died rather than listen to Radio 2 in the afternoon fifteen to twenty years ago but as it now seemed to be a retrospective Radio1 playlist with a beard, she told herself it didn't matter.

It did though. 'Who Are You?' by the Who came on, asking the ultimate question, and her spirits soared, but turned out after ten seconds to be merely the jingle to introduce 'The Mystery Voice'. "What a great question!" enthused the presenter shortly afterwards, and again Megan was appalled to find out that the Great Question was a 'factoid' about the only country in the world to begin with the letter 'Q' (Quatar). She realised that Radio 2 wasn't always like this but she missed the edge there had been when the radio played your songs when those songs – and even the trivia – were *Now*.

It would have been all right if the Ministry of Education didn't make her feel equally redundant at a time when surely she was at her peak and should have been leading the march of learning, rather than resisting its trivialisation. She unearthed some notes she'd made a couple of years ago during The Cultural Revolution Course Unit No. 26 ("How To Run A Department" (naturally, she'd added an 'i' after the 'u' in 'run'):

Where's the fun?

Where's the self-deprecating wonder?

Where's the stuff you said was gospel last time

And have only left out because teachers said No?

Where are the writers and readers, tomorrow and today?

Where are the pimple-real teenagers

Being taught by real nervous-breakdown adults

Who might, after twenty years, actually have some ideas of their own?

Oh yes and - where's the door?

She binned the rest of the course notes with grim satisfaction but retained this to include with her letter of resignation to Dafydd or Welch (or whichever County apparatchik/bureaucrat/salesman was going to be Head). She sighed. 'Golden Years' by David Bowie shivered across the Radio 2 airwaves and it brought back that golden time just after she left school but before the unskilled wage slavery had driven her back into 'education.' She turned the radio up and threw down all the result-driven crap she was sorting. The music reminded her of how curiously liberal and idealistic they'd all been - and how completely she'd believed there was a real man – a real hero - out there somewhere with whom she could make the visions come true. What had happened to all that 1970s dreaming?

3

'White Man In Hammersmith Palais' by The Clash blasted the hot street. Back in those great days when we all had No Future, that was what music did. Young Megan crossed it, making even a Sainsbury's uniform look sexy. A punk student in an outgrown school type blazer, thin tie, tight trousers and Elvis Costello circa 1978 specs, was putting up a step ladder in the new – and closed-within-a-year - plate glass bus terminus.

"*Megan?* It's Dafydd."

"Dafydd? Taff!" Megan called out to him, excitedly. "I thought you were at University?"

"I am. Cardiff." He grinned and then climbed up the step-ladder. He shook a can of red paint spray. "I'm just bringing the bus shelter graffiti up to date."

"What for?"

"It's important. The struggle. It's changing."

"What struggle?"

"The workers. You know." He went into lecture mode. "Love and Peace is passé. Punk rock is marginally more honest, revealing that life is sexist, racist and class-ist, but it's still just a pimple on the ass of capitalism. It's time to take the fight out onto the streets."

"What fight?"

"Well ... politics."

"Politics? You was never interested in politics."

"I don't mean like Callaghan versus Thatcher. It doesn't make any difference who wins that one."

"Doesn't it?"

"Na. In fact it will be better for the workers when Callaghan's out of office because then we'll have a straight fight between naked capitalism and naked labour. It's the steelworkers and miners who'll change this country. Not parliament.

"In fact, I've just written an article for *Annibynnwr Sosialydd* about an old Pantysycham legend of a two headed creature with the body of a dog, one head native collie, the other a Welsh sheep. The heads are perpetually and ineffectually torn two ways. Now an uneducated worker might just think it's about a collie that's been able to rob the local abattoir of a severed sheep's head before running happily out into the public highway or something. But it's much deeper than that. It's a *symbol* of the Welsh worker's divided culture and consciousness. The collie is Cymru, the sheep England. (Or have I got that the wrong way round?) Anyway, do you want to come up to my place for a coffee? We could discuss it."

"I've got to get back to work Taff. I'm a worker, remember?"

"Dafydd. My name is Dafydd. Please come."

"*I'm* doing 'A' levels now you know. On day release. Up at the college of knowledge."

"Which ones?"

"English and Sociology."

"Sociology! *Great!*" Dafydd sneered sarcastically. "The bourgeois substitute for revolution."

"Well I like it. It gets me thinking. I didn't too much of that at school."

"Thinking's no good. What you need now is action." He made a clenched fist salute.

"I like a change from action. I get enough of that at work. And I can't really talk to Brian." She paused. "What do you think? I might apply to the Open University."

"*You?* Really?"

297

"What are you going to do when you leave?"

"It's not called 'leave'. It's called 'Come Down'. I don't know. The struggle is bigger than any one person or what she/he does. I suppose I'll find a way of getting Socialist Realism into the workplace. My old man can get me into the steelworks. Then journalism maybe." He added hastily, "Only not *The Guardian*."

"What about teaching?"

"*What?*"

"What about you becoming a teacher?"

"You must be joking."

"I'd like to become a teacher," said Young Megan. "But I'd make it interesting. Teach people to think for themselves. Not like we were."

Dafydd had by now sprayed JOBS in giant red letters across the bus shelter. He checked quickly for police - or other agents of capitalism - then got to work on the rest of his slogan.

"I've got to go Taff - Dafydd. Be careful won't you?"

Dafydd gave a deprecatory wave without looking at her. The ghost of a valley that never got laid.

" See you then." She crossed the road quickly, turned the corner and burst into tears.

4

Megan could feel them on her cheeks now. Tears for all the wasted years that ached between her and Dafydd every time they passed in the corridor. For the child-teenager she'd been. For the children she would never have now.

"You little shit," she whispered as she remembered Young Dafydd completing JOBS BEFORE PROFITS and getting down off his high ladder.

"Get stuffed Fascist!" retorted the slender unbalding, uncompromised, unjobbed crusader with the can...

When was it exactly that Young Taff had become Old Taff? When was it that JOBS BEFORE PROFITS became JOBS FOR THE BOYS? Megan stopped binning for a moment, went very still, seemed to make her mind up about something, again, yes, again - but properly this time - and headed for the stairs.

5

Dafydd sighed and went back to his notes.

"If I could break that question down into seventeen parts, Mr Carmichael Hunt. Firstly, what I could offer to this job is the fact that I grew up here among these mountains and came to school up these very lanes."

Megan appeared in the doorway behind him, unseen.

"I have this country in my blood. You could mine it from my veins like Welsh coal and iron. When those red shirts bring a tear to my eye, it wells up from the buried faults of my broken land. It's my place see. And in the pupil's faces I can still see myself. I know what these children dream about and what they dread and hope for and I think I know what they need. No 'National Framework' can give you that."

Megan applauded.

"Duw, Megan how long have you been there?"

"Long enough. Is any of that true?"

"Most of it. Believe it or not."

"I believe it."

"Thanks. What are you doing here anyway?"

"The Head summoned me. And I wanted to see you. Where's the opposition?"

"Getting on famously with Troll last time I looked. He's been in there almost an hour, giving the interview of his life no doubt, selling them the line about working as a team and getting on with your subordinates. Talking about it all as brilliantly as he'll actually do it badly. I'm the opposite. I do it better than I talk it."

"I don't know. That sounded quite convincing."

The bell rang and kept ringing and then cut off. Perhaps it finally had a choice?

Dafydd shifted closer towards her. "You smell nice."

"Do I?"

Silence.

"I never did get the chance to ask you." The bell rang again long and hard. "You don't have to go do you?"

"No. Not this time. Never did ask me what?"

He stepped off the cliff. "What is a nice girl like you doing in a place like this?"

"I could ask you the same question. Unfinished business I suppose. Anyway," she moved closer to him, "who are you calling a nice girl?"

"I thought you might have applied for this job. You know you could do it better than most of us. Is it because you think it's been fixed?"

"I'm sure it has. But I'm not here because of the job... I used to enjoy the time we spent together."

"When?"

"When we were ...young."

The bell went again. It just didn't care!

A caretaker swayed in. "Jusht testing the bells." He swayed out again.

"I've been thinking a lot lately. You wouldn't believe what's been going through my mind trying to get it straight for this interview. The purpose of education, or lack of it, youth, the past, you. But last weekend I stopped, just for a few hours. I really stopped. I shelved the marking and the bullshit application forms, got totally off my face and went up the mountain at dawn. I watched the red sun come up over the lip of the world and, Megan, it was like I was sixteen again. It was like... Eden.

"And I thought, whatever I'm on this planet for, it's got to be more real than scrabbling for this promotion - and feeling like Munch's *Scream* in a suit. Teaching's not the problem. Not exactly. If you can get all the Carmichael Hunting and Welching and Trolley's paper chases out of the way. But there must be something more than that. Something to do with finding out who you are – deep down in the bedrock. Finding that place where no one can threaten you or usurp you. Because it's just – you. Finding *that*, is what gives everything else significance..."

Megan knew he was speaking the truth but he was doing it on the other side of the room. "I'm nearly convinced. But there's something not quite right. So listen to this. Because you're not going to get another chance. Nobody, nobody I know anyway, and certainly not you, gets to that place alone. Not without loving someone. I know what I'm talking about, believe me. But I'm not sure that you do, quite. Dafydd, look at me. You know I'm going at the end of this term. This is your last chance to say something to me I know you've been meaning to say since long before I earned these grey streaks. I've waited long enough. I'm getting on, Dafydd. I'll wait until the end of today and no more."

"Oh God."

"Say what you're going to say. And you needn't worry. The answer's yes."

Silence.

He looked at her. Her eyes were like the sea. "Will you marry me?"

Megan laughed. "I'll think about it."

"What!"

"But this is all so sudden. I hardly know what to say. We're both so young!"

"What!"

She laughed again. "Of course I'll marry you."

The interview door opened. Dafydd and Megan jumped up guiltily. Dafydd pretended to be sipping his water, Megan to be adjusting her eye make up. Out came Norman Welch looking super-confident. Carmichael and Robin Hunt were smiling behind him. Carmichael came forward very reluctantly to Dafydd.

Robin Hunt said severely behind him, "My brother has something to say to you, Mr Thomas. Carmichael."

Carmichael glared up at Dafydd.

"*Carmichael!*"

Carmichael shuffled, then muttered, "I'm sorry I was short with you earlier."

Dafydd spat his water over the wall. And then attempted not to drown in laughter. Megan, in her agitation not to join him, fixed all her attention on constructing one eyebrow in hyperbolic detail – and then forgot the other, conducting the entire evening's subsequent Eisteddfod with one eyebrow. They finally got themselves under control by not looking at each other. Then Megan sat down on a child's chair in the corner and loudly split her tights, which started the whole whooping dam-burst of giggles all over again.

Troll exchanged a triumphant look with the panel, like one who has finally secured the bridge against a foe.

Norman grinned, "You two seem to be getting on very well. Mind if I take your place, Dafydd?"

"Frankly my dear," chortled Dafydd, "I don't give a damn."

Major Llewellyn-Jones fixed Megan's laughter-collapsing face and dysfunctional eyebrow with a serious eye. "I'm afraid we're not accepting your resignation Ms Morgan. We're going to need you so I'm asking you to reconsider. Mr Riley has just been taken into custody for hospitalising a parent."

Carmichael Hunt frowned, making a note. "Does this sort of thing happen very often?"

"Only at times of particular pressure, " said Dafydd. "In other words about twenty times a term- usually around parents' evenings or after Rhys has vandalised a teacher's car - or asked a female member of staff to spend the night with him at his love palace. It isn't funny, Megan," he said, his voice squeezed into a whisper by merriment. "Mr Rhys Senior is sadly one of those parents who complain when his own child is punished and when everyone else's isn't."

Major Llewellyn-Jones groaned. Inspector Robin Hunt coughed. "Mr Thomas! Remember my brother will be deciding today whether this school has a competent leadership team or whether it needs to be taken over by County or even the Ministry. This is not the way to present yourself. Mr Thomas! Mr Thomas, it's time for your interview."

Carmichael Hunt made furious notes.

Dafydd recovered himself at last. "Ok – but just give me a minute would you? Megan, I think we were interrupted...-" He leaned over Trolley's stony face and kissed her.

"Dafyddnotnommmmm- " she said.

They began rocking back and forth on the chair. A screw came out of its base. Norman Welch, shocked, picked it up and offered it to Trolley who asked why on earth would he want a screw? Dafydd and Megan melted into mirth at this but didn't stop kissing – it was hard to tell where the laugh ended and the kiss began. Troll suffered a general paralysis of the brain at so many school rules being broken at once, but nobody, least of all he himself, noticed the difference. Welch all but capered in the air at Dafydd's evident career suicide.

Dafydd finally emerged from his kiss. His lips felt blessed. Surely he would never speak ill of anyone ever again? Surely he would interview like a god. "See you later, gorgeous." He winked at Megan and made his way into the interview room. He would be Headmaster. He would be her hero. Nothing could stop him now!

Mr Welch picked up Dafydd's interview notes from the chair. "Hang on, he's forgotten his lines!"

"That's very sporting of you, Norman, old boy." Megan beamed. "But I don't think he needs them."…

6

Carmichael Hunt, increasingly self-conscious as the situation between Megan and Dafydd developed, stopped matters there. He indicated his calculator. "This is scandalous. I have not on any occasion during today's events had a chance to say or do anything that fits into any of the five Assessment Objectives laid down in the Government Regulations for Novels, viz:

I rarely achieve a connective let alone a paragraph; sustain no effective argument and am susceptible to no recognised analytical terminology. Not only am I a laughable fiction, I fail to enact five of the six Government-approved non-fiction text types - Chronological report, Explanation, Information, Discursive Writing, Persuasion and Evaluation. In short, I appear to be nothing more than a height joke and the most rudimentary text type categorised as Instructions.

I belong to no clear literary genre or period, nor do any of my parts – however small- at any point in the narrative have any kind of relationship with a whole.

My functional language, form and structure cannot be evaluated as anything but alien to the style and preoccupations of the novel.

I am unlikely to be interpreted as anything but a caricature villain by any reader, no matter how ingenious an examiner's questions nor how controversial a critical approach is applied – and, finally,

I will always be read the same way, no matter what historical, cultural and other contextual influences on cultural study occur. I am the eternal little Hitler, the timeless half-pint tyrant. At one point of the text I am even given the ironic nomenclature of 'Goliath' while the audience is repeatedly and gratuitously and hyperbolically reminded both directly, and through heightist innuendo, that I am four feet tall! (For the record, though it's beneath me to dwell on it, I am five feet six and a half.)

None of this is satisfactory. It is not even adequate. 'River Deep, Mountain High' is, in short, a failing novel which I seriously doubt even Special Measures can redeem.

In consequence, I declare it - *closed.*

EPILOGUE

The Mountain

I stepped into an avalanche
It covered up my soul.
When I am not this hunchback that you see,
I sleep beneath the golden hill.

1

Per corer migliori acque le vele... Oh God what an interview. As
Dafydd drove down valley to the St Margaret's Home For Redundant Men, he relived the worst moments. He nearly caused two
accidents on the Pantysycham Exchange as he screwed up his eyes
against its continual replaying in his mind. He only just stopped
the car from mounting the pavement and ramming its bonnet
through the window of *Pantysoch Hosiery*.

The panel's incredulous exchanged looks. The sardonic si-
lences. The initial impression as he tried to look them straight in
the eye while sitting down on a chair lurchingly six inches lower
than expected – a chair brought in especially from the local primary school for the Inspector. And after an hour of squirming, the
Idiot Governor's question, "Now you've told us why you think
you should get the job, can you tell us why you think you
shouldn't?"

"I think I've just done that," he'd quipped. Inappropriately.

And all of this with a kid in a facing window holding two fingers up just above Carmichael Hunt's head.

Until - "Excuse me," Dafydd had said at last, mid answer, lunging forward to interrogate the "unacceptable behaviour" of a kid who, if his later written punishment lines were anything to go by, heard the entire rebuke as "Will you be quite? Yore biavuh is atroshus. Compleetli unexceptibal. Sea me owtsid mi yofis. Munday mawnin at nin! Now on yore way in silents! "

Not so much an interview, more a cry for help.

Dafydd *had* ended well, though. "Like our SWATs-busting Welsh Advisers, I believe a school is a crusade rather than a government audit. And I would lead it accordingly."

Then Trolley's priceless retort, "No doubt you would also like a cordless telephone, a Labour Government, and a Welsh Assembly, Thomas, but we've got to live in the real world...."

2

Dafydd steered the Lada over the roaring shingle of St Margaret's carpark, halting under the vandalised celebrity tree. Some local boyo made Godot had planted it in 1986. Sinatra was singing *There was a girl in Portland* as Dafydd entered Limbo Hall, the tv room. Most of the occupants had been divorced or otherwise evicted by wives driven mad by useless lumps still expecting to be fed, serviced and laundered like the heavy industrial males they used to be: the ex-movers and ex-shakers of an ex-coalfield. Dafydd took in the sharp old-male smell and a table display of industrial pots and pans labelled *Piserau*. He wondered if this was the Welsh word for incontinence. A poster advertised 'The Valley Inheritance.' His father looked up.

"Well?"

"They gave me the job."

"Never!"

"Thanks for the vote of a confidence."

"No! I mean – no, well done. I can't believe it! Sorry. I mean – wow! And I got onto my computer course today too. Well done, Son. Well done. Wow! Wha hae! Ha ha ha! Ha ha ha! Whoo hoo! Whoo hoo! Now maybe we can all look to the future."

3

Dafydd drove up valley under the last remaining railway bridge. He shivered. Troll's house dominated both bridge and road here and Dafydd recalled how as boys he and Ramo had once played knock out ginger in his terrifying porch by mistake. It's about time I got over that, he thought. He parked under some Victorian railings and ran up his mother's worn steps. He gave her the news then rose to go.

"Won't you stay for a cup of tea?"

"Can't mam. I've got the English Department's Eisteddfod school play. Why don't you come?"

"That new American agony aunt thing is on. *Miami Advice*. I can't miss that now can I?"

"Yes."

"Is *he* going?"

"Who's he?"

"You know very well who."

Dafydd coughed. "He said he'd try."

"His son's made a Deputy Headmaster today and he still won't stir himself. Hasn't he got any pride left?"

Dafydd sighed. "Headmaster, mam. And no he hasn't. But he got onto that computer course today. And he'd a be a damned sight more likely to come if he knew you'd be there."

"What is this play anyway?"

"*Romeo and Juliet.*"

"Your father doesn't like love stories. He walked out of *The Sound of Music* in Cardiff. In 1966.

"He had to walk out. He had tickets for the game. He told you."

"*Why* did he have to go?"

309

"They lost anyway."

"What's that got to do with anything?"

Dafydd couldn't explain. "It's a love story for men *and* women. Set in the valleys. Produced by a woman who has this coalfield in her veins, actually. She's wonderful, Mam. Wonderful... Dad would like it."

"Aye, and dragons might fly."

"They just might. Why don't you ask him?"

4

The outstanding success of Megan's *Romeo and Juliet* was only marred by Trolley's insistence on pupils changing out of their costumes back into school uniform in between each appearance on stage. At the end he thanked Megan cursorily then introduced the main business of the evening: the news that no-one could go home until the stage and hall had been cleared for Monday Morning Assembly.

It had been an exhausting enough day already and Dafydd knew he would have to overrule Trolley on his own ground.

"What Mr Trolley means," he announced, "is that Monday's Assembly is cancelled. So we'll clear up then."

Trolley's body was paralysed with rage. "Call that leadership! That's another tradition you've thrown out with the bath water, Thomas. It will be all downhill from here," he said.

"So we'll go downhill - like a river. Maybe we'll finally get somewhere."

"And do you even know that Norman Welch has resigned? What are you going to do about it?"

"Give his workload to you– it's not as if he *did* anything."

Trolley had never looked so much like the Black Knight of Arthurian legend who had guarded a stream and blocked all progress to the grail. Perhaps he *was* the Black Knight of Arthurian legend. He'd been around long enough. He gave Dafydd a hard Paddington stare that Dafydd faced down.

"My hero!" laughed Megan behind him. But her heart ached. She felt as exhausted as the local mine. She had always hated that day-after-Boxing-Day feeling when a play came down. She'd lived every scene, every line, with these teenagers, rehearsing the thing every evening for months and every weekend for weeks. *That* was her life, up there on stage. And now it was gone. And she could hardly take Romeo home with her could she?

Well maybe it was time she found him in real life. "Dafydd, I need a drink. I need several drinks probably. And when we've done that, Old Boyo, you're going to take me home... Where's the nearest pub?"

"The Marquis de Sade at Ychafi."

"Where's the next nearest pub?"

5

"The Old Viaduct" in Hiraeth (Ifor's local) was opaque with smoke. The jukebox was playing 'Golden Years'.

Don't let me hear you say
Life's
Taking you nowhere,
ANgel...

Tommy and some of the underage cast gathered at the jukebox, furtively lacing their pints of 'Tristram' Shandy with magical realism from a paper bag. 'Tristram' Shandy didn't alter your grasp of time and space or the plot exactly. It just took it all the way to its logical conclusion and left it hanging there, in absurd detail, with a tipsy smile all over its face. No. It was the magical realism that did it. Keeping a wary eye out for PC Plot, the kids negotiated Ploughman and Shepherd – who were respectively chewing off a half-pint barman's ear and grilling a captured waitress in protest at their Lunch and Pie being sold off, prior to eating both - and became increasingly absorbed in Ms Morgan's liaison with their Headteacher.

"Any jukebox requests, Miss?"

"Yeah! Get lost!"

They giggled themselves into fits and left. A clacking game of dominoes kept reaching a stalemate in the corner.

"What are you doing in here tonight, Dai? Isn't it your diamond wedding anniversary."

"Aye," growled Dai, going cross-eyed. "Sixty yers with the wrong bloody woman!"

"You've only 'ad one row," protested Joyce (the barmaid).

"Aye, and it's lasted sixty yers!"

Prolonged Male Voice Laughter.

Dafydd groaned. "Shall we go somewhere a bit more neutral?"

"My place or yours?" said Megan.

"Is that a rhetorical question?"

"I'm too tired to know the difference. What do you mean?"

"Yours might be better."

"I'm not so sure."

"I am."

"Why? Have you got an inflatable sex doll on the bed or something?"

Dafydd nearly dropped his pint.

Joyce pretended to mop the table, making mental (and completely unpunctuated) stream-of-consciousness notes.

Megan went on. "Your wine-guzzling friend over there just told me. The one watching porn on his mobile while munching giant packets of Diet Bombay Mix and betting loudly that you can't get Diet Penmawr Mix in Bombay. He tells me he's cutting down on the alcohol by switching to 'medium dry' white wine but he seems to think 'medium dry' is the glass size you and I know as a half pint, wiped dry of its former contents with a tea towel. This is not my idea of a romantic mise en scène, Dafydd. Shall we go?"

6

By the time Dafydd and Megan were parked high up on The Mountain (drinking themselves into neutral territory with a second bottle of half decent Côtes du Rhône), Bridge Street, Trollbridge was watching tv, washing up the last cups and saucers, putting out the milk-bottles, sipping cocoa, nodding off over half a page of a crime thriller and putting out the light. Soon after it was, mostly, sleeping peacefully.

Hours passed. Then, around 2.30 am, a burglar alarm sounded briefly but turned off as the spare key of Dafydd's flat did its work. Morfydd, a little deflated, suddenly brightened as Brigadier "Bullshitter" Davies – rather splendid in cravat, Cavalry twill, puce cummerbund, Sinatra trilby and blazer - turned on the light in Dafydd's room and came in.

"O!" she cried...

7

Brian Jennings (53) editor of the *Trollbridge Morning News* looked at the dummy of tomorrow's final edition just as Friday night became Saturday morning.

He read the splash headline, LOCAL PISS HEAD FLASHES WOMAN.

"*That's* the sort of front page Trollbridge needs to wake up to," he insisted. He put a call downstairs to the works.

"Print!" he said.

8

Dafydd and Megan climbed the mountain path in cloudy moonlight. A car could be heard in the distance. It was four in the morning. They had been walking a long time.

"How much longer? I'm not really dressed for this."

"Well, you could always *un*dress."

"Tch. You're drunk."

"Like *you* aren't! And who in their right minds would try this sober?" chuckled Dafydd, swaying back from a shale avalanche on the edge of Lovers' Leap.

"Careful," giggled Megan.

Dafydd became aware of a pressing matter. "Excuse me a minute. I must have a pee."

"Another one!"

Dafydd found a discreet thorn bush and unzipped his flies. A slim shadow joined him half way through. "Psst!"

"My God! Who's that? Meg?"

"No. You - thirty years ago. You've done it then!"

"What!"

" You and Old Megan. You've done it!"

"Yeah - all the more reason for not dying of a heart attack now! Don't sneak up on me like that."

"Sorry."

"Still, yeah, I have, haven't I? Listen, I thought we'd stopped seeing each other- "

"Don't worry. I won't cramp your style. As a matter of fact I'm just saying goodbye. You don't need me anymore."

Dafydd felt a sudden pang. "Really?"

"Really. So long, old man." The boy flashed his older self an encouraging grin. "Give her one for me, eh."

"I beg your pardon!"

"A kiss, I mean. Give her a kiss for me. I only ever had the one.... Mind you, it was worth all the others."

Dafydd agreed quietly, a little nervous now about all this talk of kisses.

"Well go on!"

The man and the boy shook hands in farewell, their eyes meeting for a moment, and then Old Dafydd walked back towards Megan.

"Who were you talking to over there?"

"No-one," he mumbled.

"Dafydd?"

"A little communion with my younger self, that's all."

"Never heard it called that before!"

"No – I mean it. I've been seeing him all day. Myself about 15 or so. And at the most inconvenient times… But he's gone now."

"I'm glad to hear it. Bit late to find out there's madness in the family." But Megan was thinking of her own little self-communion back at Mam's old house earlier. "Pity he's gone actually. I always rather liked him."

"He's still here – just three decades older – in me. And wondering, tragically, why you never let him know you 'rather liked him'!"

"I hinted at it – loads of times. But he never seemed to believe me."

"He had very low self-belief."

"Well- believe it now."

She nestled against him. They took in the view together. The moonlight made everything stand breathlessly still, including time.

Megan stirred, "Why is it so warm?"

"We're up near the Marw, above Penmawr. There's a hot spring and underground lake under that twmp. Remember the local legend?"

"No."

"One day, the twmp will open and the Druid Merlin will return, bringing dragons."

She saw – or imagined - something move up above them. And out of the corner of his eye, Dafydd also saw – or imagined - the two children they'd been move out of the shadows above him. The children turned and came down the mountain, hand in hand. Were they leaving their elders at last to get on?

Megan grabbed Dafydd's hand tightly and they peered into the moon-filtered blackness above the Llanffyluchaf hills. "Dafydd, it's Trolley!"

"No!"

"Yes it is!"

The deputy headlights of his car had raised a shadow ogre out of his furtive stance.

"What's he doing?"

They looked. They saw. They couldn't believe their eyes.

"He's dumping illegal waste! All those decades of litter assemblies and he's *dumping illegal waste!*"

Dafydd jumped up. "OI! Troll!"

Megan threw her fags, "OI!! *YOU* BOY!!"

The shock produced a brainwave inside Trolley's skull. He travelled faster than Dr Who's Tardis into the modern world, or at any rate, as far as the 1960s. His eyes, as if scratched at birth by some melancholy chance that had prevented him seeing the beauty of the world, saw it at last, face to face.

He began speaking gleefully aloud, in tongues. "*Red saint drops H and introduces hell* (6)!" Strange music filled his head and coursed through his veins. "It's not STALIN. Or LENIN." His stony eyes lit up. His heart started beating again. "It's LENNON! *LENNON!* YEAH YEAH YEAH!!! YEAH YEAH YEAH! YEAH YEAH YEAH!" He was screaming like Fran the Fan on the back of those original Parlophone Beatlemaniac singles sleeves now. "IT MEANS *PSYCHOANALYSIS* WAS RIGHT AFTER ALL!"

No-one ever saw Troll move so fast. It was partly the shock of being yelled at in the mountain dark by lovers, partly the nemesis of being caught dumping litter, but mostly the alacrity of a man who wants to get back and complete a cryptic crossword that has defeated him all day. Troll broke his own primordial schoolboy record for the sprint as he made it across the boulders, down some shale scree and back to his car. They heard its boot slam and the frantic ignition and then watched his car headlights blaze away through the Llanffyluchaf woods (with the car's Motorola radio live-from-the-past Light Programme playing a jazzed up orchestral medley of ELEANOR RIGBY, YELLOW SUBMARINE and ALL YOU NEED IS LOVE) before reappearing a couple of minutes later in the distance negotiating the lane. His full beam briefly exposed a bollock-naked Norman Welch up in his bedroom admiring his own reflection in a mirror.

Dafydd tried to breathe between renewed bouts of laughter, accidentally dropping his asthma inhaler over the side of the mountain as he did so (it fetched up later in some scree next to Megan's ciggies), and finding this funny as well. Megan brushed tears of hilarity from her cheeks. They had witnessed the seismic re-animation of Troll, his hair a veritable moptop of verve, his heart beating late '60s time. And it rocked.

Feeling easy at last, they turned upward again and climbed past the old signal box to the twmp. Dafydd looked across the bald, moonlit moors under the stars and felt oddly and intoxicatingly that he was looking not across the Marw but at the sea. Megan smiled at him.

"We could go to Florence," she said quietly.

"Florence?" he asked, miles away. "What's wrong with this?"

"For our honeymoon, you fool."

"Ah!" Dafydd felt a glow of warmth at this. Easter sunshine over the Pontevecchio under a powder-blue sky and Megan. And heaven's own painters-and-decorators providing the mise en scène. "Sounds good. If only Michaelangelo had got his proportions right, he would've been the perfect sculptor."

"You mean the *David*'s head is too big," said Megan knowledgably. "That's only because he designed it to go on top of a building. You're supposed to look up at it, in the heavens. *What a piece of work is man; in countenance like an angel-* ."

"I didn't mean the head," smirked Dafydd. "I meant the *penis*. It's all out of proportion..."

"How do you mean?"

" It's *enormous!*"

Megan gaped at him.

Dafydd laughed. "Had you going there."

The teachers looked down together at Lloegrbach, golden streetlamps stitching it into the void. Beyond it, in a brilliant ribbon down the twenty-mile valley, they saw the lights of the various towns all the way to the Channel.

"Sleep tight, ya heaven-seeking Friday nighters!" called Megan.

Dafydd thought of all the (now-sleeping) valley pubs and nightclubs, little hell-halls of souls hammering and bellowing their way into oblivion, trying vainly to stave off the working week to come. Forever. Never looking life in the face without a blurring drink in the hand.

"Mind you," sighed Megan, "my idea of heaven would be a Sunday night actually looking *forward* to work the next day."

In their modern world of endless meaningless engagements, skating over the surface of life, each individual soul more and more craved solitude and real contact at once – it was why so many took refuge in the walkman perhaps – but here for a moment they had peace *and* companionship at the same time. They shared the world and in doing so recognised it, saw it properly. In their present mood the view was less Lloegrbach – Welsh Little England – than *Logres*, the (recovered) Lost Lands.

They were at a watershed. The roar of the Afon Marw – its source was nearby – filled their ears. This water had been in the sea already, in the sky already. And would be again. He realised – or remembered - what he had always known: Everything flowed, as it always did and would, through everything else.

He had been teaching it all his days but you had to experience it to really know. You had to climb the mountain to find the sea.

Megan was remembering by heart that poem she'd once written into her biology book, decorated with a border of flowers, hearts, roses and the names of her latest boys (including a Dafydd its referent assumed was someone else). She announced it on the night air.

But when his prayer is crushed between our lips
And kisses come inside me like a bee's
And draw my honey from me, every drop,
A stillness comes upon me as of ships
That, tall and stately, slide beneath the sea's
Uncharted depths. Oh God, I whisper, stop...

"Except," she laughed, drunk with the words, "I could never understand why she wanted to stop! *I* never would." The suddenly flooding moonlight revealed her face.

"Would you Adam and Eve it, Meg, you and me up here like this after all these years? I won't be running away this time."

"Better late than never," she said.

Then she thought about it. "Na. Better *now* than ever."

"Exactly. And for Monday morning's assembly, I'm going to do *Suzanne*."

"Does she know?"

"Very funny." He fell over and realised he wasn't entirely sober. He lay on his back and breathed in the mountain air, more deeply than he remembered breathing before. "No. It's the Assembly I was always afraid to do when I was a Prefect."

She lay down beside him on the coarse grass. "Good."

"Then I'm going to appoint you Head of Curriculum. And then we're going to get rid of that PR factory down there and start a school."

Day was breaking in the east like a red dragon lifting its wings to fly, eternal and thrilling as Genesis. It would come down and take them up to heaven. Her eyes, sea-grey now in the daybreak, gave him a look that could drown a planet let alone a man. She moved slightly. He opened his mouth to ask her why on earth she was crying and found hers, unbearably soft. Kiss. *Gusan.* Wild as whimberries. He felt something break in his heart and realised it was singing.

Look at that sky, life's begun,
Nights are warm and the days are yo-ung...

Cymru, Not Wales. Wales meant foreigner. And this was home....

1989-2007

Author's Note

"River Deep Mountain High" is my attempt at The Great Comprehensive School Novel. There have been many great Public School Novels (and Campus Novels) but I am not aware of a single State School Novel, despite the rich and popular comic field it offers. I have taught English in such schools for a quarter of a century and learned in them for the best part of a decade before, so here is a version of the comedy show I found there. The book is dedicated, with respect and affection, to everyone who's ever tried to teach me, everyone I've ever tried to teach and to all the peers and colleagues who were there at the time.

All the characters and incidents in "River Deep Mountain High" on the Friday it narrates happened. But only in my Shandy-intoxicated imagination. To quote my protagonist, if I recorded what *actually* happened, no-one would believe me.

Gareth Calway.
Sedgeford, Norfolk,
November 2007.